Psypher

David Twede

PublishAmerica
Baltimore

First printing

Disclaimer: Although this work was inspired by actual FBI investigations of questionable Internet communications, it is a work of fiction. The events described are imaginary; the settings, names, incidents and characters are the products of the author's imagination. Any resemblance to actual institutions or persons, living or dead, is purely coincidental.

ISBN: 1-4241-4565-1
PUBLISHED BY PUBLISHAMERICA, LLLP
www.publishamerica.com
Baltimore

Printed in the United States of America

Dedication:
To Freedom and Responsibility

For something supposedly free, speech has likely cost the United States more gold and blood than any other freedom.

Acknowledgements

Thanks to all who helped this work, especially Special Agents Greg Stejskal and James Reeves (now retired) for key information about criminal cases and FBI operations. Sandi who has encouraged me since birth.

Wednesday, January 29

Ann Arbor, Michigan

Special Agent Tim Delbravo hated his replacement firearm.

It didn't have the same solid weight of his regular piece, didn't feel as smooth or as safe. After getting out of his truck, he checked the safety again and made sure the gun was secure in his shoulder holster. Sweat formed under his heavy coat as he approached the convenience store. Flashing lights from police cruisers strobed off Michigan-gray snow clumped around the gas pumps. A dozen reporters chattered at the perimeter, talking over the herd of police radios. An officer loaded a 10-round clip into his handgun.

Tim Delbravo would never get back his compact—an old matte blue Smith & Wesson rubbed shiny around the grip and barrel—after serving him for a decade in the bureau. For three months during his suspension, the Office of Professional Responsibility kept Tim's old companion locked in a container. It was evidence.

At the helm of this current emergency paced Henry Kaplan, the Resident Agent in Charge. Kaplan was digging a trench between the yellow police streamer and line of squad cars. He wore his usual green polyester suit and gray hair grease-combed over a bald spot. In his shaky hands he raised a small bullhorn, searching over it for the on-switch. He reminded Tim of an old man hunting for a raincoat while his house floods.

The last thing Tim needed on his first week back from suspension was an edgy Senior Resident. The chances of a shooting rose with each ticking second, and Tim hadn't broken in his new Sigma Series 9mm at the firing range.

"Travis McCurty," the Senior Resident's voice crackled out of the horn. "This is Special Agent Henry Kaplan of the Federal Bureau of Investigation."

The reporters fell silent, and like beggars, stretched their hands with pocket-recorders and microphones over the police ribbon.

"Travis," Kaplan continued his regulation speech. "The store is completely surrounded. Release your daughter and the store clerk, lay your weapon down, and come out with your hands empty and up."

Tim squinted at the store but saw only empty aisles of beer and magazines, no one inside. He stopped alongside Kaplan and held up a printout pulled from the computers at the National Crime Information Center.

"McCurty's background, sir," Tim said. "His boss fired him this morning. I called his psychiatrist. He's manic depressive."

Kaplan ignored him, lowered his horn and grabbed the bottle of mineral water he kept on the hood of a squad car.

Tim pushed the printout at him. Before coming to the scene, he ran a quick computer check on McCurty. It was a kidnapping across state lines, and thus under federal jurisdiction. What SA Kaplan didn't know was last month in Ohio, McCurty's home state, he threatened some cops after getting a speeding ticket. They hauled him in. McCurty had called his shrink instead of a lawyer, and the police noted it in the computer. Tim called the doctor and learned about McCurty's pending divorce and custody battle.

"Sir, the doc's panicky," Tim said. "McCurty won't go in, and hasn't filled his lithium prescription for weeks. The doc says he'll swallow his muzzle, maybe kill his daughter first."

"Hey, I'd take him out myself, but we gotta wait it out."

Tim kept his voice calm. "We should send in an unarmed counselor, a negotiator."

"Negotiate what? He's not making demands."

"That's because he's suicidal. The doc told me ways to talk him out."

Kaplan waved him off. "We're busy."

"I'm not."

"You? You work computers. What you gonna do? Offer to file his taxes?"

Although only one of a dozen black computer investigators in the FBI, Tim had gained experience in hostage negotiation at the Chicago Field Office and Oakland Resident Agency, his third and fourth assignments. "I can do it," he said.

"Yeah, I've heard how you do it. No thanks." Kaplan took a quick swig from his bottle, holding his stomach. "We'll wait for orders from Detroit."

"You can blame me."

"You've taken a lifetime of blame already. No, if it comes to it, we'll throw in a can of CS or tear gas."

Tim shook his head. "He's suicidal. No gas works faster than a trigger."

"Then we wait him out, Delbravo. Now get the hell out of here."

"Kaplan, sir, he's in a convenience store. Food on every aisle. An army of cops outside. He's not going to cool down, camping on the floor and watching our flashers."

Kaplan held up a hand. "We're following procedure."

Tim knew the drill. It meant they'd shut off heat and electricity. But the doc told Tim that making McCurty uncomfortable would only depress him suicidally. His best bet, the doc said, was immediate negotiation.

"Have you tried talking with him?" Tim asked.

"Yeah, yeah." Kaplan wiped a patina of sweat off his upper lip. "Ann Arbor police called on the store phone. He didn't answer, so they tossed in an FM field phone. We're monitoring from the van, but he hasn't picked up."

"Has anyone told him how to use it?"

"Look, who's running this?" Kaplan waved a hand at him, as if shooing a gnat.

Louis Mott, a green agent in the office, walked up to Kaplan and handed him a cell phone. He spoke with a southern drawl. "Detroit's on the line."

Kaplan set down his bottle, and pressed the phone to one ear, his free hand to the other. While Kaplan spoke, Tim turned and looked into the store. He registered no movement inside. Had McCurty killed his hostages? Tim pictured bodies lying flat, blood flowing under the refrigerators. A child missing her forehead.

God help him do something before it happened again.

Before coming to the scene, Tim had fed a copy of his printouts into the residency fax machine and dialed the Detroit Field Office. Maybe they could talk some sense into Kaplan.

"Yessir." Kaplan took the phone off his ear and folded it. He handed it back to Mott, then grabbed his bottle again.

"Detroit wants all the reporters cleared out," Kaplan told them. "Unless something breaks, HRT will move on McCurty."

Hostage Rescue Team, a squad of top-flight sharpshooters, was known for using maximum force. Tim saw their decisive skill in Chicago. Each year the national team recycled eight or nine of its sixty members. It was policy that every Field Office had at least two former members of the national team residing in its wings. Detroit's team still trained and retained their sniper skills, and would excise McCurty from his hostages with surgical precision.

"But, sir, his daughter," Tim said. "They'll kill him right in front of her."

"Better him than them all."

Either way, the six o'clock news would report bodies. And if she survived, the girl would be forever tattooed with the memory of her daddy's head blown into her lap. Tim's throat tightened at the thought.

"We're doing this by the book." Kaplan tipped back his seltzer and drained it.

By the book. Right. Kaplan wouldn't chance his final year. While most senior residents spent every moment grabbing bureaucratic power, Kaplan was so close to retirement he didn't even bother pocketing office supplies anymore.

But McCurty still had a chance, if he got human touch instead of a bullet in the head. "How long before hostage rescue gets here?" Tim asked.

"Five, maybe ten minutes."

Mott smirked at Tim. "Just enough time to drive your *hairy booty* home before you shoot another hostage."

Tim hauled in a deep breath, cooling the red-hot outrage in his gut. Mott, a crew-cut blond, looked as though he had been protected his entire life by a nanny at a white picket plantation.

Tim persisted. "We should be negotiating, sir."

"Here, make yourself useful." Kaplan thrust his empty soda bottle at him. "Get me another from the van."

"With all due respect…"

"Just do it."

Tim snatched the bottle. During his first decade as a technology crime expert, the FBI's black caucus, BADGE, had revered him as a top agent. Then one screw-up, an accident, and suddenly he was back to filling drink orders.

But he would get through it.

He marched to the van, the residency's control vehicle, and yanked open the door. SA Taylor Cobbs, also known as Spike because his stiff hair jutted out in black tufts, sat behind a communications deck. Spike wore full-ear headphones and monitored digital recordings. Tim reached in the back and opened a beverage compartment. He grabbed bottle after bottle, but all the seltzers were empty. Finally, he found a full can of root beer and carried it to Kaplan, who was directing the local police as they herded reporters away.

Kaplan shoved the can right back at him. "I wanted mineral water, dammit. This gives me heartburn."

Mott's eyes and lips narrowed into a grin. "Certainly ain't the NBA," he muttered.

Tim's fist balled up. He wanted to pour the soda over Kaplan, then crush the can on Mott's head. But that would only waste valuable time.

Kaplan turned his back to Tim and moaned. "Where the hell's HRT? I really hate the waiting."

Sweat drenched the inside of Tim's coat. He had exhausted every plausible argument. Except one. He tapped Kaplan on the shoulder. "Sir."

Kaplan spun around. "Didn't you hear me?" he shouted, holding his belly. "A seltzer. Now!"

"There's no more seltzer."

"Then you go out and look until you find me one, or don't come back. That's an order, dammit!"

Tim locked his jaw and said, "Yes, sir."

* * *

"*Delbravo!*"

Tim didn't turn at the sound of Kaplan's bullhorn. The man wanted a seltzer; he was going to get it. He had dropped the can and started marching out of the main ring of his boss' circus. Cold air pelted him as he pulled off his coat and tie. He unsnapped his holster from the shoulder harness and loosened the top button on his shirt. At the edge of the parking lot, he stepped up to the store entrance.

At least Kaplan had given him the perfect icebreaker. McCurty, the hostage taker, would relate to having a boss with a keen sense of stupidity. Tim opened the door and walked into a quiet store, knowing the Senior Resident was too rule-bound to order someone after him. Yeah, he might very well be sacrificing his comeback in the bureau, but protocol be damned. A little girl's future was at stake. He sucked in a cleansing breath and began looking down aisles and over counters.

"*Delbravo, get back here.*" The store windows muffled the horn.

He set his coat and gun by the cash register and followed a whimper coming from the freezer section. He first saw Travis McCurty's eight-year-old daughter. She sucked on two of her fingers, tears streaming down her cheeks. Nearby, the store clerk glanced up, lying spread eagle in his blue and white uniform. In the corner between them, crouched a man with short red hair, pale cheeks and disturbed gray eyes. He trained his .38 revolver over the two hostages and looked up at Tim.

"Stop!"

Tim held up his hands. "I'm unarmed."

"You FBI?"

"Probably not for much longer."

Sweat gleamed on McCurty's face. He panted through bared teeth and looked confused. The hand holding his revolver shook toward Tim. "What do you want?"

"Hey, take it easy. I'm just getting a soda for my jerk of a boss."

"*Mr. McCurty, that man does not represent the FBI,*" Kaplan's horn interrupted.

McCurty glanced at the window. "Your boss?"

Tim nodded. "I hear yours had a charisma bypass too."

"Huh?" McCurty's brow arched. "How'd you know about that?"

"I know it's hard losing your job. We have to talk, but not in front of your daughter."

"I need her."

"Take me instead."

"*Delbravo!*"

McCurty glanced at the window, then asked, "Why would I want you?"

"Because," Tim pointed outside, "they get trigger happy when guns are pointed at kids. I'm not so precious. You'll have more time."

McCurty slowed his breathing. The girl stopped crying. The clerk watched him as if he were God. Tim knelt down and controlled his voice.

"I'm here as a friend, Travis. I don't want to see you lose your daughter anymore than you do."

McCurty's eyes twitched over his daughter to the clerk. "What if I trade you for that guy?"

"It's your daughter that worries them."

"Well, I need her, not him."

The cashier looked up. McCurty waved his gun toward the door. The clerk glanced at Tim with gracious eyes, then jumped up and darted out.

"Now your daughter, Travis."

"If I let her go, you'll just arrest me."

"I'm unarmed."

McCurty rubbed his cheek in thought. "You swear?"

"We'll just talk, but not in front of her."

McCurty studied the floor, then took his daughter's hand. He spoke tenderly. "Shelly, you go wait by the candy. Pick out your favorite. I'll call you back in a minute."

She hesitated, her lower lip sucked in and eyes moving from the store aisles back to her father.

"Go ahead, honey," he said, urging her on with his hand.

She walked past chips and beer, to the candy section. Tim's shoulders relaxed. Both hostages were out of McCurty's grasp. Tim started reversing when McCurty pulled back the hammer and aimed his gun at him.

"Okay, cop. What'd my wife tell you?"

"I didn't talk with her." He wouldn't say the information came through the psychiatrist. The doc also told him not to mention the lithium.

"She stole Shelly from me, you know." McCurty almost sobbed the words. "Without my job, the judge will side with her. And if I can't have her…"

"Give me the gun, Travis."

"I work…work so many long hours, like the boss wants. So much time away, then lose my family. And how does he thank me?" McCurty stared out indistinctly and relaxed his grip on the gun, still leveled on Tim. "You ever lose it all, everything important?"

Tim's mouth opened. He wanted to say yes, but he remained silent. Although he hadn't lost his family, months earlier in California, he had lost his best partner, his self-respect.

"Put the gun down. Let's go talk over a pizza and beer."

"Everything crumbling. The house, car repairs. All the time spent…I-I…I can't." McCurty moved the gun to his own right temple. "I just…can't keep up anymore."

"No, Travis!" His palm went up.

McCurty's voice went flat and slow. He thumbed the hammer. "Ever try blowing your brains out?"

"Your daughter is still here." Tim flashed a glance around the aisle. He couldn't see the girl.

"Huh, cop? Or are you the perfect good-guy? Out catching criminals all day, stoking the family barbecue by night." McCurty's eyes stared unfocused, past Tim. "Your wife probably admires everything you do. Kids get A's on every test. You save every dime for their college. Right, cop?"

Tim's demotion had been hard on his wife, Janice, and their two children. And the transfer, back to the icy-snow of Michigan winter, was hell. Janice didn't see him as such a good guy. Damn, he knew what McCurty was feeling.

"Probably haven't even missed church once."

"I'm…that's not the way it is." Although flashes of gunfire and blood pooling in a basement drain still haunted Tim, his memory had more holes than a bull's eye. The shooting in a Danville estate…The bureau matched his gun and prints, then interrogated him endlessly. But he couldn't tell them what had happened.

"You're a damned perfect gentleman." McCurty aimed the gun back at Tim. "Maybe too perfect."

Warm blood throbbed in Tim's temples. His lungs heated. He wasn't perfect at all. He had shot a little boy! "Just give me the gun, dammit."

Then something moved in Tim's periphery, by the aisle. A black figure—hostage rescue black. McCurty jerked his head and Tim dove for the gun.

A flash roared, discharging from the barrel.

He landed on McCurty, holding the gun in his grip, warm barrel, tart smell of burnt powder. Hands slid under his arms. Two hostage rescue members pulled him off McCurty and took the gun away. He didn't feel any pain, only high-pitch ringing in his ears. He stood and patted his chest. The bullet had missed him.

"I just want my daughter. My life back." McCurty sobbed as the two HRT agents pulled him up and took him away.

Tim stepped back and crunched broken glass underfoot. The bullet had shattered a refrigerator door. Inside, bottles lay in every direction, some smashed and dripping. He grabbed a seltzer—Kaplan's brand—and recouped his coat and gun, following the hostage rescue members out of the store.

In the parking lot, Kaplan jabbed a finger into his chest. "You're in a heap of trouble, Delbravo."

"Hey, I was just following orders." Tim handed him the bottle and left.

* * *

Resident Agency

The bureau keeps a satellite residency on the third floor of the Ann Arbor federal building. Tim didn't return after netting McCurty, instead he went out for coffee. After three cups his ears stopped ringing, so he put back on his tie and gray suit coat. Everyone would have returned, and his nerves had unsnarled enough to take on the browbeating Kaplan wanted to give him when he left the convenience store.

He stopped in the alcove entrance that, during normal hours, could only be unlocked from the inside. Ms. Downey, the receptionist, worked on the other side of a three-inch, Plexiglas window. He cleared his throat to get her attention. From behind a yellow-paged, bodice ripping, romance novel Ms. Downey looked up and then buzzed the door open.

Louis Mott stood just inside the bureau residency, leaning against his cubicle wall—a mauve-carpeted partition. More like a floral shop than a bureau suite, rose patterns hemmed the ceiling above the stalls, and gold-framed landscapes, hand picked by Ms. Downey, branded each wall. In the center of the cubicles lay a common area that held the residency's fax machine and Secured Telephone Unit.

Mott, still leaning against the wall, smirked a first-office-agent grin as Tim walked by. "Dumb move, dumbass," he said in his johnny-reb drawl.

"Really? You mean, getting them out alive?"

Mott tugged at the lapels on his charcoal suit. "Dumb luck. You broke orders. Now you'll be clerking for another year, wearing out your ass with *beach time.*"

Everyone knew about his suspension. But soon, Tim would get approval on the case he was building. And Mott would still be refilling staplers. Getting Kaplan his coffee.

Tim looked down at Mott's mirror-shiny Florsheim shoes. Mott knew nothing about pavement. He hadn't been born at a free clinic in the heart of Detroit, or raised in the projects by a single, Brazilian-immigrant mother. Tim had endured more street-life in junior high than Mott would learn his entire career.

Instead of trading another insult, Tim headed for his cubicle sitting in the farthest corner. He threw his overcoat on the chair and eyed the papers and lame work covering his desk. Paper mounds nearly buried a year old photo of his family: Janice with their children, Tasha and Reggy, aged nine and eleven. On a stand next to his desk sat the computer terminal that connected him to the National Crime Information Center, the FBI's criminal database. Tim handled most of the computer legwork for the residency, because his initiation into the bureau included a year with CART—the national Computer Analysis and Response Team.

No sooner had Tim seated himself at the computer than Kaplan marched into his cubicle. His gray hair, normally looping over the bare crown, flopped soggy around his ears.

"Real stupid, Delbravo, playing the hero."

Tim didn't even flinch.

"I conferred with the SAC"—Special Agent in Charge—"and he's considering another suspension. Your life here is over, mister."

Tim had seen agents go down for less. But he had good reason for disobeying Kaplan. He knew more about McCurty's situation, and the Field Office wouldn't fire him outright because he succeeded. But he could face another demotion, unless he shined the right shoes.

"For now, you're chained to this chair." Kaplan plopped a stack of envelopes on his desk. "Stuff these FOIA requests. We need them mailed today."

Stuff envelopes? "Can't Ms. Downey do it?"

"She's got important reading…" Kaplan started leaving, then rotated around before Tim could even close his mouth. He threw a CD on Tim's lap. "And scan this, when you're done. My computer can't read it."

"Right." He watched his boss leave and then examined the CD. The words on the top were crossed out with permanent black marker. He angled the disk toward the light so the reflection revealed the blocked-out text: *Ecosphere II*.

Dammit! Another stupid game—a bootleg copy even—from Kaplan's grandson. The jerk wanted him to spend bureau time fixing a game disk. Well, the hell with it!

He tossed the CD on top of the envelopes. Kaplan had him trapped, and soon enough he wouldn't have any legitimate work to do. As an agent, he would fade into oblivion, unless he could get transferred or get assigned to a case. But Kaplan would never give him a chance.

That was all the more reason he had to find a case for himself.

Shoving the envelopes and game disk aside, he returned to the computer terminal. Somewhere in the bureau's files, he would find and build his own investigation.

CASE 1

"Thank god for the Net, or I'd be stuck with the losers around here."
—Kurt Victor

Thursday, January 30

Moscow, Russia

Fifteen-year-old Laurie Dunlap read the slasher story as if it were a treasure map. The computer monitor showered her with luminous, erotic horror, taking her across the Internet and back home to America. She missed the States; Moscow just didn't compare. And no movie compared to reading straight from the slasher's own mouth.

"Ooh scary," her friend Paula said. They shared a wide teak chair, ornately carved with vines and swirls. "I like it. Let's e-mail him."

"No—too gory. What if he replies?" Although protected by half-a-world's distance, Laurie only exchanged e-mail with the best authors on the Internet newsgroup *alt.sex.stories*.

"But I *want* a reply." Paula leaned past her, grabbing for the computer mouse.

Laurie's reflexes jerked, causing the mouse to fall on the carpet. She stared at her friend in amazement. It was like gazing in a mirror. Both had chestnut hair, cut shoulder-length and combed flat from a middle part.

"My house, my rules."

Paula scowled and reached down for the mouse. She put it on the desk—an antique European escritoire of walnut and brass that Laurie's father cherished. All around the den, hundreds of unread leather-bound books lined the stately walls.

"I hope you get caught, Laurie."

"No you don't, because you'd be in trouble, too."

"No way. My parents don't care what I do at home."

"But you don't have a high-speed Internet connection." After that, Laurie shut her mouth. She didn't want to anger her friend or make her leave. Getting scared alone was no fun. And Laurie had no other American friends in Moscow.

"That's not fair," Paula pouted. "I did most of the work building our webpage."

Laurie ignored her, going back to the newsgroup. The next few stories in the list were from *RipPantiesMan*, a dark author who never gave his real name. Laurie rarely e-mailed guys cowering behind forged Internet aliases.

Snuff-porn writers and graphic scan artists lived at *alt.sex.stories* and hundreds of other lecherous newsgroups. They used the groups as repositories and showrooms for their latest wares. Like pictures and notices pinned on a grocery store bulletin board, anyone could post anonymously on the newsgroups.

Laurie scrolled down, clicking to a new author. He listed his real name—Kurt Victor, at the University of Michigan in Ann Arbor.

"Hey, that's where your dad teaches," Paula said.

"Used to."

Her father, though still payrolled at U-M, collected just enough on his investments that he could be treated as royalty in most former first-world nations. With all their money, Laurie's parents still loved working late, leaving her to study with the Russian maid. Well, even the third world has its Internet. And this author was from her hometown.

Laurie pulled up Kurt Victor's story, entitled *Romancing*. A personalized disclaimer headed the rest:

This story contains a lot of ugly stuff. Send me e-mail if you want to see more.

Dozens of requests trailed it. She scrolled to the introduction and bit her lip with building anticipation.

My friends and I think more about raping than necking; more about cutting into a bitch than caressing one. That's why we don't call them "girls" or "women" cause then they'd be just people. "Whore," "bitch," and "slut" makes you see them as they are.

For most of you, I write this to turn you on. For the rest, I write this to annoy you.

To me, ultimate pleasure is complete control. Where kidnapping is romance, torture becomes foreplay. Rape is the act, and snuff, the climax.

Laurie's eyes sparkled with eagerness as she continued reading.

In his story, Victor takes a Japanese girl who trusted his offer to help her find a store. Lured into his car, she is gagged and held helpless. Taken to an abandoned shack. Bound with cords to a rusty folding chair. Her shredded clothing tossed aside. Cooking gel slathered over her by monstrous hands.

The details turned wholly barbaric. A hot curling iron, and clamps. Metal rods and splintery wood. Then a long-handled butane lighter, and a flame engulfing the half-conscious victim.

Paula swallowed, a disturbed smile running across her flushed cheeks. "Wow! We gotta e-mail him."

Laurie nodded breathlessly. "Yes. And print it, too."

She began typing out a message after her friend clicked the *print* command. Before she finished her e-mail, the Laserjet spewed out a hard copy. As the first sheet escaped, Paula and Laurie grabbed it together, provoking another fight. Paula shouted at her, she yelled back. With all the commotion, they failed to hear a man enter the den.

"Hello, gals."

Paula gasped and whirled around, almost falling off the chair. Laurie turned pale, rotating at the sound of her father's voice.

"Homework or fun?" Roger Dunlap looked down smiling.

Laurie attempted to hide the printout under the chair. Paula blushed.

"What is it?" Dunlap blinked curiously.

Laurie answered with short breaths and wide eyes. Getting caught frightened her ten-fold more than any slasher story on the Internet.

He reached out and grabbed a corner of the paper. She yanked hard, ripping it in half. She could only watch as he read. Slowly his mustache turned down. With dark eyes he skimmed the rest, his frown growing into a storm.

21

* * *

University of Michigan, Ann Arbor

President John Alexander Kladstein gazed out of his large office window, thinking about what a difficult job he had. Overseeing the University of Michigan's $6.1 billion annual revenue and four multi-million dollar construction projects required long hours. It came with the office, the prestige and the perks. Still there were those days when the academic-snobbery became too much, and he would give anything for a hot blond in a red convertible and long stretches of coastal highway.

He was about to head to another meeting when Deborah McGuire, the Vice President for Alumni Affairs, knocked on his open door.

"Deborah." He smiled and touched the back of his head, patting down his hair weave.

"John, we have a problem." She carried a tan satchel and crossed the maize and blue seal emblazoned on the carpet.

Kladstein pulled at the tails on his Raffinati suit coat, then motioned for her to take a high-back leather chair. She sat, crossed her legs and smoothed her navy blue skirt.

"What's up?" he asked, sitting behind his mahogany desk.

"An antsy alumnus."

"Who?"

"Roger Dunlap." From her case, she lifted out a yellow pad with scribbled notes. "You've met him. He stayed on as faculty in the Eastern European History Department. Made millions in the book-and-lecture circuit when he accurately predicted the collapse of the former Soviet Union and post Soviet terrorism. Now he spends most of his time on sabbaticals. He's in Moscow currently."

"Donations?" Kladstein eased back in his swivel chair, noting that one of his framed diplomas hung tilted.

"A quarter-million per year for the last five, and—"

"He has a complaint," Kladstein finished, rolling his eyes. Another whiny donor. They always thought their contributions dictated how he should run the campus. But he had to keep his investor happy. No one should be surprised to learn that he managed a business, not an educational institution.

"He said his teenage daughter's friend was playing with their computer. She stumbled into a graphic rape fantasy on the Usenet."

"Why should we worry?"

"It was written by one of our students."

"Another student." Damned kids. "Who, this time?"

McGuire re-crossed her legs, giving him just a peek of her smooth thighs. She glanced at her pad and underlined some notes with a fingertip. "Name is Kurt Victor—a senior in Secondary Education. He just started his student teaching. Has an A-minus ave, and is the Math Club treasurer. His father is a field engineer for some Microsoft consultant subsidy—Digisat, I think. The mother teaches at Urbana, an anthropologist. She's on sabbatical in Africa."

"What can we do? I mean, it's a sick hobby, but we're supposed to tolerate student views." He certainly didn't want to lose his academic reputation over this. Hell, the press called him the "*Diversity President*" after all.

"I had someone at the office verify the story, and they tell me it's pretty sick."

"But what does Dunlap expect?"

"He wants the student expelled."

"Is that all?" He sang the word "that" with deliberate sarcasm.

"No. He also wants the story removed off the computers."

"Right. We can't have a story where everyone will read it."

"You don't think we should do anything?"

"Expel a student for an essay? Think of the press we'll get." Kladstein rubbed the back of his neck. If it weren't for attention-deaf, hyper busybodies like Dunlap, they wouldn't even worry about this Kurt Victor.

"He's expecting a suspension, or said he'd find another place for depositing his tax write-offs."

Damn. She was siding with the dollars. He felt outnumbered. But did it have to be his responsibility? "Send it to the Regents. Maybe it violates the student code."

"No, I already checked." McGuire swayed her legs, gorgeously long legs. "John, you know the Regents won't meet for two more weeks. Dunlap is calling back on Monday."

Kladstein was too proper to swear in front of a lady, but damn, he needed Dunlap's millions, not some heavily publicized conflict. Bad press came and went; dollars taken in survived as long as the buildings. He had no choice— pitted between the liberal focus of academics and the conservative notions of his investors. Other alumni would grow cautious when their cohort didn't get the university's ear. Like it or not, he couldn't half-ass it this time.

"All right, all right—the whole nine-yards. You can help me draft a suspension. You call Counseling right away. I'll get Legal into it." With hands pushing down on his desk, he added, "No lawsuits."

* * *

Field Office, Detroit

Tim found Assistant Special Agent in Charge Robert E. Givens sitting at his desk in the Detroit McNamara building. The ASAC's office looked spotless, except for the few papers on his blotter. Tim knocked on the open door.

Givens looked up. "Tim. I was going to call you."

"I hoped you wouldn't have to."

"Well, your RAC wants another demotion for yesterday's stunt. I'm trying to convince the SAC you don't deserve it."

"Thanks, Bob. That was partly what I came to ask."

"Sit down."

Tim sat on the other side of the desk. Givens wore a black wool suit and black silk tie. Ever since training with him in Quantico, Tim had never seen Givens dress any other way. In California, Givens headed the largest team at the Oakland residency. He scrutinized part of Tim's review after the Danville mishap. Now he worked as an ASAC at one of the top field offices. Givens had risen so fast in the bureau, even Tim was tempted to buy a black suit. But then, light gray had always been his best color.

Givens stacked his papers and brushed off the desktop. "SAC Hansen wanted to chew you up. I promised him and Kaplan I would talk with you. I don't have to tell you how close you are..."

"I know. It was stupid."

"Yes, but I think we both know why you did it." Givens smiled at him. "What's it, six months since the shooting? The leg healed?"

Tim nodded. "Just a limp now and then."

"Good, good. You know, I still think the demotion was unfair."

"You won't hear me arguing."

"Fine. Then let's hold another review."

"What?"

Givens reached into a drawer and pulled out a sheet. "Forensics and ballistics reports from California."

"I've seen all that."

"No, this is new. They re-examined the guns and analyzed the photos. We should ask for a new review."

"You mean, let an inspection team rip open my scars?"

"I know how you hate OPR, Tim."

The Office of Professional Responsibility investigated internal matters, mishaps and just about everything they wanted. In Tim's case, OPR hadn't held back at all, exposing everything about him. They gave him a polygraph. The bureau used lie detectors as often as paper shredders, and Tim's exam was inconclusive. It got so personal, he referred to this internal review as *Official Privacy Rape*.

"I just want to forget the whole thing, Givens."

"You can't. Either way, you'll have a second review before coming off demotion. I just think we can narrow the gap. You shouldn't have even taken the fall, Tim."

Tim had heard this all before. The whole process—internal affairs, crusades of blame—was vintage FBI. When the inspection team interrogated him after the shooting, they asked as many questions about his dead partner, John Robinson. Yes, Robinson made mistakes too, rushing in without backup and shooting when talk would have better soothed the kidnappers. But once Tim had gotten shot in the leg, he couldn't remember anymore. Nothing except the dying, vacant eyes of a young boy. He could never get those out of his mind.

The lab had matched the bullet that killed the boy to Tim's gun, not Robinson's.

"This new report only confirms my suspicions, Tim. I still think your partner must've emptied his gun, then grabbed yours."

Like the first time he had heard Givens' theory, Tim felt stuck—an ethical crisis. Should he, like the bureau, take the easy way out? Maybe it didn't matter to them who took the blame, as long as it reduced media attention. A dead agent couldn't talk.

He had sensed this was their reason—not that he was blameless, but that he was alive, and an eleventh year minority.

"I don't want to go through this right now."

"Now or later—"

"Not now."

Givens studied him. "All right. Just read this." He slid the report across the desk. Tim took it.

"I came here for another reason." Tim reached down to his briefcase and pulled out a two-page brief. "I want to start a case. A computer investigation."

Givens took the papers, and looked them over. "There's not a lot here."

"It just happened today. I want permission to prepare a full brief."

"How soon?"

"By tonight or tomorrow morning at the latest."

"Fine. Fax me all the details by tomorrow morning. I'll give it some thought. But you have to go by the book. No more stunts. When you come up for review, you better look as saintly as a dead pope."

* * *

Student Affairs Office

That evening, VP Mary Carter handed President Kladstein the least threatening memo first. Now that she was a year from retirement, the President finally visited *her* office. It was serious, and she didn't want to get him angry.

After reading it, Kladstein looked up. "I can't believe Counseling found nothing abnormal about Victor."

Mary forced a smile and shrugged. She never trusted psychologists anyway.

"What about his computer account?"

"I've got that memo here someplace." Mary searched her cluttered desktop. The inseparable piles crisscrossed in layers, each connected into one large mass. Twenty-two years of service and she had only seen the color of the desktop wood once. From the top of this heap, she grabbed some papers and handed them to him.

"I think you'll be disappointed," she said. Earlier that day, Kladstein's tenacity had surprised her—he hardly gave a minute per year to student affairs. But this one had his full attention.

"Why?" He paced around her desk.

"The Network Security Division suspended Victor's computer account and tried to remove the story. But it takes time for the cancellation to be okayed everywhere off campus."

"How long?"

"I'm not sure, it's so technical. Days?" She handed him another sheet. "Here's the latest finding."

Mary wondered if she should have started with the worse news. Building up like this might only make John angrier. While the memo kept him absorbed, she glanced outside her window, watching the snowflakes stream down. Student-pedestrians cowered under furry hoods and slid on ice. The cold wind whipped them with a vengeance. It seemed to prophesy the swelling fury behind this predicament.

"That sonuvabitch." Kladstein looked up from the memo. "He didn't just pull her name out of a hat."

"No. She's real and lives in the same dorm as Victor." Mary held up a manila folder. The bombshell: Victor had used a classmate as his story's victim. "Here's her confidential file. She's a Japanese exchange student, studying in our English Department."

Kladstein found a seat.

"Here's a photo." She pulled out a picture of a young Asian girl with innocent eyes and a delicate smile. "Even his story descriptions match her looks."

Kladstein held his mouth open for a long moment. "We better do something. Call the authorities."

"They've already called us. Campus police have his e-mail. The FBI called them, and want you to okay a dorm search."

"Absolutely," he said. "Let's just keep this hushed. Protest season's coming. If the media gets the girl's name…"

"It may be too late." She closed her eyes and rubbed her forehead. "*The Herald* called only fifteen minutes before you arrived. They wanted confirmation of Victor's story."

Friday,
January 31

Residency

Tim stood in RAC Kaplan's office, wishing he had called in sick that morning. He had stayed up past midnight pulling together details for his case-request, and faxed it to Givens just after one-thirty in the morning. He woke late and ran to campus for more information before dashing to the residency. When he arrived late, Kaplan pulled him into his office and closed the door, chiding him about schedules and procedures.

"You are a damned flea, Delbravo. Biting the hell out of my last days." Kaplan yanked open his top desk drawer and grabbed a bottle of Tums antacid. He popped a handful of the tablets in his mouth and rubbed his winter-white forehead, which wrinkled as he chewed.

Tim took a step back. "Are you through with me?"

"Just starting. Sit down."

Tim hadn't taken a seat, hoping not to get cozy while his boss railed on him. He pulled out the chair set in front of Kaplan's National Crime Information Center terminal. The computer, dusty as always, remained off. Probably hadn't been turned on since the day they installed it. He always had Tim or Mott recover information from the terminal at Tim's desk.

Kaplan mumbled something, then reached over and grabbed a coffee mug from the top of a paper mound on his desktop. Papers slid off, landing on the tan carpet specked with shredder overspill and crumpled papers around a trash can. Only a few pictures broke the white sea of walls. A plaque on the desk read: *What part of "go to hell" don't you understand?*

"You think you're so clever, don't you?"

Tim shrugged. "About what?"

"Don't give me this crap. You skipped over my head, straight to the field office—to your training buddy Givens. Made me look like an ass."

Tim bit his tongue, holding back a comment about Kaplan's polyester green suit, how his bulging pants were splitting just above the crotch. "You mean the case-request?"

"Damn right." Kaplan squeezed the antacid bottle open and popped another tablet. "Giving me an ulcer, you are. Can't help but cause problems. First California, now here. Why can't you just give me some respect?"

Tim didn't reply.

"Hell if I know why, but the ASAC gave you the go-ahead on the computer thing you sent him."

Tim shifted into a chair and struggled to keep from smiling. Givens had come through for him.

"You report to me, dammit." Kaplan bared teeth. "And don't think about me releasing you from your office work."

"No, sir."

"You won't have this for more than a day, if I can help it. One screw-up, and I'll drown you in envelopes. Understand?"

Tim nodded.

"Go to your buddy again, and I'll let everyone know you're a momma's boy."

Tim didn't reply.

"You're supposed to give me a rundown, then I got a fax from the Attorney's office for you."

"A fax?"

"Yes, a fax. Now give me a review."

"You want to hear about my case?"

"Yes, dammit!" Kaplan slapped the desk.

Tim straightened in his chair. "It's an interstate threat. A U-M student published a rape-fantasy on the Internet. He used a real name for his victim, a female student."

"What? Campus called *you*?"

"No. I did a search on NCIC for reported incidents in our area—anything to do with computers or the Internet. I guess a man in Moscow told DC, but they only made an entry in the database."

Kaplan smirked. "Half the frat-kids probably write up their fantasies. What're you gonna do? Arrest every guy with lousy pickup lines?"

"The story speaks for itself." Tim didn't have it with him, but when he had first read Victor's story—*Romancing*—the blood in his face retreated. The guy was sick, a snuff-porn preacher, who advocated rape and murder as openly as TV evangelists extolled donations and offerings.

"Yeah, well, one story don't make a rapist."

Tim knew it wasn't top-line investigation, but he had to start from the ground up. "He's making plans. Several weeks ago, Victor e-mailed an accomplice. A guy named Alven Hando from Toronto…"

"Wait. How'd you get the e-mail? That's private, ain't it?"

"I called campus police. They had already seized his account and gave me his e-mail this morning. They'll search Victor's dorm once they find the roommate."

"Damn! Just let campus police handle it." Kaplan frowned and munched a last antacid before throwing the empty container on the floor.

"If you'd read, you'd realize it falls under international conspiracy to commit rape. There's two of them." He shouldn't have to explain this to the RAC. "Campus can't go after the accomplice in Toronto."

"So just have the Royal Canadian monkeys pick him up."

"I was going to give them a call as soon I got the green light."

"Well, you only have that temporarily." Kaplan tossed a fax sheet at him. "I'm filing an override to your buddy's boss. You got too many reports pending here to screw around with a go-nowhere case."

* * *

Despite Kaplan's threat, having a case excited Tim. He had a chance to prove himself again. The excitement, however, soon gave way to a nagging feeling.

The symbiotic relationship with rapists and junkies always bothered him. What he wanted was to stop the sickness and do some good. And that meant he must wade into the perverseness of criminal waste.

He studied the e-mail. Victor and Hando had traded almost a dozen messages during a two-week period in December. The important parts of the

PSYPHER

transcript took up a couple of pages. Alven Hando first e-mailed Victor after reading his story in the newsgroup. Victor quickly replied.

December 12th, Victor e-mailed Hando: "Dude! It's so great to find another blood-licker. Thank god for the Net, or I'd be stuck with the losers around here. BTW, I just downloaded a rippin' scan. *Real* full length images of the Mahaffy girl that Paul Bernardo licked, luscious mini skirt, ripped just right! She's dead in the last two frames. I'll give you the net-address for it."

Same day, from Hando: "We positively must meet soon. I would fancy doing someone together. Thank you so much for the URL to that fab rape image. Just seeing it makes me shiver with utter delight." Hando signed the message: "a.k.a. The Psypher."

Later that day, from Victor: "Yeah, you know, it reminds me of the bitches I've seen here. Sooo Nice! I have to make a bitch suffer! I've been telling myself, 'Go on Kurt, it'd be slick.' But the fear of going to jail always stops me. Soon enough we'll lick some butt! BTW, what does 'Psypher' mean?"

December 13th, from Hando: "Psypher—because my identity, my being, is enciphered so no one can find me. I want to do someone, but I am not exactly clear on how to proceed. The parts of the stories you have sent inspire me wonderfully. I want innocence and youth. Surely, the younger the easier to acquire and control."

December 14th, from Victor: "You know, I've been thinking too. Hell, I'm not sure how young for me, maybe fifteen. But they gotta be virgins. YEAH! And you know you can control any bitch with rope and a gag, do anything we want. Be the first and last to do them. I know how, and can't stand waiting. Just thinking 'bout it anymore don't do the trick. I have to DO IT."

December 15th, from Hando: "When you decide, please, just tell me and I'll be there. Who do you have in mind?"

Same day, from Victor: "I know a certain ho. A virgin Asian. I'm working on the story. Maybe by January. Problem is, all of my ideas have so much mess. Where? is the question. I just picked up a copy of that post 'Blood Lust' and it horned me up. But I don't want no blood in my room. So I got me an excellent plan. A virgin abduction. As I said before, my room is right across from the girl's bathroom—it's a co-ed dorm, you know. I'll wait until late at night, grab the ho when she goes to unlock her dorm. Knock her out with a

31

metal pole, and put her into one of those trunks like a foot locker or a duffel bag. Then hurry her out to my car and take her away. I could carry out the best of the stuff I wrote. Whaddaya think?"

December 16th, from Hando: "I'm there with you. It sounds fab, like the Teale-Homolka killings. I only wish it were as easily accomplished for me. To be, that is my quest. Expiring someone will breathe new life into me and draw out my true self."

December 17th, from Victor: "Hey, it's finals week here. A rough one 'cause I didn't study much with all the yappin. My folks are gonna cut my allowance or something if I don't pull out some kinda trick. I don't think I'm gonna write for a bit. But watch the stars, maybe a test run."

December 21th, from Hando: "Please excuse the interruption, but I have been waiting, re-reading our earlier messages. Each time I do, they arouse and awaken me more and more. We must get a plan and come together on this. I will give you more details as soon as I find out my situation. I do not always know where I will be from day to day."

December 26th, from Victor: "Alrighty then. I'm home for xmas. Doing e-mail on long distance, so can't talk too much. But let's shoot for January, right after I finish this Asian story. When you come up, we'll ping-out plans over some great coffee and donuts at this place I used to part-time. Let's trade phone numbers so we can call, okay dood?"

That was all Tim had, but it sufficed to enflame his adrenaline. He had to find evidence and stop the planning. Although Victor never actually gave the victim's name to Hando, it did appear in the newsgroup fantasy. Of course, Victor told the university his story was purely fiction. But the bastard created the fantasy while eyeing a girl who lived down the hall from him. A Japanese girl with the same name as the girl in Victor's fantasy. A girl who was anything but fiction. They couldn't let it slide.

From the messages and stories, he made a list: objects and items that Victor wrote about. Odd particulars like curling irons, cooking gel, a steel-wire whisk, and metal poles. Ordinary objects such as kitchen utensils and bags and suitcases. And various tools that could be bought at any hardware store like wire, rope and a ladder. He would go to the dorm search and compare his list with what Department of Public Safety officers found.

The university also supplied him with transcripts of every phone call made from Victor's dorm room. Some of the calls would have been his, others belonged to his roommate. None were to Canada, so it didn't appear Victor had called Hando from the dorm room. One local phone number in particular had already been highlighted—the number to the university's Internet Service Provider, which connected Victor to the network through a modem on his computer. A modem, since those older dorms still were not wired for high-speed Internet, and most students weren't loaded enough to get broadband any other way. Victor must have been using it a lot, since it was the most frequent number on the transcript.

Next he read over the fax from the U.S. Attorney that Kaplan had given him. U.S. Attorney Sam Grand wrote that the messages and stories were enough to indict Victor. But Grand wanted to wait; he gave the FBI the weekend to also find the accomplice, Alven Hando.

Tim just couldn't understand; the attorney wanted to wait the weekend? A weekend was three days too long for letting this sicko roam free. Ensuring Victor didn't flee the campus would take time enough, leaving Hando to remain completely concealed. Didn't Grand realize that either could do it? Somehow, Tim had to protect the girl. She'd be vulnerable until they made the arrests.

But then a weekend might not be enough to find Hando, he also worried. Hando, "The Psypher," the big zero could be anyone. According to the Toronto police, Hando's Canadian Internet account had been killed on January 10. Nothing more about him was known, not even if Hando was a "he." Hopefully, the Mounties understood the gravity of the situation. Just to make sure, he would have to go to Canada.

Kaplan's threats didn't scare him. This was a legitimate case, and ASAC Givens would back him.

He read the university files, which painted Victor like a damned kitten. Victor, who scored 300 points above average on the SAT and maintained nearly an A-minus average at the university, was not as stupid as he made out. Not as brain-dead as he sounded just to seem "cool." His whole file was chock full of nice remarks—*exemplary* student teaching, *high* marks, a *model* dorm resident.

Victor was squeaky clean, according to the university. He aspired to teach computer science at a junior high school, his advisor in Education had noted. He'd been tutoring for money—rich elementary-school kids, whose parents wanted them to learn computers. Tim only had the name of one family, but he would do some checking and questioning. Maybe they could reveal something more about the suspect.

From a large envelope, Tim pulled out a glossy photo; it'd arrived by courier ten minutes after he'd left Kaplan's office. The print was a blown-up passport photo of the girl—Yoshiko Kamahara. Even though grainy and blurry, Tim could sense innocence and fear in the image. Staring at it, he sensed a responsibility to her and possible redemption for him. "Nothing must happen to this one," he told himself quietly.

He grabbed his list and left the office.

* * *

Lawrence Hall

Tim had a hell of a time finding Victor's dorm hall. Parking was worse. The University of Michigan sprawled along the Huron River Valley. He carried the list he had made toward the dorm building, hoping to find a match and provide evidence for a sure conviction. The campus police would execute this search, but he was after a witness or physical evidence that could solidify the circumstantial self-deposition of Victor's story. But in case Victor had more of this weaker validation, he had brought a portable USB drive for copying computer files. And after the dorm search, he would get the U.S. attorney to file for a warrant to search Victor's vehicle.

A cold draft followed Tim into the warm residence building. Its name, Lawrence Hall, was new, taking the most recent moniker from the latest donor. Tim couldn't remember the old name; campus buildings changed names these days as often as multinational corporations merged. The hall appeared medieval under the weak lighting, and he could see smears and stains across the thick plaster walls, matching the dimpled streaks on the tiled floor. The lobby remained as quiet as a library, and just inside he found campus officers standing over a table with a student who looked Asian-Polynesian. The young man wore a heavy lime-green coat and carried a stuffed backpack. It was the roommate—Ned Lovanah, he was sure. Tim walked up to them.

"All this just for my permission?" Lovanah hoisted the forms and glanced at the cops.

"Covers the department," the tallest officer said. "You know—against illegal search and seizure."

Tim slid his credentials to the other officer, who looked and handed them back. He watched Tim with admirable eyes.

"So what rights am I really giving up?" Lovanah took off his coat.

"None," the first officer said. "We won't touch a thing of yours. Guaranteed. You just come show us what not to disturb."

Lovanah sat. "So where's my roomy?"

The officer glanced at his partner. "He's not allowed on campus, right now. We can't tell you why."

"Doesn't matter. It's as good as the transfer I never got." He grabbed the pen, and without reading them, he signed the forms.

"You put in for a transfer?" Tim asked.

The student looked at him oddly. "Wouldn't you? I mean, the guy's weird—makes funny noises, talks to himself. And he's obsessively neat—I can't even leave without making my bed. It's like having a mother for a roommate."

Tim took the opportunity for witness testing. "Mr. Lovanah, have you ever heard Kurt Victor speak about girls in the dorm?"

"Not really. He just goes on and on about cleaning stuff." Lovanah set the pen down and handed the waiver to one of the officers.

"How about stories and the Internet?"

"Yeah he loves the Internet. Mostly I avoid talking with him."

"He talk about someone named Alven Hando?"

"Not that I know."

Strike one for the witness angle. Maybe they would find collectibles in the room. He motioned at the hall, and the officers began marching down it with him and the roommate in tow.

The shadowy halls were narrow, and the plaster emitted a moist odor. Where the lobby had been nearly deserted the labyrinth and rooms bustled with activity. A few students read from textbooks. Others seemed to disregard the fact that they were in college. Frisbees zipped down the hall. Students left the showers, walking around in towels. The dorm rooms he could see looked as though a fleet of helicopters had cleaned them. Afternoon soaps and sour grunge music blared from many. One student threw a book across the hall, others laughed and yelled.

It was a damned playground.

They reached the dorm room. It stood in the middle of one long hall, right across from the double doors that led to the set of adjoining bathrooms. Male and female quarters: dark, damp, dreary halls, brightened by student horseplay and foreplay. Amidst all the activity, the two officers opened the door with a key and walked in. Victor's dorm, a ten-by-ten-foot cave, had no kitchen, no sink—just a single closet, two beds and two desks. It was not quite as dark as the halls because of a window, but it radiated the same musty smell.

An officer flipped on a light. Compared to the other rooms, it looked as tidy as an art gallery.

The officer shook his head. "It's so clean, he's gotta be hiding something."

"Yeah. A maid." Tim handed his list to the taller one. "Pay strict attention to this. Bag anything that matches."

The officer nodded.

Lovanah began pointing out everything that was his or Victor's. On a small desk sat a computer. When asked, the roommate said it belonged to Victor.

The campus police were husky, both about the same height, one a little shorter and heavier than the other. Both had sharp, military haircuts and determination in their brows. They glanced back at Tim, as if checking to see if he approved. He could feel their apprehension, eyes on him tense and trying to look bold like meter-maids working alongside the department captain. Each held a pen and pad. One had a camera and the other carried plastic bags for collection if needed.

The shorter one turned to him. "Sir, what does it take to get in the FBI?"

Tim smiled. "A failed psychiatric exam."

He looked back dumfounded. The other officer nudged him back into the search.

While they explored the closets and bed, Tim inspected Victor's desk. A new computer with a flatbed scanner and color printer, a bookshelf and a telephone sat on the desktop. On the corner of the wood top, and on the floor below, Tim spied something shiny. He bent down and found specks of metal. The spots on the floor appeared round and dull. He picked up some flecks and examined them. The metal felt soft and deformed easily. Lead solder, used to connect electric circuits and devices. Tim had soldered his share of wires while serving in the army.

He stood and looked over Victor's bookshelf. Rows of *SciFi Monthly* and computer books lined the shelves. He opened his case notes and checked a copy of Victor's course transcripts. As he suspected, Victor had taken no electronics courses and only one computer class. Yet he owned several hard-core computer books ranging from programming to UNIX. Yeah, Tim knew these. What had it been—fifteen years? He was burning through these very subjects at Wayne State University before studying computers became popular.

Choosing computers as his career had been the last thing Tim would've guessed before his second year of college. In high school, he did passing in math, no better than an eight-year-old armed with a calculator. He had struggled so hard his first year at Wayne State that the next summer in boot camp at Fort Bragg, he felt like he was having a vacation. The army, at least, let him get six hours of sleep every night. He was posted on electronic communications duty in his platoon, which gave him his first introduction to anything approaching a computer. The army had taught him as much about hard work as the streets had taught him about hard life. It also paid for the rest of his college.

"Sir." A campus officer tapped him on the shoulder. "Here's the inventory of what we found." He handed him two pads, both with scribbled notes. "I'm sorry, but nothing matched your list except a fork. We didn't even find a *Penthouse* magazine."

"Did you guys check all the way under the mattress?" He smiled.

The officer's eyes darted. "Nothing there."

No physical evidence. This was not good. Maybe Victor left some more incriminating documentation.

"And the computer?" Tim shouldn't actually do the checking since the bureau didn't have a warrant; he was only invited along.

"It's over there." The officer pointed.

"Yes, but did you check it?"

He glanced at his partner, who shook his head. "I'll look at it."

They walked over to the computer and seemed confused, since they couldn't even find the on-switch. Tim made a loose offer to help. The officers moved aside.

The suspect owned a fairly nice Windows machine, and with his portable backup drive, he backed up all the data files and made a list of the applications. He found a typical word processor, web browser, and interestingly, satellite tracking software—not amateur or shareware, but the professional SatTrack code. Victor's record showed nothing about an interest in astronomy or space science. Tim also found a document along the way that caught his eye—a story with a file date from the week before.

He read it. In the story, another real-as-hell sounding fantasy, Victor kidnaps an unnamed "Asian" girl at knifepoint. He takes her to an isolated place off Route 23 in northeast Ann Arbor, and tells her to strip, take out a toolbox from his car, then forces her to sort the tools that he eventually uses to rape, beat and mutilate her. After harrowing torture, he kills her by fire.

A short paragraph prefaced the remainder—an introduction, or something, to convince the reader that it was real.

I am planning it well. It will be my first abduction. My first real rape. The Asian ho. My first experimentation with all the devices of pain I had originated before. I am aroused and haunted by the torture of this target more than any other girl on campus. Her innocence, I will have it. Do her as soon as I get the courage.

* * *

Northeast Ann Arbor

At five o'clock, Tim stood on the porch of a large home in the richest area of the city. It was cold outside, where the snow covered the ground and the sky reflected its color. He knocked a second time and waited until the door cracked open. A lady, dressed in purple sweats and holding a baby, gazed at him.

"Yes?"

"Mrs. Sarah Farnes?"

She nodded. "Can I help you?"

"I'm Special Agent Tim Delbravo, with the FBI." He set down his satchel and flipped open his credentials.

Her eyes grew large. "What…Uh, what?"

"I only need to ask a few questions."

"Questions?"

"About the tutor you hired for your oldest son, Robert."

"Robbie? What did he do?"

"Nothing, Mrs. Farnes. It's about the tutor. Can I come in?"

"Sure," she said softly. She hefted the child on her hip and pulled the door wide. Tim followed her into the warm entry, where an assortment of plants heaped up around a clock and short table. On one side, stairs led up, and the other opened into a family room. She stopped under a low overhang. He expected her to offer him a seat, but she didn't.

"I only met the tutor once. He worked with my boy, but…"

"Mrs. Farnes, does Robert keep his computer in his room?"

"Why? Did he do something on it?"

"No. Is he here?"

She looked at the stairs. The baby pulled on her dark hair.

"I just want to ask him some questions. Look at his computer."

She studied Tim, pursing her mouth, then turned toward the stairs. "He's in his room."

She rose the stairs, and Tim followed her. At the top, she asked, "Should I call my husband?"

"If you want. I'll only be a minute."

She guided him across their teal carpet and up to a door plastered with *Stay Out* signs and rock posters. Robbie's room. She knocked on the door.

"Robbie?"

The door opened. A boy with brown hair and braces gazed up at them. "What?"

"This man is from the FBI. He has some questions for you."

He looked at Tim, then sighed. "So ask."

Tim, shocked at Robbie's lack of surprise, cocked his head and looked into the bedroom. More posters hung on the walls and ceiling. An empty fish tank covered a small dresser, and on the desk sat a computer with a glowing monitor.

His questions would likely solicit the kind of information a twelve-year-old boy hid from his parents. He turned to the mother. "Is it all right if I speak with Robert alone?"

"Why?"

He stared at her, moving his eyes back toward the hall. "Boy stuff."

Mrs. Farnes objected, but Delbravo took her aside and privately reassured her. He told her what he would ask and promised to debrief her afterward. She shifted the baby on her hip and watched her son. "All right, I guess a minute alone wouldn't hurt."

Tim walked into the boy's bedroom. Robert closed the door.

"This your computer?" he asked the boy.

"Yeah. Am I in trouble?"

"No. You had a tutor from the university last month. Kurt Victor."

"Yeah. He came here twice."

"What did he teach you?"

"Nothing. Just set up the computer I got for Christmas."

"Do you have an Internet connection?"

The boy nodded.

"Did Mr. Victor help set it up?"

"Yeah, so?"

"Did he talk about sex on the net?"

"Dunno." Robert looked away. "Maybe. Will you tell my mom?"

"Hey, you're not the bad guy. I only want to know what Mr. Victor did here."

"He just set up the computer."

"I'm going to take a look at it." Tim put his satchel on the desk next to the computer. From it, he pulled out a portable hard drive.

"What do you want?"

Tim sat behind the monitor. "Just a look."

"Don't you need a search-thing?"

"Are you hiding anything?"

"I-I...Uh, I..."

"I can get your mom."

"No...no. Look, Kurt showed me stuff, you know."

He hooked the drive on the USB port and started looking through the files. "What kind of stuff, Robbie?"

"You know. Guy stuff."

"Don't worry. I only want to know what Victor showed you. Just so we know he wasn't doing anything wrong."

Robert sat on the bed. "He showed me where to get free pictures."

"Pictures?"

"Girls."

"Oh. Just girls?"

"And...and stories."

Tim looked back at the kid. "Anything Mr. Victor wrote?"

Robert nodded. "It was on some kind of group."

"A newsgroup?"

The boy nodded.

"About a Japanese girl?"

"That's right."

"Is that all?"

"I didn't like the story. Just the pictures."

On the computer, Tim found several JPEG pictures little Robbie had downloaded from adult sites. Robbie couldn't have had a hard time finding it. The computer porn industry grossed several billion dollars a year—about an eighth of the total sex market. The erotic newsgroups endlessly flooded readers with massive images and video, grabbing about a fourth of all Usenet traffic in less than a percent of the total groups. Nearly every fetish—pre-teen, bestiality, bondage, torture and so on—was catered on the groups. Where the cops would cuff any adult handing printed porn to a kid, it wasn't illegal to send digital porn to a minor. Congress had passed a public-appeal act outlawing it, but the Supreme Court ruled their legislation unconstitutional.

Tim asked, "Did Victor say anything about the story?"

"Just that he wrote it. He was proud. It was stupid, I thought."

"Did he say that it was real?"

"Nope. He made it up."

Damn. Unfortunate, but expected. Tim scoured the boy's hard drive for anything uniquely matching Victor's story text. It came back without a single result. Tim felt his jaw tense. Damn.

"Did he talk about a guy named, Alven Hando?"

Robbie looked around the room, twisting his mouth. "No."

"Anything strange?"

"Not really. He just showed me stuff, took me out for ice cream once."

"Thanks, Robbie." Tim got up and collected his equipment.

"That's all?"

"That's it." It wasn't much, but at least it gave confirmation of Victor's authorship.

Saturday, February 1

Detroit

Tim looked up and squinted at the early sun rising above Lake Erie. It chugged into the ice-blue sky like a tugboat hauling Montazuma's gold into the slums of Detroit.

Usually such a scene would inspire Tim, but he felt uneasy, unsure. Although he knew Victor was dangerous, the dorm search gave him nothing concrete for conviction. The Farnes boy hadn't given anything solid either. Even with Givens going to bat for him, he couldn't work it forever if his case continued slipping away. As much as he hated leaving the perp unwatched, and Yoshiko unguarded, he had to go to Toronto and look for Victor's accomplice—The Psypher, a.k.a. Alven Hando. But first, he hoped to get a little reassurance about everything.

After admiring the sunrise, he crossed an empty street and examined his mother's home on the other side. The two-bedroom concrete row house looked so much smaller than it did when he was a child. It'd been gray and red back then. Now it stood forest green with yellow trim and abutted brightly colored houses on either side—all peeling thirty years of paint. He could see a light on in his mother's kitchen. She was awake.

Though he loved the old house, visits to this neighborhood had never put him at ease. This morning, he would tell his mom about the case. At least he could excite her.

He tromped up her plywood steps, creaking over splinters to the entrance. His mother's porch was screened in, and he opened the flimsy gate quietly so as not to wake the neighbors. Inside he wove around an assortment of garden tools, ceramic statuettes and plastic trolls—none of which would ever be planted in soil since his mother had no yard. Hardly a day had passed as a kid when he hadn't come home with his knees all bloody, pants torn and palms all roughed out on the pavement.

Her door was locked so he knocked with a single knuckle. After a moment he heard her scuffling footsteps. The kitchen window curtain flew up and little eyes peered out at him. His mother threw open the door with a cry of delight.

"Oh I'm so glad to see you!" She hugged him closely.

"Me too, Mom."

He pushed quickly inside, closing the door behind. No sooner had the door closed, when a swarm of memories buzzed around him—the faded yellow-brown tile floor in the kitchen, the wobbly Formica table where he'd spent hours studying, the shag carpet leading upstairs, and the aroma of home-cooked meals and her cheap department store perfume. She still held him by the waist and stretched up to kiss him on the cheek. Pink curlers tucked under her hairnet hit him mid-chest and she seemed so small now, reminding him of his grandmother.

She squinted at him. Her choppy words still reflected her antique Brazillian roots. "You look tired, as usual."

"And you always say that." It was his way—looking weary. Everyone thought he looked sleepy, but he was wide-awake, busy soaking up details.

"What are you doing here?"

"Get dressed, Mom. We're going out for breakfast."

"Breakfast? My son's taking me out for breakfast?" She harped and whooped, sliding in pink slippers around the sink. She reached over and turned off the burner, looking back incredulously. "Not a call in weeks. And then...Poof! He's here to make up for lost time."

"Come on, Mom."

"What's the occasion? Has the FBI fired you again?"

"No. Just get changed." Was she still worried about him getting shot? Her visits during the suspension had been comforting, though, after getting shot, the bureau lost its charm with her. As it had with Janice, his wife. The new case, he hoped, would spark new esteem in his family.

She moved to the stairs, and about halfway up she called back. "Where we going?"

"To Denny's."

"Oh, gracious me! The one where they kicked out them others?"

His mother had been big on civil rights in the sixties, so Tim was taking her into the former all-white sections of Detroit. "Royal Oaks."

"Oh, good! Is it just breakfast, or can you stay longer?"

"Just breakfast."

"Oh."

While waiting for her to dress, Tim inspected the kitchen for items needing repairs. The wood in the cupboards sagged, warped and rotting some. Chipped paint suspended from the ceiling in spots. But for the most part, the house seemed in better condition than he would've expected. As always, his mother kept it immaculately clean.

Seeing his home again stirred a lot of feelings. He'd been so eager to move out at eighteen, but he still felt comfortable there. On the kitchen table he saw a pair of colorful salt-n-pepper shakers. He picked one up and sat at the table, remembering the little dwarf painted on its side. When Mom wasn't looking, the shakers had been toys for he and his younger brother, Cedric.

Cedric. Why the hell did it always turn out that way? Like almost everything he valued, Cedric had been stolen by this jealous city. Tim was in Quantico when it happened—only a year married and Janice six months pregnant with Reggy. When he had flown out, the house was more cluttered than he'd ever seen it. His mother was a wreck.

He shook his head and felt his jaw tighten. He couldn't bear to think of Cedric's death. He turned to find his mother descending the stairs, dressed in a flowery blouse and a conservative white skirt with hat to match.

"You got a case you working on?" She walked down the hall, removed her hat and then entered the half-bathroom on the main floor.

"Yes, I do." He smiled and stood straight.

"Don't they give you Saturdays off?"

"I have a meeting in Toronto tonight." He would work the weekend with the Royal Canadian Mounted Police, trying to locate Alven Hando.

"You sure it isn't a job interview?" She fixed her hair.

"No."

"Why not?"

He put the salt shaker down. Why did she do this? Sometimes he wondered if she had Alzheimer's; she couldn't seem to remember his feelings.

She came out of the bathroom.

"Mom, I don't want to leave the bureau. You know that."

"I don't know why; they don't respect you. And it's so dangerous." She replaced the hat and grabbed a handbag from the stair banister. "You'll go out like Cedric; leave me all alone. Make me live my years without family so I can die in line at the supermarket."

He could feel her eyes on him, but he wouldn't look into them. Maybe she did worry, but he wanted her admiration. It seemed no one in his family appreciated what it took to stop criminals.

She said, "I called them, you know. After you got shot."

"Who?"

"The FBI man—what was it? Robert somebody? He knew you."

"Bob Givens?"

"I told him you should quit."

"Mom!"

"You know what he said? He said, you didn't really deserve the demotion. But what will they do? Nothing. You're a black man in a white man's maze, Timothy. Not even getting no cheese for all your work."

He rose from the table. "Are you ready for Royal Oaks?"

"I suppose so," she mumbled. "But it won't cheer me."

Sunday, February 2

Apartment

Janice Delbravo had given up waiting for Tim. She rose from the dining chair, still dressed in her cream-lace camisole, and eyed the red wax pooled high in the candleholder. Her roast dinner had grown cold; Tim was late coming back from Toronto.

She had put kids to bed, shelved the books, stacked the videos and prepared his favorite meal in hopes of spending the evening with him. She licked a fingertip and pinched out the first wick. Before extinguishing the next, she heard the front door open, then the sound of Tim's coat rustling and his shoes scuffing on the entrance tile. The door creaked shut and the lock clicked. She turned and saw him, rumpled shirt and haggard face, coming into the dining room.

"Sorry, I'm so late." He dropped his case and walked to her.

She felt his arms wrap around her back. "It's all right. You look tired."

"It's not an act this time." He rubbed his hand across the small of her back, smoothing the camisole. "Seeing you in this…maybe I'm not that tired."

They kissed. "How'd it go up there?" she asked.

"No luck. The Canadian perp is still a ghost."

"Sorry." She squeezed his arm. "You got a couple of calls. Campus police."

His mouth dropped open. He rushed to the kitchen. "What happened?"

"They were looking for someone. She wasn't in her dorm Friday or Saturday night. Some Japanese girl."

"Not good!" He snatched the phone, then jerked open a drawer and pulled out a phone book. "Yoshiko. I just knew it."

"Tim." Janice grabbed his hand. "You don't have to call back."

"What?"

"They found her late today, in another dorm across campus. She spent a couple nights with a Japanese girlfriend. I guess she was scared. She's safe now."

Tim heaved a breath and lowered the phone.

"I'm sorry." Janice pulled up her camisole and held his hand. "I should have said that first. Please, don't…"

"No, no. I'm just stressed, tired of seeing snowy freeway." He returned the phone and looked over her at the table. "That looks good. Too bad I ate on the road. Is it warm?"

"No, but I can reheat it." She released him. "Or save it."

He stepped to the pot roast, tore off a hunk and put it in his mouth. "It's good…but I'm more interested in your after-dinner plans."

She smiled. "You go upstairs, get ready. I'll put this away and come right up."

"Don't take too long." He turned and left.

She cleared the food and dishes, feeling odd in the kitchen wearing only a lace bra and string panties under her camisole. She knew Tim liked this particular outfit.

She pinched the last candle and then rose the stairs. At the top, she found Tim in his navy blue robe, standing in their children's doorway. She hugged him from behind until he reached around and drew her to his side. In the room, she saw Reggy and Tasha in their beds. Reggy had kicked off the covers again and stretched like a cat by the fireplace. Tasha held the quilts tight around her neck, curled up underneath.

"I missed you guys this weekend."

She didn't respond. They had discussed it many times; he should know her feelings. He could work less, spend more time at home, but he just wouldn't.

It was the curse of having earned so many commendations for his work; it was never enough. He'd had his glory days, and now that was over. Couldn't he just be satisfied with a safe desk job?

"Promise to be home more this week, Tim."

"I promise." He kissed her, kissed her long. Then she felt herself lift up. He carried her down the hall and buried his head between her hair and neck.

"Let's go to bed."

Monday, February 3

Federal Building

Monday morning, Tim hung up the phone after speaking with U.S. Attorney Sam Grand. Yoshiko Kamahara, the object of Victor's perverse desire, was in Grand's office waiting to be interviewed. Without physical evidence from the dorm search, she became their strongest hope. If Victor had harassed or even approached her, then they had an airtight case, Grand had said.

Ever since getting the victim's photo, a gnawing sensation began eating at Tim. The small file the university supplied about her only bolstered his agitation. On paper, Yoshiko seemed so likable and harmless and innocent. And Victor wanted to upset all that—to intimidate her virtue—the sonuvabitch.

In the court offices, Tim found Grand's door cracked open. He knocked politely.

"Come in."

He pushed the door and saw the U.S. attorney first. Sam Grand smiled in that baby-face-way he always did, which was why he looked half his real age.

Next to him sat the Japanese student. Her eyes regarded Tim softly like a caress on his unshaven face. But he also felt her stare drill him, like she might see his past. Would she trust him if she knew how badly he had screwed up in Danville?

In her picture she looked older, but she was really just a child. So young like…In a flash, he envisioned her delicate face bruised and bleeding. Just a broken child. Then he saw her there in Grand's office, an adult. She hinted a respectful smile at him.

"Come in, Agent Delbravo." Tim had forgotten to enter completely and Grand had to remind him. He found a chair just off to the left of Grand's spotless desk. The attorney's office appeared as if no one except custodians ever worked there. And possibly an interior decorator or two.

On the desk sat a paused micro-recorder. Grand picked it up, but before he turned it on, he looked at Tim. "I've explained everything about this to her, and she understands and wants to cooperate. I was just about to end my questions. Basically, building up to the release forms."

Tim nodded.

Grand turned to Yoshiko. "I have a few more questions for you, Miss Kamahara, and then we'll let Agent Delbravo ask some more before you sign those forms. All right?"

She nodded, one downward stroke of the head and then up. Not the usual bobbing that most people do. She studied them. Grand started the micro-recorder.

"Ms. Kamahara, I called your father in Japan. He says the decisions are yours to make. We want to know that if for any reason we need you to testify, would you be willing to do it."

Yoshiko considered this and then spoke politely with a moderate, understandable accent. "I don't know. I would like to be…confa…dental," she stammered.

"Well, let's see how it goes. If we really need you, then I'm sure we'll coach you thoroughly." He cleared his throat and grabbed some papers that were stacked neatly on his desk. "One last question. How did you learn about the, uh…story, that includes your name?"

"When the lady at the university tell me."

"Mary Carter?"

"Yes, that is her name."

Grand paused briefly. "Have you read the story?"

"I saw some of it."

The attorney squinted and spoke gently. "Is there anything additional about his portrayal that seems…particular or highly accurate of your person?"

She looked at Tim, then at Grand, eyes blinking and cheeks twitching up. "I'm not sure. I could not read it all; I got scared."

Watching her, Tim felt strangely disquieted. Despite her flat features and small eyes, he saw something very familiar in her manner. The tears peaking around her lids and the soft quiver of her lips reminded him of John Robinson's oldest daughter. He remembered how his partner's girl had struggled when her father was killed. Tim could do nothing, say nothing to alleviate the pain she carried. And he always felt he owed her a debt for leading her father to his death.

Tears streaked down Yoshiko's smooth cheeks. "I was so scared," she repeated.

Grand reached out and patted her hand. She took his in hers and bowed her head respectively. Tim felt ashamed that he had not comforted her first. Just like he hadn't with Robinson's daughter.

This time, he could not shun payment. He would never forgive himself unless he did all he could to protect Yoshiko, and bring in these bastard rapists before it got out of control.

Grand supplied a tissue and Yoshiko wiped her eyes with it. The attorney smiled at her and spoke softly. "Why don't we let Agent Delbravo ask some questions now, all right?

She pursed her mouth and nodded in her manner, sniffling and turning to him.

Tim sat up nervously and began speaking. "First, I want to say, it is a pleasure to meet you. Second, I want you to know we will do everything we can to protect you from these threats."

He really meant it. Bowing, she gave him a thin smile. He promised himself that he would not let anyone harm that smile. At least he could feel good that nothing had happened to her during the weekend. He would have never forgiven himself for not insisting on her protection at the start. But it was turning out all right. They would stop it before it went any further.

"Now most of my questions are for our verification," Tim continued. He looked at his sheet. "How long have you been at U-M?"

"I come from Hikone, Japan, to Michigan two and a half years ago."

He cleared his throat and read down his list. "Have you lived in Lawrence Hall, dorm 309 for the entire time?"

"No, I first live in Baits Hall, on North Campus for one year, then I moved to Lawrence."

He made a note of this, remembering that Victor had resided in Lawrence Hall, the same room his entire time at the university—two halls across from her current room. "Have you ever met or seen Kurt Victor in your hall?"

"I don't think so."

"But you've seen the photo of him?"

"Yes. But I don't think I know him."

Damn. Tim looked down at his sheet. "Our records indicate that your Linguistics class last semester is the only class you ever had with the subject. Is that correct?"

Her eyes folded. "What do you mean 'subject'?"

"The subject or suspect, Kurt Victor."

"Only Linguistics 210, but I don't remember seeing him."

"And no one who looks like him has ever bothered or even approached you."

"I don't think, not that I know," she said. Her face appeared worried now.

It was not looking good. Apparently, she hadn't stumbled into the suspect—which was better for her safety, but worse for their investigation. Maybe she hadn't recognized him. Or maybe he just had one of those common, boy-next-door, kind of faces.

Grand watched her warmly, his hand cupping his chin. Yoshiko sat cordially with her hands resting in her lap. Tim wiggled a pen in his right hand and continued. "During the past two or three months, at any time, have you ever been approached by a strange person?"

"No. I usually go only with my friends."

"Can you write a list of your friends' names?"

"My friends?" Her face twisted anxiously. "Would he go after them?"

"No." Tim swallowed hard. If she ever did, God-forbid, disappear, her friends might know whether she was safe or really missing. "It's just protocol. You can get me a list in a couple of days, okay?"

She nodded.

"Just a couple more." Tim looked down at his list. "Have you ever received any strange letters or notes or items in the mail or at your dorm room in the past three months?"

She shook her head.

"How about strange phone calls, breathers, hang-ups?"

"I don't have a phone."

Tim forced a smile. "That's it. Thanks, Yoshiko." He glanced back at Grand, shrugging his shoulders.

It just wasn't going to be as easy as they thought.

* * *

Tim worried about their case after learning Yoshiko had never seen the subject. After she left, Tim spoke with Grand in the foyer of the court offices.

"Any news about our warrant?" Tim asked.

Grand scratched his chin. "Well, good and bad. The bad news is, the judge wouldn't okay a search for Victor's car."

"What? The car is used in every story, including the new one I found at the dorm."

"Yes, and that's part of the problem, says the judge. You searched the dorm without a federal warrant. I can't use anything from that search in the affidavit."

Tim bit his lip. "The university had waivers from both students."

"Yes, but they're for policy breaches in campus housing, not criminal activities."

"Damn. And the e-mail?"

"That's okay. Judge said we can use all the e-mail given to us. A federal officer did not extract it without a warrant."

"Look, Grand, I'm sorry about the dorm search. I thought the waivers would be enough."

"I don't blame you. I'll file a petition with the Circuit on the matter. I think you did what you had to."

"Will we have enough with the rest?"

"We could always use more evidence," Grand said. "Today, Victor hired a lawyer to challenge the suspension on campus. I'm sure he'll fight the charges as well. The other problem..." He paused. "I'm worried about the Internet aspect. We're treading new ground on this."

Tim nodded. "The media will pay service. But why worry about the Internet?"

"The judge will. Why shouldn't we?"

"Because, Internet or not, it's still a threat." Tim stuffed his fists into his pants pockets. "What if they had called each other, or sent postal letters instead of e-mail?"

"Yes, but there's no precedent for this on the Internet. A case like this, and the whole law is up for grabs. It's new, unregulated media."

"It's a bunch of Limbaugh wannabes playing on the world's largest soapbox. And rapists taking pointers from each other."

Grand snickered. "Well, we can take two of them out of the game."

"Not both," Tim said. "We're playing hide-n-seek with the accomplice. The only 'Hando' we found in all of Canada was a 78-year-old man in an Ontario hospital."

"Great." Grand slapped a desktop. "It just pisses me off to think these jerks live in separate countries, and can still plan together like this."

"Yep. That's the net. There's an international support group for every vice. *Alt.sex.stories* is only the tip, and Victor and Hando are the first in a long line."

"Well, I'll give Victor's attorney a call," Grand said. "Good news is, you can plan on picking him up right after lunch."

Tim nodded. The difficult part was just starting. He knew it had to be by the book. That meant taking a partner to the arrest.

* * *

Attorney's Office

Special Agent Louis Mott rode with the black agent in the *bucar*—a dark Pontiac sedan supplied by the bureau—and he didn't even feel like complaining. Delbravo drove them past U-M's Medical School, over the Huron River into an older residential area. Mott felt funny assisting the black agent and all. But that was the bureau for you—they're big on political correctness and all kinds of never mind.

At least it was getting him out of the office. Kaplan had him so hog-tied to pulp and print that Mott didn't know a gray Michigan sky from its snowy roads. They were going to make an arrest. It was Mott's second arrest, and that was great, too. But he wondered what all the hubbub was about, since Delbravo hadn't said a thing.

Delbravo pulled the bucar off Broadway, near Plymouth Road. Mott hadn't got any lunch since he was pulled away early. And damn! He even forgot his 10mm. Regulations dictated that they must be armed for an arrest.

"Damn!" Mott said. "I left my Roscoe. Did you bring yours?"

"You don't need it."

"Don't need it? Regulations say—"

"I know regulations." Delbravo patted his coat. "I brought mine. That's enough."

Mott blinked at him incredulously. He didn't even know what kind of gun Delbravo carried, but it was probably a wimpy, low-caliber revolver.

"I want to be armed, Delbravo. I have no idea who we're doing."

"It's a routine arrest."

"And I still want a gun!"

Delbravo reached into his holster, pulled out his firearm and tossed it on Mott's lap. "You can hold mine, if that will make you feel better."

"I want my own."

"Shut up."

Mott picked up the gun, a Smith & Wesson Sigma 9mm. It felt light, even for a carbide frame. Too light. He ejected the clip.

It was empty.

"Shit. This ain't even loaded."

Delbravo didn't say anything.

"I said this isn't loaded."

"There's an ammo case under the seat."

Every bucar kept an ammo case, but that wasn't Mott's point. Delbravo was carrying an unloaded weapon. Totally against regulations. He cursed to himself, worried that his record would be stained. Just getting his start and some tar-munching ape was going to ruin it all for him. He would just have to make sure he didn't take the fall.

He pulled out the ammo case and loaded Delbravo's clip, then slid it back in the gun. He watched Delbravo from the corner of his eye. The guy seemed so casual, like he was going to get the oil changed, not make an arrest. Mott vowed he would never get so burned out. He just needed to find something local to keep his southern blood boiling. Everyone up here was so damned impassive.

Delbravo stopped the bucar in front of an old Victorian home, spiking the curb with the front tire and parking just behind a corroding red Celica which leaked antifreeze into the snow. He shut the engine off and exited without a word. Mott hurried behind Delbravo on an unshoveled path, crunching icy snow up to a bright pink door. The off-white house was outlined with blue trim, and on a pole hung a yellow and red shingle announcing: *Daniel Clevor, Attorney at Law.*

Before knocking on the door, Delbravo tossed a pair of handcuffs to him. "Hold these, Mott. And note the time of arrest."

Delbravo pushed a buzzer. Mott noted it was just before one p.m. After a moment, the door opened and a man with thin hair and glasses stepped aside without a word. Mott almost laughed. It was great to put that kind of fear into people. That was the one thing he loved most about the bureau.

Delbravo showed the man the warrant and told him they were there for Kurt Victor. After Mott entered, the man explained that he was Victor's attorney. Then he showed them from the entrance to his office.

The lawyer apparently lived there and kept his workplace beside the entry. Inside his office, a young man sat. The kid wore jeans and a brown sweater over a white turtleneck. The lawyer introduced the young man as Kurt Victor. The kid's listless eyes stared at the agents from behind a pair of wire-frame glasses. He wasn't all that tall and looked thin with a narrow face and a sparse mustache, basically like any common guy. The high-back chair he sat in practically dwarfed him. Delbravo walked up to him and flipped out his FBI seal.

"Kurt Victor, by order of the Attorney's office of the United Sates of America, I am placing you under arrest for violation of Title 18, United States Code, Section 875(C). Willfully transmitting a threat to injure the person of another in interstate and foreign commerce."

Delbravo glanced back at Mott while pointing at the boy with a tilt of his head. "You want to *Mirandize* him?"

Mott smiled and began reciting, "You have the right to remain silent..." as he placed the cuffs on him.

Immediately after he acknowledged that he understood the Miranda, Victor looked at Delbravo. "What's your name, Officer?" he asked.

Delbravo, apparently surprised at the inquiry, answered after a pause. "Special Agent Tim Delbravo."

The lawyer observed his client. Mott gazed about the room, watching everyone's expression. Arrests could be so much fun.

Victor cracked a thin smile. "Well, Mr. Delbravo, your case is bullshit!"

"Be quiet, Kurt!" shouted the lawyer.

But Victor didn't heed the counselor and added another prediction. "You'll regret this day."

"Kurt, I said keep your cool!" Clevor put a hand on his client's shoulder. "I'll have you back by tonight. You've got no record and no judge is going to hold you on a simple computer fantasy. Just stay calm for a few hours till I get your bond."

Victor nodded, and Mott helped the black agent lead him out. On the sidewalk, Mott watched Delbravo grab the kid by his shackled hands, almost lifting him as they moved to the sedan. Mott was surprised. He'd never seen Delbravo so alive.

The lawyer shouted at them from the door. "I'll call your father, and follow you to the federal building later. Don't worry about your car either!"

Delbravo shoved the boy into the sedan and slammed the door. In a minute, they were pulling back onto the road, tires squealing. Mott latched his belt tightly because Delbravo was driving as if the Klan were on his tail.

* * *

Residency

Tim placed Victor under the care of two U.S. marshals for an hour. His stomach pained him and sweat started forming on his brow. He just had to make this case work. That meant perfect investigating and reporting.

At his desk, he hovered over his computer terminal and punched in information about the arrest, using a few fingers on each hand. Touch-typing had never come easy for him unless it was computer code. But he easily kept up with the colossal and slow National Crime Information Center system. Tim didn't know how much the database currently held, but a couple of years ago, it had files on over ninety million persons stored into five levels of classification—all in all, hundreds of millions of files. Even simple call-ins from the public had to be entered, according to protocol. Like real criminals should get in line behind curious nobodies. Right.

To store all these files, DC had bought the best storage media around. But they forgot to buy the faster processors. With all the crime-backlog and primitive technology, it was like trying to get on a flying jet from a tricycle. The system continued at its snail pace as Tim punched in Victor's information, making him wonder if he would finish before Victor's bail hearing.

He continued on the reports when the phone rang. He answered, moving to a form.

"Timothy Delbravo?" a woman's voice said.

"Yes. This is Special Agent Delbravo."

"Please hold for Senator Euler."

Tim cursed silently; there was no time for anything.

"Agent Delbravo, I'm glad I could reach you," said the senator. He had a strong, farm-talk accent. "I'm Senator Jack Euler from Nebraska. I wonder if I might have a word with you about the Kurt Victor arrest."

Tim was shocked that he would know about it, but then he was a U.S. senator. "I don't have time right now," he said. "I could fax you some notes tomorrow."

"That will be too late," the senator said. "The media is trying to destroy my legislation, and I need your help to show them how important it really is. You help me; I help you. That's all I'm asking."

"Help how?"

"Do you know about my Internet Protection Act?"

"Some." He stopped working on the forms. He was about to get a lesson on Internet law from a senator.

"The smut on our computer networks is horrible, Mr. Delbravo. It's turning the Internet into a red-light district, if you know what I mean."

Sure do, Senator. Most congressmen were quite familiar with red-light districts.

"We're coming to a vote, you know…"

"Senator," he interrupted. "What do you need from me?"

"Well, sir, you know our Communications Decency Act and then COPA were overturned in court, but now we've reworked them. The Internet Protection Act is a law that requires computer manufacturers to include an onboard chip, we call it the Decency Chip. It's like the V-Chip we already have for televisions. Once activated for kids, the D-Chip monitors information content coming in through communication ports, cutting out the indecent material."

"Senator, I don't think I can help you there."

"Sure you can—with supporting testimony when I bring this up for a vote this Thursday. Friday at the latest."

"I'll be in court on Thursday."

"Even if I have to twist the judge's arm, we'll get you out. Friday too. This is important."

"So is my case."

"We're talking the same thing. Your criminal posted that violent pornography."

"Victor wasn't arrested because of online pornography. He's planning to rape someone, Senator."

"Yes, yes. His story is just horrible. And that other one—he got away, right?"

"We don't know who he is."

"Right. Well, our D-Chip will also check outgoing material. To ensure the sender's real identity is intact. No more anonymity. Just think how that would've helped you."

"Senator—"

"You know, a kite without a string attached won't be any more free to fly. I'm trying to keep our great computer networks soaring in a turbulent society."

Blah. Blah. Blah. Tim wished he could shut him up. He knew firsthand about all the problems on the net. But no laws, no speeches and no grandstanding was going to change it. They just didn't have the manpower to hunt and herd all the offenders.

"And there'll be no censorship, Mr. Delbravo," the senator continued. "It's a matter of choice. Adults who want the…this stuff can get access with an encrypted password. It's impossible to break our encryption."

"*Tell the parents,*" Tim wanted to say. Kids are notorious for being better at computers than mom and dad.

"You fly out to DC in a couple days," the senator said. "We'll meet before my act is introduced on the senate floor. Once you've testified how it will help this Victor case, I'll see about a promotion."

The promise enticed Tim briefly, but he knew Euler was playing games with him. Tim wouldn't let some senator add his name to another reaction list of tokens just to get promoted.

"Senator, I honestly can't say that your act would've stopped our assailants."

"Don't question my judgment, young man. I'm on the senate appropriations committee. If you won't help, I'll get the FBI to appoint someone who will. That Victor case is too valuable. You understand?"

What a jackass. "All too well, Senator."

"Then you cooperate with my aide. He'll be around to coach you the day after tomorrow."

"Senator, I need to be in court now. Please excuse me."

Tim hung up.

* * *

Detroit

Two hours later, Tim left the District Courthouse. The Magistrate had listened to the preliminary evidence Sam Grand presented, and admitted the defendant into the Milan Federal Prison without bail. Next would come a grand jury indictment. Everything proceeded according to protocol.

But Tim felt nervous. Slighting a senator wasn't the smartest thing he had ever done. It worried him. His case was in for a lot of attention, he realized, and he had to be careful. One mistake and he could be replaced.

Everyone emptied the courtroom and entered the pristine city hall with its waxed floors and polished columns. Tim moved over as Grand passed him and plunged onto the stairs leading outside. A crowd stood there, speaking to reporters. Several of them mobbed Grand as he came out. Tim remained inside, letting the attorney field all the questions. He could hear the hubbub through the glass it was so loud.

Grand acknowledge the media interest, using singsong declarations about "precedence" and "for the children" and "net decency." He made sure they knew how important the case was.

By the large number of ambitious news reporters, Tim guessed they already knew it. He stayed back, waiting for the impromptu press conference to end. Tim had had a gut-full of reporters after the shooting in Danville. The matter barely remained classified.

* * *

Residency

"You promised to be home," Janice told him.

Tim cranked the phone against his ear. "I'm sorry, Janice."

"It's almost midnight, Tim. Again."

He looked down at his desk clock ticking off the seconds. "Once this case is over, I'll go back to a normal schedule."

"Normal? That's you going for promotion after promotion." He heard teeth grating on her end. "We don't want an agent-of-the-year. We need a husband and a dad—not a framed commendation."

Couldn't she just understand? If he sacrificed now, they would have time later.

"It's short term, Janice. I need your support."

"And we need yours."

Tim felt like a stretch toy. Demands pulling every limb—Janice, the children, the bureau, and even Yoshiko.

He shook his head. "It's the middle of a case. Lives—living, breathing people could be hurt if I don't do my job."

"Your living, breathing wife and children are in misery because you do it too much."

"But if I don't work the chance now, I could lose my career. Start over as a meter maid. Do you want me back on the streets?"

"No..." She sighed. "Just do what you have to. Then after this case, promise to spend time at home."

"I will."

They spoke for a moment longer, then he wished her a good night and hung up. His hands stabbed back on the keyboard of his NCIC terminal. He had finished entering all of his case information into the National Crime Information database and set it crunching on the data. Given Victor's and Alven Hando's e-mail, the NCIC system would anatomize each author's writing until it had a distinctive signature against which it could compare further writings.

He disconnected from the NCIC, returning to the main menu. One option led him to the outer network, into a server that would connect him to the Internet. He navigated to the Usenet and scoured articles from the *alt.sex.stories* newsgroup. Once directed, it furnished him a long list of subject and author lines. He read each line, pages and pages of them; the primitive newsreader on his bureau desktop did not have search capabilities. Several of the earliest user-posts spoke of Victor's story, and the University of Michigan's pending suspension against him. They had dates preceding the arrest that day.

Tim found a couple of amusing counter-posts. One entitled, "How I hurt

Kurt," conveyed the feelings of a bold gal who wanted to see Kurt Victor strung up by the nostrils. Another anonymous post called, "Victimizing Victor," detailed the grueling torture of Kurt and his murder by acid wash and drowning in boiling grease. Scores of replies followed the counter-posts, threatening the gal and other author with vile acts. This virtual violence went on for days in the list, only subsiding at the end, when a new topic ransacked the group's obsession.

At the end of the more than 2000-post heap, he found dozens of posts regarding Victor's arrest. They had just started that evening. The newsgroup had gone wild with inflammatory remarks and conspiracy theories about the FBI and the University of Michigan. Most of them were so wrought with four-letter words and toilet talk, it soon grew tiresome, and he found himself nodding off to sleep.

The basis of his search came from suspicions that Hando might post something now that his friend was in jail. Most of the users, like Hando, used pennames, and Tim believed Hando might take on a new alias now that his friend had the world's attention. He planned to feed every alias-written post through the NCIC for a writer's match in order to find Hando, if he was still out there.

Then he discovered he wouldn't have to. In the middle of this last cluster, Tim found a post signed by Hando himself. He pulled it up.

From: Alven Hando <hando@in1.toronto-net.ca>
Date: 3 Feb, 21:13:48 - 0500 GMT
Subject: The Smell of an Education

Hades help us all to learn some smarts,
While a campus' money hits the charts.
Now the brilliance of one student body
Is suspended and stamped like a nobody.

Something stinks and reeks like shit,
When creativity is raped and plundered.
Damn school, they'll regret their fit,
When they see the mire, they'll rue the blunder.

——Alven "poet against prudes" Hando

Hando used the same e-mail address as he had with Victor over a month before. The same address that no longer existed when Tim and the investigators in Toronto had checked. By the date of the post, he learned that Hando had posted only a few hours ago, much after the hype of Victor's arrest. Yet Hando did not mention the FBI or the police or any legal involvement. Of course, in Canada, the news might not be so big.

Most worrisome, the last stanza sounded like a threat against the university. A mire, they'll regret.

Tuesday, February 4

Milan Federal Prison

On Tuesday, Tim watched Kurt Victor's attorney escort the accused into a conference room in the heart of the federal prison. Victor wore a brown jumpsuit and loose shackles on his feet, none on his hands. There were no guards inside the room, and Tim suddenly felt the burden of immediate prisoner security rest upon his shoulders. It was eight in the morning. His early schedule had been upset when U.S. attorney Sam Grand called an impromptu meeting to negotiate Victor's plea. Depending on the outcome, the rest of Tim's day could fall under Grand's grip as well.

He and Grand shook hands with Victor's attorney, Daniel Clevor. The lawyers wore dark suits. Tim had on his light gray Penny's special. He and Grand sat across a cheap conference table from Clevor and the accused. Grand placed some sheets on the tabletop and began speaking. "As you know, gentlemen, we are here to offer a reduced penalty in return for information about Mr. Victor's accomplice. Whether Victor met Hando in person."

"And if my client had," Clevor said, "what does it get him?"

A good kick in the teeth. Tim didn't think they should let the bastard plea down the punishment. But then, if it also netted Hando...

Grand replied, "A three month suspended sentence and reduced $2,000 fine, for the identity of Mr. Hando or information leading to his capture."

"Ridiculous," Clevor said. "You want me to give you Hando, so you can use him to build a bigger case against my client? We'll get a dismissal. You have nothing."

"We've got plenty. We have your client's e-mail. He was conspiring to rape the girl."

Clevor pshawed. "Yeah? Tell the girl, and the university. This supposed threat sat on newsgroup bulletin boards for over a month before anyone did anything. My client did nothing to pose a threat during that time."

"Since when did one month constitute the statute of limitations on harassment and threats?"

"Look what you're saying. Harassment? The girl didn't even know she was allegedly threatened until you told her."

"It doesn't matter. The statute doesn't say the intended victim has to know. The Secret Service doesn't tell the President about every assassination plot, but they still make hundreds of arrests."

"Well, this is no assassination plot," Clevor said. "All you have at most is a puerile story."

"And e-mail with specific plans."

"I doubt that my client's e-mail will be admissible. You had no probable cause except a story, no warrant."

"The judge already ruled on that. The dorm search evidence wasn't admitted, but the e-mail was. It's in our affidavit."

"And my client's personal correspondence was gathered without cause, except for a fictionalized story. You have no physical evidence. Kurt has no priors, never harmed, stalked or even met the alleged victim. Your case is awash in circumstances, nothing more."

"Look, fellows, we're here for one reason." Tim leaned forward and faced Victor. "Do you know Alven Hando, Mr. Victor?"

Victor didn't speak.

Grand held up a paper. "If you do, we can end all this now. Suspended sentence and a modest fine."

"My lawyer told you," Victor said, "you've got no case. I'm getting out."

Clevor said, "We want immunity and no fine."

"No way." Victor gaped at his lawyer. "I'm not giving them more fuel against me."

"I'm negotiating for immunity, Kurt."

Victor curled his lips angrily. "I don't want them to get a thing. We're fighting for freedom of speech."

"This is about your accomplice." Tim drummed on the table. "Why would you protect Hando?"

Victor remained silent, looking at him with crooked lips. Tim continued, "In your e-mail, you mentioned meeting up in January. Did Alven Hando come down to Michigan?"

Victor folded his arms and leaned back. "Should I care what some guy does?"

"That's enough, Kurt." His lawyer held a hand up to his own mouth. "If you want the deal, then you tell them what you know."

"Read this." Grand slid a paper to the lawyer. "If we find out your client knows anything more about Hando and doesn't tell us, we'll indict him on obstruction and hindrance. Understand, Mr. Victor."

"Bite me." Victor sneered at Grand.

Tim clamped his hands on the edge of the table. "Look, you little…" His nostrils flared and his lips hammered together, then broke open again. "I've got a lot of work to do, so you listen to Mr. Grand. Tell us where to find Hando, then we'll all go home."

"Look, I never saw the guy." Victor stood freely and stepped back, rattling his chains. "I'm outta here. Hanging in my cell beats the hell outta chatting with a couple of 2nd-string G-men."

Tim leaned across the table and grabbed Victor's elbow. "Sit down!"

Victor jerked his arm, pulling Tim over the table until his grip failed and he slapped the table top to keep from falling.

"Watch it, stable boy." Victor held his hands in fists.

Clevor stood. "Gentlemen, we'll see you in court." He grabbed his client and yanked him out the door.

* * *

Sheriff's Office

Delbravo's appetite had dropped out as fast as his case seemed to be sinking. All their evidence resided in documents and one confirmation from a twelve-year-old. Bargaining with Victor contributed nothing. Without the victim's eyewitness of Victor, no physical items in the dorm linking him to an actual plan, and a stretch for the motive, he grew worried. Grand sent him to find more evidence. Which meant longer hours, and getting local cooperation.

An hour after meeting with the accused, Tim stood over the desk of a deputy in the Washtenaw County sheriff's office. He introduced himself, and the deputy grumbled his own name—Mikels. Mikels didn't offer him a seat.

"Let's get on with it," the deputy said through a large gray mustache. "I've got a lot to do."

Tim couldn't believe Mikels was busier than he. It took a lot of pleading to get Detroit to approve the funds for local assistance. He didn't know where the money would come from, but he got affirmation on the phone only an hour before. And clearing his day felt like Tim's last dental exam. He wasn't excited at all about relying on the locals to do his work. But he didn't have a lot of choices.

"We'll go out after you read these," Tim said, handing the deputy copies of Victor's story-posts. He would have Mikels take them to likely spots fitting the suspect's written geographical descriptions. Hopefully, with some local familiarity, they would find the location of Victor's proposed rape.

Taking Victor's stories, Mikels stared at him under bushy eyebrows. "Go where?"

"Out searching for spots."

"Spots?"

"That was all explained in the fax the field office sent."

"Sure, but I can't go out searching. We wouldn't make it to one place before I use up the time on the bureau's charge account."

Tim leaned against Mikels' desk. "We're paying for one-man day."

"Not according to the fax I got." Mikels lifted a rolled-up sheet.

"What?"

"They said I could charge only a half-hour." Mikels smirked.

Tim took the fax and unfurled it. The top registered the sending office as Tim's residency. It was signed by RAC Henry Kaplan. Dammit. The charge account, which came from Ann Arbor's budget, had been cleared for only a half-hour by Kaplan. He was surprised Kaplan gave any at all.

"I guess you won't need me, then." Mikels rolled out his file drawer and lifted folders from it.

"I do. We have a guy threatening rape."

"Whoop-de-do."

"Look, if I don't get your help, his charges will be dismissed."

"Look, you." Mikels lost his smirk. "We're on a tight budget here. I ain't the FBI's lap dog."

Tim searched unsuccessfully for a seat. "The money's been approved. You got the wrong fax."

"It had my name on it." Mikels set down his folders. "When you get it cleared up, you can reschedule with two days' notice."

In two days, they had a preliminary hearing. Tim couldn't wait. His day was planned already. "Okay. Half-hour. You read the stories, then break out some maps."

* * *

Freezing rain poured while Tim spent the day alone, traveling around the county with a camera. The directions given by Mikels pretty much led nowhere, but there was enough in Victor's stories to go hunting. All in all, Tim traveled over a hundred miles, filled his digital camera card to the brim and narrowed his scene-list down to two probable locales: An old abandoned schoolhouse in northeast Ann Arbor and a utility shed off an Interstate rest stop.

The rest stop was unremarkable except for one possible connection to an "unpublished" story by Victor where he figuratively left the victim on the "flat roof." On the other hand, the old schoolhouse bore several remarkable connections to Victor's fantasy. Particularly a bell tower from which Victor, in his story, hangs the victim's bloody clothes like a flag at half-mast.

Tim snapped several photographs of the red brick tower, and mapped out the entire perimeter of the one-room schoolhouse. The deserted spot did seem to provide just the elements Victor wanted in his fantasy.

But would detailing the scene prove anything? Even if the schoolhouse matched the stories perfectly, Victor could just claim he used it as the basis for his *fictitious* scene. Grand had thought it would help, since their list was short on evidence, but Tim had his doubts. There just had to be something else they could use.

By evening time, he was ready to go home, but he knew he couldn't stop— not yet. They still hadn't a clue about Alven Hando. He was somewhere on the Internet. Tim's knowledge of the latest networking technology had not kept up with the rapid-pace of engineers. With all the caseloads, he'd had little time to read trade journals since graduating a decade earlier. He knew he needed help.

The Detroit Field Office quartered only two other agents with computer training, from whom Tim was required to get his assistance. He had met them briefly when he first arrived in Ann Arbor. It had taken him all but five minutes to realize that their support technician—Mark Striker—knew profusely more about newer technologies than the agents did. Striker was just out of trade school and still traded video games with kids.

The Internet teemed with wild anarchy, and Tim needed a computer junkie just as wild. Although it was breaking protocol, he called Striker first.

* * *

Detroit

In a closed fish-tank office at the Detroit Field Office, Tim found technician Mark Striker seated before a large computer monitor. He wore ratty jeans and black headphones attached to an MP3 player. Other than the computer devices and the table they sat upon, the room was bare. Tim opened the glass door and immediately heard brassy hiss leaking from Striker's headphones.

Striker didn't notice him until Tim knocked loudly on the glass. Abruptly Striker turned and gaped with large brown eyes. "Oh—hey! Tom Bravo. You called; I almost forgot."

"Tim Delbravo." He held out a hand. Striker squinted at it and then shook.

"So what can I do you for, Mr. Delbravo—or have they sent you to rag about my beard?" Striker rendered a playful smile and rubbed his chin, which had a couple of days' growth. He kept his brown hair short, but the sides were shaved in a wavy pattern. His left earlobe appeared irritated and pink. Looking carefully, Tim noticed a hole—a pierce for earrings.

"Like I told you on the phone, I'm trying to find a suspect on the Internet."

"Yeah," Striker mumbled, fishing a candy bar from a frayed pocket in his jeans. "Good luck."

"We certainly could use some. Apparently, our guy has a computer account in Canada. He's used it for a newsgroup post last night, but it doesn't really exist."

"He made it up, then."

"But it was real. He received e-mail with it a couple months ago, from the other suspect."

"Oh, this that U-M student?"

"His accomplice."

69

"And his e-mail address?"

"In Canada. It just disappeared."

"Disappeared—how?" Striker looked away, returning to a text window on the large monitor. His mouse and pad sat on the left side, the buttons reversed.

"The account just vanished. Even the host computer site is gone." Tim knew that all Internet accounts required a site that hosted and gave users access.

"No host?"

Tim shook his head, pulling up a seat and then landing hard on it. He glanced through the glass, out over the vacant offices. The field office monopolized the 26th level of the McNamara high-rise just off Michigan Avenue. Tim had always hated his time in field offices. With the SA in Charge and other officials cruising through at all hours, it was enough to give any special an ulcer.

"Can you give me the headers?" Striker asked with the end of his candy bar sticking out of his mouth.

"Sure." Tim opened his satchel and retrieved some printouts. Every e-mail or post on the Internet had a header—a record of when and where the message originated, where it passed and to where it should go. Tim handed the stack to Striker. "Here are some of the messages he sent. With headers."

Striker took the papers and glanced at them. He pointed at the top of one message. Reading through the header, he denoted the different stations that the message had traversed. In this one, Striker explained, the starting point differed from Hando's e-mail address.

"It's a fake."

"But then how did he get e-mail, if it was a fake address?" Tim asked. "I mean, you get mail returned if the address is wrong."

"Oh the e-mail address is real, or was at one time, so he could get mail there. But he's shooting back blanks."

"Blanks?"

"Sending back forged paths, so you don't really know what server he gets or sends his mail from."

"But he's getting connected somehow," Tim said. "Just like anonymous letters getting delivered by the mailman, e-mail still has to cross real computers to go someplace."

"Sure." Striker pointed at Hando's message, at the header. "He's going through an elite site."

"Elite site?"

"It's a cracker's network that loads up the header with crap, so it doesn't actually reveal where the user came from. It's great for fake-mail."

"So this is a hidden site?"

"Yeah, and apparently this guy's using one all the way out in Europe—a real snobby-elite. Doesn't let just anyone use it to send fake-mail. Your guy has connections."

"Really?" Tim studied the printout more carefully. "How can you tell this from the headers?"

"Oh, it just comes with experience. I got to know some of the elite addresses before coming to work here."

"Can we get the perp's address from the site?"

"You want to trace it?"

"If it's possible."

"Sometimes it's possible, but never easy—not this one." Striker chewed the last bit of his chocolate. "There're few guys I know that can fudge headers this well."

How had Striker met these hackers? "Can you get together a list of names?"

"A short one, but I don't think it'll help. Most of them are hiding across the Atlantic or rotting in jail."

Just great. Canada was big enough—now Tim had to search the rest of the world to find this Hando character. Every ticking moment he felt his chances slip away.

* * *

Apartment

At nine p.m., the earliest Tim had arrived home in a week, he knocked on his children's bedroom door. He felt reluctant to be handling a fatherly problem. Tim never knew his own father. Even though he had sworn to break the cycle of his ancestry's fatherless pedigree, growing up without an example often took its toll on his own paternal role.

"Come in."

He entered and saw Tasha first. She sat on her bed, untangling braids in her hair.

"Daddy!" She smiled broadly and rose from the bed.

"Hi, honey." He smiled back. On the other side of the room, Reggy lay on his bed. Pain soaked Tim's stomach. His demotion forced them to live in a smaller place. In California, the housing market had tumbled just before his transfer came. The money they lost was all part of the censure he'd received. Now his son and daughter had to share a room. Reggy was nearly a teenager, and needed privacy.

Tasha reached her arms around his waist and hugged him. "I got an A on my math test today," she said.

"Really? That's great." Tim smiled and then glanced at Reggy. He seemed to ignore everyone.

"Tasha, will you go help your mom? I need to talk with your brother."

"Sure, Dad." She bounced over to her bed and grabbed a small pink bag.

Tim watched her leave and then turned to his son. "Hey, Reg."

Reggy moved his mouth silently and tossed a baseball above him. He caught it and turned it over in his hands. Tim walked closer, noticing his son's black eye for the first time.

"Mom tells me you had a little fistfight at school."

Reggy tossed the ball up again. Tim reached out and grabbed it out of the air. "Your Tony Clark?"

Reggy nodded. He had caught the Tiger's MVP foul ball at a game they went to a month before. Clark signed it after the game.

Tim sat down and handed the ball back. "What happened?"

Reggy looked at the wall. "Just some kid."

"Some kid with fists for brains."

Reggy smiled. "He said I was a pat-brat."

"A what?"

"A cop's kid. Saw you on the news." Reggy dropped the ball. "Now no one wants to be around me."

Tim heaved his shoulders. "Did you fight back?"

Reggy shook his head, still looking at the wall.

"Why not?"

"I dunno." His eyes darted around, looking moist. "I guess I'm a wimp."

"No you're not. You're just a good kid."

Reggy rolled his head. "I don't even know how to fight."

It was probably true. Tim had learned while a young boy in Detroit. "Well, then you're going to learn."

"How?"

"Your old man knows a few things about self-defense."

"They teach you in the FBI?"

Tim nodded. "Defense moves. To counter an attacker. I'll show you." He stood up and took off his coat.

"Now?"

"You bet."

"Can I get lessons, too?"

"Sure thing."

Wednesday,
February 5

Federal Building

Tim's morning started worthless and full of Kaplan's paperwork. Just before lunch, he had a visitor from Washington. Senator Euler's aide, Dan Buck, wanted Tim's case notes. They sat at a small table in the vending area outside the RA, drinking coffee Tim had purchased for both.

"Is this all you have?" the aide asked, holding up the manila folder Tim had given him. It did not mention or reference Yoshiko Kamahara by name.

Buck's voice resounded both strongly and delicately. It would've almost lulled Tim, had he not felt so edgy. He sipped from his cup, eyeing Buck's perfect hair and teeth, molded from a Hollywood action figure. The aide wore a hand-tailored suit and a large green bow tie over his distended larynx. He held his head with an air of intelligence. Buck was definitely a congressman in training.

"Mr. Delbravo?"

"Yes?"

"There's nothing more?"

"That's it," Tim mumbled. "I need to get back to work soon, if that's all."

"Just a minute." The aide smiled and fished in his briefcase.

Tim wanted to leave. He felt cornered, especially after the encounter with Euler; he couldn't repeat his impoliteness.

He glanced around, searching for a safer escape route. Vending machines stood over the ceramic floor. Inside them, rows of identical snacks lined one after the other, waiting to be purchased. It reminded Tim of this aide somehow—a line-up of look-alike congressman waiting to be bought.

"This is for you." The aide handed him a paper with congressional letterhead.

"Okay."

"It's a memo offering our support in your investigation," Buck said. "Our constituency is made up of pro law enforcement minded people like yourself. They believe Senator Euler is a godsend. Like Jesus cleansing the temple, Euler is clearing away the depravity and foul language on the Internet."

Tim had grown up with the Bible, and he always understood it was for his words that Jesus was killed; crucified for what his government thought should *not* be said in public or private. Wouldn't Jesus be in favor of people *choosing* speech for themselves? But then Jesus had said something about that which comes out of a mouth is what defiles a man.

"With this one chip," Buck held up a small case with a small square piece in it, "parents won't have to worry about Internet indecency."

"Right," Tim blurted. "And how long until someone cracks it?"

"Forever." Buck's green bow tie bobbed up and down as he spoke. "That's why we put the encryption on-board."

"On the chip?"

"Yes. It's the only way to stop misuse and indecency."

Encryption to stop indecency? On the chip? It didn't make sense.

"I'd think the FBI would be grateful," the aide said. "Don't you?"

"I can't speak for the FBI on these matters, Mr. Buck."

"Surely you can give a personal endorsement."

"I need to get back to work." Tim began rising.

The aide's eyes grew large. "But Euler really needs a testimony for the Act. The success of your case is exactly what he's looking for."

"Well, if I can get back to work…" Tim scooted back his chair.

"Look, Mr. Delbravo, Senator Euler is on the appropriations committee. He could put in a note about your cooperation when they pen the next FBI budget."

"Well, that's a very nice offer, Mr. Buck." Tim turned.

The aide rose and grabbed his arm. "You must fly out tomorrow."

Tim didn't know how to respond. He felt his anger rising. Hadn't he made it pretty clear he wasn't interested? But this aide and Euler were so adamant in their persuasions and testimonies. All for his sake.

"I don't get it, Mr. Buck. Why am I so important to you?"

The aide smiled proudly at him. "We need you. We need the FBI and especially agents like you that handle cases of extreme importance. The facts and reality of it are in your daily work. It is the FBI that will ultimately enforce decency on the Internet."

"Yeah, and that's what worries me," Tim responded. "You know, it's hectic enough worrying about half-assed threats and harassment on the Internet. Now you want to nail every thirteen-year-old typing the F-word on his keyboard?"

The aide looked angry with Tim. "Well, that's the price we have to pay for—"

"But it's misguided! You're focusing on gnat-sized issues. With kids raping and killing other kids, but all you can see are four-letter words. Get a clue."

"Dammit! Don't piss us off, Mr. Delbravo." Buck grabbed his full cup of coffee and pitched it into the trash. "Euler will spit down your throat, if you don't speak his language."

"I can't go. I have a case."

"Try and hold it tight, Mr. Delbravo." He gave Tim a snarl, then left.

* * *

Residency

Assistant Special Agent in Charge Bob Givens wanted to appear unconcerned while he waited in the cubicle for Tim. But everyone at the Ann Arbor RA watched him anxiously, and RAC Kaplan kept peeking out of his office. Having the ASAC lounge around the residency was enough to make even their coffee nervous.

Givens wasn't accustomed to spooking people. In fact, he had never been one to get noticed much—just below average in height, always conservative clothing, and voice just above a whisper. But just being the ASAC had its own shock value. Others may enjoy it, he knew, but he never liked putting off anyone.

The fact was, he wouldn't have gotten such a high-ranking promotion if he hadn't *received* Tim Delbravo's legendary *confession* months earlier. Givens reproved Tim for taking the fall, but there was no deterring him. OPR had just accepted it. Then with that review wrapped so nicely for him, DC presented Givens with an assistant lead at the Detroit Field Office. But he would've gladly passed it, if it could help Tim. As it was, maybe he could still help his friend.

He pulled out some papers from his brown leather case and acted occupied—preoccupied, rather, which in fact he truly was. What's taking Tim so long? he wondered. The receptionist had told him that Agent Delbravo went out into the hall for a brief chat with someone. That was before his meeting with Kaplan. It had been something like a quarter-hour since he left the RAC's office. And now Kaplan was watching him again.

"So, sir." He smiled at Givens. "How's the clan?"

"The clan?" He stared back at Kaplan, noticing a large ketchup stain on the sleeve of his green suit.

"Your family." Kaplan gulped a smile.

My family? he wondered. Didn't the RAC remember why he waited? He had told him that he needed a chat with Delbravo. Before Givens could answer, the residency door buzzed. Delbravo walked through and raised his eyebrows upon seeing him. The lights in the offices highlighted gray hairs just above Tim's ears. Givens greeted him quietly the moment they made eye contact.

"Sir." Tim stopped and stood rigidly.

"Come on, Tim. You used to call me, Bob. We were training-mates, after all."

Tim nodded slowly, still holding firm in his position. Givens walked over and motioned to the door. "Let's go out for a bit," he said.

"Well, I'll catch up with you later, sir," Kaplan said, waving at him.

Silently Tim led them out into the hall. Once the door closed, Givens spoke again. "I came by because I had to meet with Kaplan."

"Oh? I'm sorry."

Givens chuckled. "Just thought I would see how you're doing."

"Not toilet training anymore," Delbravo said without looking at him. He continued walking down the hall toward an alcove where the lone stairwell lay. "Thanks for the vote of confidence."

"I knew you would do great. Have you read that new ballistics report yet?"

"Not yet. The case is taking all my time."

"You read it tonight, understand? We'll talk about a new review after."

Tim gave a slight nod.

"How's the case going anyway?"

"Good."

"How's Janice?"

"Fine."

"And your children—they like it here?"

"Kids are fine, Givens." His answer came fast, almost too fast, as if Tim were annoyed at the question. He stopped at the end of the hall and studied the carpeting.

Givens reached a hand to his shoulder. "Tim, I wish I didn't have to say this."

Delbravo rotated and stepped back, causing Givens' hand to slide off.

"I got a complaint, Tim. SA Louis Mott filed an allegation saying your weapon wasn't armed for the Victor arrest. You know—"

"I didn't need it, Givens." Tim looked him straight in the face.

"It's regulation. I can't—"

"We arrested him at his attorney's."

Stay calm, Givens told himself. With any other agent, he would have reprimanded heavily at the first interruption. But Tim needed someone on his side. And he owed him. Still, regulations were regulations and he couldn't allow Delbravo to get so loose it required someone higher up to intervene. He was just nipping this while he had the chance.

"No excuses, SA Delbravo." Givens kept his voice firm and deliberate. "If it happens one more time, SAC Hansen will step in."

Tim mouthed the name back, rolling his eyes. They both knew well what that meant.

"You keep it loaded. And read that report. Understand?"

"Yes, sir."

* * *

Tim had seen countless guns bagged as evidence, but never his own. In California, months earlier, they had taken Robinson's and his guns, and analyzed them. Robinson was dead; Tim couldn't remember what had happened, even after loads of psychiatrists tried to bleed his memory—his post-traumatic stress memory loss. Somehow, they had to lay blame for the death of Michael Miller, shot with a bureau gun. And somehow, Tim never felt right laying it on Robinson just because he couldn't remember.

The new ballistics report, like the first one, had essentially the same information. The bureau had sent the weapons to the two-floor laboratory in Quantico. The lab sent back a first report, the one used in all of the questioning.

The new report listed, in the first column, the slugs and firearms recovered at the Danville, California, crime scene. The adjacent column identified rounds fired into a water trap by the same firearms after the incident. At the scene, an ungodly eighteen bullets had been collected, most of them shattered on walls or photographic and electronic equipment in the Danville estate basement.

Five rounds had dodged fragmentation by plunging into soft tissue. Three people killed: one of the kidnappers, Tim's partner, and one boy. Ten 9mm slugs came from one agent's gun, a single from the other. Two from a .357 revolver, another five from a .38, which killed his partner and ripped apart his own leg.

He remembered the shooting, the commotion…the monstrous appearance of the kidnappers. Fear on the faces of their hostages. Guns being raised, then going off. But he couldn't remember what happened after they began firing at the agents. His memory wouldn't even call up exactly when his leg had been shot.

The next line of the report indicated a 9mm slug from Tim's gun matched the one recovered from Michael Miller. His gun had only been fired once, the single bullet that killed young Miller. John Robinson's clip was empty, and they recovered all ten shots in the estate basement or perp's body. And like the old report, finger prints analysis showed that, although Robinson's gun had only his prints, Tim's firearm had two sets of prints—his own and his partner's.

That was why Givens always believed Tim had not shot the boy.

Both agents had powder traces on their firing hand, and because of messy prints on the metal grip of his old gun, it wasn't clear who had fired it. None of the evidence was conclusive. So, with the partner dead, it boiled down to Tim's word.

What had Robinson been doing with both guns?

Every time he asked himself, he recalled Robinson's smiling face, his jokes, and his huge appetite for sour kraut hotdogs. Robinson was the best he'd paired with in Oakland. Tim took his wife and children to Robinson's home last Fourth of July. He drank beer with John, talking about old cases until two in the morning. They found everyone else crashed in front of a video playing on the TV. Their kids had become good friends, and hardly a week passed when he wasn't dropping off his boy at his partner's house.

Today, he could remember little more: The wracked hurt on Robinson's face in the estate basement. Vague flashes of gunfire. Then a gun, with his sweaty fingers around the casing, wriggling in blackness. And he could almost remember feeling the recoil when it went off.

Or did he?

After so many hours on the firing range, his sense of recoil was second nature. Did he really experience it in that basement? Or was it a mind trick, an old habit?

Somehow he knew it didn't matter. Either way, it had been his gun that ripped open Michael, eleven years old from Dallas, Texas. Jeez, the boy was the same age as Reggy—Tim's own son.

The new report had one additional piece of evidence not mentioned before. Right after the shooting, a lab technician had stained Tim's hand with a reactive chemical that showed gunpowder and burns. They illuminated his hands under ultraviolet and took photos. Now further image analysis of the powder marks said that Tim's spray patterns were few and light. They striped across his hand in an uncommon pattern, and didn't conclusively match the typical form of a firing position.

He threw down the report on his desk. There was no way he was going to dig up his partner's resting place. He couldn't change the eulogy they had given him—a twenty-one gun burial, flag and apple pie. And how could he face Robinson's wife if he were to scapegoat her husband now?

No, he was going to work this out his way.

Thursday, February 6

U.S. District Court

"The prosecution opposes the motion, your honor." U.S. Attorney Sam Grand rose from the west pew of the Detroit District Court, sweat running down his nose. He had seen and even argued many cases where the key evidence came from documents, not witnesses. That shouldn't give any reason to dismiss this case, so how could the judge even consider the abrupt motion?

"Counselor." Judge Arthur Truante looked over his bifocals at Grand. "Do you have any reasons why I should not review the motion? Or do you just oppose it because it's your job?"

"Judge, I came prepared for a bail hearing, not to argue against dismissal," Grand said, thankful there were no reporters in the session. Only Delbravo, Grand and his assistant sat on the prosecution side. The defendant and his lawyer remained before the defense table. Behind the defendant sat his father. Victor's mother was still researching abroad in Africa or Asia, Grand had heard.

Truante rubbed his bushy eyebrows and twisted his mouth. "I need an opinion, Mr. Grand, if I'm to consider your opposition."

Grand, familiar with Truante's usual support for prosecution, expected the motion to get tossed right away. Truante, however, didn't seem to be in a hurling mood. Grand opened his mouth, but for the moment nothing came out.

"Your honor." Daniel Clevor, the defense counselor, stood in the silence. "Mr. Grand is stalling. The prosecution has no witness that can testify of real intent. Their entire case is built upon a story, whose whole purpose was purely fictional, evidenced by Victor's sworn statements. Confirmed by the fact that he posted his story in a public newsgroup determined for 'stories' from its very title: *alt.sex.stories*. This case seems to be a misunderstanding."

Grand could almost feel Victor's angry eyes upon him even though he held his back to the student. The sensation often touched him at hearings. He shook the feeling and countered: "We have more than a story, your honor. The affidavit quotes three e-mail messages, in which Victor discusses plans with another man, his accomplice."

Clevor raised his head. "But they never apprehended this would-be accomplice, Alven Hando, to whom was addressed the *private* e-mail messages. It would be patently unreasonable, however, to assume my client's communications caused their only foreseeable recipient, Hando, to fear violence from Victor. Hando clearly demonstrates his desire to continue such discussions in his replies. And until Mr. Hando is found, if he even exists, the Court can not allow his testimony to be given as evidence—it's all inadmissible hearsay."

"Agreed," Truante said. "Mr. Grand, do you even know if Hando is a man?"

"It would be fair to assume that."

"Why, why?"

"The language, your honor. His words."

"*Typed* words. This Hando could be a ten-year-old boy, or a 70-year-old grandma."

"It would be hard to believe."

"But it is all possible, isn't it?"

"Yes, theoretically."

"See, counsel. Without knowing who makes the threat, there is no way to evaluate if their plot is just play or dangerous. A five-year-old can hardly fulfill. Now an NFL linebacker is another thing."

"But, your honor, the charges are filed against Victor, who we know can fulfill."

"Without knowing Hando, it's only half of the story, Mr. Grand. In preparing your brief of opposition, it would be well advised to not use statements from an unknown witness."

"The accomplice is not a witness," Grand replied. "The charges are built from the words of Mr. Victor alone—in whose e-mail is written: *I have to make a bitch suffer! I've been telling myself, 'Go on Kurt, it'd be slick.'*"

"Mr. Grand, all he's done is tell his thoughts. We're not punishing Mr. Victor for having lecherous thoughts, are we?"

"No."

"Then what would we punish him for?"

"Violation of the threat statute in Title 18. Victor wrote: *'Just thinking about it anymore don't do the trick. I have to DO IT.'* And. *'I don't want no blood in my room. So I got me an excellent plan. A virgin abduction.'*" Grand drew in a quick breath. "I take these statements as motive and a plan, which usually follow sincere intent."

Clevor brushed his suit coat. "Speculation, since these wishful e-mailings do not mention or refer to a specific person to whom my client intended harm."

Grand interjected, "The victim's name comes out of the story."

"Granted," Clevor said, "but we've established that is not real. At most, my client expressed in his e-mail only fleeting hopes to seek pleasure from harming another. An unnamed other. Hopes and desires go unfulfilled all of the time, your honor."

Truante nodded with Clevor. Grand felt his heart sink as he looked over the inset bookshelves behind the bench, then at the high gabled ceiling. His eyes followed the terrace leading up to the judge, reminding him how just before the hearing he had dreamed about sitting upon that fine rostrum.

"Admittedly, this is not a murder case," Grand said at last. "It is a case to *prevent* murder. Injustice would be to dismiss this threat and not take it seriously, thus allowing more of its kind to bubble up the conduits of computer communications. Victor did have a target and a plan, your honor. Please act to protect a young woman from being seriously hurt."

Truante swallowed, and Grand thought he saw sweat glistening on the top of the judge's brow. Clevor began approaching the bench, but Truante held a hand up. "Counselors, I have heard enough and have decided to take the motion to dismiss under advisement."

Grand's mouth dropped. He closed it instantly and felt his heart racing. This was so unlike Truante, who often left the stand with the defense crying at their table.

Truante cleared his throat. "Also, I am already disposed to grant the motion to release the defendant on bail of $10,000 and remand him into the custody of his parents, unless the prosecution can offer a substantial reason not to release him." Truante aimed his attention at Grand. "Counselor?"

What the hell was Truante pulling here? After skipping the bail hearing, Truante wanted to throw Victor on the streets without so much as a perfunctory yawn.

"Judge...I..." He dredged up nothing in his mind except dread. Now Agent Delbravo must find Hando. Without the accomplice, the judge would not perceive the combined threats as viable and the prosecution's case would be positively dismissed.

"Counselor?"

Grand's hands began shaking. "May I approach the bench?"

"Both counselors may approach the bench."

Grand and Clevor walked up the platform, arriving together. Grand held the banister, feeling this was as close as he would get to the other side. From four feet up, Truante stared down at them. "Sam?"

Grand said, "I need time."

"I can't give you anymore, Sam."

Grand looked into Truante's eyes, which reflected a kind of uneasiness.

"Arthur—Judge, I don't understand. With the motions and hearing changes, our schedule is running loose." Grand felt water running down his back and condensing on his chest. He had exhausted all of his artillery in opposing the motion to dismiss. "I sense pressure. Are you troubled about setting a precedent on regulating the Internet?"

"Nothing is pressuring me, Mr. Grand." Truante glared at him with angry eyes. "Unless you have an opinion about pretrial release, sit down and take it like a man."

Grand brainstormed, putting his mind into overdrive. "May we delay the conclusion?" he suggested. "At least until a full psychiatric evaluation can be performed to determine the measure of danger Victor poses to the community."

"Your honor," Clevor interjected. "Both the university and we have completed psychological evaluations. Both gave Victor a clean bill."

"But," Grand protested, "we want a *psychiatric* not psychological evaluation, and from our own professional. The university's people are not as well trained in applied criminology."

Truante gulped. "I can't afford the delay, and I don't see the point, Sam."

"Maybe the appellate will."

The corner of Truante's mouth twitched. His eyes dropped. "It must be done quickly. By tomorrow morning."

"Yes," Grand promised, hopeful. He didn't dare question the expeditious turn around.

"And the Government must abide by the analysis, whatever it may be."

"Yes."

The judge nodded. "I'll allow it, and make a decision before the weekend."

Friday, February 7

Milan Federal Correctional Institution

The viewing area did not have one-way glass. Instead, Tim, Sam Grand and Assistant Prison Warden Forsyth watched a large black and white monitor connected to a camera in the examination chamber. In it, Victor sat before the prosecution's psychiatrist, smiling and cooperating. Tim wished the exam, already over half an hour long, would pick up. The doctor was still on inkblots.

"What'd you all say this bastard did?" Warden Forsyth asked Tim in the viewing room. Forsyth's roundish body held up his bulbous head. The warden looked at him with tiny pupils swimming in dingy white.

"Threatened to rape a girl."

"Rape, huh?" The warden spread his massive lips. "Lots of opportunity to be on the receiving end here." He ripped apart the word "opportunity" with a choppy, staccato intonation and laughter. "Your boy's mighty cute."

Tim turned back to the monitor. He could barely hear the speaker box, so he stood and dialed the volume higher.

On the monitor, the doctor held up a card. *"What about this one?"*

Victor studied the card—an inkblot spiraling outward and mirrored in a bizarre pattern. Tim would've guessed it looked like road kill on a cloverleaf freeway connection.

"*Another cloud,*" Victor responded with a smile. "*Maybe a summer breeze.*"

"*And this?*"

The next card had a squarish blot with gouges shredding through it. A bullet-ridden building, Tim guessed.

"*Um. Maybe a sunny day. Or high clouds.*"

Tim shook his head. It seemed the kid was playing with them. All he interpreted were soft fluffy clouds, a warm day and grassy hills. But no way did the blocky diagram look like a cloud.

In the chamber, the doctor set down the cards and reached in a box. "*I'm going to give you some paper and a pencil,*" the doctor said. "*I want you to draw something that reminds you of your childhood.*"

Tim watched Victor take the pencil and paper, and begin the task. Assistant Warden Forsyth stood and began talking with Grand.

Tim watched carefully, trying to tune-out the man's gibbering. Victor drew round images and formed them into pictures of little bunnies. All of them lay fairly close together, smiling and maybe playing.

"*You continue. I'll be back.*" On the monitor, the doctor stood and headed for the door, leaving two guards to watch Victor's artistic competence.

In Victor's sketch, some of the bunnies carried objects now. Tim's college training had included a couple of psychology courses and he only learned the famous cases. Victor seemed to have taken the same class. His images were perfect, maybe too contrived, following classic textbook examples. Tim breathed hard as he observed.

The viewing room door opened. The doctor walked in. Grand left Forsyth talking to himself and huddled around the monitor with the psychiatrist.

"What do you think, Albert?" Grand asked the doctor.

On the monitor, Victor's bunnies now played with flowers and licked lollipops.

The psychiatrist wrinkled his nose and shook his head. "I don't know, Sam. I mean, it's archetypal." The doctor sighed. "I can't really give you anything. As far as I can tell, this boy is rational."

Rational? Tim's fist balled up. Victor was remarkable—a real pro—the jackass.

* * *

The Diag

At lunchtime, Tim walked across the busier part of campus. He had just picked up Yoshiko's list of friends. Even though it was cold, many students swarmed *The Diag*, as it was called. The diag had two crossing walkways that converged into a large concrete square that fronted libraries, computing facilities and several of the science department buildings. All around the square, situated in a disjointed fashion, there were tables, booths and shanties from campus organizations and student run "stores." The shanty stores were a new twist—a so-called scholarly mall from which the latest student body used profits to fund campus movements and politics. Here they held rallies against the government and campus administration. The diag also catered the annual Hash-Bash and Queer Kiss-in—celebrations of mind-altering hallucinations and alternative-mating relations.

Today students poured out shouts against the *censorship of Kurt Victor*—like Victor was some poster-boy for the repressed student body. Victor the con-man. He had passed their evaluation with flying colors. By afternoon, the judge would finalize the bail decision. Either way, Tim's load would wind down, and he could make it up with the family. Spend more time teaching Reggy defensive moves.

He rested, thinking on a cement bench along the diag and watched the protest build with stored energy from the media. News people had flocked to the U-M campus in a free-for-all since the arrest. Like a bunch of rocket boosters, reporters pumped the students full of motion, then falling away to watch once the momentum was built. The crew pointed dangling carrot-like microphones at the protestors.

Though most of the demonstrators favored Victor, a smaller, more pacified gathering had set up a table across the square with the slogan: *Remember the victim, not the Victor!* Now a crowd of smoking protesters concentrated around the pro-victim corner. One young man with short, blond hair stood on a bench, speaking to the crowd.

"Victor is the real victim!" he shouted over them. "And so is everyone's First Amendment rights. No one has the right to outlaw words!" He held up a banner that read: *Stop the Kampus Kop Klan.*

Cheers and whistles encouraged him. Microphones lifted up and flashes from cameras flared out. Onlookers collected in the back, filling the square.

"He threatened to rape a girl," said a black female student with a purple coat. She rose on the table of the opposing perspective and glared at the young man on the bench with hands on her hips. "Since when does his right to write override her right to privacy and protection?"

Few students applauded her. Cameras and reporters shifted direction. The boy and girl debated back and forth, shouting louder at each exchange. The young faces and book bags slumped on the cement reminded Tim of his own college days. He never had time to get involved in campus politics. It took all of his effort to keep his scholarship.

In his childhood neighborhood, no one could believe it when Tim got the scholarship. Only three years before going to college, he was heading straight for jail. In the city, glue runs had been Tim's charge when he turned fourteen. The older guys had put him up to squeeze hard epoxy in the door locks of parked cars so they would be abandoned overnight and easier to steal. It now seemed like child's play with what today's fourteen-year-olds did in their gang.

One afternoon in Tim's fifteenth year, Officer Reginal Lidel snatched him on a glue run. After driving him home, he let Tim off with a promise to go with him to a Lions Game at the Silverdome. The real bargain, as it turned out, came after the game.

For the next two years, Tim would race to finish his homework every day. He'd never done a lick of studying before, but somehow with the incentive of having a father-like friend and the games and nights out in the patrol car, his schoolwork all seemed so easy. There was no doubt why he had wanted to become a cop.

From his pocket, Tim pulled out his keys, fondling a penknife dangling from the chain. The bright yellow and blue knife had been a prize Officer Reginal Lidel won in a shooting competition. Tim was only seventeen when his friend gave it to him. After they awarded him, Lidel had walked off the range and to the stands in full blue regalia. Without a word, he just handed the certificate and penknife to Tim. It was the closest he ever saw that man come to tears. Later on, his friend put an inscription on the blade. "God keep you, son," it said. Of all his possessions, Tim valued that penknife like life itself.

Their friendship all ended as abruptly as it had started when some punk drug dealer took Lidel by surprise on Livernois Avenue in Detroit. It had nearly torn Tim apart. Jeez, how he missed Lidel. He had wanted a father for so long, and when he finally found a semblance, his world destroyed it. Like some kind of jealous mistress, the city killed everything he valued.

And now, his case was dying too. And everyone seemed more concerned about how Victor going to jail would affect the Internet rather than the intended victim. The students continued their arguing, now high-pitched screaming in the diag.

"Cool off, feminist bitch!" The blond student supporting Victor spit in the direction of the black girl on the other bench. Another student with straight black hair and dark glasses joined him on the pro-Victor table, and lit a cigarette. He exhaled a puff of smoke and put his arms up as a prizefighter would in triumph.

People yelled and pushed forward. Cameras flashed. The black girl, now allied by a man with a ponytail, gave the middle finger to the two on the bench. Students cheered and rallied, urging the smoker to leap from the bench to her table where he removed the sunglasses. He took a tight drag from his cigarette, and smugly exhaled in the female student's face.

She stood firm only blinking and grimacing.

Then several things happened at once. The ponytailed man pushed the smoker and the crowd propelled forward. The table toppled, those on it slipping off. Fists flinging up and out. Students jumping onto benches and others falling underfoot. It was an all-out brawl. Bodies rushed at the edge, others running from the grass into the fray. Flash bulbs, cameras and microphones pushed from the boundary, holding the volatile mass together. Reporters smiled eagerly. Campus police charged, bully clubs in hand.

Tim quickly wove his way from his end of the diag toward the boundary and State Street beyond. He still heard the commotion behind and turned to look from his safer vantage. The police quickly brought the strife under control. They detained a couple of students, and reporters took photos.

It was over.

"Crazy dips," Tim mumbled to himself as he spun around and started his retreat to the RA. On his left side, a chain link fence guarded an older building. Brick piles, excavator tracks and a blade from a bulldozer left telltale signs of renovation. Old stone on the building face rose uncovered and scarred with unfinished repairs. He marveled because the whole campus always seemed to be under construction. On the other side of the fence, Tim spied a man walking toward him. He'd seen the man already—on Liberty Street below the federal building.

The man seemed to be moving closer. He wore a thin coat and carried a black camera bag. His face wrinkled as he squeezed through a gap in the fence.

With the construction crew gone for lunch and sidewalk empty, Tim walked south along State Street. The man shadowed him, which was annoying. Behind his sour face, there was a hint of wide-eyed hope. Must be a reporter—someone who wanted a statement from him about Victor's evaluation. He decided to stop and let the man pass or ask his questions.

The fence ended at this point on campus and muddy tire tracks led across the snowy ground into the quartered site. Tim stood there. As he neared, the man breathed tautly and then stopped beside Tim.

"Timothy Delbravo?" The man's voice was jagged.

"Yes, and you are?"

"You work for the FBI?" The man squinted even more. The questioning worried Tim.

"It's no secret."

The man's eyes seemed to brighten at that—as if a load had been lifted from him. "I have to tell you something," he said. "I've waited too long."

A confession, Tim was sure. Like a walk-in off the street, they would come in to the bureau-offices after holding their guilt and unload the whole thing to the first agent they saw.

The man scraped the snow with a boot. He shifted his hands inside his coat pockets and let a grin fall wearily off his lips. The informant's smile, Tim recognized.

"I saw you on the TV," the man said, "talking to reporters a few days ago. Do you know who I am?"

Tim felt a shiver under his heavy coat. "No."

Steam poured out through the man's dry lips. "I came from Dallas to see you. I'm Amos."

Tim blinked, shaking his head. Meant nothing to him.

"Miller." The man's eyes misted. The corners of his lips quivered and then fell down. "Amos Miller. My son was in California. Danville."

Tim's memory called up the boy's face. Then the eyes reappeared—the boy from the estate basement. His mind began spinning, heart racing and mouth mumbling, "Michael Miller?"

"That's right. A clerk gave me your name, Agent Delbravo." Amos Miller pulled something from his camera bag. "I just wanted to thank you for shooting my son."

Amos raised a small revolver. It fired.

Tim's ears exploded as he lunged for the cover of a dislodged bulldozer blade. He fell hard on his hands, sending lightning bolts through his arms. The bullet still caught him, he knew. Not only because he felt pain, but also the force of impact made his leap fall short of cover.

"You killed my son!"

Another shot rang out, this time missing as Tim felt sharp pain from the first hit. The bullet had grazed his left thigh—just off to the side, near where he'd taken it in that basement with the boy. He counted two more shots before scrambling completely behind the shield of the large scoop. Instinctively, he grabbed for his shoulder holster, then stopped himself. He kept his weapon loaded now, and there was no way he could shoot Michael's father.

"Bastard!"

He peered down at his leg. Only a narrow fleshy trench, small trickle of blood. It looked better than he would've expected. Holy Mother, it hurt, but Miller—he had how many shots?

"Come out, you sonuvabitch!"

A clap of gunfire echoed, followed by another ting and hiss of a slug ricocheting off the thick steel between them. Six shots, Tim thought. Amos carried a revolver, probably a .22 caliber with six loads. The first hit him, three misses before reaching the shield and two since.

Tim twisted his head around the scoop. Amos searched frantically, his brow high and desperate, his teeth bared and steaming. People in the streets cowered behind mailboxes, parked cars and tree trunks. Just then Amos saw him, raised the gun and pulled back. Tim ducked, hearing the inept click of the hammer. It was empty.

He tried to stand but a scream from his leg yanked him down again. On his elbows and one knee, he dragged and pulled himself out.

"Bastard! Killed my boy! My Michael." Amos sobbed, repeating his son's name.

Tim crawled further, nearing Amos, who fumbled in his coat and pulled out some ammunition.

"No!" Tim shouted, hastening now on the painful leg. Amos ignored him, absorbed in trying to get the revolver's cylinder open. Moving and straining over the snow, Tim couldn't quite tell when Amos had reloaded. He reached him just as the cylinder snapped shut and the gun started rising. With nerves scorching his leg, Tim leapt high enough to lock onto Amos' waist. As he fell back, Amos fired. The crack blasted Tim's ears. Everything was rushing down. Tim waited for the sting of another hit. It did not come, however. He'd not felt the impact this time. Somehow he was over Amos and pulling the revolver from his hand before it could fire again.

"You murdered him!"

The campus police arrived.

"You should be dead!" Amos cried as the officers pulled Tim off. "You should have died with my boy in that inferno dungeon."

They began cuffing both of them but Tim hardly noticed. His gaze was fixed on Amos' grief-torn face. In it he saw Michael as powerfully as his memory had ever shown it.

"I wish you were dead!"

More than the searing flesh in his thigh, Tim felt Amos' loss, his pain. As reporters took photo after photo, a horrible thought struck Tim.

If blame for the boy's shooting had rested on Robinson, Amos would have felt the agent's death justified and appropriate. It would have given this father some closure. As it was, Tim knew Amos blamed him, and he was alive.

Still alive.

Amos wouldn't even have the joy of causing him much more than a small flesh wound.

The Detroit Herald

February 8—Yet another multi-car pileup on the Information Superhighway was cleared late yesterday.

U.S. District Court Judge Arthur Truante dismissed all charges against Defendant Kurt Victor, the University of Michigan student arrested earlier this week for allegedly transmitting threats across the Internet.

"Victor did not violate the law, as it is currently written," Truante wrote. "Perhaps with changes proposed in Congress by Senator Euler, my ruling would have been different."

Citing insufficient evidence as the reason for dismissal, Truante explained, "A lot of careless speech makes its way across the wires connecting our networks, and who's to judge what is real and what is fantasy? The prosecution has failed to show a specific threat here...[Their] spirited investigation fizzled into a rescue operation once they realized Victor's writings were only tasteless pieces of fiction."

Some argue that the dismissal sets a precedent over the regulation of computer network communications and ensures their future as a medium for free speech.

Max Ulquist, Director of the Center for Technology and Democracy in Washington cautioned, "While this case may have implications in U.S. law, the Internet is international and any precedent or law set in the U.S. will ultimately fail where foreign law differs."

Senator Jack Euler of Nebraska has legislation pending in Congress he thinks should help. "Had my D-Chip law been enforced, this would have never have happened," he said.

When asked how a chip would have stopped Victor from writing his story, Euler only commented that it would have stopped Victor from transmitting it.

Upon release, Kurt Victor issued a statement. "Free speech is the endowment of all enlightened cultures," he wrote. "These rights are one of the first things dictators remove. I'm glad the case was dismissed."

Victor has been invited to speak at Michigan State University and a number of other college campuses. Anne Hinzman, general counsel for the ACLU's Michigan student-chapter, indicated that several people have stepped forward with donations to pay Victor's legal fees. He asked his attorney, Daniel Clevor, to file a suit against the university if they don't reinstate him.

Victor's status at the U-M is likely to improve. "If [Victor] wants continuing academic status, we would halt any suspension proceedings," said Mary Carter, Vice President for Student Affairs.

The dismissal has muddled the situation for the U.S. Attorney's Office. "A dismissal can still be overturned by the appellate court. Especially a travesty of justice like this," said Samuel Grand, assistant general counsel for the government's case.

CASE 2

"The parts of the stories you have sent, inspire me wonderfully."
—Alven Hando

Tuesday, February 11

Mud Swamp

Black silence enveloped Deputy Detective Sherrie Marshall when she cut the Bronco's engine. Out in the middle of nowhere, the border around Mud Swamp seemed closed down for the winter, especially at night. Sherrie opened the door and stepped out into the freezing air when she caught a glimpse of light behind her. A lone Northfield cruiser, flasher going full-tilt, sat empty at the head of a trail leading into the bogs. Although she was one of the first at the scene, only one squad car didn't feel right. They didn't know if it was accidental or intentional. A boy, hardly into puberty, had been incinerated at the swamp.

She grabbed a flashlight, some film and a camera from the Bronco. Before locking up she tapped under her arm to ensure her Glock 9mm still hung in her shoulder holster.

The cold air did not completely freeze the marshy odor. She knew the area from maps and a few trips. Nearby fields encircled the swamps, and at the southern edge lay Independence Lake—a county park. In spring and summer, the swamp area filled so much the deepest part took the form of a second lake. Sherrie could only guess what it looked like in the winter—a desolate, frozen marshland. A wasteland housing a burn-homicide.

Not somewhere she wanted to be shivering at five in the morning.

She followed boot prints down a south trail, holding her wool-lined parka close. Loose fitting blue jeans wrapped around her long johns, and a purple skier's band warmed her ears. The frosty path led down a slick descent. Now far from the cruiser's flashing globe, darkness prevailed. Few folks lived in the area. She reached a tall maple falling over the path, and saw a figure coming up the trail carrying a flashlight. His wide brim hat labeled him as a small town cop. The officer, a portly man, wore a heavy coat and breathed loudly as he climbed the trail. He was chewing tobacco and spat his wad onto the white snow. As she neared him, he smiled at her with gummy teeth decaying under a coat of brown spittle.

"Hello." He almost sang the greeting and pushed his free hand toward her. "Officer George Parkin."

Sherrie winced inside upon shaking his hand. "Deputy Sherrie Marshall."

Parkin spat again. "Where's the detective?"

"That would be me."

"Oh." His face wrinkled in sarcastic astonishment. "At first I thought you were one of those young, glamorous reporters."

Sherrie sighed. "What do we have, Officer?"

"Unidentified male." Parkin rubbed his nose. "Burned, maybe with gasoline or something. I noticed scorch lines on the skin."

"Let's allow the M.E. to decide that. You just show me the body."

"Sure thing, miss."

"Call me Deputy Marshall, or just Deputy, please."

He tipped his large brim. "Deputy."

"How much further?" she asked. She could see hints of the swamp now: dry snake grass and stagnant cat tails poked through white crust as if to escape.

"There." He pointed his light at an icy clearing about ten yards ahead. "Mud Swamp, or Lake, as some have it."

Sherrie aimed her flashlight and found flat ice. Stalky poles speared the ice like winter rigor mortis. In the middle, continuing from the path, a trestle made from small logs spanned the pond. As they got closer, Sherrie could smell the aftermath: smoke and burnt hair, opened flesh and…What was it? She detected a hint of some kind of accelerant. Not gasoline, but something else.

Above the bridge sat a scaffold; benches sitting in a disconnected line—

wood, old and decaying. Parkin stopped. "That's the observatory spot for professors. But it don't look like it's been used for a while."

"Professors?"

"I'm told U-M owns this part of the bogs."

Sherrie pointed her light all around. "Where's the body?"

"Oh, it's on the other side of the bridge." He started off toward the catwalk but she stopped him with her arm.

"Wait. I want to get some pictures."

She pulled the camera off her shoulder, attached a high-capacitance flash and loaded film in it—the department hadn't splurged on a evidence-proof high end digital camera. Aiming it, she took several pictures of the swamp as well as close-ups of the catwalk and benches. Then she crossed the trestle, snapping frequent shots. Her lace-up boots pattered on the ice crust, sounding like tap dancing on potato chips. As she approached, the scent of burnt flesh grew stronger. Eventually, it overwhelmed her memory of the accelerant. She would have to wait for the lab to identify it.

She examined the ground, noting that all the tracks coming across matched Officer Parkins' shoe print.

"Any other tracks?"

"On the back side, to the south." Parkin stayed back now.

"A single set or more?"

"Single, I think."

The boy's, probably. Sherrie moved forward. The swamp cut a circle, thirty yards in diameter, through the forest. The catwalk split it down the center. On the other side, the flat ground rose only inches above the frozen waterline. The officer pointed to her right, to the south. She could see the scorched earth at the edge and melted ice part way into the swamp, all tracing a circle.

In the middle of the burned circle lay a blackened fleshy body, barely perceptible as human. Part of it dipped into the swamp. She could make out the head and possibly ears, one eye socket emptied and the nose ashened by the fire. The victim, probably twelve years old, wore no clothes, and her mind cowered at the thought of this kind of foul play. Just horrible. How could someone do this? Sickness filled her stomach and she had to turn away until her nausea passed. The boy had died on his back with the front exposed, burned grossly between his legs.

The stench was strong, but not as bad as other homicides she had assisted.

She flashed several photos, circling the scene at various zoom levels and burning through two more rolls of film. Parkin watched her in action, rendering an apparent expression of pride that he was working a homicide. Sherrie made a wide sweep around the dry half of the scene, snapping rapidly to the end of the third roll.

From what she had seen in the dimness of their flashlights, she had no doubts about accidental death. This was intended.

Although the body was almost entirely black, scorch marks carving deeply on the victim indicated the use of an accelerant. The boy may have been doused from behind, apparently lain in a pool of the flammable fluid. The forensics lab would run spectroscopy on everything to determine the accelerant, fibers or other products they could trace back to a suspect.

She combed the area and found several objects near the victim. A foggy, blackened mason bottle, probably used to carry the accelerant, sat in the scorched area. A short plastic tube, stained with a white powdery substance, lay two yards from the outer edge of the burned section. Further away, all around, she found a half-dozen yellow Polaroid pull-tabs with the prints missing. On the south side, she found a strange indentation in the icy mud. Three holes poked the ground about an inch deep in geometric arrangement. The ground was frozen, and she surmised that a heavy tripod had made the holes. But it didn't make sense. An expensive tripod for a Polaroid? Did Polaroids even have tripod guides? And why even shoot ancient Polaroids when digital was so much easier?

With a micro-recorder, she made point-by-point notes of her theories and impressions. The first ones often proved right. Details were best anatomized immediately, which was why she kept the recorder with her at all times. She would go over them repeatedly in a controlled environment, pick at each impression and hypothesis until one stood above the rest. She would never enjoy reviewing a homicide like this one. Her first time solo and already she was questioning why she had wanted to be in homicide so badly. This was an especially cruel scene. Something she would have to work hard at removing from her memory. It was no wonder homicide detectives take earlier retirement than most cops.

Sherrie heard a ring. From her coat, she pulled out a cell phone and answered.

"Someone from the M.E.'s office is on their way." It was the sheriff. "Crime unit should already be there."

"Good guess. It's no accident."

"Right. I need to know if the victim is named William Ramey."

How could he know? "Just a minute."

She turned to Parkin. "Do you know the victim?"

"Hard to say," Parkin replied. "He's so burned."

"Do you know William Ramey?"

"Yeah," Parkin said, smile missing. "A boy that lives just down the road a mile. He'd been playing at the school grounds with some friends until evening. They said he just plain disappeared, never went home…"

"Deputy?" the sheriff voiced on the phone.

"Yeah, Sheriff. Very probable it's Ramey."

"Let me know what the M.E. finds."

"How'd you know already?"

"Feds called."

"The feds?"

"They already knew the name and that it was a burn."

"How did they know?"

"They just did, somehow. They're sending someone over this morning. You clean up. Take good notes, then pass it off."

* * *

Apartment

The phone woke Tim early that morning. He first thought, in his drowsiness, it would be a rude salesman. Janice lay asleep next to him.

"Tim, it's Bob Givens." His voice was urgent over the phone.

"It's not even six."

"I need you to get to the office. Call me back on the STU."

The Secured Telephone? "You can't tell me now?"

"It's bureau-confidential."

"Will it get me out of the session?"

"No, Tim. That's still mandatory. You can't afford to break the rules."

* * *

Swamp

"Who found the scene?" Sherrie asked Officer Parkin.

He spit on the trestle where they stood. "We got a call from Mike Fieldman. He lives a block back past the elementary school, just at the border between Northfield and Webster."

"What was Fieldman doing up in the middle of night?"

"Working." Parkin lifted his cheeks into a drooly grin, which deflected her eyes.

She wrinkled her nose at it. "Working what?"

"Well, I guess a pipe burst in his place about four in the morning. He was outside turning off the main, and says he saw an orange glow through the trees. He could smell smoke and decided it was a fire down in the gully. He put on his boots and tromped down from his place." Parkin sniffed hard, pulling at his nose with clamped fingers. He wiped his fingers on his pants and resumed. "Fieldman's worn a small trail that winds down from near Kearney Street around the swamps. Says he gets firewood near there and sells it. My pa and I used to cut wood near here. In the winter, I'd go over to Independence Lake and play hockey. I lost quite a few pucks in those cat tails around there."

"Anyway," Sherrie hinted.

Parkin smiled back at her. "Well, Fieldman is giving a statement to my partner, right now. So you can get the full account later."

"I want you to tell me what Fieldman said." The woodcutter would have been the first person on the scene and she wanted as many accounts of his story as she could get.

"Well, Fieldman says he got near the place, but the fire had mostly died. He said he could smell something awful. Knew it wasn't no dead animal, but says he couldn't place it, so he started following the scent. When he reached the body, he knew right away it was a dead person. Smart man, Fieldman. Instead of looking around, he immediately went back and called us. We got the call at just before five."

"Did he see anything else?"

Parkin scratched his neck and twisted his mouth around. "No, not really. Fire'd been going maybe twenty minutes before he got there. But it was mostly burned out, he says. Just sparks and ash left. A fire on a frozen swamp won't burn for long."

Sherrie walked around the scene again, cursing silently because Parkin's tracks had marred some of the scene detail. On the south edge, she found a smaller set tromping both ways. She wanted to follow them, but the suspect was long gone; it had been over two hours since Fieldman said he saw the flames. And she didn't worry about the prints melting in these temperatures.

On her tape, Sherrie started a suspect list—people familiar with the spot would comprise the bulk of it. The swamp was remote and used by very few people. Possibly university staff would constitute the top half. Fieldman and neighbors would file below them, all people she would have to check out.

Thoughts about the victim living so close to the scene haunted her mind. As she pondered theories, she remembered something. According to Parkin, Fieldman had seen the first sign of flames at around four. He went to see for himself, and then "immediately" returned home to call the police. Parkin said the call came in just before five. Almost an hour later. After getting his statement, she would have to time the trip from Fieldman's house to the scene and back. Suddenly Fieldman was being bumped to the top of her suspect list. She clicked off the recorder and loaded the camera again.

Before Sherrie could finish flashing another roll of film, three members from the crime unit arrived. The on-call forensics officer, a tall lanky fellow named Dale Jobian, made a beeline for the body. One of the other two had several evidence bags and a stretcher. The last, a new technician just assigned to the night crime unit, carried Jobian's camera and fingerprinting equipment: carbon and magnetic dusting powders, tape cards, and a bio-organic solvent for hard to get latents.

The crime unit swarmed the scene like ants, carrying off bits and pieces of the body of evidence. Jobian stood before her, waiting for further instruction.

"I got a lot of pictures," Sherrie told him. "Victim is a young male. Burned with an accelerant, probably sexually assaulted. I found at least eight collectibles outside of the main burnt area. Tracks lead south, very probable. Get molds of the best ten, but hold off on tracking them until we complete everything else. Give me a floral vacuum at three feet beyond the burnt diameter and along the entire trail south a little later. But first do an examination of the body, without moving it until I return."

Jobian stared awkwardly at her. "Where are you going?"

"I want to check on an after-the-fact witness while his mind is fresh."

He nodded. "I'll have to go back to HQ for the vacuum and filters. My wake-up call said it might be accidental."

"Not in the least." Sherrie shook her head. "We got a full blown H."

* * *

Residency

Tim unlocked the RA just before six a.m. and limped inside. No one was around, which was fine now that Victor's charges had been dismissed; Tim would probably spend a lot of time stuffing envelopes in his cubicle until he could get transferred. Even Louis Mott had gotten paired up on a brick assignment—an undercover op following the militias in their region.

He walked to the common area and picked up the STU-3 handset. Why Givens wanted to talk secured, Tim had no idea.

The phone rang in short intervals. He cupped his chin, noticing the few whiskers standing out; he hadn't shaved that morning.

"Tim," Givens answered cheerfully. It sounded feigned. "Go secure, okay?"

Tim turned the STU's encryption key and punched the SL button. The LCD registered *MinSL* for a confidential mode only.

"How's the leg?"

"Much better, Givens." Tim felt uncomfortable calling him by his first name. But after all the years they knew each other, "sir" was not right either.

"And Janice?"

"Fine. Everyone's fine." Tim exhaled a long breath. "Is my family's health classified?"

"No." Clearing his throat, Givens' tone changed. "Tim, we've been with you on the Victor case all along. The media kept it on our minds. Now DC called early this morning. It's another computer post on that same newsgroup."

Tim felt his stomach turning. They had retrieved another sex-assault threat from the Internet newsgroups. "Is it Kurt Victor again?"

"No, Alven Hando, this time," Givens said. "But we should question Victor when we find out what motel he and his dad are staying in while they fight the U on his suspension. Apparently, Hando posted from the same site as before, up in Toronto. CART passed Hando's message through the writer analysis system and came up with a match. Near perfect—97% likely."

"Any more clues where Hando might be?"

"No. Apparently, the post was uploaded in Toronto from a falsified account just before four this morning. And," Givens' voice went softer, "he used a name. William Ramey."

"Is he real?"

"He was, Tim. A twelve-year-old from Webster Township. Sheriff has a homicide team on site now."

Tim felt lightning pass through him, a fire in his feet streaming up to his throat. William was the same age as Reggy. And Michael.

Son of a bitch!

After the encounter with Amos, Tim had felt his bite go soft and his taste for the kill go sour. He was ready to file for a transfer. He would take an analyst position in the labs or somewhere they could chain him to a desk. Then Victor got released, and he started writing his resignation in the hospital bed. Hadn't he promised to protect Yoshiko?

Givens said, "A prelim phone report from the county gives an M.O. that appears identical to the post. Subject used lighter fluid, and took pictures among other repugnant things." Givens paused briefly, but Tim said nothing. "Look, Tim, you can handle it. You're good with the media. You know the most about the case."

He spat silence. A molester, a snuff-porn freak had tortured a child. *Another boy.* In a way, Tim wanted to jump at the case, but he felt dark walls closing around him. Heavy air suffocated him with thick fingers around his throat.

"Tim?" Givens paused. "I'll fax the file to you right now. And I'll okay your request for a better computer, once you take this."

"But..." Tim stammered. He could be suspended for refusing an assignment. But did Givens know what it all meant? "It's a child, Bob."

"I know. You, better than anyone understands what's at stake. Look, SA Kaplan is not the answer man. You'll be reporting to me on this one."

That meant Kaplan would be out of the loop.

"And I'll cough up any RAGs that you might need. I'm pulling for you; I'm even putting in a request to the SAC for reinstating you back to GS-13."

GS-13? A promotion! "You...they'll strip my demotion?"

"The whole ball of wax, Tim. But only if you accept. Otherwise the SAC won't go for it."

So this was the catch—the fine print. In order to absolve his mistakes, he had to slide down them once more. It had to be a sure thing, not just a possibility.

"When will you know, Givens?"

"Maybe in a few days. But I need an answer right now."

"Now?" He wanted to think about it.

"We can't hold up the investigation, Tim. And we need you. Just say yes."

Somehow, he knew Givens would fulfill. He trusted Bob. "All right, Givens."

"Good, Tim. Good."

* * *

Swamp

The sun was just rising when Tim found the swamp. He followed a well-worn trail from the dirt road down until he was staring at Hando's handiwork. Several brown uniforms surrounded the body, already lifting it into a thick bag, dark green in color. One man directed the others.

"Special Agent Tim Delbravo." Tim held out his credentials to the man in charge.

"Dale Jobian." Jobian raised his gloved hand, covered in ash and dirt, then lowered it before Tim could get a hold. "I'm the assistant county examiner."

Three men lifted the body of a barely recognizable human boy. The left leg held on by slivers of bone and tissue, it was burned so badly. Tim averted his gaze back at Jobian. "Tell the M.E. not to do a destructive examination. We may send it back to Quantico for a full work up."

Jobian nodded.

"Who broke the scene?"

"Deputy Marshall. She's back there." Jobian jerked a thumb behind them at the south edge of the swamp.

Tim saw a lone figure standing above a trail, holding a flashlight. He nodded his parting and walked around the taped-off perimeter to where Marshall studied the ground. A camera and duffel bag hung around her neck.

"Deputy Marshall?"

She looked back and stood. "Yes."

"Special Agent Tim Delbravo." He held out his credentials.

She looked young and pretty: sandy hair, petite facial features, slender build. Her face at the moment was not cheerful, and her voice sounded a bit frustrated. "They told me you were coming."

"What do you see?"

"Foot tracks." She dabbed a finger in the air. "They lead right through that bog there."

Around the swamp lay long stretches of turbid marsh. The tracks led south, directly into the heart of a cattail forest.

"I don't want to upset them trying to follow," Marshall explained. "I was trying to see where they lead."

"I know where they go."

Her eyebrows dipped and she studied his face. "How…what…how long have the feds been tracking this guy?"

"Not long enough. Come on, I'll show you where he came in at." Tim began moving south between the pools of quagmire.

She followed. "You going to let me in on how you know, or just take my first homicide without a thanks?"

"Anyone tell you the bureau's angle?" he asked as they walked across the driest ground.

"Nothing. But I will give you everything I have. No juris-dispute."

"Thanks." He knew she was only acknowledging that the FBI had ultimate authority. When all was said and done, the bureau could pretty much take any felony case it wanted. But Tim didn't care about jurisdiction. "I want to ask if you would stay on top of local details for me. You know the county and the type of people in the town near the incident."

"Oh, I intend to keep on this, if the Sheriff allows me," she said. "I want to nail the bastard just like everyone else."

He smiled at her, and in the slight glow of the rising sun, he could see her grinning back. He liked her. If she could stay on, then great.

She walked beside him over short stalks and around wet patches. "So what's the history?"

"Have you heard of the Kurt Victor case we built?"

"Who hasn't? I guess the judge dismissed him."

They neared a clearing. In the dimness, Tim could just make out a road ahead.

"It's on appeal," he said. "Victor, besides posting his story, was e-mailing a suspect in Canada, making plans to abduct a girl. His accomplice used an alias, a fake computer account. We refer to him as Alven Hando. The Ontario Provincials never found him."

"So you think there's a connection here?"

"Hando, not Victor," he explained, "posted a snuff-porn story on the same group from a hacked account. He named the victim and detailed his plans in story form. It appears he posted it at the same moment Bill Ramey was being killed."

"The same time?"

"Yeah, it's confusing." Tim had read the faxed story several times just to be sure that detail was correct. "Supposedly he posted from Canada, but the boy was in Northfield, more than a five-hour drive from Toronto. And before he begins the story, he had a line at the top about a live broadcast for those who knew how to get it."

"You mean like television?"

"Possibly." He shrugged.

"How? I mean, do you think he has a transmitter or a station?"

"Not sure. But he mentions a camera."

"I collected half a dozen Polaroid print tabs."

"Polaroids? Why that?"

"Not sure, maybe to leave the tabs for us to discover. And oddly I found three triangular marks near the body."

"A tripod," he surmised.

"In the story, too?"

"No, but it makes sense. He has to have one to record the broadcast."

"Where's his telecast?" she asked.

"Not sure. He doesn't give any more info about it."

"But there's a story."

"A two-page tragedy, more like it. It starts with children sledding on Monday by an unnamed elementary school."

"Whitmore Lake Elementary. Down the way," she said, wiggling a finger eastward.

"Right. Then Hando finds William Ramey alone on his way home in the dark and abducts him. He carries him to a truck and rolls him in a tarp, tying it up so the boy can't escape."

They reached the edge of a dirt road. Tim held up a hand. Deputy Marshall stopped.

"Here's the road he probably drove in on."

She looked around. "We're at Independence Lake Park."

"Yeah. In his story, Hando duct-tapes the victim's mouth and leaves him in the truck bed, then drives to a lake by a public park. None of the places are particularly named, but I'm sure this is it."

He had mapped the most probable entrance/exit before coming. With a finger, he motioned to center of the road where shallow tracks continued east. "Those his?"

Marshall tiptoed into the center of the road and bent down while Tim remained on the shoulder. She walked along them a few paces, looking up and down the road through her telephoto lens.

"Same boot prints." She snapped a couple of photos, then returned to roadside by him. "Looks like he kept stopping. About every ten yards the feet come together. He entered the bogs about thirty yards west of here."

"Let's go find the other end." Tim walked east, studying the tracks from the roadside. "He writes about coming into the park after snapping the lock on the gate. Then the story says he drove to the north edge of the loop going around the lake and parked. We should see the tracks stop up ahead where he got out."

Marshall walked beside him. "There's only one set of tracks the whole way."

Tim nodded. "Hando describes carrying the victim and a backpack full of items, and the trip wears him out. He has to make several stops carrying the boy—just like you saw. I don't know how he could predict it so accurately."

She slowed. "Makes my stomach turn. A serial madman prophesying the grisly details beforehand. But why would he describe what he did? It only makes life easier for us."

"Well, first of all, we can't say he's a serial killer. This is the first hit we know of."

The tracks ended where a clean pair of tire prints began. Two sets of four-tire tread marks connected by a three-point turn around.

"Just like clockwork. Get some shots, Deputy."

She lifted her camera, hinting a smile at him. "Call me, Sherrie."

"Okay, if you call me Tim."

She nodded and aimed her lens. "All the planning. He must have experience."

"Maybe, or he's just read a lot of stories about it. Now he's creating his own. A part of the allurement, I guess, is to see how well you can plan it, and how close the fulfillment gets."

She rejoined him at the roadside, and they continued walking fast toward the park entrance. "So he gets admirers by showing off his plans," she said.

"In that much, he fits the psychopath identity. He revels in the attention his violence gets. But if he really is a budding serial killer, then we've got something new."

"Has the bureau built a profile?"

"Not yet. But one thing is clear, our suspect is the kind of pedophile we strictly call a mysopedial pyromaniac. That is, a child molester that likes to torture and torch his victims."

"Sounds like you know the subject well."

"More than I'd care..." he admitted. Besides the experience his cases offered, Tim had spent time in the academy learning the profile techniques that garnered so much hype in Hollywood. They had been new, eleven years earlier. He couldn't do a full-fledged profile himself, but he could start one until DC granted his case some expert opinion.

"There have been kid-killers before," Sherrie said. "What's new about this one?"

He saw the steel gate, red shafts as thick as ankles, just ahead of them. "Serial killers work alone, scared to reveal who they are to just anyone. But now, with a barrage of reverse-therapy newsgroups and chat rooms on the Internet, Hando's trying to hook up with someone."

"You mean, he meets other killers online? That's horrible."

They reached the gate, which swung slowly in a breeze created by the risen sun. Sherrie captured photos of everything as Tim examined the lock. The cut metal twisted in a distinct manner. Markings on it would offer exact identification of the bolt cutters that had snapped it. Provided they got a hold of the cutters.

He studied the ground without disturbing any tracks. Hando would have had to get out of his vehicle to cut the lock. Shoe prints led from the road to the gate latch and back. One of the foot tracks fanned in the snow, like he had almost slipped then reversed a second time right near the gate connection. Something had made Hando stop and turn back. At the pivot, where Hando had turned back, the toe of one shoe print pointed into the trees. Tim's eyes followed the ground in line between the print and the treeline.

On the snow, he found some broken twigs. Recently broken from branches hanging over the fixed-end of the gate suggested that Hando had disrupted the tree. He scrutinized the branches and found thin strands of yarn or wool.

"Sherrie."

The fibers, brown or black they appeared, must have come from something worn by the suspect. Clothing about waist high, for Tim, had snagged in the branches, pulling the perp back for a moment.

"What is it?"

"Fibers. Get me some tweezers and an evidence bag."

She fished in her bag and handed him a fresh pair of tweezers and a steel button receptacle with autoclave tape still binding it shut. He peeled the tape and opened the container. Once uncovered, the vessel was no longer sterile. Working the tweezers, he gathered the fibers from the branch and placed them in the receptacle.

"Good eye," Sherrie said as he closed the bin and handed it to her. "Let's get the forensics team down here. We can get casts of the tracks, then sweep and powder the rest. I'll take you to see the M.E. after that."

Tim looked at his watch. He was due at the doctor's—the damn shrink—in half-hour. He couldn't afford to skip. "I've gotta run, Sherrie, but I'll catch up with you, in say, an hour and a half or two?"

"Look for me at the sheriff's office." Her lips formed a quick smile as he nodded his departure.

* * *

Clinic

Tim watched Psychologist Frank Toller tip back his coffee mug, wondering how he might shorten this mandatory session. The bureau required him to see a doctor before they would allow him to continue his case, and he was prepared to say anything just to have a quick ending.

"Tim—is it all right if I call you Tim?" Doctor Toller asked.

"Sure, Doc." He forced a smile and picked lint off his suit.

"Comfortable?" Toller brushed his thick gray mustache. He wore a slightly rumpled sweater and scuffed Cole-Haan shoes.

"Plenty." He stopped himself from squirming over the thin blue felt on his seat.

"Tim, I'm sure you are familiar with protocol. You've been through a few visits like this…"

He didn't reply. The less he said, the faster it would end.

"How's your leg?"

"Fine." After a four-day weekend of rest, his leg was actually doing well—almost better than his left hand that was sprained during the shooting. The doctors had to remove his ring for all the swelling, and he hardly noticed the leg.

"Any pain?"

"A little," he said. The heater came on and blew over them. He stomped his black boots. Drops of water were still on them, edges evaporating and some gone, leaving only dull gray splotches behind.

"It's just a scratch," he added. Thirteen stitches worth.

"Amos Miller will be happy to hear that."

"Amos?" His eyes perked up.

"Yes. He called here yesterday—under advisement of his psychiatrist. He asked how you were, wanting to thank you for defending him." Toller drew a finger across his mustache. "The prosecution is honoring your request, did you know?"

"No. What'll happen?"

"Amos accepted a plea to misdemeanor assault. He'll stay under care at Dallas Parkland in rehab. How do you feel about that?"

"It's good, I guess. But I don't think he's crazy."

"No?"

"Nope."

Toller wrote on his pad. "What does your family think?"

"About Amos?" He glanced at the wall clock.

"About the case, the shooting."

He stared at the doctor. It was no innocent question. "What should they think?"

"I don't know, Tim. Have you spoken with your wife?"

"Oh sure. I talked her ear off."

"And what does she think?"

Tim shrugged and looked at the clock again. "Sad for Amos. That losing his son would be so hard on him."

"Hard enough to make him seek revenge, punish you."

He didn't respond. He turned his gaze to the window.

"Do you think he was justified?"

Justified? Tim aimed his glare at Toller. "Of course not." He bit his lip. "I mean, I'd be mad as hell if someone shot my boy, but I can't condone revenge like that."

"Of course not." Toller wrote a note. "But what about Michael Miller?"

He did not want to talk about the boy. It had taken him months to get away from the boy's dead stare. Then Amos had shot those eyes right back into him. He felt his hands grip the edges of his seat and his feet squeeze together. Then realizing he looked tense, he shrugged and pulled out his key chain, hoping to give a signal to end the session.

"Tim?"

"What?"

"How do you feel about Michael?"

His eyes moved around the room. His mouth opened and closed several times but only his breath escaped. Don't think about the boy. He averted his gaze to the window, rubbing the grooves on his keys with a fingertip.

"Tim? Tell me." Toller sounded agitated. "How do you feel about shooting Michael?"

He breathed hard and anger shot out uncontrollably. "Yeah, Doc. I killed that boy. Is that what you want to hear?"

"I want to know if it bothers you still. For some inexplicable reason, you can't remember any of it, but you get quite angry whenever anyone brings it up. Like you don't like Michael."

Don't like Michael? What the hell was the doc thinking?

"How do you really feel about him, about shooting him, Tim?"

"Feel? What the hell difference does it matter what I feel?" He scooted to the edge of his seat. "The boy is still dead! I should have been the one protecting him. But instead I killed him."

"Maybe you did, just perhaps you're right. But do you think you are punishing yourself for it?"

Tim shook his head, blinking back moisture.

"A lot of people are counting on you to move on. Especially you," Toller said. "You can work yourself to death, but there's more to life than work, and your children need your love."

"My children?" He sat back again.

"Yes. It's obvious that you've been neglecting your family from the number of hours you work. Why do you feel justified in abandoning them to pay some kind of penance?"

"I'm not abandoning them. I wouldn't do that, Doc." He clutched the bright yellow and blue penknife on his key chain, holding it solemnly and remembering what it meant. How much he missed Lidel.

Truly, the doctor had a point.

"You have to let the accident go, Tim. Quit punishing yourself. Quit trying to find recompense in overtime and superhuman feats. Realize you made a mistake, just a mistake that can't be changed, and move on."

Tim heard his breath rasp through clenched teeth and shut his mouth. How could he realize anything if he couldn't remember any of it? The doctors couldn't explain the suppressed memory by his injuries. But he knew enough to not speak about it with shrinks.

He stood and grabbed his coat. "You're right, Doc. I'm ready. I'm moving on. I already got the next case."

* * *

Field Office

At ten-thirty in the Detroit Field Office, ASAC Bob Givens put his coffee down on his desktop. Special Agent in Charge Phil Hansen and Doctor Toller stood over him.

"I hope you know what the hell you did," the SAC said. "There's no way I would've approved handing Delbravo this case."

"Our deal, remember?" Givens rocked back in his chair. It moaned under the weight he had added since accepting this desk job. "You gave me Tim's reigns when I came to this F-O."

"You should've waited till after the evaluation." SAC Hansen looked at Toller "The doc certified Delbravo isn't up to snuff."

"No," Toller interjected. "I said SA Delbravo is self-dejected. Success will bring him out of it. But I also worry about his lack of family time."

"I'm not worried about this guy's mental health." Hansen turned back to Givens. "Hell, this is a murder, Bob. And Delbravo didn't prove himself on the threat case."

"He did great," Givens said. "Blame the prosecution. Besides, there wouldn't have even been a case, except Tim smelled-out something we all missed."

"Anyone can smell manure when it passes under their nose." Hansen pushed his hands against the desk.

"But no one else had the stomach to clean it up."

"Everyone else had better to do." Hansen shook his head. "And nothing's cleaned. It stinks just as bad, so why give him a homicide *and* a promotion?"

"My discretion." Givens stared at the SAC. Regretfully, he half-wished he hadn't requested Tim be transferred with him when he accepted the promotion. Why did he think he could be Tim's lookout?

"You really want to stick your neck out? Anymore screw-ups, and I'll be looking for two replacements."

"Gentlemen," Toller interrupted. "I think the question should be, regardless of Delbravo's condition, whether he's the right man for the case?"

"Yes," Givens said firmly.

"The guy doesn't even load his gun." Hansen snickered. "What kind of an agent is that?"

"I already instructed him. His gun was loaded when the father shot at him."

"Sheesh. But he didn't fire back. He's scared. What's he going to do if there's more shooting?"

"He got the Silver-Mark at Quantico's range two years ago. Besides, we need him more for his computer experience."

"What about SA O'Neil and Parker?" Hansen asked. "Our resident computer geeks."

"Phil, neither has a computer science degree or the experience Tim has."

The SAC wrinkled his mouth and looked off indistinctly. "And when he fails?"

"He won't," Givens said.

"I was asking the doc." Hansen looked at Toller. "Is Delbravo going to flip out in the middle of this?"

Toller shook his head. "I doubt that, but he does need success."

"And if he fails?"

"It could go either way, in that case. He could still win over his doubts if he fails. But he has the best chance if he captures the assailant."

* * *

Sheriff's Office

The trip to the doctor's took over two hours. Just before lunch, Tim arrived at the Washtenaw County Sheriff's office in Ypsilanti. He knew little about the office, which took up two floors and had rustic carpet. Deputies, men mostly, scurried about with paper work, coffee and the occasional perp or witness to be interviewed. In the RA the bureau kept vital statistics for all local enforcement agencies: city, county and state police that could assist FBI investigations. The sheriff's office had, Tim remembered, about fifty deputies and a dozen detectives. It was huge compared with the FBI office in Ann Arbor.

In his past experience, Tim had never known county sheriff offices to quarter many female detectives, if any. Sherrie Marshall was probably the sole woman dicky and one of a handful of female deputies. She would fight for territory, he knew, probably learned it in her struggle to make detective.

He found Sherrie at her desk in an open office arena with five rows of paired desks facing each other down the line. She greeted him with a smile and stood, stretching to her full height. Tim couldn't help notice her gray wool pullover and her jeans…She wore model-fitting Levis like a perfect hug. Her perfume smelled like smooth skin after a bubble bath. It certainly would be a distraction, if they worked together.

She offered him her own seat and plopped herself on the edge of the desk, feet swinging. He wondered how long ago she had graduated from college.

"Sheriff's giving me the day to work this," she said. "Maybe longer, if I can keep my other cases up to date."

"Good." Tim put his brown satchel on the floor. "Did you see the M.E.?"

She nodded.

"Any perks or extras? Semen maybe?"

"They swabbed everything, got anal and oral smears, but the M.E. doesn't think any residual tissues survived the incineration. The body's pretty torched. Won't be sure till tomorrow."

"Damn. And fingerprints?"

"Doesn't look too good. We usually only get them at a third of our scenes, and those mostly come from the cashiers where the perp bought his supplies. He wiped everything and wore gloves, we think."

"That's what he says in the post."

"We did get something." Sherrie hopped down from the desk and snatched a couple of sheets. "Near the tripod marks, I retrieved half a dozen skin flakes. Small pieces lying on top of the perp's footprint, so they're fresh."

"Victim's or the subject's?"

"Preliminary blood typing shows different than the victim." Sherrie handed Tim a sheet of paper. Lab results.

Tim shook his head. "You know, it always amazes me when forensics can sift through the mountains of particles and come up with a few key pieces of dust. Especially when the scene is outside and the ground is nothing but dust and dirt and mud."

"That's why we use a floral vacuum."

"What, more powerful?" Working computer crime, Tim often missed out on hearing about the latest forensic techniques. He knew the industrial vacuums they use to clear-out carpet at a scene had about five-times the sucking power of the best home-class vacuums.

Sherrie shook her head. "Unlike the interior breed, exterior sweepers use low power. They just grab the loose stuff off of the dirt ground, items that recently fell and haven't settled. Although, we have more levels of filters and an electrostatic separation unit."

"Electrostatic, like in footprint lifters?"

"No, it's part of a dust separation unit. The filters separate by particle size. The electrostatic module separates by electric charge. You see, most nonconductive items have static buildup, especially in the dry winter air. Human hair, skin and some fibers tend to be charged. Metal, rock and others usually have no charge. Other fibers, rubber and plastics have the opposite charge of the human particles."

"This is great. So what do we know about these skin flakes?"

"Dandruff."

"And a secretor," he said, scanning the lab sheet. About a fifth of all people do not secrete white blood cells in their urine, semen or sweat. Blood-typing them with their secretion helps, but with DNA profiling, the bureau had caught even non-secretors.

She handed him another sheet. "And the lab just sent back the results of a quick-n-dirty chromosomal orcein stain. They confirmed what we suspected. The perp's only got one X."

"A male with a bad hair day."

"Yep. Though, we can't get a definite hair color, but it's improbable to be blonde. More likely brown, maybe red at the fairest, since the skin melanin content is high-average for a Caucasian. He also uses a typical non-conditioning shampoo, according to the mineral oil content. Maybe we should recommend Head-n-Shoulders when we catch up with him."

Tim chuckled as he glanced over the last page of the lab report. It was highly technical. "You seem to know quite a bit of forensics."

"I studied criminology at Ohio State, minor in forensics. I wanted to go into an examiner's office, but I just couldn't stomach the smell. But my heart's still in it. I sit in on the occasional class at the med-school here."

"Well, it seems to pay off," Tim said.

"I'm guessing your labs will try to get DNA markers for matching, assuming enough skin sample is left from all the other tests."

Tim put the papers with his case file and rose. "Let's go back to Northfield, if you have time. I want to do a thorough reconstruction; dissect every piece of dirt. Maybe Hando gave us more clues than he intended."

* * *

Bronco

Sherrie drove since her Bronco was much better on rough terrain than Tim's bureau-issued sedan. She had to move a stack of papers and trash from the passenger seat for him. Her cell phone lay in a charger. She took it out and stored it in a pocket. In her line of work she was rarely in the office and police-band radio was just too much of a nuisance, barking all emergencies as they happened. Cellular phones struck quite comfortably, but they were insecure and she had to be careful what she said on one.

They belted themselves in and she drove out to Carpenter Road. As she pulled onto Highway 23, she felt a surge of nervousness in the pit of her belly. She had never worked with the FBI before, so she was breaking new ground. And going back to the swamp provoked unpleasant thoughts.

"Did you read the list of items recovered from the area?" she asked.

"Yeah. It all matches. I brought a printout of the post for you to read. We'll go over it at the scene."

"What about the powder on the tube?" she asked. "The lab put a small amount in a spectrometer. It looks like a narcotic, but the spectra didn't exactly match anything in our drug database."

"I'm not sure, but he writes about taking a 'rimshot of rhapsody.' I'm betting it's some kind of drug he snorted. He calls it 'rhap' with an 'h' and talks about 'rhapping and rimming.'"

"Rimming," Sherrie repeated. "It sounds sort of familiar. A sexual thing."

Tim shifted in his seat. "I'll let you check it out then. It might be a local jingle that I never learned."

She passed the Plymouth Road exit, continuing north. "You know, it seems to me this is local job. The person that did this has been in Washtenaw County long enough to know about the exact place at the swamp. I mean, it's so secluded."

"True. And this drug sounds rare. Maybe we could shake down local dealers for names or faces. Why don't you send the sample to the DEA for more analysis?"

"Way ahead of you. Filled out the paperwork half-hour ago." It was routine for local police to hand-off large or rare drug problems to the Drug Enforcement Administration, a federal agency dealing with national narcotic trafficking. Even the FBI, which clashed on territory with the DEA, passed them the names of a lot of street dealers. She changed lanes. "So is it typical for a serial killer to use drugs?"

"First, let's hope he's not a serial killer." Tim shifted in his seat. "But yeah, there's precedence for drug use. Some say Manson did. Henry Wallace confessed to a cocaine addiction. And Andrew Cunanan probably had drug ties."

"Would our perp have been coherent enough to handle computer posting and cameras and all that while on drugs?"

"Not sure. I can't even say what equipment he handled, since it isn't mentioned in the story. Just the rape, torture and killing, for the most part."

"But you did say he posted his story on a computer, and at the same moment he was killing the Ramey boy."

"The date on the post coincides with a time after he had abducted the boy. There are lots of ways this could happen. He could have posted it remotely from this area to his Canadian site, using a laptop. He could have forged the header date, having posted before leaving Toronto. Or he could have scheduled a delayed post from Toronto, using 'at.'"

"At?"

"Yeah, a computer command," he said. "Think of timers for your house lights. You can set them to come on at a time when you're not home. Hando might have programmed the post to upload while he was down here."

"I'm not as good with computers as you, so excuse my questioning."

"Well, I'm not too much of a people-person. I'll stick with the computer-clueing, if you'll handle interviewing. We need to get with the victim's parents—the Rameys—soon."

"You just got my first interview notes."

"Yes, but I want to check out a few things."

"I'll call them." She passed a loud rig and waited for the noise to subside before talking again. "I've always been a little confused about the Internet. I mean, why can't you just search out where he called from in the LUDs or phone company database?"

"For one, there is no dedicated database for Internet exchanges. It works differently than the phone networks."

"Well, I don't even know how the phone system works. All I really know is you pick up your phone and dial, then someone answers. The phone company keeps track of it all. Doesn't the Internet work pretty much the same way?"

"Yes, and no." Tim sighed. "You really want the full lecture?"

She nodded. "Why not, professor."

"Okay. Let's talk about the phone system first. Think of Amtrak. The phone company is like a train system. Making a call from Detroit to Los Angeles is like hopping on the rail from here to LA. There isn't a direct line of tracks connecting the cities. Amtrak decides when to switch tracks, which cities you pass and so forth until it gets your train on the one line leading into LA. The passengers don't drive, they don't switch the tracks, they don't decide on the stops. And there's really only one kind of service, all using the same tracks.

"Likewise when you make a phone call. You're the client, and the Baby Bells serve you. They assign your phone line a unique number, switch your calls and keep track of communications in their central databases, like the LUDs. That's why we cops can trace most any call, almost instantly and even after it's disconnected."

"Okay, I think I sort of knew that already," Sherrie said. "How's that different than the Internet."

"In the servers. While the phone company is like trains, the Internet is more like a highway system. With a highway you could drive yourself, decide the stops and interstate changes, go anywhere the road is paved. Of course, you'd need to understand how to navigate the roads, how to read the maps and follow the connection protocols. Same on the Internet. If you don't know, well then, like hopping on a taxi, you can have your Internet Service Provider do all the driving for you, which is what virtually everyone does. Much easier."

"So a hacker drives himself, right?"

"Right," he said. "The biggest difference for tracing hackers on the Internet is that while the phone companies keep calling information accessible to law enforcement, Internet providers can be mega-corporations or acne-faced, high-school dropouts. The database of connections is spread out among all providers, rich and poor. All over the world, in every kind of file format. And worse, the Internet databases can be deleted at the whim of each provider."

"There aren't laws?"

"Not internationally. Hell, not even nationally. A hacker who knows what he's doing could set up his own server, or go to hacker friendly servers in Budapest or Niger, then anonymously relay any message from there. Ten minutes later, the server admin deletes any record of who requested the exchange. It's completely insecure."

"You're saying you may never find this guy."

Tim shook his head. "I don't know. When he was just planning with Victor I searched for him online and even went to Canada. He seems to be nowhere."

"Or in two places at once," she said. "You were saying he could be anywhere when he posts."

"He could. In fact, he doesn't even have to be at his computer, if he schedules it. This makes it harder to find him, but not much more than if he had called in his story to a news reporter. The difference might be this broadcast. A broadcast goes everywhere, and we may find it and follow the signal back to him. I'll check on that as soon as I can get a decent computer."

"Such an elaborate scheme," she said. "All for the attention of a whacked-out audience. You think he'll do it again?"

Tim cursed under his breath. "At the end of his story, he claims to have found an even better spot for the next round."

* * *

Apartment

Tim dragged himself home late that night after an all-day scene reconstruction. Their efforts since lunch gave very little: a couple of theories about the make of Hando's car, and how he had hauled the boy into the swamp.

Tim seized the overflowing mail on the kitchen table and sorted through the stack of mostly bills. Another letter from BADGE, the FBI's black caucus, requested that he consider re-joining. He tossed it into the wastebasket. When he had first joined BADGE years earlier, he really believed they could change the discrimination he'd tasted. But when he was suspended, *they* canceled his membership. Now that he'd been decorated with a second gun wound, they wanted him back.

He turned and saw Janice enter the room.

"You're home late. And you left without saying goodbye." She wore a bathrobe. Her hair was combed out and she looked beautiful to his tired eyes.

He dropped the mail and put his arms around her. She squeezed tight around his back, pulling on the top of his shoulders. They kissed.

"I'm on a homicide," he said.

She stood motionless in his embrace.

"Well?" He smiled.

"Good for you," she said matter-of-factly. She relaxed her arms, then looked away. "Beth called me today."

Robinson's widow kept a long-distance friendship with Janice. She rarely called when he was home. "How is she?" he asked.

"Still hurting. Still hates the bureau. She can't seem to shake off any of it."

"Sorry to hear that." Tim let go of Janice.

"She found some pictures of you and him. She's mailing them."

He nodded, not so anxious to see pictures of his former partner. Oddly, he wanted little to do with Robinson right now.

Wednesday, February 12

Residency

Tim knelt down and ripped open the first of three boxes. It contained an LCD monitor for a new office computer sitting in a box next to it. He had requested funds from the Field Office for a nineteen inch monitor, but seventeen was the most Bob Givens would approve on such short notice. At least now Tim had a real computer to help him chase down Hando. It would compliment the dinosaur NCIC terminal, rather than replace it, since both had their unique purposes.

Before he could even lift the monitor out of the foam packing, U.S. Attorney Sam Grand walked into his cubicle. Grand's blonde hair looked a bit rumpled and his face was minus its usual smile.

"What's up?" Tim asked, standing back up.

"I'm writing the appeal for the Victor case. I need you to revise this affidavit." Grand held out a sheet.

"Maybe next week. I'm real busy right now."

"Week's a little long. I have a circuit judge willing to review the whole file by the end of this week. Can you at least give me a short version?"

"I'll try," Tim said, "but Victor's case is peanuts compared to the murder."

"That's why we need this, Delbravo." Grand heaved a tired breath. "If we can roast him with more charges, maybe he'll talk about his former accomplice, now turned killer."

Tim looked at Grand. "How much do you think Victor knows about Hando?"

"Well, he was hiding something at the plea bargaining."

Tim had believed that too, but he doubted Grand's plan would give them what they needed soon enough. "Well, even before our case took a nose dive he wasn't cooperative. You think appealing the same case will make him talk?"

"I don't know," Grand said. "It's worth a try, unless you can think of worse charges we can use to sweat him."

Tim thought about little Robbie Farnes. "Victor gave porn to a minor when he helped set up the boy's computer."

"Yeah, you put that in the original file." Grand wrinkled his mouth. "Hmm. Tough call. It was on the kid's computer, not on paper. The current statute only explicitly penalizes distributing printed or video-recorded pornography to minors. We can't prove it wasn't already in the kid's possession. Victor probably wouldn't cave in for a nebulous charge."

"Well, Victor's not the only person that knows Hando. Hando's a popular guy on the newsgroups these days."

"Can you find us some of his net buddies to broil?"

"If I could get into Hando's e-mail account I might figure out who really knows him." Tim looked over the boxes containing his new computer. "But when I get the e-mail, I will probably have Hando himself."

Grand nodded. "That's why we need to turn the heat on Victor. He's back in town, negotiating a return to campus. Victor's the only human link to Hando, and if we add the minor distribution on top, maybe he'll squeal."

"We can try, but won't it take months to get a new court date? I can't wait while my guy, who knows where, goes writing and living some more of his fantasies. Besides, the case could get dismissed again before Victor even begins feeling warm."

"Well, that last dismissal still has me spooked." Grand rubbed his brow. "You know, last week I spoke with a district clerk, a good friend of mine, and she told me that Judge Truante got pressed to hurry the case. The same day we argued against the dismissal, Truante was getting calls from some congressman wanting updates about it."

Tim's eyes grew big. "Euler? Buck?"

"She didn't have names," Grand said. "Who is Euler Buck?"

"Two guys: Senator Euler and his aide, Dan Buck. They gave me their hellfire and damnation speeches just before the dismissal."

"Oh, well doesn't sound like hellfire scared the judge too much."

"Or maybe the senator wanted the case dismissed to throw more fuel on the fire under his Decency Bill."

"Oh, a conspiracy." Grand chuckled, then waved. "See you later, Delbravo."

* * *

Sheriff's Office

Sherrie sat before the DataGeneral computer terminal, networked from the sheriff's office to national crime systems. She pretty much hated computers, the Internet and practically anything with a keyboard. They drained away time through your fingers. Her search in the drug databases had given nothing about Hando's drug rhap. She was about to log-out when someone called to her from the hall. She turned and saw big-britches Mark Hannor, the Sheriff's second in command. He entered the computer station cubicle with a sneer filling his lips.

"What are you working on for the DEA?" Hannor asked. He stood over her with bold sunglasses covering his upper face.

"Why?" Sherrie didn't want to volunteer anything.

"You got a fax." Hannor held up four sheets.

Sherrie reached out, but he pulled away.

"Nuh—uh." Hannor shook his half-opened mouth. "Sheriff wants to know about the DEA. You're not on narc duty."

"It's for the Ramey homicide."

"Which budget?" It was a poisoned question.

"Mine."

"Your which one?"

"My free time."

Hannor snickered. "Why pucker on the FBI's ass? They can't promote you." He tossed the fax sheets at her. "Just don't forget us when you're a DC-star, babe."

Sherrie watched him leave then carried the fax to her desk. Her current caseload stared from towering heaps. But she made space for the DEA report and read it.

Two pages had plots—spectra. Only the last sheet offered an explanation, if she could call it that.

"*...Signals across the entire NIR and visible spectrum,*" it read. They had sent the sample to their "wet labs." A copy of the report went out to New York—an Agent D. Priestly—for some reason. Apparently, Hando's rhap had Sherrie, the FBI and even the DEA baffled.

* * *

Residency

Tim felt ready for some hacking. Empty computer boxes lay scattered on the floor. From his desk, he had scooped up his forms, stapler, pens and even the family photo; kissing in the air at the image of his wife and kids before throwing it with the desktop clutter into a drawer. He needed every inch of space for the second computer he had tied into a secure government network. After Grand left, he spent an hour battling to arrange the set-up, and now he was ready to go after Hando. The trail was already a day cold.

He scanned all the newsgroups, looking for Bill Ramey's Internet address, but could not find it. Apparently, the boy had not posted to the Usenet groups, making him wonder how Bill had met Hando. Tim dove into the *alt.sex.stories* newsgroup where he hoped to find Hando's original post. He examined other posts along the way, noting the names of other users were strange. With titles such as: *Snuff Finder, BloodSurfer, AbyzzMaul,* and *TyMeDwnPlz,* hardly anyone, like Hando, was giving his real name. The little chickens were afraid. He envisioned white-hoods and basement hiding places, where like Klansmen, these bastards would hunch over their keyboard, plucking letters until their attack was complete. Then they would laugh hysterically as they sent the latest material—some kind of virtual hanging, coed raping or bondage whipping.

On *alt.sex.stories,* several new messages about the Ramey murder filled the halls of this virtual coffee shop. It was the latest excitement. Tim read through them, his temperature rising with each one. They discussed the "broadcast" as though it were a sitcom. Did they know it was real—that a boy had actually been murdered? Two of Hando's fans used European accounts. One from Norway was exemplary of many, saying:

"Only the real kill has the power to keep me so aroused. And this was live-action! I had to skip classes to see it. But it was worth every bleeding minute! Keep it up Hando!"

From Norway—across the damned ocean. There was one from Australia and others from around the world. It was an international sickos convention, gathering for the broadcast. Somehow Hando had televised and transmitted it on something like a global-access channel. How he broadcasted at the same moment as the slaying was puzzling. Since airwave transmissions could be located by following the signal strength back to the source, Tim had a chance of finding Hando once he found this broadcast.

He counted the number and type of posts on *alt.sex.stories*. With over 2400 postings in a month, the newsgroup received around 80 posts every day. There these posts remained, like cheap candy in a bowl at the doctor's office—or worse—the poisonous Halloween candy from an insane neighbor. And any kid happening by could just grab a piece—stories and images free for anyone with a computer and a connection.

He returned to the post Hando had uploaded from Toronto early Tuesday. Somehow, he thought, the key is in the header. Mark Striker had shown him this much.

Path: newsfeed.fbi.gov!news.sprintlink.net!
nn.ic-net.com!news.wimsey.com!info.metro.com!
news.zip-per.net!news.doplo.org!news.net.net!
in1.toronto-net.ca!hando
From: hando@in1.toronto-net.ca (Alven Hando)
Newsgroups: alt.sex.stories
Subject: SIZZLING SWAMP part (1/1)
Followup-To: alt.sex.stories
Date: 11 Feb, 03:54:19 - 0500 GMT
Organization:
Lines: 965
Sender: hando@in1.toronto-net.ca
Message-ID: <1mmmummm1@in1.toronto-net.ca>
NNTP-Posting-Host: in1.toronto-net.ca

According to the path statement, Hando's message had passed nine computer sites. These were traceable, Tim knew. Starting with *hando* at *in1.toronto-net.ca*, it next passed *news.net.net*, then *news.doplo.org* and so on until it reached the last destination: *newsfeed.fbi.gov*—the FBI's news server. Each site was a distinct place on the Internet, and although the path suggested that the story had originated in Toronto, he had his doubts. Anyone with enough knowledge of Internet protocol could forge accounts, falsify paths, and send messages under false identities.

Anonymous messaging. It was not much more difficult than writing a fake return address on a paper envelope and mailing it from a different city so the postmark doesn't reveal your true hometown.

Hando, the clever bastard, would have forged all the e-mail headers he could. With the place, the account, the ID and hosts all fabricated, Tim wasn't sure about much of anything. Not even the date, which looked as though it had been posted at the same moment the victim was killed.

Something was real, his gut told him. At least the FBI news-site in the path was real. With that much certain, he could start from the bureau's site and work backwards. To do so, he must learn the art of hacking a post as well as Hando had done.

"Back to school," he told himself. Hackers, who loved bragging about their skill, would have some kind of online "hacking for dummies" guide. Tim would learn their black art.

* * *

Downtown

Sherrie hit the streets when answers didn't come in offices or labs. She walked to State Street, and after a quick chicken salad on rye in the nearby sandwich shop, she monitored pedestrian traffic around the pool halls and party stores. She needed information and contacts—street punks that snitched for bucks.

It wasn't smart going into pinball lounges and halls. She stood out— smoke and cue sticks just weren't her best look. She preferred the plainclothes of an up-class detective.

Just outside a drug store, she spied a skinhead that had given her tips in the past. He wouldn't know much about sex-deviants, but he might know about rhap and it was better than pacing in the cold.

The skinhead dressed mostly in metal, with hints of black leather and dark denim underneath. His head was skin-shiny, not even a dark smudge to imply he once had hair. Small red and black tattoos covered the base of his skull and what she could see of his forearms.

This one went by Kyle Cercs. His favorite color was green since he was a chameleon—not the kind that could always fade into the background, but a mood chameleon. He could be cooperative or mean spirited, depending on the situation. If he needed cash, he got cooperative.

She pulled out her wallet and passed him, implying an offer. "I want something."

"I don't need any green," the skinhead clicked, walking even faster. They were moving past a stereo shop across from campus.

She grabbed his arm, slowing him to a near halt by a café. "That's okay, since I haven't formally offered any."

"I said, I don't need you," he squawked, looking away and shaking her grip from his coat. "I heard you ain't A-squared or Ypsi police anyway."

"No I'm with the county, the sheriff."

"So go find some cowboy. I ain't your bitch," Cercs said and walked away.

She grabbed him again and threw him against a stone wall, but not so hard to hurt him. He squinted his eyes, blinking apprehensively. She moved in tight, their breaths intermingling until she could smell his beer-weed mouthwash.

"Have you heard about the kid that got burned at the swamps?" she asked.

His eyes opened wide and he smiled impishly. "The pyro-kid."

"Is that who did it?"

"No." He pulled her hand away from his collar. "That's what I heard the vic is called."

"Who did it?" She blocked his escape with a wide spread stance.

He looked around, turning to see behind him. They had stopped near the entrance to what was referred to as "The Arcade." It was a walkway through the buildings, connecting State with Maynard Street. Inside sat clothing shops, specialty stores and a post office branch. People walked in all directions at this place, and Cercs gazed nervously at them.

"Come on," she said, grabbing his coat. "Let's cross to campus. You have something to tell me."

He hesitated, but she kept her grip and Cercs seemed to follow without much of a fight. They bisected State to the northwest point of campus where a couple of men begged for handouts. She stopped by a vacant cement bench.

"Who did it?"

He seemed a little more relaxed, mood changing on cue. "I only know a little," he said, pausing to look at her wallet.

"What? You want some greens now?" She only had about twenty, but Cercs was cheap.

He nodded, and she fished out a five-bill. He snatched it and hid it under his leather jacket. From the corner of his mouth he made his disclosure. "From what I've seen the guy's a new scrub around here. I'm betting he's pissed out his brains. Stinking crazy." He stopped, looking at her wallet again.

She grabbed his left arm. "That's all I get for five? Anyone can tell me he's crazy."

"Okay," he whined. He glanced around, searching the crowds. His eyes were filmy-red and dilated, his forehead creased. He lowered his head to her ear and his odor enveloped her again.

"This one's free. Won't cost you a nigger's dime," he swore. "You know I don't like faggots."

"So you're saying the guy is—"

"Let's just say I hear he's into things even fags wouldn't do." He forcefully pulled her hand off and started fading back.

"How do you know this?" Sherrie half lunged at him, but he was already out of reach.

"The pinch is he hangs at the *Autarchic Franchise*. Try it there."

The skinhead ran. She ran a few steps and then decided to let him go, even though she'd never heard of the place. He couldn't know any more or he would have cleaned her wallet. Right now, she needed to tell Tim about the DEA's riddle and Cercs' tip.

* * *

Residency

The odor of uneaten meatball sandwich pervaded the office, since it grew cold before Tim could finish. Greasy wrappers still littered under his chair and a large mug with a ring of coffee stained a stack of papers on the floor. The crowded desk still lay mostly neat, except for cables snaking between the two computers. Tim studied the newest screen. He was making progress and even a late lunch didn't disturb his search.

On the newsgroup *alt.2600*, Tim had found a Frequently Asked Questions guide, in which hackers published many of their tricks and gags. One section of the FAQ taught him how to post a forged message on the public newsgroups. It included a *perl* script, complete recipe-instructions and user-friendly code to automate posting remotely. A user could write his message, then feed it to the program and let it post remotely at any time he wanted. Create an alibi for himself.

Tim tested the programs referenced in the hacker's manual by forging a post in a test group, and then on the same newsgroup, *alt.sex.stories*. While waiting for his message to upload, he re-examined Hando's post-header. Though the subject's account was forged, the path his post had traversed was mostly real. Tim *pinged* each site to determine whether the site existed, and searched online where the physical address and owner of each real site. The first three sites on the path were false paths, contrived by Hando, making the first real location his message had reached, *news.zip-per.net*. This *zip-per.net* site actually resided in a town not far from Ann Arbor.

It was impossible to tell from where Hando had posted by just examining the header. From examination of server logs, Tim learned Hando's message had reached the Usenet—the FBI news server anyway—only minutes after the time-stamp his header indicated. It was posted at the same time the murder was happening. Maybe Hando scheduled his task to do it for him. Or maybe he had a laptop computer and a wireless card or cell phone modem. Of course, common wireless would probably not reach to the swamp and a modem wouldn't have the speed for transmitting full video…

In any event, it appeared the date and time were not falsified. So Hando had devised the plan in advance, releasing his story and some kind of broadcast just moments before executing the particulars. More than premeditated murder, Hando had prophesied the victim's responses and pain with excruciating detail.

Tim went to look for his own trial post on *alt.sex.stories*, and found three new posts, signed by Hando, waiting on the newsgroup.

This time it wasn't stories, but digitized pictures. Tim just stared at the subject line of the three posts: JPG image of pyro-kid, actual scene (part 1/3)…(part 2/3)…(part 3/3).

On his computer terminal loomed the culmination of a fantasy. Not computerized fiction—but a terminal fantasy of a deadly reality. A dream gone nightmarishly true.

It mocked him. Rather than feel incensed, however, he went numb. *You must go on,* he told himself. Investigate and incarcerate. But his limbs and mind were frozen until he caught his fists hammering against his thighs. He lifted them to the keyboard, stabbing until he had extracted and decoded all of the posts. The computer finished loading, and he read Hando's intro:

"Many said they missed the broadcast. Remember, you can get access by chatting on the IRC in the right places (just ask around). But for those that didn't get to the show, here are some stills. Believe me, the video is much better and is aired just once. Only during the kill—real-time, my friends."

The attached images exhibited Bill Ramey. Three scenes of a boy's torture and death. As gruesome as Tim could not have imagined. He breathed hard, standing wildly and pacing—trying to sort out the illogic of it all. But his mind was caught in an infinite loop. A nausea, a depression, crept through him. It made its way to his throat, almost escaping. He shot up and fought it back with tight-mouth swallows.

Then he heard the RA entrance buzz open. From around the corner, Sherrie Marshall appeared. She wore a gray waistcoat over a yellow sweater. "I got a tip," she said upon reaching his cubicle.

The images were still blazing on the monitor. A list of the stories and messages on *alt.sex.stories* displayed in the back.

Sherrie motioned at the screen. "What is that?"

He really didn't want to discuss it but he knew he must if they were ever going to find Hando. "Our subject must have digitized the Polaroids of Bill Ramey. He posted three pictures."

Sherrie glanced at the listings on the screen. "Hey, 'pyro-kid!' I just heard that."

"I guess that's what Hando calls Bill Ramey." Tim hoped she wouldn't ask him to recall the images. He would prefer to send them off to the lab with a copy of her film for analysis.

"I found six Polaroid tabs at the scene. Are you sure there are only three images?" Sherrie stood over the computer.

"Three's enough." Tim leaned on his desk. With Sherrie's presence, his stomach calmed, feeling maybe even a little empty. Then he saw the cold meatball sandwich and decided he wasn't really hungry. Coffee sounded more appropriate.

Sherrie jumped in the chair by the computer. She tapped on the keyboard and pointed excitedly at a subject line. "Tim, did you see this?"

He bent over to look. She had started a search on the newsgroup for any message or story that contained the word "pyro-kid" and found another post. It was a request for re-post.

Someone wanted Hando to re-post the story about the pyro-kid.

"Look at the date," Sherrie said.

The request was from two days *before* Bill Ramey was killed.

"What the hell!" Tim shot toward the keyboard. "Here, let me drive."

"If the story is a re-post…" Sherrie began but failed to finish. Tim took control of the computer and opened a command box.

"Yeah," he said. "I'm going into the archives. I haven't had a chance to search the previous month."

He guided his web browser into a Usenet archive site, which kept news posts from the last few years. He typed in "Hando" as the search word and waited until it listed all hits or matches, revealing two posts by Hando dated four and ten days earlier. One was entitled pyro-kid bogs me. The screen listed the other as marshland meltdown.

Tim read through them, finding nearly identical stories as the last post they already had about Bill Ramey—except the victim's name was missing from the first two. All of the same detail and premeditation, only days earlier than they had thought.

"He was planning this for a while, right out in public," Sherrie said.

"Yeah. He was modeling it on the computer. Like computer car designs and blueprints. Only Hando refines his sickness and abductions with the newsgroup sickos. They tell him the good parts, what to use. Almost a conspiracy to enact murder."

"Just imagine all the arrests," Sherrie said, smiling.

"I'll send the messages to DC for psycho-analysis and ID." He stood. "Right now, I need a break. Want some coffee? My treat."

"Sure. Let me just look up something in the phone book." She looked around on his desk. Tim dug under some piles and found an Ameritech phone book for the Washtenaw area. She took it and flipped pages like a child opening a birthday present.

"What are you looking for?"

"The tip I mentioned was that our suspect hangs out at a place called the 'Autarchic Franchise,'" she said, mostly absorbed in her search. "Ever heard of it?"

"No," he said, wondering why she had waited so long to tell him this. "Is it a club?"

"I guess."

"What's *'autarchic'*? Some politically correct new sex thing?"

"Not sure. Got a dictionary?"

"Not here."

She gave up her white and yellow pages hunt after trying several places. "It's not in here. Maybe it's new. Call information."

He agreed. He picked up the phone and dialed the operator, who in turn, asked for a city.

"Probably in Washtenaw County. Check under the entire area code. I'm looking for the phone and address of an establishment called, Autarchic Franchise."

"How is that spelled?" the operator asked.

Tim wasn't sure. "Try, a-u-t-a-r-c-h-i-c, f-r-a-n-c-h-i-s-e."

He could hear the keys clicking on the other end and after a moment of silence she said, "There's no listing."

"Anything with the word 'Autarchic'?"

"I'm sorry, sir. I don't find anything."

"Try the first few letters. And try every area in the Midwest."

She did and found nothing.

"Anything under Franchise?"

Her keys clicked. "About three hundred places."

"Thanks." He hung up, shrugging at Sherrie. "Nada. Where did you hear this?"

"A skinhead told me."

"A skinhead? How would *he* know?"

"Just did."

Tim rose. "Well, either he's feeding you crap, or there's no Autarchic Franchise."

"Or it's not in this area. Maybe the skinhead knows, or maybe it's in Toronto with Hando."

"True." Tim sat at the computer. "Maybe a company search on the Web." He clicked to his web browser's search page, typing "AUTARC*" for a wild-card search. The icon swirled, bits flew across the world. In the end, it gave him dozens of approximate matches. Most of which connected to sites about Australia, authors or automobile pages.

"Ready, then?" Sherrie stood.

"Just a minute." He guided his browser to a digital Webster's page. "I just remembered there's an online dictionary."

"And I almost forgot," she said. "I got a fax about rhap this morning."

"What'd it say?" Tim typed the word.

"Nothing helpful. They can't nail it down."

"They?"

"The DEA."

Tim nodded. "That's right, Don't Expect Anything…"

"What?"

"That's what we sometimes call the DEA cowboys. Don't Expect Anything."

He looked at the screen. The dictionary found a match.

autarchic *adj.* : Dictatorial and despotic.

* * *

Café

The coffeehouse, a place just off Main Street called Café Connexion, was new to Sherrie. It wasn't crowded at just before three in the afternoon. Four of the twenty-something tables were occupied by typical Ann Arborites or career-students. Halogens softly lit the scene and mellow music breezed around them.

The Café Connexion was apparently so named because it offered several terminals with Internet connections. Two ways to get wired: caffeine and computers. Sherrie asked Tim if he had come to Café Connexion in order to use their computers.

"No," he answered. "I didn't realize they were wired. I was trying to escape the dip-sticking things."

She ordered a cappuccino. Tim bought a black coffee. They sat at a small table protecting the far corner of the establishment from desertion. Sherrie sipped her cappuccino and licked a slivery froth-line off her upper lip. "So how's the tracing our hacker?"

Tim rocked back in the small wood chair, the seams and legs creaking under him. "I'm barely out the door. But I've been thinking of a different route. Maybe we can get Hando through the real world."

"How so?"

"Through a rhap dealer." Tim grabbed his coffee, but just held it.

"Undercover?"

"Yeah. I think I'll call Detroit and bring in a RAG."

"RAG?"

"A Rent-A-Goon." Tim rocked back again.

"I could do it."

"No. You're not on the payroll. It's my butt if anything happens."

He was right, of course. And Sherrie was better at sifting and analyzing clues. "Have you given any thought about motive?" she asked.

"I don't think I'll ever understand why someone would do this."

"Yes, but why Bill Ramey?"

He nodded. "A few weeks ago, right after I arrested Victor, Hando up'ed a post about revenging his friend's suspension. 'A mire' the university would regret."

"The swamp connection?"

"That and the fact that Bill's mother is staff in Family Counseling at U-M."

"And the father?"

"Works for Ford in Dearborn."

"But, Tim…" She paused, setting down her cappuccino and noticing that he hadn't even touched his coffee yet. "But why Bill? I mean, there have got to be lots of staff with kids."

"I'm thinking Hando met Bill online. He made friends and learned that Bill's mom worked on campus. I've seen it happen before. Have you called the Rameys?"

"I tried them this morning," she said. "They weren't home. I'll keep trying."

"They probably get calls from the newspaper; won't answer anymore. Maybe we should go there."

"Let me try calling first." She didn't want to catch them at a bad time.

He nodded. "Until tomorrow, then we'll drop by unexpected if we have to."

Sherrie sipped her cappuccino and watched across the café. The other patrons were bound in serene colloquy, a soft hum-hiss of intellectual gabbing. The coffeehouse displayed flyers and bulletins about volatile events and demonstrations. Activism and politics were meat-n-potatoes for many Ann Arborites. Even on Valentine's Day, a queer movement held a kiss-in protest.

Tim put down his coffee. His eyes remained fixed on the table.

Sherrie held her chin up with a palm, watching him. He was attractive: a large man, mature but not old, not fat or gray or…well, he didn't seem shallow. His firm jaw and thick neck topped a good foundation of shoulders. Yes, attractive. Her eyes followed down his arm to his left hand gripping the table. It looked sore, but he wore no rings on his hand. Embarrassment settled in as she realized how obvious her probing might seem. She looked up nervously and her gaze suddenly met his.

They were tired but penetrating eyes—deep bronze eyes that soaked in details. She had only known him for a couple of days, but she realized that Tim was the kind of person that could rock back casually or lounge about and still catch more detail than someone with a video camera and microphone. A man that seemed to be sleeping through a conversation, he could remember every sigh and eye-blink days later. Surely, he had noticed she was looking at his ring finger.

"So, what's our next move?" she asked.

"We'll get a RAG. For us it's the same old. I'll keep on the computer, if you'll track the drug info and call the family. Try to find out more about this place, the Autarchic Franchise, too."

She nodded, grabbing her own cup. The cappuccino tasted good at this place and she liked the serenity. She glanced around again, eyeing the other people—couples. They looked so content and happy. Her gaze wandered from face to face and eventually she caught herself staring back at Tim then jerked her head as if startled by a bee.

"So…uh," she stuttered. "How long you been with the bureau?"

"Almost twelve years," he said proudly.

"It's great, I hear."

"Usually, but it takes a lot out of you. Hard life, catching criminals only to lose yourself."

She watched his face deepen with arcane thought. Like something was pulling his eyes back to revisit a day long ago. "You ever have to shoot a perp?"

Tim stared at her with wounded eyes. He sipped from his cup and released a reverie with a loud sigh. "I guess I better get in touch with Detroit soon, if we want a RAG."

Sherrie felt twangs of electricity shooting from her gut, worried she went too far. Her question must have been highly personal. She wanted to crack this case with him and to be his friend, not offend him. He sat up evenly, looking out over the small crowd in the middle of the café. His face showed no anger or hurt, nothing except a wall of blank expression.

* * *

Residency

Like the ever-faithful and passionless sentry, receptionist Downey buzzed them back into the RA. She handed Tim a message to call back Agent Deacon Priestly with the New York Division of the Drug Enforcement Administration. He held the note up so Sherrie could see it as they walked briskly back to his cubicle.

"I love the bright colors here. Not like the drab grays and browns in my office." Sherrie tossed her coat onto a chair.

Tim didn't answer but again noticed the tight sweater she filled so well. Immediately he chided himself for thinking about it. He grabbed his phone and began dialing New York. With the receiver to his ear, the cord tangled as he squirmed and danced to remove his own coat. Before he could unweave himself the receptionist answered. He asked for SA Priestly, and she transferred him.

A deep voice resounded over the line. "This is Special Agent Priestly."

"Tim Delbravo with the FBI. Got your message. This about the drug?"

"Yes," Priestly said more softly. They passed introductions and a short history about their respective cases. Priestly was the case agent in the Big Apple for the new drug, Rhapsody. He also called it IC4D, explaining that users talked about rhap expanding vision past 3D, to a so-called fourth dimension of consciousness. The DEA had spotted it hitting the streets for only a few weeks, mostly in NYC and one sex club in San Francisco. Ann Arbor was the third place it had surfaced.

"What I need, SA Priestly," Tim said, "is some clue for an entry. Where is our undercover going to find the dealer?"

"Clubs, gay bars, and particularly at pharm parties and underground raves. It's going out almost exclusively to young wealthy kids," Priestly said. "Yours is the first outside a social scene. I'd like to come out, make a trip to Kalamazoo."

"Kalamazoo?"

"I'll explain when I get there. You sure the bureau can handle a drug-bug?"

"We'll make an exception this one time." A slight smile broke Tim's granite lips. "In the meantime, should I send out a goon, or should we wait for you?"

"Not me," Priestly said. "Users are young and usually white. I'm black, in my late thirties. I'll be out in a day or two, so get your cloak-n-dag rolling now."

"Right. Fax me whatever information you can soon. Thanks." Tim hung up. He turned to Sherrie who had been watching him throughout the whole conversation. "We got another break. The stuff is handled mostly by young kids in sex clubs, gay bars and parties. Now we know some possible entries."

Sherrie folded her arms, supporting her sweater's cargo. "Do you guys have anyone young enough to handle it?"

Tim nodded. "You know the town. Where's a quick entry for our RAG?"

Sherrie concentrated. "There were some flyers in the café. Friday's Valentine's. There's a kiss-in on campus and parties afterward."

Thursday, February 13

Liberty Street

The morning was a warm 15 above zero Fahrenheit, ten-degrees higher than the average over the past week. Tim walked from a single booth café across Liberty to the federal building. In the slight breeze just beginning, his trench coat flapped. He was about to enter through the main doors when a man leaning against the mirrored entrance lurched toward him.

"Agent Tim Delbravo?" he asked. His lambskin parka rubbed against Tim as he wriggled to block the opening.

Tim halted, maintaining a grip on the door handle. "Yes?"

"I'm Phil Thomas from the Detroit Associated Press. Can I ask you a few questions?" The reporter clutched the doorframe with gloved fingers.

"What about?"

"Your investigation of the boy that was murdered."

"What about it?" Tim worried reporters would be all over Mr. and Mrs. Ramey now. Sherrie had finally found them home late last night. She scheduled an interview with the Rameys for Friday.

"Have you found the suspect?" The wind mussed the newsman's perfect hair. "The guy named Alven Hando."

Tim bobbed his mouth open in surprise. "Hando who?" Although the murder was public knowledge, the suspect was supposedly still a confidential matter. Only certain people at the FBI and the county deputy helping him should know of the subject.

"Oh come on, now," the reporter said, smiling keenly. "Surely you heard about the story in today's morning edition of the *Washington Post*?"

Tim walked a step from the building. "No, I haven't."

"It was bottom front-page." The reporter followed him, letting the door close. "Senator Euler has a bill going for a vote tomorrow. He's using your case to give credence to the vote."

Great, Tim thought. Jackass senators and their privileges. Now the suspect would know he was the subject of an FBI investigation.

"What do you have to say, Agent Delbravo?"

"No comment." It was the only response allowed by the bureau. Tim stepped toward the door.

But the reporter lunged back at the entrance. "Wait! Euler claims you're a troublemaker. You've been reprimanded by the bureau twice, isn't that right?"

He glared at the reporter. "You guys really don't know how to do your own digging, do you?"

"Yeah?" The newsman narrowed his eyes into a grin. He pulled out a carton of mint filtered smokes. "Euler's got you pegged well. He says you're really against his D-Chip. That, here the FBI has blatant Internet crimes, and they've assigned an agent opposed to improving the law."

"I never said that!" Angrily he faced the reporter, uncaring that his every word would be plopped in sound bites on every doorstep in America. "I'm concerned with real crimes, real violence and threats. Apparently, Euler seems concerned about politics and deals."

"Sounds like an accusation," the reporter said, lighting a cigarette. He sucked hard and exhaled with his lips pointing at the sky. "You know something?"

Tim shook his head and pulled open the door. He had already said too much. He closed the door and caught one last glimpse of the reporter.

The bastard was smiling at him.

* * *

141

—

Zip-per.net

Tim drove to Milan, twenty minutes south of Ann Arbor, arriving just before lunch, then driving around for half an hour before he actually located the little shack that housed *zip-per.net*. It was the first place Hando's murder post actually reached on the Internet, according to the header. The site owner, he hoped, would provide him with a strong link to Hando's identity.

Tim knocked on the front door, but there was no answer. He waited in the profound silence of the area. For acres around, only wintry fields and the distant hum of a polar gust tarried.

Before driving out, he had located the owner's name and phone listing in Ameritech's database, and connected to *zip-per.net* from his computer. Right away it displayed a banner warning that cops weren't welcome, and not in such nice terms. It was an *elite site*—an illegal board, where once you got to know the owner, and for a small fee, you could get full access to the system files. Files that likely included illegally copied software packages, and designer drug and bomb making instructions. Anarchy info.

In the bureau's NCIC database, Tim found loads of information about the owner, Jez LeFerril. LeFerril worked at a computer fix-it shop in Ann Arbor, and was suspect in an ongoing investigation of copyright violations. Tim had called the shop, but they said the man had left work already. Now Tim waited for him in the black bureau sedan.

The shack housing *zip-per.net* looked as though it wouldn't survive another winter. The walls rose just slanted. The foundation corners crumbled, leaving a gap large enough for obese field rats to sneak in. Apparently, it had only recently got electricity and phone service. The lone utility pole that strung the cables was made of green wood.

It was easy to suspect that LeFerril and Hando were one and the same, upon first examination. But Tim really didn't believe such a theory. Hando, who hacked like international spies, would never have used his own site for posting such incriminating messages. No, LeFerril was probably completely unaware of what Hando had sent through *zip-per.net.*

Tim flipped through his case file, reviewing some of the details received that day. Scene photographs and Hando's digitized pictures were being analyzed in the DC lab. Spectroscopic analysis revealed that Hando used a typical lighter-fluid accelerant. There were no fingerprints on any of the items. The fibers Tim had found by the snapped gate lock were getting analyzed by FBI lab coats in Quantico. So far they determined them as wool, stained brown with a unique dye, a vegetable oil based dye the lab hadn't determined yet. Tim would check the report and determined the victim had not worn anything wool the night of his abduction.

The foot tracks and tire tracks showed that Hando wore size-eight American-made boots, and drove a small foreign vehicle. By analysis of the tire imprints, separation distance and turn-ratio, the lab had narrowed it down to nineteen different car models.

On the victim, the M.E. found tiny fragments from a green tarp identified as the common canvas that could be bought at many stores in the area or nationwide. The tube with traces of IC4D or rhap, was an ordinary drinking straw. On one end, the lab found smudges of tissue. They rated the blood type as A with a positive Rh factor, matching the victim's blood type. From the skin flakes, the county already determined the subject was O-negative, a pretty common type. Not a whole lot to help Tim.

He mused over the details until an old Ford Escort Wagon pulled up and parked over the snow. The driver stepped out, eyeing Tim's sedan. His dark hair was long and twirled into a ponytail pulled back right from the edge of his beard. He wore a dull green-gray coat and heavy winter boots, and could almost pass for a homeless off State Street, he was so dirty. The man went to the warped door of the small gray shack and began unlocking it.

Tim stepped from the sedan and beckoned to him. "Mr. LeFerril?"

LeFerril turned back. "Yeah. Who are you?"

"FBI. Special Agent Tim Delbravo." He pulled out his credentials and unfolded them.

The man smirked at him. "So *special*. Every one of you, somehow."

"Yep. The bureau loves us all." He put his badge away. "I need to talk with you, Mr. LeFerril."

"Am I being arrested?" LeFerril asked as he re-locked the door and pulled out his key.

"No." Not yet, anyway. Tim stopped about three feet from the man. "I just want to ask you some questions about a user on your bulletin board system."

LeFerril eyed him carefully and then glared past him at the sedan. "And if I refuse?"

"Then I go back and get a warrant, and we tear down the house in search of whatever we can find." He eyed the shack. "I am only interested in one of your users. I don't give a damn about copyrights. But if I have to get a warrant, then my partners will give a damn."

LeFerril glanced off indistinctly, sighing. "Who?"

Tim suppressed a smile. "I don't know the real name. User ID might be Hando."

"No one by that name on my system."

"He posted a message to the Internet through your system. I just want to see the records from February eleventh."

From his jacket LeFerril pulled out a cigarette and lit up. "I don't keep records of activity more than a day. Not enough room for that, man."

Tim knew he was lying. A guy running an illegal board would keep records of anything not self-incriminating. Just for insurance.

"Is that so?" Tim said and slowly turned back toward his sedan. "Well, I'll just have to get a warrant anyway. Got to be sure in a murder investigation."

He began the retreat to his *bucar*, but LeFerril halted him with a cough and choke on his smoke. His cigarette and face lit with surprise. "Did you say, murder?"

"Yes. And if I have to come back with a warrant, and find you do keep records, I'll indict you for aiding and abetting a premeditated. Maybe even as an accomplice."

"Look, man," LeFerril said nervously. "I don't want any part of this. I'm sure I can get the backup of the past week, and give you the records. Just give me a chance to go in and do it."

"I'm coming in." Tim stepped closer.

"I can't let you in."

"You don't have to worry unless you are a part of it."

LeFerril unlocked the door, shaking his head. "Not a part of any murder. I am offering you hands up, man. Just keep your word."

They entered. The shack was a maggot mansion; dingy clothes and crusty dishes were stacked everywhere in the single room, blankets strung for a curtain over the only window and another tattered one acting as a partition in the middle. What might have been the kitchen area was so filthy that Tim almost hesitated to go further, thinking that he ought to call in Health and Human Services.

Besides the partition, he saw a closet or tiny bathroom. However, he failed to examine it further, worried what might be living there. He didn't see a television, a couch or a table. There was no sink or refrigerator. LeFerril's furniture comprised a bean bag chair, a lone mattress sprawled low on the floor, a glowing electric heater and two cardboard boxes with some macaroni and cheese cartons inside. He wondered how LeFerril cooked it.

The man was dirt poor, rolling-pennies poor. LeFerril had to have enough computer skills to sink a middle-class income, and still he lived in a heap in the middle of nowhere.

LeFerril parted the tattered barrier that divided the one-room-hut. Tim followed apprehensively, wading through piles of greasy chip bags, empty beer cans and pizza boxes. Against the wall, with piles of trash protecting either side, sat an irregular board and concrete-brick desktop. On the desk lay a top-line Sun Fire computer server, a tape drive, DVD burner and a brand-new Hewlett Packard laser printer.

Tim chuckled to himself, realizing how few people would ever suspect such equipment in this ratty hole. A perfect hiding place.

LeFerril reclined in an old chair and Tim stood because he couldn't find another seat. Other than the food wrappers and computer equipment, only a tall, rusting file-cabinet kept the room in the new century. LeFerril touched the computer keyboard and the monitor returned from screen-saver hibernation. The screen was filled with the image of a Valentine's Day heart and the blinking inscription: 1 day more. I'll be yours forever.

Tim didn't want to ask what it meant.

LeFerril's fingers flew at Mach-two as he pulled up command boxes and spawned UNIX tasks to retrieve the data.

"What day?" LeFerril asked.

"February eleventh, at about four in the morning." He leaned against the files. In a second, the user-logs were burnishing on the screen. Tim looked down at them.

"What did the guy do?" LeFerril growled.

"I can't talk about the investigation."

"No, I mean on the computer, man. What did he do on my system?"

"He posted a message to the newsgroup *alt.sex.stories.* It went through your machine on its way out."

"Not on my site."

"How so? The first real pointer on the post's path is your site. *Zip-per.net.*"

"I don't feed anyone else from here," LeFerril said. "*Zip-per.net* is a dead end. Like a cul-de-sac on the info superhighway."

"How do you send e-mail and message packets?"

"I only receive or send initial packets of data. Not set up to play middleman. I'm still expanding."

Tim lifted his brow. How could this be? Did Hando forge a *real* path? He knew *zip-per.net* was the first real place on the path Hando's story reached. Most hosts can act as *wayposts* for e-mail and news posts, but LeFerril was saying his site was an exception. "Did anyone *begin* a post from this site to that newsgroup at four on the eleventh?"

LeFerril ran through the data on the screen. He pointed at one item. "Yeah, here's an IHAVE request from another host to upload a post to *alt.sex.stories* at 3:54 a.m. on Feb eleven."

"That's it!" Tim got excited. "Where did it come from?"

"All I have is an IP address. 198.137.241.31."

"No user name?"

"No, just the IP address."

Tim knew that the IP address was a string of *octet* numbers. Each site on the Internet had a unique 32-bit number, like a phone number or street address, and there were databases with the name of the owner for each number.

Tim suggested that LeFerril try matching the IP number to a real name via *ypmatch, host, whois,* and other UNIX commands. None of them found a match. The number didn't show up in any of the usual registers or databases.

"Try pinging or connecting to it," Tim instructed him.

LeFerril issued the command and it returned several "request timed out" lines before ending with the sterile "no answer from 198.137.241.31" that meant it existed but was not up and running at the moment. It was real, but not plugged in. Some sites didn't have dedicated connections, but rather connected to the Internet by phone only when they needed to make an exchange.

"Tell me, what speed was he connecting at?" Tim asked.

LeFerril scanned the logs. "His upload speed was a steady one-k-per second."

It was probably a dialup, an ancient modem. Good, because phone calls can be traced, once Tim found Hando's Internet Service Provider.

"We done, man?"

"Not quite." Tim made a note about the IP number in his brown casebook. "I want you to try looking at three posts made yesterday. One from last week and another the week before."

He handed LeFerril a sheet with the times and names of the three image-posts Hando put up the day before, as well as for the former story posts from weeks before. LeFerril searched his logs for each and found, in every case, identical IP numbers as the first.

"I can't tell you anything more," the computer man said.

Tim rose. "Fine. Just get this place cleaned up for the next time I visit or I'll bring the Health Department."

LeFerril released the mouse and stared at him. "What do you mean 'the next time'?"

Tim just smiled at him and walked past the blanket divider.

* * *

Residency

For Tim, the Internet was a mishmash of anarchy and juvenile playground. Hando was a punk, hard to spot in such culture. He blended well, and Tim worried he would keep uploading untraceable filth. But the suspect had added another clue in his case file. On the newsgroup just the day before, Hando mentioned that live video of his exploits was broadcasted. He had promised that other newsgroupees could get access by "chatting in the right places."

Chat rooms had to be the most active part of youthful Internet society. Unlike the newsgroups and e-mail, each chat room carried real-time conversations, electronic text flowing between dozens of people on computers all around the world. And this was similar to how Tim believed Hando did his live broadcasts.

There were hundreds of thousands of different chat rooms, some—many—of which were not widely publicized. Few of the chats were archived, and some conversations were so secret, the chat room itself was destroyed after use. Tim had no idea what chat room to search. Hando's hint was to "*just ask around.*" Tim couldn't even do that much without arousing suspicion. At least not until he ditched his FBI account and learned to hack his own net-persona.

For this reason, he went back to the newsgroup, and back to *alt.sex.stories.* Maybe there was more information hiding in the messages. When he connected to the news server, he immediately found a recent post by Hando.

Subject: Not live, but real all the same (Video: SQUEAL.MPG)

Hello all,

Attached is a little treat I concocted during the night. I think you'll find this delayed "broad"-cast almost as lively, though, now she's dead.

>:-)

Enjoy!
Alven "Is it live, or is it memohex?" Hando

<attached MIME: SQUEAL.MPG file>

Tim retrieved and decoded the attached video file, fearful of what it would reveal. He had a video player application and opened Hando's file. The movie, in mostly black and white, was compressed digital video, something a bit more grainy and jumpy than seen on television. It lasted for over three minutes.

The video started with an empty room brightened by lights shining from behind the camera. Night lights and car headlamps shone through an old single-pane window with wood shutters. The thick plaster walls and ceramic-tile floor looked like something constructed around the turn of the century. Then abruptly, like a scene cut-in, there appeared a young girl maybe fourteen or fifteen years of age. She was tied to an old black iron-belly stove. Within the first few seconds, her clothing was ripped off leaving white innocence exposed, followed by a quick zoom-range over her entire developing body. Tim felt sickened by the kind of freak that would degrade a harmless child. Two children now. There was a close-up of her frightened expression. The eyes looked supernaturally terrified, almost ghostly.

Then the real sickness began.

Through all of the torture and beating, Tim could not make out the perpetrator. Gloved hands and forearms, and black pants were about all that appeared from the edge. At one point, the attacker waved his weapon close to the window, smashing the glass into little pieces that seemed to fall in slow motion. Near the end, he could hardly recognize the girl, and black-blood coated everything—the walls and floor and stove, the last of which was now smoking. The glove hand appeared with a canister of lighter fluid in the last few seconds. Spraying the girl and stove, the room quickly filled with tall flames. It finished as abruptly as it had started, showing just the empty room again, now blurred and apparently burned almost to destruction.

Tim had to reign his repulsion because he knew he had little time. Certainly he could do nothing to save this victim, but there would be the next. For now, he had to find this place and gather every clue as fast as possible. As much as he hated it, that meant watching the video, freezing and zooming segments to determine where and what and how. He would have to dissect every brutish frame.

Scanning the perpetrator's gloved hands and pants yielded little if anything. Zoomed stills of these only indicated that they were heavily blurred and out of focus; all of the attention had centered on the girl, whose face was significantly more resolved than anything else in the scene. Beside the long butane lighter at the end, the other instrument of death had been a baseball bat. From the beginning, with the video frozen on the frightened yet still unharmed face of the girl, Tim captured and printed the best front and side profiles. He would need them for victim identification.

He scanned the room next, starting with the antique stove. The name was blurry—it was a Fischer and had white powder all over it. This, Tim postulated, might be the same drug found on a straw at the Ramey scene. Or it might just be flour. The window view gave the most revealing details. Centering on it, he found faint and blurred images of neon signs. After grabbing a frame, he loaded it in his photo editing software. With a little deblurring and sharpening, he recognized the letters: W-H-I-T with several more that were indiscernible. Underneath these were three distinct letters: D-E-P and two trailing letters that he couldn't make out. A building in the outside view had old Victorian architecture, hanging signs and perhaps antique street lanterns. It looked like something right out of a history book.

Then it hit him. He was looking at Ypsilanti's Depot Town, in the town just east of Ann Arbor. The old preserved storefronts there lined the banks of the Huron River on its way through the city. Across the street from the murder scene had to be the Whitmore Taffy Factory. Which would put the scene probably in a restaurant or…

Tim dug out his city maps and placed the taffy factory. Across from it was a bakery—the Depot Town Sweets Bakery. Immediately he seized his phone and called the Ypsilanti police.

* * *

Depot Town

The sun had set and the bakery was closed by the time the police and Tim arrived. With warrant in hand, he directed the officers to force entry into the bakery. They marched in, weapons not out, but ready all the same.

Surprisingly, the police had received no reports of fires anywhere in Depot Town for months. And the bakery manager, who had worked during the day, told them on the phone that he knew of no such fire. Tim was beginning to wonder if he had the right place.

Once they reached the back where the Fischer potbelly sat, he was no longer unsure. Everything—the black stove, the white walls, the single pane window—was nearly, if not exactly, as it looked in the video. Except nothing was burned. Nothing was destroyed, and neither could he find any indication of a struggle. No body, no glass from a smashed window. The floor looked recently mopped. Tim knelt down.

"I thought you said there was a fire," one of the officers said.

Was he dreaming? He looked under the stove, where the mop had neglected the floor. Black soot covered it. He studied the stove surface, looking for more traces of fire or blood.

"So what are we supposed to do?" another cop asked. "I got to write up this one. And creative writing ain't my strong point."

Everyone laughed. Tim rose and looked them over. He wished he had called the sheriff's office on this one. Sherrie Marshall might have been more understanding. But YPD had local jurisdiction.

"I want this place swept out," he said finally. "Everything in bags. And does YPD have a field serologist?"

"Yeah. You already asked for the forensics detail," said an officer with a mustache.

"Okay. Have the forensics team get some Luminol in here."

The officer cursed. "Luminol? Who the hell's paying for that?"

"The bureau will."

The officer went back to the building entry. Tim continued studying the lack of clues this scene gave until forensics staff marched into the bakery area. They began coating the area with chemicals. He had seen Luminol used before. The spray was a fluorescent dye with a blood-heme specific antigen bonded to it. Once it came into contact with even miniscule and micro amounts of heme-iron, it would fluoresce under ultraviolet light. What couldn't be seen with the naked eye would show up under this chemi-illumination.

He walked back out into the bakery display area. Officers were seated, some with coffee from an all-night shop down the street. He leaned against a seat and tugged at his scalp.

When did the mutilation occur? Hando had written it was from the night before, but the scene appeared clean. How had he done that? Maybe the owner of the bakery was in on it. He at least could give them a list of who had access to the bakery.

Tim looked around, but oddly, the manager was nowhere.

It would take time for the forensics process to complete, so he found a payphone. Before leaving the residency, he had uploaded Hando's video to the Detroit FO for full image analysis. He wanted an update. A mutilation was high priority and someone there would work all night if needed to get the analysis done.

They just had to prove he wasn't wrong.

Mark Striker, the FO computer technician, answered the call.

"Delbravo, we just popped it up. Got our first view a second ago. Man, this jerk is one cruel sonuvabitch."

"Yeah." Tim swallowed. "How long will it take?"

"There's just me and SA O'Neil here right now. I can stay late, but O'Neil's got a gig of some kind."

"How long?" Maybe he would have to go and do it himself.

"Jeez. I mean, how can you expect me to know? There are so many things that can be done. Takes time."

Someone tapped Tim on the shoulder. He turned to find the forensics staff leader motioning back at the scene. "Just a minute, Striker."

"We're done," the serologist told him. "You need to come see."

"I'll call you later, Striker." Tim hung up and started following the field serologist back. "How much did you find?"

"Nothing."

"Nothing?"

"Well, almost. We've scanned every inch three times." The forensics officer stopped at the doorway.

"Almost?"

"We found some small traces of crystallized blood on the corner of the steel counter. It's probably been there a while. The corner must be catching unsuspecting workers as they walk by."

151

Tim looked in the bakery area, which was now darkened. Two brown-jacketed officers moved about with foot-long UV lamps and filtered viewers, inspecting the room's contents carefully. Nothing illuminated under the lamps. The serologist pointed at the floor, which—like the walls, doorway and window—was wet, covered in an acrylic-smelling solution.

"Anything on the floor?" he asked the serologist.

"No."

"Was it mopped?"

"Maybe, but even if it had been diluted in soapy water to a hundredth normal-concentration, we would have picked up a minute amount of blood in the floor cracks. Easily. I mean, our dye solutions report down to one part in five million."

Tim bent over the stove. It would have been difficult to mop the stove handles and crevices. There had been a lot of blood on the stove surface in the video. As he got close, he could tell the exterior had a different chemical coat on it. It smelled more like alcohol and looked yellowish on the steel knobs. "Is this Luminol?"

"Not on the stove, because it's made of iron and copper. Some of the Luminol will light up—like it was bonding to heme-iron. So we used a solution of Toluidine on it."

"Toluidine?"

"Yeah. Toluidine fluoresces under UV when it contacts glucose and heparin—the anticoagulant released in the skin upon injury. It occurs almost exclusively in mast cells—you know, blood vessels and the likes."

"Oh." Tim felt somewhat embarrassed that he didn't know this. "Well, there was a lot of blood in the images I saw. How do you think he got it up?"

The serologist shook his head. "I doubt it was ever there—least not for a few months. The chemicals would have showed anything that recent."

Tim leaned against the doorframe and watched the brown-jackets cleaning up. "So we've got no blood."

"None."

"Great. Just great." Tim stormed back into bakery lobby and surveyed the half-dozen YPD officers lounging about. From an FBI folder, he pulled out some copies of the girl's face profile.

"All right. Listen up," he announced. "I want copies of these passed to every teacher in your school districts, particularly eighth through tenth grade. This is the victim."

"You mean there really is one?" an officer asked.

Several of them laughed quietly. Another pointed at the image in his hand. "Look at her eyes. What? She abducted by aliens too?"

That solicited even more laughter.

"This is not a joke!" he shouted. "A girl has been killed somewhere. Maybe not here, but until we're sure, we need every teacher to view these photos."

"Do you know how much time that will take?" an officer said. "We don't have the time to play the FBI's bid every time you see a spook."

Nearly all of them nodded. Even the sergeant who had remained quiet the entire time voiced his agreement. With the lack of clues, Tim almost wondered if he had seen a ghost.

* * *

Detroit

Tim had his theories about the lack of evidence. Even though it was after midnight, his determination spurred him to the Detroit Field Office where his video was getting scrutinized. Inside the offices, hardly anybody but the night guard was around. Striker sat in his usual locale—the fishbowl office. He wore his headphones again and didn't hear the knocking on the glass, so Tim entered. Immediately he heard the tinny music coming from the earphones. He approached the tech, noticing that he had three scenes from the bakery blazing on his monitor. At first, Tim was shocked because the images, which came from a black-n-white video, were oddly colorized.

Striker didn't notice him until Tim grabbed a chair and sat down, causing the tech to lose the earphones and jump out of his chair with a shriek.

"Sheesh!" Striker fumbled at the keyboard, closing out the displays. "Why the hell are you sneaking up like that?"

"I didn't mean to scare you." Tim chuckled.

"Yeah, well. Give a guy some warning next time." Striker held a hand against his chest and breathed heavily. His eyes blinked warily at Tim, and he rubbed his left ear, where an empty, pink-red hole still drilled the lobe. "I thought you were maybe someone else. Maybe out to check my hair length or something."

"Was that my video?"

"Oh that?" Striker adjusted himself back in the seat, grabbing the mouse on the left side. "Just didn't want others to see such personal images. The girl, I mean."

"Good." Tim relaxed. "So what did you find?"

"The video is a pastie."

"A pastie? You mean a computer animation." Tim had suspected this.

"Kinda. We call it a pastie because it uses some real parts pasted with fake or synthetic parts."

On his monitor, Striker displayed a gray-level image of the girl. Using the computer mouse, he cut out the head portion, leaving it detached from the torso. "It's kind of like collages we did in first grade, where you take a head image from one magazine and paste it on the body of another picture."

Tim leaned forward to look. Another image-slice displayed the bakery without the victim. "Well, some of this picture is real. I was at the bakery. And the animation is too detailed for all but the best computers."

"Yep. The room is real. The face might be too. But the body is a computer-gen forgery. Has misregistered correlation from frame to frame. Blood looks faked. Like virtual ketchup."

He zoomed on the girl's torso and clicked a filter button. Bright colors ran up and down in a striped fashion across her body. Hardly any of its original gray remained. The bloody parts particularly transformed rainbow bright. The lone bakery scene, however, had a mere handful of color dots over its plaque gray surface. The face cutout had some color and more gray mixed. The eyes and mouth appeared particularly colorful.

Tim pointed at the face. "Look at the cheeks and forehead. They're all gray. As real as the bakery."

"Probably. Could be real—maybe pasted on the synthetic body. It's a more detailed synth, if it's faked."

One thing was sure, their subject had access to the bakery. And to photos of young girls. "We could still have a serious situation."

"Don't know." The tech grimaced. "Do you know who the girl might be?"

"No. I have locals passing out her profiles in the schools tomorrow." He would get the local news to broadcast her photo, and check missing persons in local states.

"What other leads you got?" Striker asked, staring at him keenly.

"Not much."

"Anything unusual about the M-O?"

Now where was this going? Striker didn't usually ask the questions. "Hard to say—with only one complete, and another possible murder."

"Well, I'm betting this one's a ruse. He's yanking your chain, Delbravo. Wasting enforcement resources."

"Then we'll just hit him with a child stalking charge or at least get him on production of child porn."

"Not if she's all synth. I don't think it's illegal to do animations. Even realistic ones."

"Congress passed a law. It's supposed to make synthetic child porn illegal, when the President signs it."

"Yeah, well I heard about that, but ain't the ACLU holding it up?"

"I don't think so."

"Still, what're you going to do if you can't tell?"

"What do you mean?"

Striker shrugged. "Tell if it's real the next time. You gotta wait till it's processed first. If the guy's good with computer synth, it could take hours to deconvolve. Meantime a real crime's in progress."

Friday, February 14

Residency

Tim arrived at the residency just before seven in the morning on Valentine's Day. Alone, he spent hours scrutinizing *alt.sex.stories*, followed with a rereading of everything in the growing case file. He plotted ways to find the IP number that LeFerril had given him the day before. He read about hacking and the latest frills on the Internet.

The idea that Hando was broadcasting his pollution, even creating some to throw them off, really burned him. The sonuvabitch just had to be caught.

Snuff broadcasts, he had thought—at first, envisioning some kind of wacko television transmission. But people all across the world had viewed it, and the uploaded video file last evening had been digital. For computer video and sound, users chose the worldwide web. The web could transmit almost any computer communication, graphic and sound, as long as the programmer knew how to code it. And multimedia, even real-time video, was possible given a bit more technology. A sort of demented web TV.

He would focus there, except... The discussion on the newsgroup made it sound as if Hando had transmitted from the swamp. "Real time" and "live-action" video, they had called it. Tim knew that modems, even the fastest available, could hardly transmit at live video rates. He could think of no way to transmit amateur video across the globe except on the Internet. And even then, he would need a fast server for all the users wanting his snuff video. Somehow, Hando had found a way to break the public bandwidth barrier in remote locations like the swamp. Somehow, he was able to push out video from his server fast enough for dozens, if not hundreds, of would-be rapists.

As Tim studied and analyzed at his desk, he heard someone enter the RA with a key. He cocked his head and heard the door of the receptionist's booth crack open.

Immediately he rose and seized a carton that had lain on his desk. He carried it to the entrance, where he saw Ms. Downey taking off her parka.

"Ms. Downey, can you get this off by courier to Quantico?"

She looked up at him, then bounced her gaze to the Plexiglas facing the hall. He couldn't see what had caught her attention. She reached down to the desk and pressed the underside. A buzzer sounded and the entrance flew open, almost hitting him. RAC Kaplan entered, wearing a Cardiff hat and carrying a long umbrella. He looked at Tim and narrowed his eyes.

"I got a call from a sergeant at Ypsi PD." The RAC motioned his hand toward his own office door. "Let's talk."

Tim turned to follow. "I don't have much time."

"Agent Delbravo," Ms. Downey said before he left. "Here's the courier box and a shipment request. Did you want that overnight?"

He turned. "Same day, if possible."

"Same day?" Kaplan had stopped. "Where the hell to?"

Tim looked back. "DC. The lab."

"What is it?"

"Ashes and other collectibles from a clean-up last night."

"Ashes from that nonexistent fire?" Kaplan's mouth drooped into a subtle grin. "YPD told me about your emergency. Come on." He started for his office again.

Tim grabbed the courier packaging from the receptionist and followed the RAC. Inside, Kaplan threw his hat and coat on a rack behind the door and then stared at him. "You ordered Luminol—with the RA's account number. What the hell were you thinking?"

"I got whiff of a probable homicide. Downtown Ypsilanti. I needed immediate help."

"Help? Half a dozen local lab rats, officers and gallons of spy juice? You were on one helluva spending spree. Did you clear a budget with the Field Office?"

"Didn't have time."

"Well, you're SOL. The RA won't cover it on overhead. Not on my budget."

Tim knew Givens would cover it once he got word about the bakery rape. Why was Kaplan so bent out of shape? "Can I go?"

"You're not mailing that crap." Kaplan pointed at his package.

Tim bit his lip and forced his breathing to remain steady. "The Field Office will cover the postage."

"I'm not paying for the courier to come here."

In other words, he would have to take the package to the Field Office himself. Another two hours wasted. But he didn't have the time, not with all the visitors coming.

* * *

Residency

Tim decided to forego the trip to the Field Office, and instead, used his own credit card at a Fed-Ex drop-off. He labeled the evidence Same-Day and Special Care, then returned to his office.

Inside, a young man, clean-shaven with jet-black hair and blue eyes, waited for him. He eyed Tim like a cat watching fish.

"Harald Olson," the man said, holding out a hand. "I'm your secret."

"Secret?"

"Your goon. Undercover. Operating name is Colin Cantrell."

With black hightops, frayed bleached jeans, a white turtleneck and a red leather jacket, the rent-a-goon was already incognito. A real cover boy, Tim thought.

"Aren't you overdoing the costume a little?" he asked, sitting behind his desk.

"Not really." Olson almost sang the words. "I've done everything from drag to suits now."

Tim pushed a rolling chair with his foot. Olson caught it and perched himself up on the seat, keeping his feet high and arms hugging folded knees.

"Won't you blow your cover coming here?"

Olson shook his head. "I use the basement service doors."

Tim nooded. "You got the brief I faxed?" He eyed Olson's earlobes, but found no rings.

"Yep." He lifted some sheets.

"Once you locate the supply line for rhap, the dealer will lead us to the subject. I suggest you start on campus, at the kiss-in."

"So I go after the supplier by pumping a bunch of sex-addicts." Olson grinned jauntily. "Could be fun."

Tim stared at him. Could Olson be gay? A bureau drag-RAG? As far as Tim knew, the FBI was still privately hostile to gays in its ranks. But then, the bureau was once adverse to having blacks as special agents. He, himself, had spent many extra hours proving he was not just quota-filler.

"Why you looking at me like that?" Olson had lost his grin.

He closed his mouth and shook his head. "Nothing."

"What? Don't you like gays?" Olson jeered, pitching his voice.

"I never said that. I'm just surprised that…" He felt embarrassed. He didn't want to discuss this with Olson.

"Don't worry, Special Agent Delbravo," Olson said, uncrossing his legs and flattening his voice. "I'm straight as a snake, with a wife and a bambino on the way."

Tim felt his mouth drop, then slammed it shut.

Olson laughed deeply. "I play the part well, SA Delbravo."

"That, you do," he admitted, wondering what Olson would do when he was propositioned during undercover.

* * *

The Diag

Olson drove his rental to the center of campus, spending almost a half-hour searching for a parking place. The diag ballooned with students everywhere; demonstrations were in procession. On one end, a group distributed flyers about an affirmative action rally that night. At the other end Olson found a crowd more his type. The south half of the square had filled for the annual Queer Kiss-in. On black risers, he saw a guy setting up microphones and posters.

In the square several gay and lesbian couples endured the cold and a crowd of onlookers as they chattered, hugged and shivered. It looked like more of a queer huddle than a kiss-in.

He walked from the north end toward the steps of the graduate library, smoking an unfiltered cigarette. He waded into the group as a speaker took his turn on the platform. One couple, two young guys, kissed upon the speaker's gesture. They both looked at him as he passed by. He smiled back and puckered on his cigarette.

The game for now was to wait. Infiltration took time. But he could hurry the game, if he found the right opening. He scoped the scene for probable contacts. He needed a crew of unconstrained types—those looking for thrills rather than politics. In the group of around 100 supporters, he didn't really expect to find such types. Hell, the deviant-type he was after would probably be unacceptable by the tolerant crowd here.

On the risers a microphone tuned-up again and another student stood before the crowd. He was dressed in heavy winter denim and knit accessories. Olson seemed to have over-dressed for this event. A second guy joined the student on the riser, grabbing the speaker's hand. In the midst of the crowd, a young man handed out flyers. Olson caught up with the distributor and took one. It announced a celebration right after the Kiss-in at *Haut Bar*, a new gay bar in Ann Arbor.

Suddenly, the crowd formed a spontaneous line. He found himself pulled in the middle and felt bodies pressing against him from both sides.

"Everyone take the person to your left," the speaker said.

Olson felt a hand wrap around his waist, and looking, found a pair of brown eyes gazing up at him.

"I'm Rob. What's your name?" the brown-eyed fellow asked.

Before he could answer, the speaker called out the next instruction. "Kiss your partner, then trade with the next in line."

Olson felt a tug pulling him down.

* * *

Restaurant

After SA Olson left, Tim hardly had a chance to continue working. Special Agent Deacon Priestly with the DEA had arrived from New York. Priestly, a black man, was not as tall as him, perhaps a little huskier and had a mustache. He went out of his way introducing himself to people in the office. He joked and talked a lot, especially about women.

Before Priestly—the drug bug—would get down to business, he insisted on lunch. Tim suggested a sub-sandwich place, but the Bug wanted a "sit down and enjoy" meal. So Tim took him to the *Khubilai Feast*, a Mongolian cuisine, which had been quick for him in the past because it was self-serve. Along the banquet counters, canisters held raw meats, vegetables, sauces and spice. They each filled a bowl and handed it to cooks working at a round grill. Chefs dumped the bowls on the grill and used yard sticks an inch thick to stir and hit and dig at the meat and vegetables as they sizzled. While their lunches cooked, Priestly ordered a large mug of beer. Tim asked for water and coffee.

They sat and Tim asked, "Can we discuss the case now?"

Priestly took a long draught from his mug and exhaled with approval. As he prepared a tortilla, he asked, "You read the report I faxed?"

"Yes, but I can't say I understand all the chemistry." Tim dug a fork into his bowl.

"Sorry. Many of us special-op types at DEA have chemistry or pharmacology background. The jargon is second-nature. The gist is, rhap is at pharms and raves."

"Yeah, so you said on the phone. And why is it you had to leave New York to come here and tell me this again?"

"Until three days ago, I would have wondered too." Priestly rocked back in his chair and exhaled a long satisfied breath, patting his belly as it contracted.

"So what's changed?"

"Remember in the fax I wrote that rhapsody is a mix of two Schedule I compounds: MDMA and methyl-phenidate hydrochloride."

Tim shrugged.

"That's chemo-babble for ecstacy and Ritalin."

Tim nodded. "Okay...yeah. So Michigan has lots of Ritalin abuse." He had seen reports that the number of kids dealing Ritalin from their prescriptions was on the increase. Other kids wrote their own orders from laser-printed mock-ups of actual prescriptions.

"There's more." Priestly looked across the restaurant at the other patrons. "Did you know that the medical school here performed the only systematic investigation for the benefits of ecstacy?"

Tim shook his head.

"I'm not surprised," Priestly said. "It was classified for decades. Now this county has the largest public repository. Gobs of simple ecstacy recipes are openly available. A second-year chemistry student could whip out a batch in his lab class. Rhap is not much harder to make if you can get Ritalin."

"Are you saying rhap is coming from here?"

Priestly belched. "We did some tests on samples snatched from The Village, in New York City. The powder bags were manufactured in Kalamazoo, Michigan. Just a few hours from here."

Tim saw a connection forming. His mind began whirring. The relevance was more than just Hando's use of rhap during the crime. It went much deeper.

* * *

Haut Bar

Part café, restaurant, art studio and particularly saloon, *Haut Bar* was the largest gay-owned tavern in Washtenaw County. Olson walked around, taking in the place. Haut Bar had two floors. The downstairs area featured flashy walls with black and white photos of people and places common to the gay community: muscular dykes and drag-queens and famous protests. Art pieces and modish statuettes peppered sites along the walls and large flowing bar. Three bright red chairs—named Moe, Curly and Larry—cushioned those reading at the small library of gay literature. Near these sat a computer wired to the increasingly popular, national gaynet and a couple dozen gay newsgroups on the Internet.

The curvy hardwood bartop mirrored the naturally stained floors and stairs. One of the bartenders handed Olson a free Margarita.

"Thanks." Olson took a sip. "Sure is getting crowded."

"This is nothing." The bartender, a brawny guy in a green and white striped apron, wiped down the counter surface. "Tonight we'll be way over fire codes. It's Friday."

"There that many gays in Ann Arbor?"

"Hell no. We get 'em from all over—ever since the frats took over Pashins."

"Pashins?"

"Once a gay bar—our last competitor." The bartender grabbed a fish bowl and replenished its diminishing supplies of condoms. Then he held up a packet which declared its contents as *mint flavored*. "Want one?"

"Free?"

"Yeah. We try to keep up a safe rep here."

"Thanks." Olson took it, knowing he'd toss it first chance.

The bartender glided his rag down the bartop and continued serving others. Olson had never been gay, and never expected to be either. In high school two of his buddies came out. At first, Olson had avoided them, but they'd been friends for so long that he eventually drifted back to hanging out with them. He learned a lot about the culture, but often felt uncomfortable going to bars with them. Now it was academic, and part of his job.

He glanced around the club. On the bartop surface, he saw a stack of cards. He reached out and grabbed one. Written on it was a name, address and short bio of a person he didn't know. A pick-up card for random-pairing games. In the extremes of the barroom, dark and very crowded, he saw same-sex couples dancing and necking.

The party already seemed to be in full swing, and all kinds of people mingled, all very loud with clothes to match. Gays and lesbians mixed, wearing leather vests, bright tights and hand-ripped jeans. This time Olson felt under-dressed with only his red leather jacket to make noise for him.

He sipped his Margarita, when a couple of young men approached him together. One wore all white with black suspenders and tight leggings. The other was shirtless for the most part, and had ripped black denim for what might have been pants. Both were young and thin with medium dark hair. They could almost pass for brothers.

"Mondo Homo!" said the minimally-dressed one.

The man in white greeted him as well. "Fab gala, hmm?" He stepped up to the bartop but didn't sit at a stool.

Olson nodded, feigning bright eyes. "It's okay, but I would expect more." He tipped back his drink and swallowed. "I'm Colin Cantrell—new to Ann Arbor."

The one in white winked. "I'm Renny. He's Ito, like the judge."

Renny smiled at him. "What more do you expect? Maybe we can fulfill."

"I need a boost, you see," Olson said, touching his cheek with a hand.

At this Ito smiled broadly and approached the bar more closely. "What kind of boost?"

"A very unusual one. A taste for synthetics," Olson replied, turning on the stool to face the two squarely. They stood by the side of the bartop.

"I don't know about this place," said Renny.

"Sure. There're energy boosters around," Ito added. "There are places you can get a lick of ecstacy or go *au naturel* with weed. Other stuff, you name it. It's somewhere in town. A-squared's a cruiser's spot."

"How about you two? What are you into?"

"I'll try most things once or twice," said Ito.

"I'm a little more conservative than the judge here." Renny rubbed the bartop gently. "I stick with traditions: booze and men."

Olson looked away, breaking eye contact for just a moment. "Where's the best place for hitching with some rhapsody?"

Renny's eyes darted about. "I never heard of that."

Ito nodded. "That's pretty far out, fella. A new synth. I don't know for sure."

"Can you give me a hint?" Olson asked. He believed that if Ito knew about it at all, he would also know where to get it.

Ito glanced away. "I hear only rumors. You should go to *Condom Courseware* later today, this evening."

"Where?"

"It's a place just south of campus. They give out instructions to a rave after nine. Usually held outside the city. Look for a guy that might be called Babs or Babby, I think. I hear he's into supplying your gig."

Olson nodded, drinking from his glass.

"What about now?" Renny asked.

"No, I think I'll save my energy for what I really want," Olson lied.

* * *

Motel

The television played its usual assortment of late afternoon sitcoms and far-fetched movies. Olson was bored, so he turned it off and grabbed the phone. Catherine should be home. His day brightened when she answered.

"Hi, Cat." Olson relaxed his posture, sitting on the floor against the bed frame in his undershirt and loosened pants.

"Harry!"

He told her that he had checked in to the motel and gave her the number. He had an hour before meeting the local residents for dinner. She told him that she just got back from shopping.

"So how much damage?" he asked.

"What damage?"

"Damage to our little plastic collection. The one made by Visa?"

"Oh. Well, a little more than usual," she said. "I got some pacifiers and a headband with lace and a flower on it. It's really cute."

"A headband? You mean one of those brain tourniquets?"

"It's *not* a tourniquet," she said. "Come on, they're cute. And I bet you'll love it when you see our girl wearing it."

For the first trimester, he'd wanted a boy—a little buddy he could take to games and fishing. The ultrasound said it would be a girl. Catherine showed him all of the girl's stuff she'd bought already. Then he sort of fell in love with the idea of being a little girl's big sweetheart. Especially if she was a miniature of Cat.

"Pacifiers and a brain band. That didn't cost much."

"Oh, I got more than that," she said, making a smacking noise with her lips.

He could just image her wearing the stretch-suit she had bought during her sixth month of pregnancy. She'd be standing in the kitchen, probably licking a spoon of ice cream or maybe even finishing a sandwich.

"I also bought some stuff for your birthday next week."

"No parties." He'd told her this many times already.

"You're no fun. How are we supposed to celebrate?"

"What's to celebrate? Everyone does it once a year."

Her voice took a serious edge. "It's one more year of survival in the bureau. Assuming you survive this operation."

"Don't worry, Cat. Besides, save the party for my promotion. I'm coming up in twenty-two days. My first review."

"I know. I'm sure you'll get it. You've been putting in an awful lot of hours lately," she said sorely. "When you coming back from this one? I need a back rub."

He swallowed. "I'm hoping for tomorrow morning. But it could take the weekend, maybe longer. You know covert."

"What is it?" she asked. "Are you tracking some skinny unpregnant girls?"

"No." He laughed. "Quite the contrary. I'm after these fat bald guys. They raided a toupee factory."

"Harry!"

"All right. I can't talk about it, but it's just a typical investigation."

"If it's so typical, why can't you talk about it? They can't classify everything you do."

Olson's teeth ground together. *Because I don't want you to worry,* he didn't tell her.

* * *

Northfield Township

Tim parked the bucar in front of the Ramey's home. Sherrie sat next to him, unbuckling her belt.

"We're having a little residency get-together this evening," Tim said. "Why don't you come along?"

"Sure." Sherrie got out with him.

The houses in the Ramey's neighborhood all had a similar cast. Each middle-class mansion sat on a quarter-acre expanse with a gutter moat besetting it. Tim thought about the house they had left in California when he was demoted. The two-bedroom apartment here was too damn small— smaller than even his mother's house.

An older couple, wearing black overcoats, stood in the Ramey's doorway. They conversed with a lady leaning against the entry without her own coat.

Tim and Sherrie stopped behind them. The lady inside looked up at them. "May I help you?" she asked.

"Hello. I'm Special Agent Delbravo, this is Deputy Marshall."

The man and the woman on the porch turned and stared at them. Tim didn't stare back. He was too busy trying to keep a polite gaze on the lady, tempted to drop his eyes to the concrete or snow or anywhere but her wounded eyes.

She glanced back at the couple, grimacing ever so slightly. They caught the hint and began to retreat with farewells and excuses about getting on the road before dark.

"Please come in," Mrs. Ramey said.

The entry had dashes of flowers and cards and gleamed with a polished chandelier. The wood floor, however, appeared recently scuffed and soiled, suggesting a host of visitors had paid commiseration already. Tim wished he could do this by phone. No one liked discussing the details of a homicide with the victim's survivors. Especially the parents of a mutilated twelve-year-old. But without such discussions, they would never solve this case.

"Let me take your coats." Mrs. Ramey held out a hand.

They removed their coats and she took them to a hall closet. Other parts of the house sat in order—carpet vacuumed, rugs set straight, pillows laid neatly on the couch. The air smelled homey with an inference of good food in the air. On either side of the entry, divided by the stairs, sat two spacious rooms.

"I'll just call my husband." Mrs. Ramey pointed at a light blue couch in the east living room. "Have a seat in there."

"Mrs. Ramey," Tim said. "I want to get started in William's room. And the computer he used. Deputy Marshall will ask questions while I finish with it."

"Oh." Mrs. Ramey stopped. "Well, it's upstairs. In his room."

Tim followed her while Sherrie filed into the living room. At the top of the stairs, a man entered the hallway. He was tall and thin. His eyes barely danced with Tim's as Mrs. Ramey introduce him as her husband. They both walked him into Bill's room, which was large and remained joylessly quiet. The bed was made and the clothes were mostly put away. The room seemed too neat for a twelve-year-old. At least for Tim's twelve-year-old.

"The police told us to leave it untouched until the investigation completed," Mr. Ramey said.

Tim nodded. Bill really was a neat kid. The computer sat on an oak desk next to the bed. Before actually starting, he turned to the parents, and said, "Mr. and Mrs. Ramey, first let me say that we are deeply saddened by the death of your son William. We know these are difficult times, and want to minimize the time we have to spend discussing it."

Mrs. Ramey watched Tim closely. Mr. Ramey had red, swollen cheeks. He peered out the bedroom bay window, eyes focused distantly.

"Our investigation is going pretty well," Tim added. "I believe we will find the suspect."

They both nodded.

Tim opened his case and pulled out a portable hard drive. "Just a couple of quick questions while I set up. Did Bill ever mention someone named Alven?"

Mrs. Ramey face strained. "Not that I remember." She looked at her husband. He shook his head.

"What about the name, 'Hando'?"

They both shook their head, looking at him with partly veiled curiosity.

"I'll come down and ask a few more, once I've finished here."

Mrs. Ramey reversed toward the doorway. "Honey," she directed at her husband, "I'll go down. You're better with questions about the computer."

He nodded.

Tim examined the desk supporting the computer, pulling open the drawers below and leafing through a case of writable DVD-Rs. After connecting his backup drive, he flipped the power on the computer and it beeped to life. Mr. Ramey stood in the doorway, leaning against the wood frame.

First, Tim checked the configuration files. It was loaded with all of the best hardware from a year earlier and the latest software. It was connected to the Internet through a local cable provider.

"Nice system," he said to Mr. Ramey. "Did he use the Internet a lot?"

"Oh yeah. He was a genius when it came to computers."

"How many hours did he spend on his computer?" He looked over his shoulder at the father.

Mr. Ramey rubbed his head. "Judith, my wife would know better, but I'd say he spent maybe two or three hours a day at least. He didn't play a lot of games, though. He was searching for his homework and emailing."

Tim nodded. Obviously the parents didn't truly monitor their child's computer use. Probably had no idea a computer could be used for anything but an education or games. He guided his way across the files and logs. Eventually he settled in Bill's computer communication folder. Apparently, Bill had been connecting to a dozen chat rooms on many servers, including *zip-per.net* and some other local sites.

From log files, it was apparent that Bill had indeed spent many hours on the Internet. Tim found e-mail indicating he had communicated with several people. Bill had downloaded files and posted on the newsgroups.

Tim had suspicions. Using a utility he found on the hard drive, he shuffled through it and found over three dozen pornographic JPEG and GIF images. Graphics that Bill had hoarded from all across the Internet.

He quickly disregarded the images so that Bill's father wouldn't see. He didn't want to taint the last memory of their son. He planned to make a thorough search later after he made a backup of all the files on Bill's computer. Before he started the backup, he searched for *Alven Hando*. Almost expectantly, the computer came up with fourteen matches.

He turned around to see if Mr. Ramey was still there. The doorway was empty. He called up the matches—all of it e-mail that Bill had saved. Hando used the same Canadian account. Most of the messages were short and revealed how Hando had befriended Bill online a month before the murder. Tim would send it all to Quantico for the psychological profile. In the middle of the exchanges, Hando had asked Bill about his parents.

Hando: "*Why do you say you don't really like yer parents? Are they like cruel to you or what?*"

Bill: "*No, they don't hit me or any of that. It's just that they ignore me. Sometimes I just want someone to listen to me.*"

Hando: "*Hey I'm here for you.*"

In the last exchange Hando requested that Bill meet him. But Bill refused—a lot of good it did him.

Tim felt horrible inside. It was a computer stalking, by a cyber-predator. A not-so-fairy-tale ogre in search of children to gobble up. It reminded him that there really exist monsters and freaks and misfits that devour innocence.

They're called child molesters.

* * *

Living Room

Sherrie scribbled on her notepad, sitting on a rounded armchair, facing the sofa where the Rameys rested. "And who was Bill's teacher last year?" she asked.

"Oh, fifth grade—that was…" Mrs. Ramey twisted her lips. "It was Marcia Ripley."

Sherrie wrote the name down. "Is she still at Bill's school?"

"I think so. She's been at Whitmore Elementary for at least five years."

"Bill is an only child, right?"

Mrs. Ramey nodded once, her lower lip quivering and her eyes bolting around the room. She tried to speak but only a squeaky gurgle escaped. She cleared her throat. "It's just…We wanted more, but Bill was a difficult birth and the doctor told me I shouldn't have any more. It wasn't easy…"

"It's all right, Mrs. Ramey." Sherrie leaned forward.

Mr. Ramey picked at hangnails with his teeth, still staring outside. He hadn't answered a single question Sherrie asked.

"What hobbies and friends did Bill have?"

"Bill was really quiet at school," Mrs. Ramey said after a moment. "He only had one friend named Matt Butterfield."

"What did Bill do for fun, after school?"

"He traded most-wanted terrorist cards and some other things with Matt," Mrs. Ramey said. "But mostly Bill didn't do a whole lot with anyone. We were so worried about it before."

"Did he watch a lot of television?"

"Not really. Over a year ago he decided he wanted a computer. We got it for Christmas, had someone hook it up with him and show him how to use it. He spent hours on it every day. It helped his homework." Mrs. Ramey looked at her husband. He shrugged back. "All the time. He would talk about computers a lot, but it just went in one ear and out the other."

Mr. Ramey writhed in his chair and spoke for the first time. "I just never thought it was important. You think you don't have time because you're so busy with work and the house and the yard. And now I have so much, too much damned time…" Tears fell over his cheek. He wiped them with the back of his hand.

The stairs creaked. Everyone turned to see Tim descending, his backup drive and bag in hand. No one spoke until he entered the living room.

"I think I have everything I need from upstairs," Tim said. "If you haven't given the deputy the name and address of every child Bill played with, I would ask that you do that. We will want to speak with all of them, even old friends."

Mrs. Ramey nodded.

* * *

Bucar

Sherrie watched outside as Tim drove slowly along Stadium Boulevard. She felt bad about little Bill. Was there more she could be doing?

"Tim, you mentioned setting up a sting for Hando. What did you have in mind?"

He glanced at her as he drove. "I worked on a child-porn case in California. Kids were being abducted. Operation: *Innocent Images*." He paused. "We set up fake clients—kids—to meet with suspects."

"You played a kid?"

"Not really. Just online, behind the computer. We got on newsgroups and chat rooms, acting like kids desperate for attention. Then set up a meeting. We'll try it with Hando."

"Did Bill meet Hando on the newsgroups?"

"There or in an online chat room."

"So what if you contact Hando online, but he doesn't want to come down from Canada?"

"He did for Bill. Besides, I'm sure he lives a lot closer than that. Remember, e-mail addresses can be forged."

"So, where?"

"I think he's hanging around here. Somewhere."

Hanging out in Ann Arbor? "Oh, Tim! I just remembered something else. That place, you know, where the skinhead told me Hando hangs out—the Autarchic Franchise. I looked the word up in a large dictionary. It has two spellings. A-U-T-A-R-C-H-I-C or A-U-T-A-R-K-I-C. The one we tried means dictatorial, remember? The one with a 'k' goes with *independence* and *liberty*. Kind of the opposite."

"Is it in the phone book?"

"Neither spelling. Not in Toronto or this area, according to the operator. But it sounds political. And Cercs, the skinhead, goes to revival at the local militia, I'd bet."

"You're right." He nodded. "And some of the guys at the residency have been investigating the Michigan Militia."

* * *

VanBrew's Grill

Harald Olson sat at a large table in VanBrew's grill. He wore sunglasses and a low fitting Redwing's cap, to help keep his identity low profile while he was still undercover. SA Mott and SA Cobbs, whom Mott called "Spike," sat across from him. Olson wondered if "Spike" was real or just a nickname. Cobbs' bristly haircut matched the first name in any case. Unlike Mott, who kept his mouth running like a leaky faucet, Spike chained his eyes to a hockey match—the Redwings—on the big screen, occasionally reaching out for pretzels or his beer. Mott blabbered on and on about how he and Spike were working on a case together, trying to build a rapport with the local militia.

"Hey, Spike. I got another for you," Mott said. "A hockey joke."

Spike barely looked away from his hockey game.

"You know why blacks don't play hockey?" Mott paused with a quick smile. Spike shook his head and shot his eyes back on the screen. "Because," Mott said, "when was the last time you saw a black guy putting hisself with a bunch of white men wearing masks and carrying sticks?" He laughed at his joke. Olson wanted to punch him.

"You're sick, Louis," Spike mumbled.

Mott abruptly stopped his chuckling and stared at Olson. His eyes fell into a serious glare. "They hog-tied you to work the fags, I hear," Mott said. "Lucky you."

Olson didn't reply. Mott was not much of a thinker, that was obvious. He bet Mott's parents first met at a family reunion.

"What's Delbravo's suspect list look like, anyways?" Mott asked, lifting a full mug of beer—his third. Spike was starting his second. Olson was halfway through the first. He had to work still.

"Delbravo said there's only one subject. Someone on the Internet." Olson watched the door, hoping Delbravo would show up soon.

"He have a name?"

"Al Hand, or something." Olson tipped back his mug. Spike cheered as number 15 left the penalty box on the TV.

"Alven Hando?" Mott suggested, watching Olson carefully.

"That's it. You've read the case notes, then."

"No. I did a little work with him just a couple of weeks ago." Mott licked his lips. "What does he know about Hando?"

Olson shrugged.

Mott looked expectant, craning his neck forward. "How long is you tied up with Delbravo?"

Olson shook his head. "Open ended for now."

"Well, just watch yourself around him. Got himself shot just a week 'fore last, you know."

Olson had heard about the shooting. Everyone had heard. There were only a few ways to gain admiration in the bureau. Getting shot on duty was automatic veneration. In Delbravo's case, the rumors ground out any chance of it. Olson had heard the man that grazed Delbravo's leg was out for revenge. The motive, though, wasn't so clear, and it was even rumored that the whole incident was classified.

"He served beach time, too, you know," Mott said.

Spike cranked his head around and listened; a commercial paraded on the screen.

"There was some talk about him shooting a boy," Mott added.

Spike flicked a peanut at Mott. "Shut up, already, Louis." He pointed at the doorway where Delbravo, a woman and another black man entered together.

Olson watched Delbravo walk to the table. He was dressed in his suit, face shaven and firm. He didn't look like an agent who had served beach time. Not at all. Delbravo watched him with firm eyes as he removed his coat. Olson felt the pins of Delbravo's glare bore into him, and he turned away briefly.

"Everybody," Delbravo said, pointing to the other black man. "This is Special Agent Deacon Priestly. With the DEA."

Mott snickered. "Don't Expect—"

"Anything," Priestly finished. "How about Fumbling Blithering Idiots. Or Fat Blubbery Imbeciles."

"Touché," Spike said.

"This is Deputy Sherrie Marshall of the Washtenaw Sheriff's Office." Delbravo pointed to the lady whose dishwater blonde hair was pulled back in barrettes.

Olson noticed that Sherrie didn't wear a ring. Apparently Spike had as well, and started dominating her attention. Mott and Olson sat quietly while Priestly and Delbravo began mowing over the menu.

"Spike, what's good?" Delbravo asked. "This is your place."

Spike glanced down at his folded menu. "It's all pretty good. Try the grilled catfish or any flamed-burger special."

Olson picked up a menu and unfolded it. Priestly turned to him. "You and I need to go over your plans for tonight."

Olson nodded. "My first question is, what does rhap look like?"

"The few samples we've snagged," said Priestly, "have either been white powder in baggies, or powder in clear and unmarked gel caps."

"So, not very distinguishable?"

Priestly shook his head. "Not really, but it's not common, so you won't find it in buckets."

"Buckets?"

"Yeah," Priestly said, nodding, "I mean, pharm party buckets or bowls."

"So where will I find it?" Olson asked.

"Not exactly sure. We hope you finger the source. We've been tracking the rhapsody stream on the outside in New York. But our undercover hasn't made the top level supplier."

"Yeah well, let's wait and see what I get," Olson said. "Undercover work isn't exactly bureau specialty."

At that, Delbravo eyes lit up. "Before I forget. Mott—Spike, while working under at the mil—" then looking around them, he softened his voice, "—at your day job have you heard of some kind of political group called the Autarkic Franchise?"

Mott turned away, thinking. Then he shook his head. "Nope."

Spike leaned back. "It's rings a quiet bell for me. Are you sure, Louis?"

Mott shook his head. "It's not there."

* * *

Rave

Just after ten, Olson went to the south campus shopping district and entered the store called Condom Courseware. He squeezed inside the crowded entrance. It was a one-of-a-kind outlet with displays, literature and sex-gear lining the walls; a modish shop for a young generation that would rather jump on the bandwagon than in a family station wagon.

When he asked about a party, the storekeeper handed him a little packet— a condom wrapper with folded directions to the night's rave party. Olson followed the instructions and drove out to the northern skirts of Ann Arbor a ways off Nixon Road. He found the scene in an abandoned barn shining with surreal light shows and vibrating to a 150-beats-per-minute pulse.

The doorman or woman—Olson couldn't tell—collected twenty dollars at the entrance. Several banners and signs informed patrons of the night's events: Pyramid pile-ups and slamming fests. Other placards raved about rave itself. One, in broad red poster paint, said, "PLURL!" Which Olson knew stood for "Peace Love Unity Respect" with the last "L" added in black marker and the word "Liberty" scrawled below it.

He entered. The barn interior stood no longer agrarian—more like something out of the cantina in *Star Wars*. His last rave, at a renovated bar in Detroit, had a more commercial edge, and Olson didn't see any drugs there. Uptown raves rarely had contraband. Underground raves, often smaller and held in transitory locations, usually bulged with cherry meth, date rape serums, or the "amphetamine-lite" ecstacy. Now the kids had a new fix: *Rhapsody.*

On a stand in the middle, the disk jockeys skipped and pranced in front of dual vinyl players and old MC500-series synthesizers which redlined at every beat. The music, which Olson guessed was progressive house because it mixed breaks with trance, was mostly bass, cranked to marrow-crunching intensities. The DJ's reminded Olson of Navajo shamans he'd seen on vacation in the Southwest. They held out hands as if calling upon the earth and tribe to unify in a deluge of falling notes and beats.

The music had its roots in techno and industrial music, which grinded their way out of Detroit's manufacturing culture. Olson's kid brother had loved industrial, mostly because it was, in his words, *"industrial strength parent repellent."*

The rave oozed of strong sexual themes, air charged outward with a lustful energy. The laser-show imagery on the wall and video screens promoted a "safer" thread. Scenes of computer-generated condoms danced and marched across the screen, evil caricatures of sexually transmitted viruses shooting chemical bullets at the cartoon condoms. It was comical, except the kids weren't laughing. Lights across the dance floor breathed in synch with the rhythmic noise from the stand. Rays pulsed and thrashed, almost stinging as it fell over Olson. His eyes caught stray beams from a green laser bouncing off a disco ball.

He walked across the inside of the south barn wall. In the middle he saw plenty of kids, black and white, gay and straight, funky and geeky. All were at a rave party—over a thousand people in a deafening tumult—dancing wildly in the center, rubbing against each other like they were chained in some ineffable link. Others hunkered together in ambient "cubicles" for "chillin' out."

Along the west end, a vintage "smart bar" lined the wall. Olson went to the bar and sat on the only vacant stool by a bottle of blow-pops and a peg advertising glowsticks for sale. Between the bar and dance area lay several sound barriers to block the uproar. Without them, it would have been impossible to pass orders. Three bartenders worked the spigots. A young girl tended nearest him, and she walked up and smiled.

"Drink or tattoo?" she asked.

"Tattoo?" Olson squinted. He'd never seen a tattoo parlor at a rave.

"Yeah. Temporary body art. Be what you want for the night." She wiped down the portable bartop. "A drink, then?"

"A beer."

"No beer. Just pop, energy and smart drinks."

Smart drinks, the once-upon-a-time beverage of choice at raves, were comprised of fruity concoctions with heavy doses of organics and amino acids. The kids thought the protein substance would energize them for the dance, replenish what ecstacy consumed in the buzz. Olson had never downed a smart drink before. He never had time because his task was always a prearranged meeting at previous raves. A handwritten placard behind the bar listed vintage drinks: Toxic Cure, Brain Boost, Fast Blast and others.

"Give me the cure," he said.

She filled a glass with red goop from a soda-spigot. "Nine-fifty, please."

"Man. Nine-fifty for a smart soda." He fished out his billfold. "I'd say you guys are drinking it up when it comes to business smarts."

She said, "You only need one or two for the whole night."

"Yeah, well, at that price it'll be a short night."

He handed her a ten and took his drink. She walked away, cleaning up behind the bar and helping other patrons. He watched the dance. The kids there were really just that. Few over nineteen. Probably couldn't grow a goatee between them all. He sipped the drink, first tasting a fruity soda-concoction. Then swallowing, he felt grit from the amino acids coating his tongue and throat. It took him several forced gulps to down it. Taste-wise, it wasn't so bad, but the grit reminded him of medicine and vitamin elixirs that moms force on their sour-mouthed brats. And the kids were gulping the stuff like it was right out of Dad's liquor cabinet.

The bartender returned to take his empty glass.

"Any hard stuff around here?" he asked her.

She glared at him and shook her head. "*Clean and Mean* is our maxim."

He put down another ten-bill. "How about something called Rhapsody?"

"Take your money. We run a pure rave in here. You want that stuff, you get out."

"Yeah, whatever." Olson took his money and got up. He rambled to the middle floor.

Swaying in a hypnotic trance, people danced and jerked, with hands up like cattails in the wind. Several kids aimed a rainbow of LED mini-lights or laser-pointers up, weaving fiery red snakes in blue/green clouds on the ceiling as they danced. Some moved in clusters, some alone, dancing with closed eyes and sweat on their nose. Fashion was mostly tank-tops and low riders or anything that hung well below your navel and pelvic body art. The rest was pockets of retro from the last thirty years: punk, five-inch heels, beads, glittery phat pants with corporate-logo rip-offs, tie dye shirts, and various layers of top-wear that were shed as the temperature increased. And it was getting warm.

A fog machine on a high platform spurted a psychedelic fog onto the floor. One DJ changed platters and vaulted about like a dancing marionette with strings of external chemicals to energize him. Despite the large size, this rave was absolutely underground. Olson had seen plenty of glazed stares and stumbling shuffles. He just wasn't sure where they were getting the look.

He peeked in a larger stall, a cubicle like structure, where a few kids sat and watched a computer screen with trippy images—digitized live-shots of the crowd overlaid with kaleidoscopic fractal patterns. The kids in the booth just stared in amazement. He was certain there were drugs among them. He entered and sat near a thin gal in a tank-top. She seemed to be without a date.

As he sat she jerked her head, black bangs skimming her blanch cheeks. Her red eyes studied him as if determining friend or foe status. She smiled vividly, tones from the video making her face melt blue to purple. The image, a new cyberscape, spun in an array of colors, drawing back her attention.

He chuckled to himself, almost feeling shameful, like he should do something. Stop them from their retreat into artificial reality, or virtual reality now.

Even with its waffled sound deflectors, the cubicle hardly blocked out the clamor. Olson found it difficult to speak and hear.

"This is great! Is there anything to make it come harder?" he asked the girl.

"This is my space," she said.

"All right. How can I get in?"

"Not with me. You go out."

"You want me to leave?"

"No." She smiled expansively. "But you can't get in this scene."

Olson felt confused, but he figured it was due to her inability not his. "Who can give me a scene of my own?"

"Not me. I used way too early. I'm already all ate up."

"Ate up?"

She nodded. "Hoping to get it back when it goes Richter at three."

He guessed she'd used up her drugs, or her energy. "Do you know someone named Babs or Babby?"

"No thanks. I'm all ate up."

Anything he said after that just passed through her like air in a fan. He got

177

up to leave. At the stall entrance, a teenager entered and handed another kid something. The second slipped whatever it was into his mouth. Olson walked to them. The first had a nose ring and reached a hand to his chest. He pressed a plastic piece hung on his neck by a string. A little yellow-green cycle-blinker started flashing on it.

"Once that snack kicks in, the strobe will rush you," he said to the other. "It's so funky."

Olson pointed at the second kid but spoke to the one with the strobe light. "You selling anymore of that? I want to be rushed."

"I don't sell." He hissed the last word, extending it in a sarcastic tone.

"I'm looking to buy," Olson said. "Want something called rhapsody."

"What's that? A designer chem?"

"Sure."

"I only hard core with Adam & Eve," the kid said.

"Who?"

He laughed. "What cheezy corporation did you get laid from?"

Olson shook his head.

"E!" The kid gave him a dumbfounded smirk. "Ecstacy!"

"Who deals?"

"Deals?" The second laughed even harder. "We got us a real-as-ripping cocaine freak. You from the eighties or England?"

He grimaced and walked away.

"Don't go straight! Just go out and around," the kid yelled as he flowed into the main-floor Pandemonium. He waded through the sweaty crowds. The mixture of human perspiration and ancient manure from the ground mixed in his nostrils. He couldn't see any heaters, but the thrashing and dancing heated the whole place into a sauna, giving him an urge to get outside.

Then he realized it. Everyone was telling him to leave, to go out and around the rave. Everything was brought in from outside. No dealing inside. They just carried it in.

At the entrance, the door-*person* gawked at him. "I'll bet you want to go out for a stroll, right?"

The attendant handed him a small ticket stub and motioned him through. Outside, a long line had formed to enter. The barn was already packed and he found it disturbing. Jamming so many intoxicated teenagers in an old rickety wood barn stunk of disaster. Besides the crowd getting out of cars and going inside, several people meandered along the sides of the barn. On the south

PSYPHER

side edge, he found a small collection of kids, steam rising from their heads like they were leaking intelligence. It looked like a deal, or whatever these kids called it.

He walked up to the group and scrutinized the scene for a moment. Each person approached a man and exchanged money for a single, small item. Definitely a drug deal. The man taking all the money was big, older than the rest. He had a small metal air-tank, and when one kid handed him an Abe Lincoln, he filled an untied balloon, probably with nitrous oxide. The kid walked away sucking on the nipple. Olson waited patiently until his turn. "I'm looking for Babs or Babby," he told the big man once at the front.

The man glanced over him. "Why should it matter who does the vending?"

He played into the part now. "'Cause I'm looking for something really special. They say only Babs can get it."

"I'm sure I can help." The man smiled.

"The music needs some words. Like rhap, maybe?"

"You mean Rhap-See-Dee?" The man lost half of his smile.

"Right."

"Wish I could oblige." The man scratched his neck. "I've been working on getting a full supply. But no go so far; just a sample. I assume you've gotten a taste then."

"Not yet."

"Okay, so I'm Babs. Who said I vend rhap, anyway?"

"I heard it at Haut Bar."

"Makes sense. But you should have heard that there's only one vendor for now. And he doesn't sell."

"Doesn't sell it?"

"Least not to me, not for money."

"Come on!" said a kid behind Olson.

Babs shook his head, looking at the others in line. "Either you buy or you fly."

Olson reached in his pocket and pulled out the clip of what was left of the two hundred he got for the whole operation. He handed Babs a twenty.

"Whoa, such a big spender." Babs held the bill up. "A single E gets me more than this and you've already spent double my time."

He handed him another twenty. Babs smiled again.

Suddenly a crowd inflated at the entrance just behind them. A girl screamed and several guys were yelling and cursing. The crowd pushed and

179

cleared room for three guys. These were hauling a body, dragging it quickly on the ground.

Nearly everyone around him ran to watch.

"She's dehydrating!" someone shouted.

"What's going on?" Olson asked.

"It's another heat-exhaust," Babs told him. "Don't tell me you've never seen anyone go over after too much shaking and E?"

"No." He shoved his hands into his coat.

"It happens. I tell people not to overdo it and to drink lots of water when taking E."

People ripped off the girl's coat and unbuttoned her blouse. She was pale, eyes closed. A boy slapped her face.

Olson wondered if he should call an ambulance. It would probably blow his cover, but he couldn't just let it happen.

Babs shrugged. "She'll be all right, once they give her some water and cool her off."

The dealer grabbed his gear and tank. "Oh. The guy you want is known as Crazy Zig. I hear he's a chemistry student at U-M. They also say he's on the net, but I've seen him in the dorms. Go to the dorm at the Union. Saturday. The bathrooms on the first floor after lunch. He only vends when the janitors aren't there."

"The bathroom?"

"Yeah. Stinks, eh?" Babs laughed and began his retreat toward the parking lot. "That ought to be worth forty."

The dealer left. The girl was sitting up, drinking water. And snow began falling.

* * *

Rave

The kid watched the older dude—the one that'd asked Babs for the designer chem—walk toward the cars and get in one. It just didn't feel right.

The kid wasn't buzzing. And what really pissed him off, he probably wouldn't buzz all night, now that Babs had been panicked away before the kid got a turn to score his fix. The older guy worried him, and he knew Roman Ponke would want to know. He glanced about and saw Ponke standing at the rave entrance.

He walked up to the Roman, a tall lanky fellow with a large nose.

"Hey, Ponke," he said. "There's some guy asking about your friend's potion."

"What, rhap?"

"Yeah. Babs gave him some directions. Might be legit, but he was kinda old. Talked like a boomer or something, and scared the vender away."

Ponke nodded his head. "If the dude dopes with Zig, he'll be sorry. Dead sorry."

Saturday,
February 15

Residency

Even though it was officially weekend, the residency seemed busier than midweek. Tim sat in front of his desk computers. Harald Olson and SA Priestly stood behind him.

"Crazy Zig," he said, typing it in at the computer. "Did he tell you where on the Internet?"

Olson shook his head.

"I'll do a search on the newsgroups, then the web."

"Glad I'm not the one that has to figure this out," Priestly said. "All this talk about nets and webs has me feeling like a bug in a trap."

Tim looked back at him. "Once you leave here, it's your game. You oughta figure it out. It's a great tool."

"No way, man. Computers and me just do not happen together."

The search engine on the computer finished. "Crazy Zig. He's got one, two…" Tim counted quietly. "Eight posts in the last month. Groups like comp.os.linux, alt.rave, and rec.drugs."

"There." Olson pointed. "That subject line says 'UC4D.'"

"UC4D," Priestly said. "It's been IC4D on everything we've seen."

Tim moved the mouse over it and clicked. "Looks like Zig was discussing drugs online with a guy from Berkeley, California." He examined the headers of his posts. "And how about that, Crazy Zig has an account at *zip-per.net*. My buddy LeFerril in the stink-mansion."

"Who's a friend?"

"Not a friend. LeFerril. He runs a suspect computer board." He turned back to Priestly. "And you know, he might have some drug files about rhap."

From around the corner, Spike entered and grinned at them. He wore a flannel shirt, dark jeans and a large belt buckle with a rifle emblazoned across it. "We're all working the weekend, I see."

"And you?" Olson asked, looking over Spike's clothes.

"Going out to Dexter for a militia rifle round-up. Strange kicks." Spike shook his head.

At the computer, Tim pointed to a line that read: Separate the methyl-phenidate.

"Drug formulas?" he asked.

Priestly leaned in and squinted. "The damn text is too small."

"I'll print it for you." He clicked on the print button.

"Thanks."

Paper hummed out of the printer across the cubicle. Tim worked the mouse, scrolling to the end of the list. "Looks like that was the last one. The Berkeley chum mentioned 'taking it underboard.'"

"Can you find it?"

"Not likely. They'd use e-mail—on their private account. Maybe with a warrant. Or…" Tim stopped and looked at his watch. It would be difficult to get a warrant on a Saturday. But there was a way, if they were careful. He closed out the computer windows.

"What?"

"We should go this afternoon to visit my buddy, LeFerril."

"Sure," Priestly replied. "What kind of guy? Dangerous?"

"Not so much. If you get on his bad side, he might screw your credit rating with his computer, but I wouldn't worry about getting shot. He probably doesn't even know the butt-end of a gun."

"Can we go now?" Priestly looked back.

"He might be at work."

"Well, I better go get some lunch," Olson said. "Then I'm off to the dorm. The johns."

Tim lifted his eyes. "Just watch yourself. Rumors say those dorm restrooms are used for more than the typical business. A lot of anonymous meetings, if you know what I mean."

"I'm sure I'll be fine."

"Hey," Spike said, buttoning his cuffs. "I assist, if you need it."

"In those duds?" Olson pointed at Spike's mud-caked boots. "Nah. A gun-running, breeder-type like you will just get in the way."

* * *

West Quad

The resident hall looked older than Olson had expected. The dorms had been an afterthought structure added six decades earlier to the student union building. It had several restrooms in the hall, each as ugly as the others. Stains streaked the stalls with the aftermath from activities college students should've known better than to engage in. He didn't want to stay any longer than he had to. He was only out to identify Crazy Zig and then he would go and get Delbravo and a court order to bring him in for questioning. But Olson had his credentials and a gun, just in case.

On his second round through the restrooms, Olson found a gang of students in the south-most facility. A sundry crew of three very different guys stood around the bays. He entered and stepped up to a urinal. This part he didn't have to fake and after a minute he was relieved.

The students stood and watched him. Olson observed them in the mirror while he ran water over his hands—a lot of good the washing did. Filth covered the faucet knobs and towel dispensers. He dried his hands, then turned and faced them.

"Any of you know of Crazy Zig?"

"Why?" asked a short and dark kid. He leaned against a stall support, eyeing Olson with narrow eyes.

"I'm looking for something special. I hear he's the only vendor."

"And what's so special?" the same kid asked, brushing his weak-attempt at a mustache.

"Do you know him?" Olson glanced back in the mirror.

"Let's say we do," said another student with lanky arms and a large stern nose. "You can get what you want for a price."

"How much?"

Apparently the third one, a redhead with freckles and acne, didn't speak. The short one answered. "Get on your knees and do us a favor."

"Let me speak with Zig first." He needed only to ID Zig, not complete the deal.

"Look!" The lankier kid held up a straw and a baggy of white fine dust. Rhapsody, he was sure. "We even have a sniffer. You can do it off me first."

"Are you Zig?" Olson walked closer. He could leave, knowing that one of these three was Zig, but he liked to be sure.

"Not me. Just think of us as the three musketeers," the shorter one joked. Olson pictured the three stooges.

The redhead moved for the first time since Olson started talking. He stuck his lower lip at Olson and wrinkled his brow. "Why do you want to see Zig so bad? We have the stuff right here. Gratis, except for one small favor."

"Yeah," the Roman said. "Isn't this what you want?"

"Sure. I just want to make sure." Olson felt himself fumble for a rationale. "Sure that it's, er, pure."

"What?" The redhead pulled out a comb from his back pocket. "This is the only source around. What do you think you're getting?"

"I don't like this guy, Zig." The Roman turned to the redhead.

"You dumbass!" the redhead said back.

Olson had made his ID. The redhead was Crazy Zig. He eyed the door and mentally calculated his retreat.

Studying him, the short kid started moving. "Where the hell do you think you're going?"

"He's trying to get away. He's a narc." The taller one raced to the door and blocked the way out.

The other two rushed Olson. He reached for his sidearm and credentials but they had him too fast. His badge spilled out of his pocket and he struggled to get his arms free. They forced his hands down and pulled him back to the mirror. With great agility, the redhead flattened him out on the bathroom floor, striking his head hard against a sink as he came down.

Olson's last thoughts echoed Spike's offer to go with him. And his, now not so comical, reply.

* * *

185

Zip-per.net

Tim folded his cell phone and slid it into his suit pocket. "Shop says LeFerril left work half-hour ago."

"So where is he?" Priestly asked.

Tim shrugged and looked outside. The snow piled about six inches deep in the fields around LeFerril's shack. The clear sky chilled them to the marrow. Even with the rental car heater blasting, Tim felt cold. Priestly insisted on driving his rental, a blue Pontiac Grand Am, and the defroster worked poorly in ten-degree weather.

They had already been waiting for fifteen minutes. Priestly kept talking, his voice cycling with the Pontiac's choke, growing louder, then soft. Tim moved and fidgeted in his seat, wondering how much longer he could take it. LeFerril's workday had ended an hour ago, and he hadn't gone home right away. Tim figured he would spend every free moment on his computer systems since he seemed to have sunk everything into it.

"Stake outs," Priestly broke the silence. "Man, they can get boring. You do a lot?"

Tim shook his head. Not in three years, since leaving Chicago for Oakland, had he done a real, all-night stakeout. There were the few hours tailing suspects, but mostly he spent his time on computers. Janice had hated it when he was out all night on a sit. He would come home tired. She would look just as tired, and dozed with him during the day. After a long stakeout near the last of them, he realized she couldn't sleep when he was out on a night sit.

"Wasted hours," Priestly said. "I had a partner that ran a brokering business on his cell phone during stakeouts. He even offered a piece to me. But it was against policy and my own principles."

"I didn't think you DEA cowboys had principles."

Priestly ignored the comment and pointed out the window. "That our man?"

Tim watched the rusty Escort Wagon bully its way through the drifts to the front of the shack. It parked with a squeal and he could just hear LeFerril cursing at the site of Priestly's blue Grand Am. The door creaked open and LeFerril staggered out. He locked eyes with Tim, then turned away and darted for his shack. Tim didn't say anything to his counterpart. He just jumped out and started after LeFerril. Priestly got out and slid in behind him. LeFerril slowed his hike up to the door. He wore the same homeless look and had ice crystals in his beard.

"Oh great. It's the *special* Lone Ranger." LeFerril flashed a sardonic grin at them. "And don't tell me. He's Tanto of the Health Department, right?"

"DEA," Priestly advised.

"Oh?" LeFerril tramped the remaining distance to his door. "Where's the baseball cap with the missing 'D'?"

"Missing 'D'?" Priestly stopped behind Tim at the door.

"On the end of DEA," LeFerril suggested, taking out his key.

Tim noticed the lock on the door was new. How much good could it do? The door itself couldn't be any stronger than balsa wood.

He inserted the key and then paused. "Why the hell you bugging me now? I gave you all I had last time."

"We have a new favor," Tim said.

"Get a warrant."

"We're not investigating you," Tim said. He knew this could be a dangerous game. If LeFerril turned out to be part of the force behind the new drug, then he and Priestly could get slapped in court with a warrantless search and LeFerril would be free. Then the man could legally refuse to help. But on a Saturday, getting the warrant was more difficult. Especially since he had little to connect LeFerril as a suspect in the investigation.

"I know my users' rights. You still need a warrant, man."

Priestly stepped closer to LeFerril, holding his head stiff and high with eyes aimed down at the fix-it man. "Do I look like the kinda guy that needs a warrant?"

"You look like the kind of guy that needs a real job."

Priestly pressed a hand on LeFerril's chest and pushed him against the flimsy door.

"Hey!" LeFerril gritted his teeth and slapped at Priestly's hand. It had all the effect of a windblown paper hitting a bronze statue. His body pressed against the door until the hinges on the door groaned and wood frame cracked near the bolt. Tim was about to stop Priestly when LeFerril gave in.

"Stop it! All right. Just stop."

Priestly let up. LeFerril heaved a breath and fixed his rumpled coat. Then he inserted the key and turned it, opening the door on loose hinges. "Won't you please step into my humble abode." LeFerril gestured with a slight bow, extending his hand. "Excuse the drab interior, my decorator has taken the decade off, and please, remove your shoes. I don't want any stains on my new hand-woven broadrug."

Priestly looked through the doorway. "And I thought being a riffraff would take up all of your time."

LeFerril scratched his beard. "Who you tracking today?"

"One of your users has been dealing in a new drug. Ever heard of Rhapsody or just rhap, spelled R-H-A-P?"

"Who needs drugs, man, when you're connected?" LeFerril parted the blanket separator. They passed over a new layer of trash into the computer area, where LeFerril sat behind the machine. He woke his computer with a nudge on the mouse and it yawned in its own way, re-lighting over a million pixels.

"We want the e-mail for a user named Crazy Zig. User ID is just Zig at zipper.net." Tim leaned on a rusty file cabinet.

LeFerril cursed and glared at him. "Do you know how many perfectly good paying users I could lose? Word ever gets out I handed private e-mail to the feds, that's it, man."

"Don't worry," Tim assured him. "If we make any of this public, we'll be sure to get the warrant first. We're just looking for information, not evidence."

"That supposed to cheer me? Warrant or not, I'm getting shut down. Either the feds or my lack of patrons." LeFerril moaned and stopped working on the computer. "Maybe I'd like you to get that warrant this time. Least I'll have a chance to clean up for visitors."

"No." Priestly darted toward LeFerril. "Just let us read the stuff. No printouts. No evidence. I promise to keep you out."

"Deal?" Tim raised a hand. "Otherwise, we can call the sheriff to come do a quick check on your lot for safety violations. You know, poor wiring, sanitation violations. We'll have to detain you in the county jail for probable cause—while we get the warrant and sweep up."

"You guys urologists?" LeFerril asked, cursing under his breath. "You really know how to get a guy where it hurts."

Tim nudged Priestly. "You brought rubber gloves, right?"

The Drug Bug laughed. LeFerril mumbled a curse, then hammered his keyboard and shoved mouse around. Soon enough the monitor furnished the e-mail listing. Tim stooped down.

"You wanna tell me what you're looking for?" LeFerril asked. "Maybe I can do a search. That's a lot of e-mail for one user."

"Do a wildcard search. Anything with the word 'hand' or part of it."

"Hand?"

"Don't figure it out. Just do it."

LeFerril typed in a *grep* command and a minute later the screen scrolled the matches.

Two hits: "*Try your* hand *at this…*" and "*a left-*hand*ed pitcher.*"

Tim examined the matches. Nothing about Alven Hando. Just common phrases. "That's all the e-mail?"

"You're lucky there's anything. He probably flushed the incriminating stuff. Wouldn't you?" LeFerril smirked.

"What about backups?"

"I told you before, man, I don't keep them for very long. Cheaper to recycle the tape." LeFerril typed at the keyboard. "Just a minute."

After a moment, he had what looked like records or logs blazing on the monitor. "Last time he deleted any mail was about a week before my last backup. There's no way to get at it. It's flushed permanently."

Priestly joined in. "Can you find me everything he says about 'rhap'? R-H-A-P."

LeFerril typed the search command. It took several seconds for the system to respond and then it scrolled pages of information.

"Judas Priest!" LeFerril cursed.

"Watch it. He could be his ancestor," Tim said, pointing at Priestly.

"What did you find?" Priestly asked.

"A lot of the e-mail is about rhap. Probably over thirty pages."

Priestly released a heavy breath. "Great. And I suppose bad. I am going to need a warrant for arrests."

"Arrests?" LeFerril shook his head. "Look, I'll make you a deal. I'll give you the printouts with my site info and Zig's ID cut out. But you promise not to clean me out, okay?"

"No can do." Priestly shook his head. "I'll be coming back with a warrant for the full record."

"I'll tell you what," Tim added. "You give us those printouts now, and I promise not to leak your name to the press."

Priestly added, "Don't go erasing anything. Obstruction is a felony."

"Be gentle with me," LeFerril said with a high voice.

"Do we have a deal?"

LeFerril grinned smugly at them, rising from his seat. He parted the divider and walked into the other part of the hut. After a moment he returned.

"Drink on it?" He held out two Pepsies.

Priestly took one, smelled it, then joined LeFerril in tipping it back. Tim took a cautious swig.

"Now it's a deal," the scruffy fix-it man said through a belch.

* * *

Student Car

"This guy is a bloody fed!" the taller kid shouted in a whisper as he opened the rear car door. The other two students carried Olson.

The car, a ten-year-old Toyota with several craggy holes rusted out by Michigan salty winters, was parked just outside the dorm hall. They exited through a greasy side door, a typically unused and deserted access.

Zig and the short student hefted the agent into the back seat and folded his legs so they wouldn't get caught in the slammed door. His mouth was duct-taped like his hands, and his eyes were loosely closed. Slow breathing. Slight trickle of blood on the back of his head.

"Zig!" the tall student cried. "A fed! I'm telling you, we're in deep flaming vomitus—"

"Shut up, already!" Zig made a fist. "I'm sick to hell and back of your whining."

"The FBI. Do you understand?"

"Of course. We've dealt with them before." Zig held the car door. "Get in back. Make sure he's out until we can get somewhere."

He followed orders, frowning, while Zig got in the passenger side. The shorter student drove. They pulled out and went around the alley, turning onto Center Street and then heading south.

"Go to 94 and take it East," Zig told the driver.

"You're crazy, Zig."

"No kidding," Zig said.

"If this guy comes to—well, we need to keep him out," the driver said. He wore glasses now. But his hands didn't tremble like the others' hands. All of them wore gloves.

"No, it won't matter." Zig glanced back at the agent. "He won't be telling anyone once we get there."

"Get where?"

"Yeah, where?" the taller kid repeated in back, his voice cracking.

"Take 23 south," Zig replied. "I'll show you a great remote spot."

* * *

Rental Car

Priestly read the stacks of papers in front of LeFerril's shack. Tim grew impatient, sitting next to him in Grand Am's passenger seat.

"You can read that back at the residency, you know," he said. "Or give them to me while you drive."

Priestly looked up. "Sure. I just wanted to read a little to have something to think about on the drive back." He shuffled the papers over the steering column and put them on the back seat.

"You're supposed to think about driving." Tim belted himself into the seat.

"Right." Priestly started the engine and pulled out onto the back roads.

With the snow covering the roads, the potholes had all but disappeared. The car rode smoothly over the dirt washboard.

"You know," Priestly said, "just from the small amount I read, I can tell that this Zig is producing rhap right here. But get this. The other guy told him how to make it."

"The other guy?"

"From Berkeley. He's probably the ultimate source. The inventor. Calls himself 'Quimica-man', whatever that means."

"'Quimica' is Spanish for chemistry," Tim said, taking the printouts.

"Well, he's definitely a pharmacologist type. Used all the right lingo in the little I saw."

"That doesn't help my case too much." Tim sighed and flipped through the sheets. "I hope Olson gets a positive ID so we can bring in this Crazy Ziggy."

* * *

Student Car

His head ached. Streamy images of glassy snow and fiery water drizzled into it. And he could hear voices. Arguing and whining. But none of it made any sense. It sounded like Chinese or German. Nothing made sense. And his arms wouldn't move. They were cramped or tied.

Olson blinked slowly, his eyes pulsating with his heart and head jolting with some kind of motion. He could see objects that looked like tinted windows and a seat and people…

He realized suddenly he was in a car. With the three-stooges that jumped him. One of them was in the back seat with him. The tall one, with the big nose that Olson would love to break.

Now the speech was getting clearer. But he decided to close his eyes— both to keep the light from hurting them and to feign unconsciousness so he could listen.

"Maybe you should just let me out."

The voice, Olson heard, came from the tall kid in back with him.

"Don't be such an asshole," someone said from the front.

Quiet. Olson felt the car slow. He peeked a look and noticed that he was slouched against the window on the left side in the back. His hands were obviously tied. His feet might be too, but he didn't dare move them to check since the student in back might notice.

"Which way from here?" someone in front asked, sounding like the short kid.

Another voice in front answered. "Take a left. It goes for about two miles and then there's this little trail that leads to an old mill."

"How do you know about this place, Zig?"

"I've cruised around here when I came out to get my anonymous account from the fix-it man."

"Fix-it man?"

The car picked up speed and Olson felt it turning.

"The computer repair guy that owns the anarchy site. You know, we did some trades. His wares for mine."

"How many people have you traded rhap with?"

"A few. This guy's cool. No one bothers him out here."

"Sure picked a remote place for a computer board."

Olson sensed the car lurching and sliding on what was probably deep snow.

"I don't want to do this," said the kid in back.

"Shut the hell up!"

Silence.

"It's too narrow, pull over and let them pass," said Zig.

"Just stop?"

"Yeah, you ain't both driving over that bridge at the same time."

Olson realized another car was coming. Now was his chance. He wiggled his hands to find the door handle, moving across the small armrest and then a lever. But he caught the electric window button instead.

Vmmm. Cold air blasted him.

"Shit! He's awake!"

"Hit him, you breeder!"

Vmmmph. The window stopped.

Olson opened his eyes and scanned the students. The redhead was reaching for him. The taller pointed at the window. Olson quickly glanced out. A blue Grand Am was coming toward them on the other side.

* * *

Rental Car

"They're stopping to let you pass," Tim said, noticing a tinted window going down.

Priestly slowed and made his way over the bridge. "Must be a smoker. I've seen them drive with the window cracked in twenty below with a wind chill of minus forty."

He nodded his agreement. He had never smoked himself—not since he was in high school.

But something sticking out of the car's window caught his eye. It wasn't a cigarette butt. As they passed, he saw a head. A man with ruffled hair and gray-something matted on his face.

What the hell?

"What was that on his mouth?" Priestly asked.

"Turn around!"

"What's going on?"

"TURN AROUND!"

Priestly spun the car around and fishtailed into a position going the other way. Tim pictured the man again, his face familiar.

"That was Olson," he explained. "He had duct tape over his mouth."

* * *

Student Car

"Shit! He's coming back," the redhead yelled.

The engine revved. The tires whirled, rubbing against packed snow and then catching with a snappish grip. In an instant, they flew over the bridge and down the back road, veering occasionally to the side as they picked up speed.

Olson breathed hard through his nose. He fumbled for the door handle and the taller kid reached for him. With all the motion and swerving neither succeeded.

Cold air still blew in, but the glass was going up. The driver had a control for the back window.

"Just hit the bastard!"

The Roman glanced back at Zig with reluctance in his eyes.

"Do it!"

He shook his head. The redhead squeezed in between the bucket seats and reached out to belt Olson, who cocked his untied right leg and kicked the redhead in the chest, sending him back into the dash. The car bounced and vacillated.

"Zig, they're gaining. They'll read my license plate if they get any closer."

The redhead rubbed his chest and looked back. "Nah, too much snow and shit getting kicked up behind. They'll be lucky to see anything. Just go faster."

"Already going fifty."

Olson watched as the redhead braced himself in the swaying motion of the car.

"Okay, keep going until I tell you. The next curve. I have a plan." Zig sneered at the tall kid. "Can you at least grab his legs?"

The Roman nodded, and Olson began to kick.

* * *

Rental Car

"Can you…read the plates?" Priestly asked, halting as they bounced. "I'm…finding it…difficult to…"

"No. Can't see with all the snow blowing around. Not even sure what kind of car it is."

Priestly bit his tongue as he concentrated. "Can you…shoot…the tire?"

"One in a million shot on smooth pavement. Impossible here." Tim held the dash and roof with his hands, bracing against the motion. As they jounced and swerved, he also hoped Priestly could drive well enough in an unfamiliar car and on foreign terrain. He attempted pulling out his cell phone as they needed backup, but with the jostling, his hands shot back to the dash for support.

"Watch the curve coming up," he warned, trying again to get a hand to his pocket. The other car was only ten feet ahead of them. Closer than he liked on frozen roads.

Then, just in front of them, the other car's left rear door popped open as it entered the curve, slowing only slightly. The Grand Am approached on its back end. Without warning a person rolled out of the door onto the snow, tumbling and kicking up snow spray. Priestly swerved to avoid the body. Tim grabbed at the dash and braced himself, horrified. The Pontiac slid and locked up, aimed directly at the person. Priestly released the brake and the wheels caught briefly, jerking toward what might have been a shoulder in the summer. It sloped up and then dipped down.

Everything slowed. Ice and snow tumbled and sprayed over them. What had been a clear sky turned white and gray and then dark as they piled into a snow-filled ditch. Tim felt the center of gravity shift precariously several times. Spinning and hurling and smashing into ice and dirt and brown grass. Then everything rushed towards the dash and he heard the screeching of bending metal and the explosion of an air bag and shattering glass.

They halted abruptly and he was left momentarily senseless. Dizzy and confused.

His first thoughts were whether the sky was still blue or if it got cloudy. Then he wondered if anyone had been injured. Was he injured? Everything was strange and something was clicking, chugging. He glanced about.

Priestly was leaned over the steering wheel, draped with the used air bag. Tim couldn't tell if he was hurt or just got the breath knocked out of him. The light was dim and cold air hovered around them. Snow and glass lay all over them and the interior of the car. They sat at a steep angle, and he felt the back of the car sliding a little. Slipping underneath.

With a thud, the back of the car landed and the angle grew steeper. More symmetric with the length of the car. Then everything was at rest and silent except for the clicking fuel pump.

"Priestly!"

The DEA cowboy slowly lifted his head. "That was not my best driving," he said half-coherently. His nose bled. Tim searched him for more injury, finding nothing obvious.

A big square of snow fell through the passenger side window frame onto his lap, letting sun brighten the interior through the remaining jagged rim of glass.

Less disoriented, Tim assessed the situation again. They appeared to be on a small hillside, at the bottom of a gully. The angle drew Priestly toward him.

They both tried the doors and found, fortunately, that at least Priestly's would open. Tim climbed out behind him to find his left thigh hurting. The same place where he had been shot. He couldn't see any signs of broken bones but it bled through his suit pants. He checked his body for other injuries. His right chest hurt, something in his pocket—his cell phone—had jabbed his muscle.

Priestly complained about his nose as they climbed over the incline. But otherwise he said he was okay. On the other side they could see the outline of a person lying in the middle of the road. Lying face down, still and motionless.

Tim shuddered as a clear sky breeze blew through them, whistling mournfully. Fields stretched around, empty and frozen.

He heard Priestly curse and watched him tramp into the road. Just watched and stood, amazed at the scene. Feeling it all like a bad dream. He limped into the road, meeting Priestly over the body, who felt the spine and neck of the person.

"Doesn't feel broken," he told Tim.

He lifted the right side and turned the man over. It was Olson: Bloody face and snow and closed eyes. Torn duct-tape on his ashen and expressionless lips.

"Is he...?"

Priestly leaned down, pulled back the tape and pressed his ear to Olson's mouth. "He's barely breathing."

Tim exhaled at length. He reached in his pocket for the cell phone, immediately realizing why his chest had hurt. A crack ran down the phone's outer shell. It wouldn't turn on or operate.

"We need to find a phone."

"No kidding," Priestly said sarcastically.

He searched around. But the fields were vast. He tried to remember the area and where they were. LeFerril's shack was probably a half-mile away.

"LeFerril's place." He started running. His thigh gave in, jolting him with electric pricks.

"Jeez, your leg is bad." Priestly rose and ran past him. "I'll go. I'm pretty sure I know the way. Make sure he's warm."

Tim nodded but he only caught the man's back. On the ground he could see the tire tracks. They had missed Olson by only a couple of feet.

He removed his coat and lifted Olson up. His skin felt cold, but another check ensured that he was still breathing, shallow slow breaths. He put the coat around Olson, then opened the eyelids to check for response and watched both pupils react as expected.

He dashed back to the Grand Am, and with some effort ripped out the trunk carpeting. He carried the carpet back and slid it under Olson. His coat acted as a blanket and he pulled the carpet like a sled with Olson as the payload.

"Face is red, raise the head," he repeated, pulling the cargo to the roadside. "Face is pale, raise the tail."

Using the angle of the shoulder slope, he elevated Olson's feet; his face was still white. Then he went over the incline and back to the car for the interior carpet, but it was stitched more tightly.

The fields around him sprawled endlessly, but searching once more, he found some dried juniper scrub and yanked them up. Fortunately the car's lighter still worked and he ignited a small fire with the brush. It only lasted for a minute, however, and the breeze carried the warmth away quickly.

Olson was frozen. Tim was nearly frozen. It couldn't be over ten degrees above zero. He got down on hands and knees and held his body just inches above Olson. He hoped he could keep them warm until help arrived.

* * *

Hospital

The ambulance came faster than Tim had expected; Priestly had found a farmer's place before LeFerril's. Both he and Olson suffered from severe exposure. Tim had uncontrollable shivering, numb hands and puffy cheeks. Olson was much worse off. The ambulance medics worked on waking him without success. The emergency vehicle moved quickly. Tim remembered seeing Priestly in the trooper car behind them.

At Saint Joseph Emergency, a medic gave Tim two warmed blankets and all the coffee he could drink. Others rushed Olson through a pair of swinging doors into a room where they administered warm saline through an IV and covered him with heated blankets.

Tim observed the action through the glass of the double doors. Two doctors or nurses worked on Olson. One intubated him and the other checked his head and pupils and heart rate.

He felt responsible. Olson was under his guidance, and now he would die like Robinson. Olson, young and a father-to-be. How could this happen again?

"You should be sitting," someone advised behind him.

He turned and saw a nurse reaching for him. She yanked the blankets he'd wrapped around himself, but he held them tight.

"I just…"

"I know, but you need an examination yourself." The lady pulled him away. "Come with me. I'm a physician's assistant. Kathy Freelon."

Tim glanced around as they walked across the main area of the ER. It was calm. Only two or three doctors with patients in the halls. One of the patients, the Drug Bug Priestly, also followed a nurse, disappearing into a small room. Tim's practitioner led him into an examination room. She grabbed a stack of records and shuffled through them. The nurse had wrinkles and stress showing on her face despite heavy makeup.

"Here, let's have those blankets," she said, taking them from him. "Remove your shirt and…" She eyed him peculiarly. "Did you have a gun in that holster when you arrived?"

Tim sat on the white-sheet table. Over his dress shirt hung an empty shoulder holster. "Yeah. The ambulance team took it. Said it was regulation. I saw them give it to a clerk at the main desk."

"Okay, you'll get it back when we release you," she promised, glancing at his leg. "You're bleeding, or were."

He looked down. The bleeding had stopped, mostly dried. But his suit pants were stained. Like they had been in Danville and on campus, red glistening, his suit ruined. He dropped his pants. The physician scrutinized his leg, cleaning it with alcohol, iodine and gauze.

"You tore a suture." She pulled out a large orange bandage, unlike anything Tim had seen before. She applied it over his injury, telling him it was a "fibrin adhesive," a new kind of patch that worked as well as sutures. She instructed him on taking care of it, when to wash it, and the best time to have it removed.

After she finished, she released him. He put his clothes back on and wandered into Emergency's waiting area. He found a phone and called the residency—no one was there. He called Kaplan at home and told him the news, hung up and then found Priestly slouched in a seat, drinking coffee. Tim took the seat next to him.

"Man, I hate emergency waiting rooms," Priestly complained.

"Gee, this is my first time seeing one from the vertical position."

Priestly eyed him, an eyebrow raised. He finished his coffee and set the paper cup down. "What's up with Olson?"

"Not sure. They're probably still working with him. I feel just horrible."

"Well don't!" Priestly clamored with a nasal sonority. "No one is to blame."

Tim sized up the Bug's injury. Priestly's face appeared clean and his nose looked only slightly swollen. "How's your nose?"

Priestly began to stand. "Tender. But it's not broken. And I can still smell a little."

"That's good."

"I guess, but these hospitals always stink." Priestly collected his coat. "How about your leg?"

"Got it dressed."

"Good." Priestly put on his coat. "Well, I'm going off to rest before my trip back tomorrow morning." He handed Tim a slip of paper. "Here's the number at my room. Call me if Olson comes out. I'm eager to know more."

"Sure. By the way, can you remember anything more about the car?" They had discussed some details briefly when the ambulance arrived. But neither could recall much.

"Only that it was red and small. Nothing about the person or people inside." Priestly waved. "I'll call you if I remember more."

He walked out of the ER. Tim sat, puzzling over why the color red seemed significant.

* * *

Tim hated emergency rooms—three times in the past seven months, all for injuries to his left leg. The first had been the worse, when he was shot in Danville, California. Waking up in the Emergency at San Ramon Regional Hospital was the first memory he recalled after getting shot in Danville. He remembered the sweet-bitter mixture of smells: blood and antiseptic, alcohol and surgical rubber.

His mind had fluttered under the weight of pain shooting, screaming from his left leg, where the bullet had ripped through the muscle, exiting without cracking into the bone. Although unbroken, it hurt worse than when he broke his arm as a child after falling from a high fence. Worse than the cracked rib's he'd gotten during combat role-playing in the army.

He had awakened, in San Ramon Regional, when they loaded him onto a gurney at Emergency's entrance. Pinpoints of fluttering sparkles had darkened his mind as it silently sank. Tim had tried to bring himself back, focus his mind. Remember how he had been injured. He'd concentrated on images flashing through his mind. He discerned a face. His wife's smile in the whiteness plaguing his mind. But it disappeared so fast. Her silhouette was masked in a haze. He couldn't see her face, could not remember the smile. No matter how hard, how strenuously he fought, the fog would not lift around her.

A brighter light, a hospital overhead, had fired down at him, bringing him back. Back with the nurses and technicians pushing his table into the trellis of confusion barely contained inside the glass cage of the trauma center. Sounds and lights tugged at his consciousness. Intercoms and voices buzzed orders, shoes scuffing and papers rustling at his sides.

His breath had echoed in resonance with heart monitors and stress issuing all around the emergency room. And the boy that was screaming off to his side, howling at several green-clad, ghost-like medics. The boy...The boy had been Michael Miller, he realized now. The boy he had shot, though he couldn't remember doing it.

He could envision three of the green gowns holding the boy down while a fourth inserted a hypo into his neck. Instruments clashed, carts rolled in and then bluntly the noises had died, leaving Tim in cold smothered urgency. Sounds fading as the boy died on the gurney.

And odors. As broken up as Tim's memories were, the smell behind this one was unforgettably whole. Not only the blood-n-antiseptic odor of the hospital. This memory had a smell not even a mountain of injuries or a river of blood could produce. It was the body-bag stench of a decaying child, the moldering innocence of a child discarded in the estate basement.

No! It was too much. He didn't want to remember!

Tim stood quickly, blinking away the memory and rambling toward the double doors where he had left Olson before getting fixed up himself. It was now empty, not even a nurse or janitor cleaning inside. He turned around and saw one of the two doctors that had been working on Olson. He approached the physician, who stood just in front of double doors reading a sheet.

"Doctor, I wonder if you can tell me how Harald Olson is doing?"

The doctor, glasses low on his nose, gazed up. "Who?"

"He came in with a head injury. Car accident out in Milan."

"Oh, yes. And what is your relation to him?"

"We work for the FBI." Tim reached reflexively for his credentials, but he had given them with his weapon to the ambulance tech. "I have my ID at the main desk."

"Right. Your partner has just been taken to radiology. We stabilized his vitals, but he was unarousable. Radiology will run a CAT-scan to determine why he's comatose. You should probably wait up there."

"Thanks," Tim said. *Comatose?*

"Oh." The doctor halted Tim. "Did you give the name of the next-of-kin to anyone?"

"Yeah. When we got in. I told them he has a wife in Troy. I didn't know the name."

"Olson's a pretty common surname. Can you call your office and get the first name?"

"I did. They should've contacted the main desk."

The doctor nodded.

"Tim!"

He turned to see Sherrie Marshall and Spike trotting from the main area. They were both dressed formally for a Saturday. Sherrie had her hair pulled up and earrings dangled from her lobes. Spike was shaven and wore dress slacks but no tie.

"We were going out for some dinner when I got a call on my car-phone," Spike explained.

"How are you?" Sherrie asked him, looking at his pants.

"I'm fine, but Olson is…is critical. They're running a scan on him. He's uh, he's in a coma."

201

Spike and Sherrie stood speechless. Tim rotated to find the doctor, but he had left.

"Does his wife know?"

"I don't know. I was too busy warding off medics myself."

He motioned to the waiting area and walked toward it. They followed as he explained the situation and described what had happened. They sat and listened, Sherrie's eyes glistening, as Tim related how he put Olson on the trunk carpet and searched without success for ways to keep him warm.

Before he finished explaining, Bob Givens walked into the waiting area. He nodded to Tim. "Thanks for calling, Tim."

"Givens."

"Sir." Spike acknowledged cordially.

"How is SA Olson?" Givens sat across from him. Tim explained the whole incident again. Everyone remained solemn until he finished.

"That's it." Givens stood. "Everyone is pairing up. Undercover as well."

"I don't need a partner." Tim did not want a tagalong, at least not someone he knew nothing about.

"Mott and me are usually paired," Spike said. "That leaves Kaplan for you, Delbravo." He smirked.

"No." Givens shook his head before Tim could protest. "I'll try to spare someone from the Field Office."

That meant Tim would not be able to choose. And anyone they could spare from the field office would be green, unfamiliar with the case, the area...He'd get a useless tagalong. Tim looked at Spike and wished he was free, but Spike had a long-standing rapport built with the militia. Only recently had he introduced Mott into the close-knit circles formed during the year-long mission.

"Sherrie's already been helping a lot," Spike said. He looked at her. "You could fill in for a while until Delbravo gets a qualified partner."

Tim looked at Sherrie. She smiled and replied, "I'd like to. But the sheriff won't give the time."

"What if we allocate funds to your department?" Givens asked her. "Get you on loan."

Tim wanted to say something, but he wasn't even sure how he felt about this building arrangement. He really liked Sherrie. She was a great cop, easy to get along with. But somehow, pairing with her full-time felt troubling. It wasn't that she was a woman, he had no trouble with that. It was the way she looked at him, the way he felt around her.

"With money, I think the sheriff will go for it," Sherrie said. "It might take until Monday to clear, but I'm willing."

"Then it's settled." Givens clapped his hands and stood. "Come on, Tim. Let's get you home."

"But Olson?"

"I'll stay here. My wife is bringing his wife here. They were trailing me by about ten or fifteen minutes. Let's get you a cab."

"What about finding who did this?"

"I've got someone from the office already assigned. They'll come take your statement tonight. We'll vacuum Olson's clothes and send them priority to Quantico, for lab evaluation."

"He was my responsibility. We have to push the lab."

"I know how you feel, Tim. Don't worry. We're talking an assaulted agent. Lab will get on it this weekend. And I hear the profile on your suspect should be coming next week."

"Thanks. But I think I'll stay. Olson has probably seen my suspect."

"No, Tim. You're leaving. That's an order. Go home and rest."

Tim sighed. He knew that there was not much he could do and he did feel exhausted. "They have Olson up in Radiology, so you'll want to wait there. Call me."

"Well, I'll keep posted too," Spike said.

Tim turned to him. "And let's get a collection going for his wife. Just in case."

Givens nodded. "Field Office can collect too."

Tim stood and began trudging toward the phones. "I'll call a cab."

Spike grabbed his arm. "No, let me drive you home."

"You sure?" Tim looked at Sherrie next to him.

"Of course. No cab is going to take you home with those pants."

Tim nodded. "I'll just get my badge and gun."

Spike and Sherrie followed him to the main desk. He waved down the clerk and asked for his gun.

"Gun?"

"FBI. It's a 9mm Smith & Wesson."

The clerk's eyes got big and it took him a moment to begin looking. After fishing under the counter—keys jangling and a box lid creaking open—he placed the firearm on top.

"That everything?"

Tim grabbed it. "Yep."

"Nice gun." Spike glanced over the weapon as Tim put it in his holster. Spike headed toward the exit. "You should see what they were selling at the militia store today. No handguns, but every kind of rifle. Semis and even some full auto paint guns, for their training exercises."

"Where's this?"

"The Founder's Franchise."

"Franchise?" Tim stopped. "As in, Autarkic Franchise?"

Spike stopped as well. "Maybe. I'm not so sure, but..."

Tim and Sherrie stared at him.

"That's right." Spike rubbed his chin. "At this store, they have a computer board in the back. A Michigan Militia computer line, called Arty-something. I'm sure it's the same name now. And Mott's been fooling with it all month."

"Mott?" Tim queried with surprise. "He said he'd never heard of it."

"I'm sure he has."

* * *

Apartment

Tim opened his front door, holding his suit coat over the stain on his pants. He did not want Janice to know he had been hurt again. Inside the entry, shoes and toys strewn about, he glanced around cautiously and then closed the door.

"Tim?" Janice's voice came from around the hall, in the kitchen.

"Yeah. It's me." He turned to go up the stairs.

"Tim, come here. I need to show you something."

He stopped before going up, hearing Tasha and Reggy playing upstairs. He couldn't exactly lie to Janice, to them, about getting hurt, ruining his suit pants. He turned and walked around to the kitchen.

Janice sat at the dining table, head bent over papers. Bills, he realized quickly by the tabulated style of print on each, and the checkbook and calculator sitting on the table. She glanced up at him and smiled briefly. He kept his coat over the stain in his pants.

"Bad?" he said.

"Uh-hm. You're not going to like it."

He sat. "How deep are we?"

"It's getting worse."

The discussion followed its usual path—usual since his demotion. Neither of them ever said a word about why finances were so tight. After taking the loss on selling their home in California when the market fell, the demotion continued draining their accounts. But even unspoken, Tim felt the pressure building every time bills came up.

"You know, Tim, I'm glad you signed Reggy up for Aikido—still that's another monthly payment."

He knew it. But the martial arts classes really helped his son build confidence. With only a few lessons, Reggy was already more assertive. Maybe even a little too aggressive. In a small way, Tim worried that it might give Reggy more confidence than he should before learning to control his anger. It was something that took Tim a while to master in the army and at Quantico when he joined the FBI.

"And this." Janice pointed to a hand written figure. "I called our credit card, to get an up-to-date balance. There's a hefty charge to Fed-Ex just yesterday morning."

"That'd be mine. I needed to get something out to Quantico, Same Day."

"Will the office reimburse?"

"Yes."

Janice sighed, brushed all the bills aside and frowned at him. "We're not making it, Tim."

He nodded.

"You look haggard." She studied him. Her eyes scanned down his face, onto his chest and landed on his lap. She took a deep breath, lifting up his suit coat. "What happened?"

"Just an accident."

"Oh my heavens! You were shot again?"

"No, no. Much worse. I let the DEA help me. One of their agents got in a little car wreck."

"Tim…" Her face tightened into a frown. "Be serious."

"It's nothing. Just a ripped stitch is all."

"No, it's the bureau." She shook her head. "It's so dangerous. I worry, really worry, Tim."

"Why? It can happen to any guy. A Pepsi truck driver has it worse, probably. It could even happen playing ball with Reggy."

She released a heavy breath. "Well, I'm glad you're all right."

"Everything's fine." He decided not to mention that they were chasing a suspect and Olson being in a coma.

"But look at those pants. That's the new suit we bought you after the shooting."

"Well, maybe the bureau can pay the cleaning bill."

Janice shook her head. Moisture collected in her eyes. He dropped the coat and grabbed her hands.

"It'll be all right. We'll make it, babe." He stood, pulling her up and embracing her.

"We have to get out of debt, Tim." She paused. "I called some schools yesterday."

"Janice—"

"No, listen, Tim." She released him. "I can teach. Part time as a substitute. Just for a while."

He had not wanted to say anything about the promised promotion, but he had to use it now. "Givens said I'll be getting a raise."

"A raise? When?"

"After this case. Maybe soon."

She studied his eyes. "But you don't really know, do you?"

He shook his head.

"I think I can work until then." She looked down as she spoke. "It'll be all right. I know the kids will be okay for a while. I won't do it forever."

Her voice trailed and she moved her gaze onto the far wall. He watched her, knowing she was trying hard to convince herself more than him. The last time she worked, they had struggled about having her quit.

It had been early in their marriage, at his second area in New York City. Reggy was about two years old then—such a sweet and curious little guy. He had just learned to climb the book cases, and he always went for Tim's favorite video—*A Raisin in the Sun.*

At the beginning of that summer, Janice had quit her teaching job without really warning him. She said she wanted to spend more time at home. She believed that Reggy was at critical point of development.

Tim, young and eager for a new home, had been livid at first. How could she do that? What did she think—that they could survive on just his income? Angry, he left and spent the evening at a bar. After a couple of beers and pool matches with a buddy, he returned to a dark apartment. He cooled off on the couch for another hour, regretting his anger. After all, he had just received his first promotion. They could afford it, if they tightened the belt a little. He almost went back upstairs after midnight, but before complete humility had stepped in, he fell asleep on the sofa.

At one-thirty that morning he was awakened by a soft kiss. Janice knelt beside him and looked lovingly into his face.

"Friends?" she pleaded. She wore the cream-colored lace and silk combo he loved so much. How could he have turned down an offer like that?

"'In poverty and in riches.'" He smiled and kissed her. "But I hope you'll be happy with less."

"It isn't vast sums of money that I want," she said. "I love just being a family. Our little boy is everything. And you and me. I just want to be simply happy at home. Make it a wonderful refuge for you. A place away from thugs and crimes and all the guff you put up with at the bureau."

Tim smiled. "But I love the guff. It's even better than that violent stuff on TV."

Janice grinned back, her eyes glistening. "This is what I want."

"We'll work it out, then." Tim meant it.

She caressed his cheek. "I saw so many of my girlfriends get pregnant. Few married. They all had to go to work. I promised I would never do that. I wanted to be different. Be a simple and full-time mommy."

"You are different. You're mine." Tim cupped her chin gently.

She lifted herself on the couch, muzzling his shoulder. He stroked her medium length hair. He loved how it was just wavy, not tight and stiff.

"I love you." She kissed him, and he hugged her back. They held each other for a long moment, and then she sat up on him, eyes sparkling in a way that always intoxicated him. In the moonlight, her figure traced a seductive outline above him. Before long, the silk slip he loved so much lay on the floor. He ran his hands lovingly across her, rediscovering excitement in the small dips and deep contours of her silkiness. It was a night that neither would forget. And three months less than a year later, their family grew. Tasha was born.

He remembered those days fondly. Money had been just as tight, but they lived ever so happily. Even here in Ann Arbor with his demotion, he was sure they could be happy. The bills at the table were so meaningless in the long term.

"Janice." He reached an arm around her. She looked just as beautiful ten years later. "I'm sorry for all of this."

She smiled at him, looking back up until they faced each other. "Hey, it happens. It's in the past. We'll be fine. The children will too."

He hugged her tight. "I love you, Janice. I always will."

Sunday,
February 16

Quantico, Virginia

Even with more than 500 agents and technicians at the FBI Laboratory Division, most of their 20,000 cases remained backlogged for months. Ken Hicks, the assistant director of Forensics Science Research, knew this was one case they couldn't afford to queue even for two days. An assaulted agent billed top priority at the lab, where normally emotions wouldn't run high.

In the basement lab, he watched his best technician, Sandra Townsend, pick up some tweezers in her gloved hands, then rotate back toward the phase-contrast microscope. Both wore white lab coats over their street clothes. He felt bad, making her work on a holiday weekend.

"Thanks again, Sandra. I know it's Sunday."

"Not a problem."

She bent her shower-capped head over the dual eyecups of the microscope. With the tweezers, she caught the few fibers extracted from SA Harald Olson's pants after a thorough field vacuuming. Hicks leaned against a table, next to other bags containing evidence from this and a related case, a child-murder being handled by the same residency where Olson assisted when he was assaulted.

"Definitely nylon twist. Short, with oils and salt," she told him, lifting the tweezers slowly.

"From a car?"

"My guess, too. Looks like common road salt on the fiber."

"The report says the agent that kept SA Olson warm, put him on carpet from the trunk."

Townsend dropped the nearly invisible fibers onto a quartz slide and sealed the top with a cover slip and index-matching fluid. "Yes, but that carpet was blue. These fibers are red."

She rose and opened the cover on a Mathesson Fourier Transform Infrared spectrometer, a large square instrument with knobs protruding out of its case. The evidence glass slide fit neatly into a corner compartment, where the spectrometer would gather the reflection values at each wavelength. She stretched a hand to the computer and began acquiring a spectrum.

She turned to him while the machine hummed through the process. "What else do we have?"

"Tire plasters." Hicks looked down at the table. "Not the best. Though, they look like brand-new tires, still snow isn't the easiest for making plasters."

"They should've had their pick. They chased them for a good distance, didn't they?"

Hicks nodded. "You know the drill. Line people never spend the time they should gathering in the field."

Field agents, whom Hicks referred to as line people, just didn't appreciate the power of physical evidence. They relied too much on the people factor. A mistake, he knew, because witnesses were commonly unreliable, and videotapes could be twisted to cast doubt in either direction. Even documents could be fabricated. But physical evidence—a bullet casing, fibers, a fingerprint, DNA—these were the most impervious to error. While they could only gather fingerprints at a fifth of all violent crime scenes, the perpetrators left hair, blood or semen three times more often. DNA analysis had become routine, and it exonerated over a third of their rape suspects; suspects that would've been wrongfully convicted before the technique. Now the court trusted it as much as their own judgments, since it cut both ways: it could prove guilt or innocence.

"How's the agent?" Townsend asked.

"I hear he's in a coma. Don't know the prognosis."

She looked away, her thin lips drawn back. Then she cast her eyes about other items in evidence bags. He was sure she felt like everyone involved. *Let's get the bastards!* An unusual sentiment among intellectuals at the lab…

The spectrometer stopped with a servo-buzz. Townsend called up the results on the computer. The monitor drew a squiggled line with distinct spikes at various locations. She gave the computer a few more commands and it overlaid a series of catalog signatures on the spectrum.

"There." Townsend pointed at one of the series. "It matches a type F dye, simple organic."

"Check the auto-carpet database."

She had already pulled open a five-inch thick catalog of all car carpet makes. She flipped the pages quickly and marked notes on a paper near the spectrometer. "It matches with two manufacturers. One distributes to all the Asian foreign markets. The other to three Japanese companies."

"A lot of models to sift through." He was afraid of this. "Let's get the calls going."

"It's Sunday."

"First thing tomorrow."

"Monday is President's Day."

"Then we'll wake someone at home, if we have to."

She nodded. "In the meantime, I'll continue with the tire plasters. The case agent in Ann Arbor asked that I cross-check them with some plasters from his homicide."

Hicks stood to leave. "Thanks, Sandra. Let me know when you get something else."

* * *

Hospital

The day after the accident, Tim still felt exhausted. His leg hardly hurt and his sprained wrist wasn't so bad, but going back to the hospital, hoping for Olson to recover, made him feel nervous. Worse was having the agent's wife there to remind him how close Olson was to leaving behind a family.

Catherine Olson sat next to her husband, surrounded by off-white plastic fixtures, antiseptic floors and light green paint. The air thickened with hushed-tension. The seconds clicked in Tim's ears as he approached the bed. He couldn't bear to get dressed up when he felt so restless, so he was tie-less and open-collared with tan cotton slacks. His new two pants suit, purchased after Amos shot him, was already down to a single pair of slacks. His overcoat was getting tattered and soiled from all of the near-death experience this month.

He looked over Olson, bandages covering him, tubes feeding him, wires monitoring. Catherine gazed at Tim and coerced a half-smile from her red cheeks, probably stained with hours of tears and worry.

"How's he doing?" Tim asked.

She shook her head softly, replacing her eyes on Olson. She didn't speak again, spurring uneasiness in the pit of his belly.

Catherine, eight months pregnant, reminded him of seeing Janice during her last few months with Tasha. Big and uncomfortable. Catherine wore that look he had seen many times when he came home long overdue from field operations. Janice would seem to age years in those hours of wait and worry.

He also saw his former partner's wife in Catherine. John Robinson's widow. He could hardly stand it. He didn't know Catherine, and anything he could say would be padding. He should be out finding the guy that did this to her husband.

"We're doing all we can to find the...the assailants," he said, as if it would matter.

Whether or not they caught the jackasses, Olson would still be in a coma, hovering near death. Olson had gone twenty hours in his coma already, and each moment longer meant his chances of coming out grew slim. All Tim could do was help indirectly by finding the assailants.

That morning, Givens had given Tim permission to work part of the search, since the assault tied so closely to his own case. Already, Tim had been to the dorm to question the managers, but none had heard of Crazy Zig. The parking lot was filled with red cars, which from each he took the license numbers and sent them to Michigan DMV for a plate check.

He came to the hospital wishing he could wake Olson. Somehow, he knew the key to this whole mess was locked inside the closed quarters of Olson's head. Inside would also be the answers he needed to capture Hando.

From the corner of his eye, Tim glimpsed someone at the door. Spike Cobbs entered and nodded courteously at Catherine, motioning for Tim to go out with him. He rose and met Spike out in the hall.

"I thought I might find you here. You need to get a new cell phone." Spike handed him a fax sheet. "From the lab. Fiber analysis. Car carpet."

"From Olson?"

Spike nodded. "Pretty fast, huh?"

"Did they get latents off anything?"

"Just bad partials. Extracted maybe two or three points total."

"They wore gloves, then?" The bureau's Automated Fingerprint Identification System required at least four points per single print to reduce the number of matches to something manageable.

"Don't know."

Tim looked over the printout. It listed the fiber type and major manufacturers, maybe three dozen models that used that particular brand and color of carpet. All designs from the last eight years.

"How's he doing?" Spike twitched nervously.

"The same."

"And his wife?"

Tim just grimaced.

"Makes you want to stay single." Spike leaned against the wall.

Just keep thinking that way, Cobbs. "What's the latest on my court order?"

"For the militia phone trace?"

"Yes."

"Still waiting. Judge doesn't like to work on Sunday. Even complained that tomorrow is a holiday."

Tim rolled his eyes. Getting a judge to sign an order on a federal holiday was on par with getting a congressmen to vote for term limits. Now that they knew the militia held the Autarkic franchise, the case needed the warrant to move forward.

"Have you told Mott the game plan?" They had talked briefly that morning about Tim contacting the militia. Spike had given him the entire folder on his case and he still hadn't begun reading it.

"I called Mott on the phone. Told him that we needed to make plans because you were coming in with warrants today or tomorrow and don't want to blow our cover. He was real quiet."

"He didn't say anything?"

"Just that a 'black G-man at a militia ought to be fun.'" Spike leaned against the wall. "He might be hanging around there. Mott and that Lonque fellow are the ones sharing computer responsibilities on the militia board."

Tim nodded. "Mott sure got tight with these bugle-bastards in a hurry."

"A natural," Spike added.

Nurses and doctors promenaded down the hall. Tim cleared his throat. "I better go."

"I almost forgot." Spike lifted another paper. "That DEA agent called the residency at noon. Left you this message."

Tim took the slip and read it. It said that Priestly had arrived in New York this morning and realized he forgot the computer printouts about rhap. He wanted Tim to find them, probably left in the wrecked rental car.

"There goes the rest of the day." Tim shook his head. He had planned to go home and spend time with his family.

"Wish Olson's wife, for me…" Spike requested, backing toward the exit.

"Yeah. I'll go say goodbye." Tim turned and rounded the corner of the waiting area.

A nurse ran by him, then a doctor. He neared Olson's room and heard voices, Catherine crying. He ran in to see her being pushed by a nurse. He grabbed her arm. She glared at him, only slightly letting up her monody. Doctors and nurses gathered around Olson, beepers shrieking and pulsing. He couldn't see Olson through the crowd of hospital green gowns. Catherine pulled on his shirt and a nurse was asking them to leave. Tim couldn't think. The commotion.

What had been a steady blip on Olson's monitor was pulsing fast and almost randomly.

"BP dropped 15 points. He's going into shock!"

A nurse pushed them again and Tim got the message. He hauled Catherine, sobbing and stammering, out of the room. In the waiting area he held her close, wondering what had happened.

"Catherine? Is he waking?"

"No," she said. She wept uncontrollably. "Just…when the…The buzzer…"

She cried and hauled in breath after breath and couldn't seem to finish. Tim held her some more and she sobbed on his shoulder. A doctor found them in the waiting area.

"Mrs. Olson?" he said.

She nodded, wiping tears and stifling shivers.

"Your husband has developed a cardiac arrhythmia as well as low blood pressure and low urine output. He's in shock. We think it's a thrombosis from pancreatic insult during the accident."

"What does it mean, Doc?" Tim asked for her.

"It means he's in an insulin-deficient coma. It means we could see him coming out in twenty-four hours, once we lower his blood sugar."

* * *

Judge's House

After Tim spent the day looking for Priestly's printouts, he, U.S. Attorney Sam Grand, and a male court recorder went to Judge Enebar's home to acquire a court order. Going to a judge's home was not normal procedure, but they had a comrade down and a child-murderer loose. Grand had said it would be fine, as long as they didn't pressure the judge.

The sun had set, and the frigid air hovered around them at the doorstep. A lady opened the door and gestured Tim, Sam and the recorder into the entry, where a small Shinto shrine, with a hanging scroll and a platform for storing shoes, decorated the hall. She closed the door behind them. She had straight black hair and folded eyelids making her obviously Asian. Her open, amiable face held a quick smile.

"Please follow me. My husband is in his den."

The wife led them from the hallway to the north. Tim heard noises, like a news broadcast or sporting event on a radio. In the den, a blazing fire flooded warm yellow light from a huge fieldstone fireplace. In front of the fire sat a glass-topped table, a large sofa and recliner, with matching cushions of Japanese brush-painted, bamboo shoots. On the far wall, stood a row of bookshelves with a liquor cabinet between them.

An older man eyed them from behind a large teak desk in the center. He held a remote control in one hand. Tim glanced at the inner wall. A muted television played a boxing match. The judge wore blue sweats and eyeglasses on top of his head, where thin strands of long gray hair shot in many directions, mostly combed backward. His wide-set chocolate eyes sized up Tim and the attorney.

"Walden," the wife said. "The lawyer has arrived."

"Sam." District Judge Enebar nodded at them. "Sit down, all of you."

Tim sat next to Sam on the sofa. The court recorder unpacked his transcription box and sat in a corner. He began stabbing at his machine, making hardly a sound.

Sam tilted his head at Tim. "This is Agent Tim Delbravo, with the FBI."

"Right. You mentioned him on the phone." Enebar turned to him. "Nice to meet you."

The judge released the remote from his left hand, leaving the match on behind them. His left palm shot over the desk. Tim rose and offered his own left hand awkwardly, which the judge gripped hard, causing pain to shoot through his, still, swollen fingers and sprained wrist.

"You like boxing, Agent Delbravo?"

"As much as the next guy."

The judge smiled at him, then shot a serious glance at Grand.

"Thanks, for seeing us on such short notice," Grand said, pulling open the briefcase he had brought. "Judge Truante is on orders this week, but he went off for the three-day weekend."

"Yes, yes, counsel. Let's move to the warrant issue."

"Agent Delbravo is assigned a homicide and has followed his suspect, using computers, to a private computer system. The suspect is believed to be using the computer to post messages on the Internet. We would like a court order to view the computer and phone records, as well as, set up a trace on the phone there."

Enebar looked over from the screen. "The computer is owned by the suspect?"

"No, it's owned by a private group. They allow public use."

"Which private group?"

"The Michigan Militia."

"Hmm. The militia." The judge shook his head. "Officer, do you suspect the militia's involvement in the murder?"

Tim straightened. "Not at this time, sir."

"How did the suspect use the militia's computer?"

"As a way station, sir."

"Way station?"

"He calls and uploads messages to the Internet."

"And you know this because?"

Grand sat forward and handed some papers over the desk. "Records of computer usage at another site, to which the militia's computer connected. The other paper has a statement from a Washtenaw deputy-detective, witnessing information received from another user on the militia system, that the suspect has employed their computer for communications."

Enebar looked at Grand. "Why do you need the militia's records? Wouldn't a phone trace be enough?"

Tim spoke. "Records of calls made to the militia will give us the suspect's phone number. If he calls back, the trace will confirm."

"How many times do you suppose he's called there?"

"At least once."

"Once?"

"Probably more."

"Once—And you want a trace?" The judge grabbed the remote and punched off the TV. "You only want the number he calls in on?"

"And any files he may have there."

Grand interjected, "Judge, the order request clearly shows our intent. We only want records pertaining to the suspect's calls and use."

Enebar glared at Grand. "But in order to get them, you will seize all the militia's computer files?"

"No," Tim said. "I don't need to take the system. Just search the files, and set up the trace equipment."

"And the phone records?"

"I'll need them too."

"If you need the phone number, then you'll get that through either a trace, or the phone records. I can't allow both."

Grand shifted in his seat. "Judge?"

"A militia computer system—notoriously political. I can't afford you seizing their records without their involvement in the crime. They'll raise hell with the appellate." Enebar turned to Tim. "The militia only has to offer you printed records of the files. And you must choose between a trace or the phone records, not both."

Monday, February 17

Autarkic Franchise

Tim concentrated on the militia. With Olson in the hospital, still in a coma, he had little choice. The militia was the next logical step in his investigation. He drove out to Dexter on Huron River Drive, which ran through the town on its way from bodies of water like Portage Lake. It continued south and finally into Lake Erie. Ironically, it never touched its namesake, Lake Huron. Around the shores of the river sat sawmills and cider-presses. The terrain was hilly for Michigan and full of tall, barren trees flowing with the river roads.

Just outside the main part of Dexter, sat the *Founder's Franchise*, home of the army surplus and gun shop. Tim pulled off the road. In the back room he would find the *Autarkic Franchise* computer bulletin board system, both owned by Grady Lonque.

The residency's file on the Dexter branch of the Michigan Militia was large enough that he only skimmed it the night before and it still took him hours. It also contained vast amounts of information about the state-wide organization of the Militia and its ties to other state militias and armed-citizen groups.

The Michigan Militia Corps, called the "Wolverines," was the second largest state militia, according to the report, compiled mostly by Spike. The

Michigan Militia was as well trained and armed as any, and was nearly the fiercest in verbally attacking the federal government.

The Wolverines' membership consisted of mostly white male, along with a few of their wives. But it was no wonder, considering that this outpost of the militia apparently had ties to the good ole-boys of the KKK. One of the larger factions of the Ku Klux Klan had kept its epicenter in Waters, Michigan where it monitored a wavering Klan membership nationwide. The background section in Spike's file hypothesized several credible links between the state militia and the Klan there.

When it came to organization, the militias, and particularly the Michigan strain, went high-tech. The militia movement was probably the first national action group to organize and direct their activities on the Internet, back in the days when it was barely a phone-to-phone *BBS*.

Hando was rumored, according to a skinhead, to hang out on a militia computer bulletin board system, and Tim worried the militia was somehow neck-deep into the affair. They were active on over a dozen militia-related newsgroups. The movement had repeatedly procured time on public-access channels throughout the community. That is, they enjoyed broadcasting their pastimes, like Hando did his. Militia members nationwide—many of which were communications experts—had skillfully connected a national chain of computers. They called their creation The Patriot Network.

The *Autarkic Franchise* was just one of hundreds of these systems. A small out-of-date computer with hardly any budget. A minor knot in The Patriot Net. The place where, Tim suspected, Hando connected to LeFerril's *zip-per.net*, and to the Internet at large.

Grady Lonque, the Franchise owner and one of the first militia members in the area, had recently purchased his store in Dexter. There he put together the *Franchise's* computer network himself. Grady had learned the skill working at U-M in the Information Technology Division as a telephone and computer technician.

Tim still hadn't had a chance to go over the details with Louis Mott. He just hoped to keep all their operations disconnected. With Sherrie still waiting for sheriff's approval, and everyone else too busy, Tim had to go without backup. Kaplan had said he would go, but Tim would rather be strung-up by a bunch of white supremacists than spend the morning with Kaplan.

He parked in the gravel outside the store and got out. The Franchise lay cozily at the opposing end of a river turn. It was large enough to serve as a ranch style house and store with three entries. Over a blue doorway hung a sign welcoming customers. He walked up to it, kicking stones and snow against the wood frame of the steps.

Before entering, Tim checked his gray suit pocket to ensure he had the court order and his gun with him. It took so much to get the warrant; he chose the trace over previous phone records, since he wasn't sure if Hando used the same phone every time. The rest of the order only compelled the militia to hand him files, not allow him to dig them out himself.

Inside, he found the store typically laid out—a full range of ammunition and guns. The aisles were packed with camping gear, hiking boots, camouflage knapsacks, canteens and other surplus paraphernalia. One entire section was dedicated to large, single-blade knives. Hunting knives and survival blades with compasses, lighters, medicine pouches, and other items stored in the handles.

Once he got two steps in, Tim fully expected to have all eyes turn on him. A black man in a militia surplus store would be quite a rare event. But to his surprise, no one even noticed him. A woman behind the counter added and tallied inventory without a head-turn. Two men continued discussing the finer points of some camping gear. One of them could have been the owner, according to a photo in the background file.

Tim meandered through the wares. Behind the main counter stood rows of rifles on a *President's Day* sale. One rifle was labeled the *Executive Veto*. A quick perusal indicated that all appeared to conform with the assault-ban regulations. Another aisle contained literature—hiking maps and camping guides, as well as political prints and tracts. A line-up of militia milieu and patriot propaganda. He stopped to look over some of it, and he began reading one pamphlet about the "Zionist Occupational Government" that the author claimed was the U.S., when a big voice startled him.

"Can I help you?"

Tim nearly dropped the tract as his eyes met the man's. A tall, burly mountain man stood in green fatigues. Had to be Grady Lonque. He watched Tim, looking kind of like a U.S. Army Santa Claus in training—without the gray-white chin and wintry raiment.

Tim opened his mouth to say something, but before he did, the man interrupted. "I hope you have a permit for that handgun."

Tim smiled and restrained a laugh. "I don't need one."

"I don't stand for no low-lifes or lawbreakers in my store. You better get out."

Tim reached for his wallet. The woman at the counter watched him. Now they noticed him. Pro-gunners worried about someone carrying?

"I said, you should leave."

He flipped his credentials in front of the storekeeper. "This should guarantee my stay."

The storekeeper scanned the badge and handed it back with a curt nod. "Sorry, Officer. Just want to be sure."

"Are you Grady Lonque?" Tim asked.

"Yep." Grady nodded, folding his arms over his belly. "What can I do you for?"

"I need to see your BBS computer." Tim looked just past Grady at a black parka—something about it looked odd.

"My computer?" Grady unfolded his arms and took a step sideways. He rested an arm on the coat racks and pulled at the coat Tim had noticed. It glimmered, like shiny denim.

"Autarkic Franchise."

Grady nodded, then grabbed the black parka that he had been eyeing. "Pretty good deal, now that winter's almost over. On sale for President's day. And it's made from all natural materials, imported, but assembled right here in the U S of A."

Tim wondered if Lonque was just trying to make a sale, or if there was something more to this. "Natural materials? That looks like polyester or nylon."

Grady smiled. "It's a hemp-cotton blend."

"Hemp? Like marijuana?"

Grady chuckled. "Probably more like the rope hemp, though it's from the same plant family as the herbal hemp. This used to be the number-one cash crop in the U.S. Now it's grown overseas."

"Let me see." Tim took the coat.

"The American Founders, like Jefferson, grew this stuff." Grady folded his arms. "But if you went to a public school, you wouldn't know that. Try it on."

In his hands, the parka felt like thick denim only sturdier and not abrasive. He tried it on and discovered that it fit well. A bit bulky, but warm with goose down insulation. The bottom hung below his suit coat. It had several pockets and an enclosure for the hood.

"Fibers are treated for wet and cold weather. It won't wear out for anything." Grady rubbed a blue coat on the rack. "Real good price, right now."

"How much?" Tim played along. And he liked the coat as well, but he had maybe twenty dollars in his wallet.

"Close out. Thirty-two fifty."

It was a damn good price. Too good. Was this an attempt at bribing him? "Thrity-two *dollars*?"

"That's right. And fifty cents." Grady turned toward the counter and added, "I don't take credit, and usually don't take a check."

It was a steal at that price. "I don't have that much cash," Tim said.

"Well, seeing how you're a man of the seal, I'm sure your checks are good, right?"

"I'm here to look at the computer, Mr. Lonque." Tim pulled out the warrant.

"Okay, make it twenty-seven even. And I cover your tax here."

"I still need to see the computer."

"That's fine. We'll go look at it. Do you want the coat or not?"

"Any warranty?"

Grady reached the counter and opened a record book. "Well, I'll personally guarantee it for ninety days, as long as you don't use it to catch flying bullets."

Tim chuckled. He could use a good parka. His overcoat was nearly ruined with all it had been through this winter. He pulled out his checkbook.

"Just let me see your ID again," Grady requested. He punched the amount on an old cash register.

He fished out his credentials and handed them over. Grady looked them over while Tim wrote the check. After Grady scribbled something on a pad, he handed the credentials back.

"We got the big guns here today. Never sold to a federal servant before."

Grady handed him a receipt. He was quite the salesman.

As Tim took the sales slip, he realized he would have to explain the spontaneous purchase to Janice. "Now let's get down to business. Your computer records."

"Which records?" Grady rounded the counter.

"User-activity."

"Sure," Grady whistled. "Come back. Let's see what we can find."

Hardly a fight. Tim was getting full cooperation. And he was prepared for a real showdown. Grady motioned for him to follow back around the counter and through a doorway.

"Mother, call me if a customer needs me," Grady told the woman. Tim couldn't believe she was his mother.

"Is that your wife?"

"Yep." They passed into a small room full of shelves stacked with boxes, cans and supplies for the store. Grady turned on a second lamp. Dust particles hovered and the air smelled musty. "This is a family business. My two boys trade afternoons helping me with the store, while Mother makes the supper."

He pointed at an old IBM compatible that looked like something bought at an army surplus sale. "That's *Auto*. It's just a real ancient computer for people without high speed, to dial in and get information. Hell, it's so basic, we're not really tied directly to the big Pat."

"You mean The Patriot Network?"

"Right. You did some checking before coming out." Grady observed him. "Well of course you would. See, we're the only local militia and we have to get information on and off the network. At least as long as we can; with these new laws about networks and so on. Anyways, I bought a chunk of net-realty at another place for connecting with the Pat. A dial-in connection, so I could save on long distance."

"Let me guess—you dial into *zip-per.net*?"

"Sure enough. How did you know?"

"That's why I'm here." Tim found a chair and sat. How come LeFerril didn't remember Grady's system was connected to his?

"Sorry, I meant to offer you a seat."

"It's fine," Tim said. "Do you deal directly with the owner of *zip-per.net*?"

"See, I never met the owner. Just been sending a check every three months by mail."

"How long?"

Grady wrinkled his brow. "Hmm. Been two years now. Their phone and address changed again about five months ago."

Maybe LeFerril really didn't remember. Or maybe he was lying.

"So, Officer, what's happened that you had to come all the way to see this piece of junk?" Grady pointed at his system.

"Someone uploaded a file from your computer address to *zip-per.net*. It's involved with a murder investigation."

"Oh sure." Grady nodded and sat behind the computer. "I think I know about that guy."

"What?"

"Yeah. Something like two weeks ago, I think, some guy sent all my users a message, bragging about how guns were a no-good way to kill. He was just plain ridiculous." Grady looked at a rifle on the wall and grinned. He sat on a stool. "Said he was into fire. Wanted to know if anyone at *Auto* knew more about flammables or bombs. And he sent a really sick story about a pyromaniac or something."

"Pyro-kid?"

"Yeah, that's it."

"I want to see that."

"See, I dumped his account and didn't think any more about it. Then end-o-last week I got a call from another user. Certs or Kirks, I think. He wanted to know if the feds were asking about him. Said they were harassing him downtown with questions about a murder. Something to do with that pyro-kid."

Tim nodded. So that was how the skinhead knew. "We have to investigate it."

"Of course," Grady agreed. "If I'd have known that pyromaniac was serious I'd have called the police myself. The message was crazy."

"Can you get it?"

"I don't think so."

Tim reached reflexively for the court order.

"See, I don't have it anymore," Grady explained. "Like I said, I dumped the guy."

"But he sent the message to everyone, so some of them probably still have the message."

Grady nodded. "Maybe. But that's a lot of mail to dig through."

"Just search for 'pyro-kid.'"

Tim folded his hands on his lap, watching as Grady grabbed the dusty keyboard and began tapping on it. The disk whirled, then stopped. Grady said, "I think I found a copy. I'll put it on a disk for you."

"Thanks." Now came the tough part. "I also need to look over some logs on your system. It's—"

"Part of the murder investigation, right?"

"Yes."

"Well, I guess it's not a problem."

Tim, surprised by all the cooperation, moved closer to the computer. "This same guy that sent the message to your system, used it to post a similar story on the Internet."

Grady scratched his brow. "I don't see how. I don't give enough juice to my users to access the Big Net directly."

"It was sent on February eleventh just before four a.m."

"You're saying he used my system to connect to another system through the phone?"

"That's what it looks like."

Grady shook his head and tapped the keys. "You mean to say anybody could just dial any long-distance number from my computer?"

"No, not just anybody. They would have to have system manager privileges."

"See, that'd be just me and one other fellow."

"The other fellow?"

"Yeah, he helps maintain the board. Part of his duties in our organization. Name is Jim Staples."

Jim Staples. The cover name for Mott.

"You said that was February what?" Grady hit the keys again.

"Eleventh. Four a.m."

Grady typed, then pointed. "Here?"

Tim drew closer to get a look. The log revealed that someone had called in at 3:50 a.m., sent some data and told the system to relay his messages by phone to *zip-per.net*—LeFerril's site—after he logged off.

"Wasn't me." Grady shook his head. "See, I never use the phone to call in. I always use the system right here."

Tim nodded. Could it be Mott? He doubted it, but he couldn't exclude the possibility. Not yet.

Grady sighed. "Must have been Staples, God help him. I would never have believed it."

"Look," Tim said, "I'm not sure it's this Staples. It could be a hacker. Probably broke into your system and got the sysop password."

"Broke into my system? Sheesh. Should I do anything about Staples?"

"No." Tim examined the cables and connections on the back of the computer. "I'll have to put a tracer on this phone line, catch every call in."

"See, I just don't know. Does that mean you'll sit back here waiting for calls? Hope he stays on long enough to trace?"

"No. It's all pretty automatic, like caller ID, except it can catch blocked numbers too. There's no waiting. We'll retrieve the numbers remotely with equipment at our office by calling in."

"Grady!" His wife entered the storage room. "There's someone a-looking for a FBI agent here."

"That's me," Tim said, turning in surprise.

"On the phone." She motioned back in the store, then left.

Grady said, "I guess I should ask you for a warrant—for my legal protection."

Tim stood. "I've got it. The tracing equipment is out in my car. I'll just catch this call first."

"See, I have to make sure," Grady said as Tim moved back into the store. "But I'm willing to cooperate with the proper papers and all."

In the front room, Mrs. Lonque handed Tim the phone.

"Hello?"

"Tim." A female—Sherrie Marshall's voice. "They told me you might be there."

"What's up?"

"I'm at the hospital. Olson's waking up."

"I'll be right there."

* * *

Hospital

Tim drove slower than he would have otherwise because the accident was still fresh in his mind. Finding a place to park at the hospital slowed him up, and he cursed as the elevator stopped on nearly every floor. By the time he reached the hospital room, he was sure Olson would be resting again and too tired to speak anymore.

But Olson was still out cold.

Tim met the doctor in the patient room. "I thought you said he was coming out of the coma."

"He is," said the same doctor that had informed them of Olson's insulin problem the day before. "It just takes time to arouse him completely."

Catherine sat in a chair next to the bed. Her eyes were red and swollen. It almost hurt Tim to look at them. Sherrie Marshall stood quietly in a corner. She wore jeans and a cotton pullover. When Tim looked at her, she flashed a smile and began walking to him.

"How much longer?" Tim asked.

"Not much," the doctor said. "He's arousable and can feel pain. He should understand when you speak to him. And talking with him will help bring out his conscious state."

Tim nodded. Marshall stood next to him.

"I'm sorry, Tim. I thought you should hurry when I got the news from the doctor."

"It's all right," he said. He would just go back to set up the trace equipment. At least he wouldn't miss anything Olson might say.

"Harry," Catherine said at the bedside, holding his right hand. "You have friends here. We're all waiting for you to talk with us."

The doctor had said talking would help increase Olson's wakefulness. Tim removed his overcoat—he forgot the new parka—and hung it up. The doctor carried a chart out of the room, promising to send back a nurse.

At the bed, Tim studied Olson. Tubes ran from his arms and nose to life-saving equipment and monitors. His face had small bruises and his nose and cheeks and lips were scabbed. Bandages wrapped his head.

Just like Robinson's. He recalled how Robinson had been wheeled into the Danville ER just ahead of him, blood staining the white strips, and his partner's face almost as bleached. He was brain-dead. Never had a chance to wake. They never could ask him what had happened in that basement.

In California, Tim had gone though the lab notes after being released from the hospital. None of the reviewing jogged his memory further. Only his gun—a vivid image of his hand around the 9mm and it going off, pointed at Michael Miller. Oh everyone had their theory. Even one psychiatrist suggested that one of the perps had gotten Tim's gun, that he had *transposed* the memory of their hand into his own. But the lab reports were clear—Tim had distinctive powder traces on his hand. And only one shot had been fired from his gun—the bullet that ended everything for both the little boy and himself.

And he just took the fall so cravenly. Givens had objected, but Tim thought the punishment wouldn't be so bad. OPR accepted his acquiescence as a confession. The beady-eyed Office of Personal Responsibility was the FBI's own internal team of Joe McCarthy's. Once the blame was cast, they dispensed a fierce censure and closed up the investigation as tight as Robinson's coffin. But Tim wasn't giving in this time. He wouldn't let Olson go the way of Robinson. And Hando the way of...The man's name escaped him, just on the tip of his tongue.

Catherine kept repeating her husband's name. Tim joined her. "Olson." He touched him. "It's Tim Delbravo."

He patted Olson's shoulder lightly. But Olson remained still. "We've been looking for the person that did this to you. Was it Crazy Zig?"

Nothing.

Tim touched his left-hand. "Wiggle a finger. Let me know if Zig did this."

Still nothing.

Tim sighed and let go of Olson's fingers. Exhaustion started overtaking him. He turned to Sherrie. "I'm going out for some coffee. I'll be back."

* * *

Hospital

Maybe she ought to go with him. Coffee sounded about right. But Sherrie didn't want to leave Catherine alone. She sat instead, just watching Tim leave. And then as soon as he went, Olson moaned and shifted his head.

Sherrie jumped up and ran to the doorway.

"Tim!"

He turned from halfway down the hall.

"He's waking, I think." She hoped it wasn't another false alarm.

Tim ran back and glanced at her with wide eyes.

"He moaned," she explained.

At the bed, Catherine stood over Olson, tears streaming and voice repeating his name. "Harry!"

Sherrie leaped to the nurse-page and pressed the button. It beeped repeatedly. Tim hovered over the bed, where Olson was moving his mouth.

"Cat," he whispered.

"I'm right here, Harry."

Olson opened his eyes into small slits, mumbling something else.

"…Hand…"

Tim bent over. "Hando?"

Olson blinked his eyes. "Take…hand, Cat."

Catherine held up his right hand. "I have it." She put it on her belly. "The baby is kicking, Harry."

Olson's lips curved up. He let his head fall to the other side where Tim and Sherrie stood. "Delbravo," he breathed.

"Right here, Olson. Was it Zig?"

He focused on Tim. "Red...A red..."

"A red car. I saw that."

Olson blinked and shook his head feebly. He mouthed something that Sherrie couldn't understand.

"What?"

A nurse ran in and saw them. "Doctor!" she called and squeezed between them, pressing a call button.

Tim backed off. Sherrie could see frustration in his brow and cheeks. She, too, was dying of curiosity.

The nurse began attaching and flipping a new assortment of monitors, hoarding most of Olson's attention for her own. Even Catherine had to move out of her way. Still Olson made another attempt to speak.

"Red..."

"Red?" Tim called from several feet away. "Come on, Harald, What's red? The car?"

"Red...air," Olson groaned.

"Red hair?"

Olson nodded. Catherine moved closer to touch his face and he turned to gaze at her. His eyes bobbed and he let a breath fall noisily from his lips.

"Olson!" The nurse cut in front of Tim. He maneuvered around her. "Is Zig a redhead?"

Olson nodded. "Yes," he hissed.

"You rest for now." Tim relaxed his stance a bit. "I'll get a whole collection of pictures. Every damned redhead in West Quad. We'll get him."

Catherine smiled at Tim and bit her lip, bleary-eyed. Olson attempted to grin through his post-comatose eyelids.

"Like you now," he said faintly.

"How's that?" Tim asked, moving closer.

Sherrie leaned in. The nurse was checking the monitors and the doctor entered.

"When you...got shot," Olson stammered.

"You mean on campus?"

Olson nodded.

Sherrie wondered what they were talking about. Tim got shot?

"I'll get...deco...rated," Olson faltered.

Sherrie watched Tim's mouth choke up, his cheeks squeezing with a bear-sized swallow.

"You're a good agent, Harald," Tim said, voice cracking. He patted his shoulder. "The best they get."

The doctor moved in and cleared his throat. "The patient needs some time, folks. We need to check him. Mrs. Olson should stay, but the rest of you will have to come back later."

Tim moved back. Sherrie grabbed her coat. They left together.

"Need backup? I'm on my own time until the feds' money comes in." Although she felt curious about Tim's prior shooting mishap, she wasn't about to risk another embarrassment like the one she'd caused in the café.

He glanced at her, sliding his arms into his trench coat. "Some help would be great. How would you like to round up some dorm-photos from campus?"

"Sure." That would be an easy one. Sherrie wanted as badly as anyone to find the red-haired freak-show that did this.

* * *

Residency

Before going back to Grady's Franchise in Dexter, Tim passed by the office for his sacked lunch. The news was unexpected.

A message from Givens indicated that CART spotted another message posted by Hando around 11 a.m.—before Tim had a chance to get the trace set up at the Franchise.

Damn!

At his desk, he logged-in his computer and scoured *alt.sex.stories*. He found it almost immediately.

Newsgroup: alt.sex.stories
From: Alven Hando <hando@who.net>
Subject: second installment coming

The time has come, the time is now.
The future is mine, I'll show you how.
Two days hence, a repost goes real.
A story of death, a life I will steal.
You know it well.
A story to sell.
—Alven "Masterful Midas of Murder" Hando

229

Tim shuddered. It was a game to Hando. A damned joke.

In two days, a repost. Something already put up; another story posted once before, but not enacted yet. Hando promised to steal another life.

Tim clutched the keyboard and directed the commands into the keyboard. His fingers flowed freely, energized with fervid vigor and anger. Pouring pure intellect and planning into the clicks and stabs on the keys, he searched for the repost.

The FBI Internet-server had a listing of all news articles for the past two months on the group. Tim had already gone through it all with a fine toothed-comb and found only three fantasies by Hando. All of them about the Ramey murder.

He felt pretty certain Hando didn't have any other fantasy posts. But maybe it was posted even earlier. Maybe in the archives. Or perhaps, just maybe, Hando had used another name.

Damn. Each month there were over two thousand posts—over six hundred rape-snuff stories—posted on the newsgroup, authored by maybe two hundred different writers. It would take him every waking moment to feed them through NCIC and find which matched Hando's writing style. And he had no idea how many months worth to scrutinize.

Hando's address on this post was different than the Canadian e-mail he had used in the past. Tim studied the header and found it actually looked identical to previous posts, excepting the new address. The path looked the same, suggesting Hando still used the militia computer and LeFerril's site to upload the post.

The e-mail address, Tim discovered upon searching online for the site *who.net*, was a forwarding box only. That is, it wasn't a real e-mail site, but forwarded all mail sent to *hando@who.net*, to another address, like call-forwarding on a phone. He couldn't immediately determine where it was being forwarded, and wouldn't dare attempt e-mailing Hando. A large nationwide Internet service sponsored the forwarding site, *who.net*. Using his FBI account, Tim sent an official request for the true address, to where mail was ultimately forwarded.

More than before, he needed that trace at the *Franchise*. Assuming Hando dialed-in again soon, they could locate him before three days. Then finding his past-post would be less essential. He had to get Givens to put a CART member on the search full-time. He should use their expertise with finding a writer's match.

In any event, he could not find anything else by Hando from the past two months. The suspect was much more clever than typical. The order was competition. And Tim was resolved to beat him.

* * *

Autarkic Franchise

It didn't take Tim long to return to the *Franchise*. Grady Lonque glimmered a smile at him when he entered the store and continued wrangling with a customer over the price of a bayonet.

Once the deal was made Grady directed his full attention on Tim. "I knew I'd see you again. You left that coat."

He reached behind the counter and fumbled under it. Grady pulled out the black parka, watching over other customers like a shepherd with his sheep.

Tim took the coat. "I had to run. An emergency."

Grady tapped his wife's shoulder and motioned at the customers. She moved to the floor.

"See, I don't have a lot of time right now."

"Well, I won't bother you too much. I just need to get the tracer set up."

"Maybe not." Grady motioned for Tim to follow him behind the counter. "Just after you left, I got to thinking about what you said. You know, how you do that trace. So I went and retrieved my own Caller ID box from my house phone and put it on the computer line. And wouldn't you know it, right under my own eyes—maybe fifteen minutes later, I got a call. Someone logged-in as the 'sysop.'"

"Just after 11:00?"

"Yeah. Did the same thing as last time." Grady rendered a proud smile. "Uploaded some kind of message to my Internet provider."

"And you got a number on the Caller ID?"

"Yep."

Tim felt excited. Good going, Lonque! "I'm surprised he didn't block the number."

"Well," Grady conceded. "You're a lucky son-of-a-gun. He probably didn't think he needed to."

In the back room, a man sat at the computer. It was Mott.

"Jim Staples, I'd like you to meet…" Grady looked at Tim. "What was your name again?"

Louis Mott turned and glared at him.

"Special Agent Tim Delbravo." Tim held out a hand to Mott. "Nice to meet you."

"We'll see 'bout that," Mott said, sneering at his hand. He turned to Grady. "Why the hell you harboring criminals?"

"Now, Jim. That's no way to treat a visitor." Grady looked down at Mott. "You have no idea if this particular federal servant is like the rest."

Tim was taken back. He expected this reaction at the beginning. And Mott kept his cover well.

"These fed-heads are all the same," Mott cursed.

A real convincing performance. Mott would do wonders in Hollywood.

"Don't get so up-in-arms, Staples." Grady shook a hand at him. "He's not here to investigate us. He's tracking some hacker or another."

"It's a front, I'll bet." Mott spat on the cement floor. "He's probably setting up surveillance right under your nose."

Grady chuckled under his breath, winking at Tim. "Well, Agent Delbravo, let me give you the number anyway. Then I got to go run a store."

"What number?" Mott asked.

"Don't you worry about it, Jim." Grady searched on the computer table. "Now, where did I put it?"

Mott grabbed a slip from under the monitor and held it up. "You mean this?"

"Here," Grady demanded, holding out a large palm.

"He'll just use it to convict another innocent person."

"Excuse me," Tim interjected, experiencing the scene all too naturally. "But if you don't give that up, I'll cite you for obstruction."

Mott scoffed at him, then tore up the paper.

What the hell? Mott!

Tim barely maintained his composure. He stepped forcefully toward Mott, teeth clenched. "You jackass!"

Grady held a hand between them, snickering and belly jiggling. "It's all right, sir. I'm sure the number is still in ID box's memory."

He walked over to the phone line. Tim watched Mott sitting at the computer. He readied to spring at any provocation. Damned idiot! It was almost as if Mott wasn't just *playing* a role.

"Mr. Staples," he directed to Mott, "where were you at eleven this morning?"

"It's none of your damned business." Mott's eyes glistened resentment.

"Cool off, Jim." Grady patted Mott's head, smoothing down his rancor as if petting a barking dog. Then he handed another slip with the number to Tim. "He got here just around the time the call came in."

"Thank you, *Pa.*" Mott bared his teeth at Grady.

Tim inspected the number. A local prefix—Ypsilanti. "Can I use your phone, Mr. Lonque?"

"Sure. Let's go out to the store," Grady said. "Just make sure you use star-6-7 to block my number from the guy's Caller ID. Can't have his retribution—don't carry the fire insurance."

Grady led him out and pointed at the store phone, then joined his wife with a customer. Tim was shocked to see how quickly Grady adapted to his requests. He picked up the phone and dialed the number. It rang and then answered with a hiss. Not a person, but the digital whine of another computer.

* * *

Residency

Ms. Downey handed Tim a message when he returned to the RA. Givens promised a psychological profile would get there that night. It was going on three in the afternoon.

He moved back to his cubicle, thinking about his next step. The more he thought about it, he wondered if Grady might have given him a fake number to throw him off. He'd been taken in by the storekeeper and for some strange reason, seemed to be trusting the man, the careful supremacist, like a colleague.

Tim grabbed the keyboard on his old terminal and launched into the reverse phone index. He searched for the phone number Grady had given him off the Caller ID box. The reverse index indicated that it belonged to a company, a large Internet Service Provider. The company had many phone lines, but the one Tim had, was billed differently. All except one of the company phone lines were paid for by the same person from their accounting department. This one number, although housed at the same address as the company, was paid by someone else. A person named Mason Jager.

Tim swung his chair over to his new computer. He called the number with the modem. It connected and displayed:

Connected to nether.net
Escape character is '^]'
Welcome to the Netherworld
Running FreeBSD
If you're new, type help at the "login" prompt.
login:

He typed help. It displayed a set of instructions, and even the name of the board owner, Mason Jager. It also included the banner: No law enforcement agents are allowed on this board.

The owner was making it clear that his system was not open to warrantless investigations. Another elite board. Hando could own the site or just use it as another transit point on his climb out of the sewer. It was ingenious. Tim had to admire Hando's cleverness—he was moving between old and new technology to make it all that much harder to track him.

A quick check on NCIC indicated that Jager had no police record, no felonies. Jager's site, a "freenet" offering free accounts, would surely hold more clues about Hando's doings. But it would take a court order to search it.

Tim sighed. "Well, there goes the afternoon."

He had no probable cause to link Jager and Hando except that Hando had used Jager's system, *nether.net,* to post his stories. Perhaps Jager *was* Hando, but Tim had no other reason to suspect it. Although he couldn't believe Hando would use his own system for hacking, he couldn't exclude the owner, Mason Jager, as a solid suspect. Still, he doubted any judge would give him permission to arrest Jager without further evidence. If he went to the business site and discovered probable cause, then he could arrest Jager on the spot.

It was late afternoon already, and if he didn't get down there fast, the business would close. Jager would go home. Tim needed to get the evidence quickly before then. If he made the warrant specific, about tracking Hando, he might get it faster. He picked up the phone and dialed the U.S. Attorney.

"Sam, it's Tim," he said when Grand answered. "I need a warrant. Quick."

He gave all the information to Grand and asked him to hurry.

"I'll rush it through. Maybe in an hour. Soon enough?"

"Should be. Thanks, Sam." Tim hung up. He seized his keyboard, and began searching for anymore information about Mason Jager and his site, *nether.net,* when a voice called out.

"Hey, Delbravo."

Tim turned in the cubicle to find Spike coming in. He had on boots, jeans and a flannel shirt. "Chopping some logs, Spike?"

Spike smiled. "No, I was just out in Whitmore with a subject, taking inventory of part of the militia's food and ammo stock."

"Hey, I want to ask you about Lonque," Tim said.

Spike found a chair and sat. "Okay, shoot."

Tim dragged his chair around to face Spike. "Your reports really make them look like a bunch of Nazis in white-hooded knickers, but I got a different feeling when I went to Grady Lonque's store."

"Yep. Lonque can be a real mystery," Spike said. "Did you know his grandfather died in the Holocaust?"

"What?"

"Yeah, he fell from a guard tower." Spike smiled.

Tim chuckled. "Good one."

"Sure. But, truthfully, you better watch him." The smile left his face. "Lonque is a real impersonator. He can be just what he thinks you want him to be."

"Really." Tim stared off, reflecting on the incident at the *Franchise*. Maybe the number was a fake and he should go back and set up that trace after all.

Spike nodded. "Yeah, a real actor."

"Mott too," Tim added. "He really put on a show for me and Lonque today."

"I'm beginning to wonder if it's a show."

"What do you mean?"

Spike tensed in his seat. "He's been doing extracurricular work with some of the real extremists. And I'm sure I don't know the half of it."

"What do you know?"

"It's not much more than a feeling." Spike leaned forward. "And I'm not ready to report it officially, but sometimes at the weekly squad meetings I see him carousing with the die-hards and laughing and joking. Then when I get close enough to listen, he shuts up. I don't know what he's doing yet, and it worries me."

"Yeah. Me too," Tim said. "Keep me posted on anything suspicious at all, will you?"

Spike nodded. Tim's desk phone rang abruptly.

"See ya, Delbravo." Spike left. Tim answered his phone.

"Please hold for Senator Euler," a woman's voice said.

Jeez. Not again.

"Agent Delbravo, This is Senator Jack Euler from Nebraska. I'm sure you haven't forgotten."

"Tried to, but you know…"

"How dare you, sir! How dare you accuse me of playing games and abusing our God-given democracy for deceitful reasons."

"I guess I got printed then?" Tim knew he shouldn't have spoken a word to that reporter.

"I should have you charged with libel!" The senator's voice shrilled with anger.

"I believe it's slander when spoken. And I only gave my opinion, sir."

"I'll have your badge! You will not ruin my hard work on the D-chip legislation. A whole year, six resolutory votes, I've waited for it to clear the Senate and House. I will not let a flag-burning, ACLU card-toting louse like you destroy this."

"No, I'm sure you won't." Tim hung up. He tried to forget it and go back to work, but the senator's threat remained buried inside his gut. Somehow he felt Euler was connecting himself more to the case every day.

* * *

Nether.net

Grand delivered, as promised, a quick, but specific warrant for *nether.net*. He apologized to Tim that it had taken so long, but said it was the best he could do on short notice. Tim told him not to worry; they still had an hour to spare.

Tim arrived at the structure housing *nether.net*, accompanied by a pair of city police officers and armed with a portable hard drive and tracing equipment. Apparently, the company was the second largest Internet Service Provider in Washtenaw County, as well as a computer outlet store, a repair shop, and a software consulting center. A full-fledged company with wings of many colors and sizes.

A receptionist directed him and the officers to where the owner of *nether.net* worked. She referred to Mason Jager as the "Boy Wonder." Heads turned from rows of cubicles as they passed by. She led them to a three-wall cubicle, where a kid, presumably Jager, sat before three computers situated around a circle. His once-blonde hair was streaked with purple dye, set long and straight in overgrown Dutch-boy style. Tim knocked on the cubicle partition, setting down his bag with the tracing equipment.

"Yeah?" The kid rotated around. He couldn't have been over eighteen or nineteen.

"Are you the owner of *nether.net*?" Tim reached into his black parka. He actually loved it. Very comfortable and warm.

"Mason Jager." Jager squinted at the two police.

Tim pulled out his credentials. "FBI. SA Delbravo."

"Holy shit!" Jager's eyes darted and his face flushed. "That was fast. Never thought it'd be the FBI."

"Oh?" Tim glanced at the officers then at their cuffs.

"I want an attorney," Jager said. "I'm not saying a thing."

"You don't have to say a thing." Tim held up the warrant. "Just move away from the computer nice and slow."

"Damn!" Jager wheeled his chair back.

The officers remained at the doorway. Tim sat before the three monitor-keyboard pairs. "Which one is the *nether.net* site?"

"All connect, but the middle one *is* nether-net," Jager said.

At the keyboard, Tim checked the system name with *uname-a*, and verified that Jager had told the truth.

"What the hell is going on?" It came from a new voice, a man's deep vibrato.

Tim turned. A man, business slacks and cotton button-up, pushed his way passed several observers and into the cubicle. The officers restrained him before he reached Tim. He looked at them, then at Tim and finally at Jager.

"Dammit, Mason. What'd you do?" he asked the kid.

"Hell if I know." Jager shrugged.

The man looked at Tim. "I'm the Boy Wonder's supervisor. Can you tell me what this is about?"

"FBI." Tim flashed his ID. "I'm investigating criminal use of Jager's site, *nether.net*."

"I didn't do nothing," Jager said.

Tim asked him, "Where do you store user-activity logs?"

"On the computer, of course." Jager grinned at him.

"What path?"

Jager told him the directory path, and Tim searched for Hando's name.

The computer found several matches. The last one showed a log-in at 11 a.m. that morning, for a user: *hando@nether.net.*

Score two! Tim stopped himself from shouting out loud.

"Do you have a warrant?" the supervisor asked.

Tim, hardly moving his eyes off the screen, held out the warrant. The supervisor swiped it from his hand.

The records indicated that Hando had logged-in from the phone line coming into the system. In other words, Hando had called Jager's computer remotely from yet another computer. The next entries listed commands instructing a second phone line to call Grady's computer. It confused Tim. First, why would Jager, if he were Hando, call into his own system if he were sitting there at the office? Second, how did he call out while calling in? Tim sent the logs to a printer sitting under the table.

"This warrant doesn't touch us," the supervisor said.

"What do you mean?" Tim asked, rotating back.

"We let the Boy Wonder keep his own computer site here. It's not an ISP like the rest of our servers. He offers free shell accounts over his private phone line here. We let him keep it here, but only because he gives out free help to our customers through it. We're not liable for what happens on his system."

"Fine," Tim said. "I'm only after data on his private system. And, if needs be, a tracer on the phone line."

"Just to be sure, I'm taking this." The supervisor waved the warrant. "I want our legal staff to look at it."

"Be my guest," Tim said. The supervisor waded back through the crowd of employees watching the show. Tim rotated toward Jager and flattened out the printout he had just retrieved. "This user," he said, pointing at Hando's username, "called in by phone. But I know from logs, he was calling out at the same time."

"Yeah, I have two lines connected to my system," Jager said.

"But you only pay for one."

"Yeah, well, I have my private line, and my supe also let's me borrow one from here. But only *superuser* can call out on the loaner."

"Why call in? Why not use broadband or wireless?"

"Yeah, I do, but I use a modem with my cell and a palmtop when I am out and about. Not often, since I'm only supposed to use it off-hours."

"Wait. So you call in on your private line, and then call out on the company line?"

"Sometimes I call in, never back out," Jager said.

"But it can be done?"

"Yeah, sure. Either line can call in or out. But like I said, I'm the only one that can do it, and if I find anyone hacking my system, they'll be roadkill when I'm through."

Jager's volunteering information signaled that he probably wasn't Hando. "Where were you at eleven this morning, Mr. Jager?" Tim asked.

"I, uh…I was in a staff meeting most of the morning."

"It's true," said a lady from the crowd behind the police officers. "Our supervisor held a strategy meeting from ten to noon down the hall. Mason was with us. Jen was there, too." She pointed at another girl in the crowd who nodded her affirmation of the story.

"Did Mason have access to any computers in there?" Tim asked.

She shook her head.

"Did he leave at any time?"

She shook her head again. Jen, the other associate, also shook her head. "Not that I remember."

"That user ain't me," Jager said. "If that's what you're thinking."

"Do you know who he is?"

"No, but I keep a record of when his account was made up."

"Address and full name?"

"No, I don't ask for personal info, 'cause it does no good. They could lie and I'd never know. But do I record when they created the account." Jager pointed at the printout. "Right there, in fact. It's shows this guy has been on my system for three weeks."

Tim looked at the paper. The first entry in his search showed a username and password creation for user *hando*, on January 29. It did not list personal information anywhere in the logs. He also realized that Lonque must have been telling the truth about the phone number.

"Okay, Mr. Jager, don't leave town." Tim grabbed his bag. "For now, I'm putting a tracer on that phone line."

He pulled out the tracing equipment and started setting up. The next time Hando posted by dialing in, Tim would phone the number and signal the tracer to give him a dump on numbers that had called it, including Hando's number. But he would have to trace both lines since Hando could conceivably call in on either.

Jager pointed to a phone cord that attached in the back of a computer. "That's the private line."

"What's the second number?" Tim asked.

Jager gave it to him. Tim needed to monitor the lines and Hando's online activity without his awareness. He needed Hando's password so he could read all his files and any more the idiot might write.

"A couple of things to remember," he told Jager as he attached the tracer. "First, you can not, will not warn any users about the trace. Second, it's a federal offense to tamper with this equipment—it's been sealed."

The supervisor entered, followed by another man wearing an Italian suit with broad stripes and cuffed pants. He had puffy gray hair and a full mustache.

"I'm legal counsel here," the suited man said. "I suppose you have identification?"

Tim pulled out his credentials. The lawyer glanced at it briefly and said, "I've read the warrant."

"Fine," Tim said, turning back to Jager. "I want you to give me the password to the suspect's account."

"Don't give him anything, Mr. Jager." The lawyer held up a hand. "Your warrant doesn't go that far."

Tim said, "I can call the U.S. Attorney."

Jager looked at his supervisor, bewildered.

"Good. Then have him explain this to you," the lawyer said. "The warrant specifically provides you a copy of certain suspect files in your investigation. It allows a tracer on the phone lines. But it does not say anything about getting accounts or passwords."

Tim cursed silently. Damned judge! Damn Grand.

"Then I'll be back with a full warrant to search all of your computers. Everything connecting to your company network." Tim stuffed the printout in his bag.

"If the judges believes that's what it takes," the lawyer lifted the corner of his mouth, "then we'll happily assist you. But I think you're sniffing too hard."

Damned lawyers.

* * *

Residency

Tim returned to the RA after six that evening. E-mail to him from the *who.net* forwarding site verified that mail sent to *hando@who.net* was indeed forwarded to *hando@nether.net*. Hando had only one real account, the one on Jager's site. Unfortunately, the forwarding service had no other real information about Hando, since they didn't require legitimate names or addresses to create the forwarding account.

Even then, Tim was amazed that Hando had posted a real forwarding address to the newsgroup. He would get bombarded with e-mail, unless he turned off the forwarding.

On Tim's desk lay a yellow message from Ms. Downey. It said DC had faxed the psychological profile. The secure fax machine sat in Kaplan's office on a table next to a shredder. Tim sorted through several transmissions until he found the one with his name on it. The stack was from DC, the suspect profile of the Bill Ramey murder. He had been waiting for it ever since learning about the Ramey murder.

Back in the cubicles all of the berths remained empty, only Tim had stayed late this evening. He perused the pages. It was from Henry Keaten, one of his favorite instructors from the academy. Keaten, a brawny, tattooed ex-marine with hair and glasses over a cliff-like brow, had helped pioneer profiling in the late 1960s. Now he was retired and had his own private profiling business for rich individuals and companies.

"*Delbravo,*" Keaten had written on the cover sheet. "*I noticed your request while passing through Virginia this past week. Your case intrigued me so I took it myself. Still with computers, eh? Go AWOL! —Keaten.*"

"Go AWOL" was always Keaten's maxim. "Go And Work to Obtain Luck."

In the first page, the words: *Mental State* jumped out right away. Keaten said he believed the assailant was post-schizophrenic and emerging into a "*complex psychopath.*" Keaten defined this as:

"*Probably someone local who is a loner, but is now emerging from his solitude and confronting his faults by mutilation of others—a little beyond your typical simple schizophrenic.*"

Tim knew a simple schizophrenic was careless, and often left evidence. They acted in fear of domination. A full psychopath, however, would use the same or a similar place and pick nearly identical victims each time with a well orchestrated and developed plan. Psychopaths were egotistical and looked for esteem in their killings, enjoying it thoroughly. Apparently, Hando was a combination, leaning slightly toward "psychopath."

Tim read further.

"The subject probably hates children because he was lonely as a child and spent a great deal of time without childhood friends. Although he was probably ignored by his parents, he likely had other adult friends, even some who might have abused him. From the details of the crime, I'd guess the assailant's age is around twenty to twenty-five."

Young teenaged or very old killers would avoid brutal violence, Tim knew. But twenty- to forty-year-old killers were usually the most barbaric. And pyromaniacs like Hando varied in their level of destruction according to age as well. By the manner of planning it on the newsgroup, Keaten proposed that the subject was keeping records to get attention. Yet he still wanted to keep his identity unknown.

The profile was helpful, but Tim couldn't name any names with it. He would get Hando's real identity online.

* * *

Apartment

That night, Tim caught up on all the world news he had been missing since the case heated up. The weatherman predicted that not only was the ground hog scared of his shadow this year, but was burrowing deep underground for the bitter arctic blast that would choke the area in the coming days.

Senator Euler made headlines. Computer corporations usually opposed to any form of censorship on the Internet were scraping their shins raw to get in the long lineup supporting Euler's D-Chip legislation. The senator, for his part, was predicting horrible future crime waves on America's networks and against the nation's children, if his bill didn't pass. He cited the "boy murdered in Ann Arbor" as a first example of more to come.

Janice brought Tim's dinner into the family room so he could eat and watch. Tim flipped off the TV, and asked her how her day had gone.

"Busy," she said, clearing the table. "You got a message while I was out. And, Tim—"

"Out?" Tim put his plate down and moved to the answering machine. It sat on a teetering stack of notes and old letters.

"I went to some of the elementary schools." Janice returned from the kitchen. "One has need for a substitute right away."

She would start working, that meant. Tim pushed the play button on the machine.

"*Hello. This is for FBI agent Timothy Delbravo.*" A familiar voice. "*Mr. Delbravo this is Grady Lonque. Sorry about calling your home. We have to talk about Jim Staples. I'll try you again later.*"

Tim grabbed a phone book and searched for Grady's number.

"Tim."

"Just a minute." Grady's personal number was not listed, but the Founder's Franchise was. He dialed the store. It rang four times and then a machine answered; Grady's shop was closed for the night. He replaced the phone.

"Tim." Janice stood next to him, holding her hands on hips. "I know what happened."

"What do you mean?"

"The accident. An agent put into a coma. It was in the newspaper. You were nearly killed, Tim."

"The agent is out of the coma."

"But I had to learn about it from the newspaper."

"It's just...I just don't want you to worry."

"So you lie to me?"

"I didn't lie, Janice. I told you we had an accident."

She looked at the ground. "I'm going crazy, Tim. You get hurt, another agent's in a coma, and you downplay it like it was nothing. Then you spend every moment at work."

"A kid got murdered, Janice."

"I know. It's horrible. But your own kids need you, too. Alive, Tim."

Tuesday, February 18

Hospital

Olson grinned as widely as his frostbitten lips allowed on the fifth photo sheet of the West Quad residents. "That's him. Crazy Zig," he said, pointing at a redhead.

"Great." Tim viewed the picture. The name below the photo was Pat Fairborne. He wrote it in his casebook. "Keep looking. Two more."

Olson, still bedridden, was recovering fairly quickly. The doctor had said he would be able to leave in a few days. Tim felt relieved.

"You think Zig is Hando?" Sherrie asked. She had obtained the dormitory photos late the day before. Funds and permissions were set, and now she was Tim's partner. At least until the bureau found a spare.

"Could be," Tim said. "I'm also checking out a guy named Jager, though he has blonde hair."

"The dandruff pigments implied dark hair."

"Well, Zig is red. I'm sure we'll figure it out soon." Things were moving now. Tim felt confident. Grand was moving carefully on the warrant this time. He said they could get one for Hando's account by mid-morning.

"I think that's the Roman." Olson pointed at another photo. The name below it read Carl Ponke.

"That's two."

Olson flipped the last few sheets. "I didn't see the third guy."

"Go through the photos again. Be sure," Tim encouraged. They had to find that last one. Even if it meant forcing a confession from Zig or the Roman.

But after another round, Olson still didn't recognize the third photo.

"Maybe he's not a student," Olson said.

"We should get a sketch," Sherrie suggested.

"Could the sheriff spare an artist?" Tim asked. "We have to sign them out from DC, a week in advance."

"I'll ask."

Tim tilted his head at the door. "Come on, Sherrie. Let's go pick up some dorm-dips."

Sherrie waved at Olson and his wife.

Tim turned back. "Hang in there. We're gonna need your help still."

"Jeez, I hope not." Olson smiled. "I've had my fill of drag ops."

"What!" his wife said. "You've been working drag?"

* * *

Residency

Tim kept his new parka on, hoping the database search wouldn't take long. He also checked his e-mail. A message from Mark Striker, the Field Office technician, said he could not locate anything written by Hando in the newsgroup archives. Even after going back over nine months ago. Unfortunately the bureau's archives didn't have any more, but there were other databases he could search.

Tim logged on the NCIC terminal and called up any records on Fairborne and Ponke. Meanwhile, Sherrie sat next to him and used the phone to get student information and class schedules.

Sherrie glanced at her watch and set the phone down. "Ponke had only one class today, already finished. We could still catch Fairborne. He has three today, the last in two hours."

"The dynamic-duo also lives together in the dorm," Tim said at the computer. "Odds are we won't find them there, so we'll send out an APB."

"Do their parents live close by?"

"Fairborne is from the Upper Peninsula, by Lake Superior. Ponke is from upstate New York. We'll send local police to their parents' homes."

Tim stood, thinking about Grady Lonque's message. The jolly gun-runner had wanted to tell him something. Time was short; he would call the Franchise when he got back from campus. "Ready?"

She grabbed her coat and stood with him. Sam Grand, the federal attorney, entered the cubicle just as they starting leaving.

"How are you, Tim?" Grand had his suit buttoned and held a manila folder. He looked at Sherrie. "Well, hello."

Introductions always came awkward for Tim. "Attorney Sam Grand, my, uh…partner, Deputy Sherrie Marshall."

"Partner, huh?" Grand extended a palm and smiled at her. "Nice to meet you."

They shook hands. Grand turned to Tim. "I almost thought I'd have to bear bad news."

"The *nether.net* warrant?"

Grand nodded. "Judge Truante was on court orders today. He wouldn't budge."

"Truante?"

"He's changed in the past weeks. Ever since the Victor case. I think he's got pressure high-up."

"So we can't get a warrant?"

"Well, since it's the Internet and the jurisdiction extends nationwide, I went to the next district. Judge Tamslen." Grand held up the file. "Pass go, collect two-hundred bytes from the suspect's account."

"Great. We'll go there before campus, then." Tim took the file. "Thanks, Sam."

"No problem. Like last time, just leave the system intact." He clasped his hands, looking at both. "By the way, do you two have dinner plans tonight?"

Sherrie shook her head, looking at Tim then at Grand.

Tim hesitated. "Actually…"

"You know, lawyer-police talk. I want to discuss investigative details for the appeal on the Victor case." Grand patted him on the shoulder. "My place. See you two about six-thirty?"

"I got a lot of work," Tim said.

"We'll make it seven then." Grand dropped his hand and turned toward the exit. "I'll leave directions with your receptionist."

* * *

Nether.net

Mason Jager's eyes about popped from their sockets when Tim and Sherrie entered his cubicle. His purple hair had faded to mostly blonde since the day before. Tim held up the warrant.

"Hey!" Jager's large pupils remained focused on Sherrie. "I've seen you, haven't I?"

"What?"

"Yeah—*alt.sex.pictures*—the cyber-cop spread. Honey, you're better in person."

"Wasn't me." She looked at Tim, rolling her eyes.

Tim sighed. "I've got the warrant for the account."

"Yeah?" Jager turned back to his three computer monitors. "Which one?"

"User Hando."

"That's right, the bastard that hacked my system. I still ain't figured out how he got in. He didn't just guess my password like they do in those cheap movies."

Tim set his equipment bag down on the table. "He probably logged in a normal account when you were on and set up his computer to capture your video stream, saw the characters as you typed in *superuser* password. Like a peeping-tom watching your TV through a window."

"Nah, I use X-authority, so the curtains were drawn."

Tim thought about it. "Well, you said you dial-in at night from home, and phone lines don't secure the video stream if you're only using x-host. He probably pulled the drapes open while you were out of the office."

Jager looked up. His mouth dropped open. "Damn, you're right. I use basic software on my palmtop—have to x-host."

Tim opened his bag and pulled out a backup drive. "I'm going to have to shut you down while I milk the files."

"Shut me down?" Jager scratched his nose. "Why the hell would you do that?"

"For a quick file backup. Then you're giving me his password so I can read any files he tries to write."

"I don't know his password, but I'll create a mirror image of his accounts on a quarantined partition. That way this hacker will still think he's on the system like normal, but he can't go trashing my system."

"Just so I can still get access to his files," Tim said.

"Sure, I'll make you *superuser* on the mirror system. You can do anything there, then." Jager looked back at Sherrie. "You should've brought her in the first time. I wouldn't have dissed you."

Tim tapped the desk. "Hurry, we've got a class to catch."

* * *

West Quad

Sherrie felt glad she had never served time in the dorms. College was bad enough. When she studied criminal sociology at Ohio State, she had lived in a sorority house the first two years and then in a cottage with two of her friends the remainder. She would have gone insane in a place like West Quad.

The halls were full of students, kids running between rooms. Loud music and yelling. "Pretty noisy, aren't they?"

"Not as bad as the dorm across campus," Tim replied. "Where Victor lived."

They walked down the wing where Fairborne and Ponke dormed together. Two uniformed deputies and a dorm manager followed behind.

Sherrie wondered how Tim would actually use the account Jager had created. "So can we catch Hando with this look-alike account?"

"Maybe." Tim walked through the hall and turned down another. "Somewhere in his files there might be a clue where and who he is or what his next move will be. If we can read his e-mail without his knowing, we can watch him planning without knowing about us. And we have the trace to snatch his phone number, too."

"Was there anything in his files?"

"I only had time to make a backup. After we're done here, I'll go back and look at them." He stopped at the end of a hall. "This is it."

Room 154L. Sherrie stood back with the deputies as Tim knocked hard. She pointed her eyes at his just-emptied shoulder holster, and nodded to herself, cupping her Glock in its holster with her palm.

After waiting with no answer, Tim knocked harder and hollered into the door. "Pat Fairborne! Carl Ponke!"

Nothing. Then a student in the next room poked his head out. "They're not there," he said.

Sherrie turned. "What do you mean?"

The student, a blonde kid with braces, blinked and twisted his mouth. "Took off early Sunday morning, like bats-out-of-final's-week. They packed up everything. Made a racket early when all of this hall was still asleep. We yelled at them to shut up."

"Do you know where they went?"

He shook his head. "Just gone. Fine with us. Fairborne was a fruit."

Tim approached toward the student. "Do you know of a third student hanging around with him?"

"No. Can't blame anyone for not hanging with Fairborne."

Tim held up a photo of Zig and the Roman. "Do you recognize these two."

"Yep. They're the two that live here, or did." He squinted and came out into the hall. "Why do you want them?"

"They just won the lottery," Tim said.

The student looked off in thought, then shook his head and retreated to a safe distance.

Tim gestured back at the dorm manager. "Open it."

The floor manager, a balding graduate student, produced a key and unlocked the room. Tim motioned for the uniforms to go in. They held up their weapons and went in. Tim and Sherrie followed.

The room, another example of college clutter, was deserted. Piles of dirty clothes towered in the far corners. Empty hangers dangled in the closets. Beer cans and paper trash lay everywhere. Otherwise, it was cleared.

The student had told them the truth. "Gone."

Tim nodded. "No stereo, phone or TV. They're gone, all right."

"We should interview all the neighbors," she said.

"Agreed. We'll come back later." Tim poked through the trash, opened drawers and looked under the bed. Then he turned to the deputies. "You two stay and watch in case they return."

He touched her arm. "Come on. Let's go to class."

* * *

Campus

Arctic air had swept down into the Great Lakes region and froze Tim's enthusiasm. The clouds over campus looked dismally heavy, as if laden with ice instead of snow, threatening to coat and suffocate all life under them. Tim and Sherrie arrived on campus just before Fairborne's second class ended, early in the afternoon. Fairborne, however, never showed. They questioned several students, who didn't provide any answers, but in turn probed back, asking why he and the deputy wanted Fairborne. Maybe the perp would show at the last class, Tim hoped. He was running out of time. The two days Hando had offered in the last post were nearly up. But he believed Hando's account and e-mail might be the link to finding him now.

Mason Jager had given him an account to access all of Hando's files and e-mail. Not only did it remove most suspicion of Jager, it would allow Tim to monitor and even send messages in Hando's username—sort of "be" Hando without spooking him.

But he hadn't had a chance to try it. Finding the roommates took precedence because direct person contact beat online data and because the classes ran on a schedule; the account, he could access anytime afterward.

Sherrie followed behind. He hiked down the aisle of the large auditorium, and scanned the group of more than eighty students for the familiar redhead. At the bottom, a female teacher stood in front of an overhead projector. The lights remained dim, and the professor didn't notice Tim and Sherrie as she explained about chemical bonds and ringed structures.

Tim ignored the lecture. He still couldn't make out the redhead. Sherrie shrugged at him. Now he listened to the lesson, waiting for a moment to interrupt courteously. But his patience was growing thin. Olson assaulted, Hando promising a new victim—he'd had enough. Time was short. Politeness could take a back seat. Tim walked up to the instructor and tapped her on the shoulder as she drew an octagonal molecule on a transparency.

"Excuse me," he said. "Do you take roll?"

The instructor shook her head, lifting her brow.

"I need to make an announcement."

"What? Who are you?"

"FBI," he whispered, turning away from the class. He discreetly showed her his credentials.

She nodded and stood at the front. "There's a gentleman here from the FBI. He has an announcement."

The class went deathly quiet as she motioned to him. He wished she hadn't mentioned the bureau, but it happened last time, too. At the front, he cleared his throat and made one last scan for Fairborne. Sherrie moved to the back, near the exits.

He straightened and spoke loudly. "We are looking for one Pat Fairborne, registered for this class. He's about five-foot-nine and has bright red hair."

No one spoke out. The same as the last class. "Anyone who knows anything about his whereabouts, please speak up."

Nothing. "If anyone learns anything about his whereabouts, please contact the authorities immediately." He turned to the instructor and offered the floor back. What a waste of a morning. If anyone knew Fairborne, they sure weren't telling the authorities. Hando, and now Zig, were just as unreachable as before.

The teacher resumed her lesson. He tramped up and marched through the exit, nearly slamming the door hinges against the frame. By the time he was outside of the building his frustration had him cursing under his breath. If they had been quicker, they might have caught Fairborne in his dorm room. Now the punk would know the feds are looking, and would stay in hiding.

"Tim!" Behind, Sherrie scurried up.

He glanced back just as she joined his side and caught a glimpse of another person—a young student wearing a fraternity baseball cap reversed over his thick hair. The student waved Tim down, slipping into an over-sized ski parka and fumbling with a large book bag.

"Hey!" the kid yelled and waved again. "Mr. FBI man!"

Perhaps the student knew something about Fairborne, but was too shy to speak up in front of his classmates.

"Slow down a minute, will ya?" The student vaulted past them and stood right in their path. "I just want to ask you something."

Tim and Sherrie stopped and stepped back to the edge of the sidewalk. The student finished putting on his baggy coat and pursed a playful smile. He chewed gum with his front teeth. Tim waited for him to speak first.

"Can you tell me why you want, uh, what's this guy, Fair...What's it?" The kid slowed his chewing and narrowed his eyes.

"Pat Fairborne. Do you know him?"

The student looked over at Sherrie and his smile grew big. "Me? Oh, I just want to know why you're looking for him."

He wouldn't play games with this beer-chugging frat kid. "Do you or don't know anything about him?"

The student hauled in a deep breath. "I know you're looking for him. He's in trouble, right?"

"Look, if you know something, then tell me. Otherwise move aside."

The kid removed his cap and narrowed his smile. "Hey, I'm sure I can help you, but first I need some information. Then we'll talk about what I can do."

Tim's forehead grew hot. Around them, several students paused to see what was happening. "I don't make deals. Tell me what you know. And give me some ID."

The kid seemed amused by Tim's irritation. "You want my draft card, or my ACLU membership? Just so you know, my lawyer loves to cross-examine cops."

"Look, you…" Tim jabbed his finger into the student's coat, then noticing the large crowd, held back his temper. Someone at the periphery caught Tim's eye.

"I…I…think you better stop touching me." The kid blinked, then gulped. "I don't really know this guy you're after."

"Then why did you stop me?" He glanced away from the kid and surveyed the group.

"For my story—the campus paper, you know."

"The…" Tim's eyes continued on the collection, his attention diverted by someone familiar. Along the rim of students, one looked at him with fearful eyes. Just as it registered that he was looking at Kurt Victor, the first student backed away.

Victor. Back in school after threatening to sue U-M. Victor, who started this whole mess. He and Hando contriving and threatening. And escaping. One through so-called justice and the other through hiding. Victor, the friend of Hando, maybe even friends with Fairborne.

Victor *will* answer his questions.

He pushed past the first student. Apparently Victor sensed the imminent avalanche about to fall on him, and began cowering through the crowd, thrusting himself between and around bodies until he plunged back onto the clear sidewalk. The crowd made an instant hole for Tim as his large frame surged behind his former case subject.

"Tim!"

He hardly heard Sherrie as Victor scurried away. He dashed forward. A few yards from the crowd, he grabbed Victor by the elbow.

"Don't touch me, you asshole!" Victor pulled his arm and jerked away.

"I just want to ask you something."

"I don't want to talk with you." Victor turned again.

Tim grabbed Victor's coat, not in a rough way, but just to keep him from leaving. "Pat Fairborne. Do you know him?"

Victor's eyes quivered. "I shouldn't talk with you. Bug off."

"You want to go down to the FBI offices? We can talk in private there."

"Bite yourself."

Tim couldn't just leave him alone. He had a feeling Victor knew Fairborne. "Is Fairborne Alven Hando?"

Victor's eyes hinted a smirk, then tried to cover it by looking at the crowd, which had followed and formed an enclosure to watch the questioning.

Tim pulled his coat and began hauling him toward a building. Maybe he could find a room and interrogate in private.

"Don't!" Victor fought against his grip. "I didn't do nothing."

Tim halted next to a snowy dirt-bed. "Oh no? You didn't do *nothing*. Nothing except harass a girl. Nothing but encourage a murderer."

"What? That's bullshit."

Tim's jaw locked. He drilled a glare into Victor. "Your friend Alven Hando killed a little kid. Something he had wanted to do with you a couple of months ago."

Victor shook his head, jaw flapping back and forth. "You heard my lawyer. It was only…just a…"

"Just a game?" he finished, gripping Victor's collar. "Let's try twenty questions. First one is, where does Hando live?"

"You arrest me for no good reason, then want my help? Go press your fat black lips on my lawyer's ass."

A volcano erupted inside Tim, anger flowing over his restraint. He hauled Victor closer to the door of a large building. "Look, you twirp, tell me what you know or I'll bust your butt for obstruction. You can play games, back in prison."

Victor's face, starting with the outer corners of both eyes and then his mouth, hardened like a clay mask. His pupils flattened and sneered at Tim. "You couldn't survive the games they play there. You butt-kissing putzhead."

Tim tightened his grip on the coat and yanked up until he held most of the kid's weight. "Where is Hando!"

Victor spat in his face. "Bite my ass."

Tim, spit dribbling down his chin, felt his free hand clench the air, making a fist at his side. He couldn't hit the bastard, but the least he could do was make him piss his pants. He held Victor's coat and shook him. Victor smiled even bigger with eyes focused just past him. Then a flash from the side cooled Tim's anger.

A camera.

Sherrie stood just beyond the crowd, her hand concealing and tugging on her opened mouth. His grip released and his fist opened. Victor fell to the ground. Flashes engulfed them. The gathered crowd gasped in unison, mumbling and pointing in amazement. Victor got up and ran. The first kid, a student reporter, aimed a camera at Tim, capturing his frown and surprise on digital memory ready for worldwide transmission.

* * *

Office

"What the hell were you thinking!"

Tim didn't want to reply to Kaplan. He sat in the RAC's office with his eyes glazed and only tokenly aimed at the man.

"Two newspapers called before you even got back to the residency. Then Washington called Detroit. And SAC Hansen yelled at me for ten minutes with words I didn't think administrators knew."

Tim focused on Kaplan now. The man's blue veins were growing over his brow like roots along a cliff. Why would the senior resident believe him? He'd been looking for an excuse to tear Tim apart, and now he had one.

"Well? I'm waiting for an explanation!" Kaplan threw open his desk drawer and extracted a bottle of Mylanta. "Detroit is demanding it. Washington is right behind."

Tim bit the tip of his tongue. What could he say? It wouldn't matter to Kaplan.

"Don't you get it? This could mean beach-time, *mister*. Maybe permanently."

Tim only shook his head. That wouldn't happen, would it?

"What? Is that a reply? 'No'?"

He swallowed. "I made a mistake." He spoke meekly.

"A mistake!" Kaplan chuckled. "You're a disaster. A lifelong muck-up!"

Tim thought about the other residents: Mott and Spike. About Sherrie and Givens and every other agent he'd ever worked with. Would they share Kaplan's sentiments now?

Kaplan took a swig from his white bottle. "Did you know that the FBI has never ever had an agent charged with brutality? You may not be the first agent ever to hit a subject, but did you have to do it right in public?"

"I didn't hit him."

"The reporter got pictures!"

"Not of me hitting him."

"The kid was flat on the ground."

"I didn't hit Victor. He just fell."

"Oohh. I see." Kaplan nodded sarcastically, his eyes big and red. "This little moron just happened to be walking next to you, and you just happened to *accidentally* push him, and just coincidentally a mob of students witnessed it. And a pesky little reporter caught it all on video."

"No! The deputy will testify. I never hit Victor!" Tim stood from the chair, the student's name hanging in the air.

The phone rang. Kaplan lifted the handset. "Yeah?"

He pulled his glance from Tim, who sat again.

"Transfer to here, Tammi."

A pause.

"Sir. Yes...Which one?"

Again, the whole event continued reminding Tim of the endless interviews and meetings after Danville, the accidental shooting. The blame he had taken, he accepted openly because it had higher purpose. The demotion, though harsh, eventually dulled after a time. Then with the promise of promotion raised, now vanishing again, he searched for some higher meaning in his actions. He had been controlled enough, hadn't he? Justified in a little interrogation?

He could excuse nothing, however, and knew Janice would not see it so kindly either. She would feel betrayed. He had struck a mortal wound against both lovers. His wife and the FBI.

If suspended, they wouldn't allow him in the office for a while. Which meant no more case and time at home, facing Janice, the children. Defeat. There just had to be some way to convince Givens.

On the phone, Kaplan whispered a curse.

"Sir?...I read it...Four?" He scribbled on paper. "Yes, sir. I can do...I am sorry about this."

Kaplan rubbed his head, messing up his hair until the bald spot it was meant to hide became obvious. "I'll keep you informed."

He hung up the phone and glared at Tim. "That was SAC Hansen. You're to hand me your credentials and weapon. He's holding a meeting about your suspension at four this afternoon."

Although Tim half-expected it, the shock was still brutal. He'd be suspended. Maybe even discharged from the bureau.

* * *

There was a time when the FBI could brag that no agent was ever convicted of a felony while working for the bureau. Tim had learned it was because the suspected agent would always resign, then get arrested his first day out. He also knew this because he saw it used on a former partner.

In an average year, a half-dozen agents would be dismissed. Perhaps a baker's dozen that would resign while under investigation. In California, the Office of Professional Responsibility had offered Tim the easy way out, but he refused, knowing they couldn't dismiss him for an accident.

His third partner, Esteban Morales, had not been so fortunate. He was not so much Tim's partner as his team leader in the New York City Field Office. There Tim spent his second assignment, almost a decade earlier. They had four agents on the team working bank robbery and major burglary cases. Tim was the computer expert. He monitored suspicious wire-transfers and computer data theft.

Morales, a stocky and short Hispanic, had achieved great notoriety as one of the FBI's top break-in artists, a man for whom hardly a lock, safe or door remained closed. He had built his reputation installing wiretaps and bugs in the most difficult places: Mafia homes, offices of political figures and millionaires, Soviet bloc embassies. When the FBI received a new director, they called in Morales to change the locks in the administrator's home and office.

Morales was one-in-a-million, regarded so highly, that by age thirty-five he was leading a crack team of agents against the most notorious bank robbers and burglars in the Big Apple. Tim, like everyone, loved him. The team was out on a case one weekend, when Morales didn't show up.

On that Saturday afternoon in a New York Federal Credit Union, where most agents banked, a janitor walked in and turned on the lights. He was about to start vacuuming when he found Agent Morales crouched behind the counter, a safe opened behind him. In a bag next to him, there was $18,000. The janitor pressed the alarm as Morales jumped up and yelled, "Halt! FBI."

The janitor froze. Morales arrested him.

The following week, the team was questioned, and Morales underwent a series of polygraph tests. His story remained that someone had called him down to the Credit Union. He went to investigate and found the door unlocked, then saw the safe. That was when the janitor had startled him, and he arrested him, thinking that he was the robber.

Morales failed the polygraphs, his prints were on the pick at the bank, and the caller never came forward. OPR also learned that Morales had amassed large debts, especially after doctors diagnosed his daughter with multiple sclerosis.

They hadn't charged him with the crime, but everyone knew what was coming when the ASAC asked him to resign.

Morales never made it to the office the day he had promised to sign the resignation. His body was found in the Hudson. Foul play was ruled out. His wife claimed she never saw a suicide note. The insurance companies settled for a quarter-million. The bureau paid some of his retirement to the widow.

Tim thought about Morales, how he must have felt cornered. How the team leader cast his life into the river to keep his family afloat.

Now after giving the bureau his all for almost twelve years, Tim's own career was shipwrecked. He would be lucky if they sent him a paper sailboat. All he could do was bail water, look back at the wasted years.

* * *

Residency

Stripped of his badge, 9mm Sigma and his anger, he left Kaplan's office. He found Sherrie reading from the case file in his cubicle. It was something else he would be giving up soon enough. The full Hando case.

His gut bubbled with the tension. He had fought and scratched his way out of the hole he fell into after Danville. Just about the time he was ready to win, to go all the way back, he would lose every last thing. And Hando would be free for more slaying. Breaking this case was to be his final hope of redemption.

"Great reading," Sherrie said, holding the case file. "You write exciting stuff."

He sat next to her. The complete shock of it all had awakened him sharply. His emotions were a raw edge, cutting his very heartstrings. "Look, Sherrie. I want you to take the entire file and copy it."

Her eyes moved across his face. "They're suspending you."

He nodded. "Just handed in my credentials."

"Oh, Tim. I'm so sorry." She reached a hand to his knee. "I'll testify on your behalf. Tell them you were only questioning the students. That they were being uncooperative so you had to—"

"But I didn't have to do anything." He felt his throat tighten, wild thoughts, angry frustrations, blitzing his mind. "I should…"

Her hand patted his knee and she lifted slightly from her chair, moving closer. "I understand, Tim."

Her gentle voice calmed him. That she understood, he had no doubt. It seemed Sherrie was the only one that did. The only one not angry, or soon to be angry, with him. A tight lump filled his larynx. His eyes blinked back moisture. He could not go home like this.

Sherrie looked at him with soft eyes. He found solace in the deep pools. Still confused and vulnerable, he reached out and grabbed her hand.

"It's okay." She hung closer to him and he hugged her awkwardly from the chair.

The swelling in his throat found his mouth, but he swallowed it back, fighting against an onslaught of emotions. They stood in silent acknowledgement. Still holding her, his feelings retreated, leaving his mind in a vacuum. The sensations wavered, as if looking for a new feeling to grab. For a long moment he remained fixed in her clutches until, slowly, a sliver of worry crept over him. That no one would see them like that.

Yet, Sherrie felt so oddly pleasant in his arms. The fragrance of her hair and the small of her back under his hands. Her arms over his shoulders and the pressure of her chest below his. It all evoked strange sensations. Uncomfortable and yet alluring.

A door burst open just beyond the cubicles.

He released Sherrie with abruptness. She looked at him, eyes reflecting anxiety.

"Tammi!" Kaplan shouted from the other side of the offices.

"I…uh," Tim halted, feeling ashamed. How could he think of betraying Janice?

"It's okay. I understand." Sherrie reached up and kissed him lightly on the cheek. "Let's go get some coffee."

* * *

Café

The air outside turned thick and began hailing B-Bs. At times it became so heavy that Tim could hear its roar as ice pellets hit the cars and street just outside the Café Connexion. He sat at one of the café computers feeling his stomach knot itself into a tight ball. Sherrie sat with him while he went to the newsgroup to check for Hando's promised story. At least he could still monitor his case on the computers at the café. They had ordered coffee and cappuccino but the cups still sat full next to the terminal.

"So they won't even let you use the bureau computers?" Sherrie asked him.

"Kaplan says to keep a low profile. Stay away from the residency. At least until my fate is decided."

"When will you know?"

"Four this afternoon." He jabbed at the keys.

"So you're not suspended?"

"Not yet."

"Well, they can't make me leave." She sounded defiant.

Tim leaned back. "Okay, Hando hasn't posted anything yet, as far as I can tell."

"Good." Sherrie sipped her cappuccino.

He grabbed his coffee, took a big gulp, then went back to the computer. "You should see the group. Besides the gazillion of posts about me supposedly punching Victor, there's a bunch of posts for Hando."

"For Hando?"

"Yeah, his forwarding account was killed, so his e-mail is undeliverable. Users are just leaving the mail on the newsgroup. Like pinning up their privates on a poster-board."

Sherrie leaned forward. "What do they say?"

"'Read my story.' Some ask Hando to use theirs on his next victim."

"That's horrible!"

"The sicko's support group."

Tim closed out the text box and sat back.

"What now?" she asked.

"Now I'll check Hando's account."

"Should you?"

"Of course."

"But, if you're suspended…"

"I'm not. And I'm the only one with the password."

"Don't get caught."

He turned and smiled at her.

"I mean it, Tim." She frowned. "Maybe I shouldn't watch."

Tim wasn't about to give in, just because he would get censured. Hando, whom no one knew better than he, would strike within a day. What was he going to do—let Hando go because of bureau protocol?

He logged into *nether.net*, into Hando's account. He bent over the keys, scanning the screen. A quick check told him Hando had not logged in since the day before. The greeting told him that new mail had arrived.

"What about later?"

"Huh?" He glanced at Sherrie.

"If he does abduct someone, can you respond?"

"If he does, I don't know. But my plan is to stop him before."

The prevention, hopefully, lay somewhere in these files. Tim checked Hando's mail file. The last delivery, unread and from someone named, "JLK," was encrypted. The header remained intact, but the message body was a large block of random characters. Completely indecipherable. Tim listed the previously read messages—five over the past week—all of which came from this same person: JLK—Jack Lacey Keller.

Only the two earliest messages weren't encrypted. Tim read the first.

"Hi, Thanks for responding to my post, Hando. I'm honored that you would take the time to talk with me. Like I said, I want to be your net apprentice. People will revere me as the right hand of Hando. I'll follow your lead if you want. But I've got a whole plan myself as well. A kid I've been e-mailing. I think he's lonely, got no dad and his mother works all the time. I bet I can set up a meeting. Just let me know."

Tim searched the other messages and files, but he couldn't find Hando's responses, giving him what amounted to half a conversation. Like regular mail, electronic letters sent to a recipient were not kept, unless a copy was made before it went out. Apparently Hando did not keep duplicates of his own replies. But the letters he had received from Keller were stored. Stored, that is, with encryption.

The only other clear, decrypted message came after the first. It was short.

"Yeah. I agree we should use encryption. I mean, we don't want our plans out. I'll meet you on IRC—the stories chat room. We'll decide on the algorithm and exchange signature-keys there."

All the remaining messages were scrambled. Damn. It wasn't going to be easy, even with the account. Tim knew Hando had to keep the tool, a program, he used to encrypt and decrypt the messages. It would be in the file system.

Besides his mail, Hando kept only five files in his directories. One, with a recent date, was called *Overtime*. Tim viewed it, but it had only the words:

UNPAID OVERTIME.

The others, older file dates, were applications or configuration files, and another application called, CryptJack. The encryption program.

He executed CryptJack, which asked for a file name, then a password-key and last, strange as it seemed, it asked whether the encryption was "software or hardware?" The final question took him by surprise. All the encryption he had seen used for mail and messaging was software. But Tim had a friend at the National Security Agency who would probably know what was going on.

* * *

Field Office

It was only 3:30 p.m. and already Bob Givens felt he was losing. Special Agent in Charge Philip Hansen, sitting smug behind his large oak desk, seemed determined to suspend, even discharge Tim Delbravo. It was just a matter of formality now. While Tim's future hung in the balance, the two of them sat calmly in the SAC's office. Black suits, files and coffee steaming like it was an ordinary mid-afternoon planning session.

Hansen would interview Tim after the meeting—still part of the formality. Then, by late afternoon, Hansen would call Washington with his advice. Givens felt sure his boss' recommendation was determined the moment the first reporter had called.

"We have to move quick on this, Bob. The Associate Director called me himself. Some senator on the appropriations committee is pressuring him to pull the reigns on the murder case."

"What?" Givens asked. "Why would a senator want the case changed?"

"I don't know, but it doesn't sound like he likes Delbravo." Hansen picked up his coffee mug. "If he pushes the AD much more, Tim will get booted by order out of Quantico. We'll just have to reassign the case."

"But that would gap the case. SA Delbravo"—Givens used the title to remind Hansen that Tim was still an agent— "assured me on the phone yesterday that he's closing in on the subject, Alven Hando."

"How close?"

"He traced the subject to his own computer account. It takes a lot of systems know-how to do that."

"Uh-huh. But he still doesn't have a real name."

"He knows the account and has good finds at the crime scene. It's all in the report." Givens pointed at the stack on Hansen's desk.

Hansen looked, but didn't pick it up. He brushed back his nearly perfect hair. "We got a call from the student's lawyer. He says he's still conferring about a suit. Or maybe a settlement. If he sues, we'll have to discharge the agent."

"Over a suit?"

"We may have to damn the passenger in order to save the ship. I can't be faulted for that."

"Phil, wait for the weekend." Givens softened his voice. "Certainly a few days won't be too long, especially if we can save SA Delbravo or the Hando investigation from a total meltdown. We don't have anyone with the computer background. None that can be spared right now."

"We'll just wait until Washington spares someone." Hansen leaned back in his chair.

"No, Phil. Yesterday, Hando threatened to make his next move. He said it would happen in two days. That's today, or tomorrow at the latest."

Hansen leaned forward. "Why didn't you tell me this?"

"I did. It's also in the report I gave you."

Givens felt Hansen's eyes pour over him. He didn't understand why Hansen couldn't just delay the suspension for a few days.

"With a senator hitting the AD, we really can't keep Delbravo on the case," Hansen said. "We'll have to bring in someone else as case agent. I don't think we can salvage his career, Bob. I know you have a soft spot..."

"That has nothing to do with it. It's the next victim that I'm thinking about here." Givens knew that it wasn't entirely true. He had owed Tim ever since Danville—when, he had his suspicions, Tim took the fall just to save the memorial of his deceased partner. Tim deserved the mercy now. "You took him into this office when no one else would. Pulled me in to assist as well. Why the about-face now?"

"Yes. I cut him some slack. He was a black agent with a serious problem. Everyone knew what that meant. And to be quite honest, Bob, just between you and me, it was a good career move."

"For me too. Why not repeat it?"

"Get real, Bob. Can't you see it?"

Givens wasn't sure. He remembered the first call from Hansen, just after Tim left California for retraining at Quantico. Hansen's offer to assist the field office astounded him. He'd not even been a senior resident, and already the big guns wanted him to assist an FO. The stars in his eyes had blinded him. Sure Hansen had remarked about how he would help Tim. It caught Givens attention, but that comment had been a mere footnote in the volumes he spoke about bureau politics. Hansen had been, was still, gunning for the directorship.

"I guess you're right, Phil. You got a lot of recognition for that move. Won't you get more this time?"

"No, no. The media will spin this brutality case against the bureau. Delbravo was a lost black sheep before. Now he's a ravenous wolf. I'm not getting my ass chewed up."

Givens' heart sank. Since beginning work in this capacity, he had never really learned to like Hansen. Now he felt at odds with everything, even his own position. He didn't need this kind of career move.

"I'm going to be honest with you too, Phil. What you just told me is quite disturbing. You used a black agent's race to play politics. And now you're abandoning him because it's inconvenient for you."

"Why don't you just say what you want to say?"

Givens sat up straight. "Did you know it's black history month?"

"So?" Hansen chuckled.

Now came the gamble. Givens shifted in his seat. "I can play politics, too. And I know how to stir up the media. Items about Tim Delbravo and other black agents here. Like Darnell Johnson, and how about Eddings? You want a media blitz. I'll give you one."

"Damn, Bob! Do you know what you're doing to yourself?"

Threatening his SAC was suicide. Yet as risky as it was, Givens knew he had to wager it. Tim was counting on him. Bob was counting on himself. After all, what did a man have left if he cashed in his integrity? Givens stared at his boss, or likely former-boss. "Give him the week, Hansen. Then black history month will end."

"Is it really worth it, Givens? Does your old friendship with this mentally unstable, go-nowhere pal mean so much you're willing to stall your own career?"

"No." Givens glared at him. He leaned forward and brushed several papers off the SAC's desktop. "But it's worth betting yours. I'm not backing off."

Hansen heaved a long breath, not answering for several moments. "Go ahead, be the lamb. Save your *politically correct buddy!*"

* * *

Tim had arrived at the Detroit office early, wearing his trench coat this time. He couldn't afford to appear the least bit out of uniform. Hansen and Bob Givens were talking in the SAC's office. He waited in Givens' office, fidgeting because every moment was wasted while Hando still roamed free.

One thing he could do was call his friend at the NSA. From Givens' bookshelf, he picked up a copy of the internal government phone registry. He found the number for the Maryland office of the INFOSEC division in the NSA. After peeking out of the office, he returned to Givens' phone and dialed the number. A receptionist transferred him to his friend, who answered after two rings.

"Dan, it's Tim Delbravo."

"Delbravo? Jeez, I haven't heard from you in a couple of years." Dan Hill's voice had a high-pitched teenage quality, overlaid with years of smoking. He and Tim had worked briefly on cases involving encrypted child porn in New York, then again in Chicago. He had been invaluable for Tim's assignments.

"Where are you now?"

"I'm in Ann Arbor."

"Michigan?"

"Yep. I got another favor."

"More pedo-crap?"

"Sort of. Not images, but e-mail."

"What is it?" Dan asked, coughing. "PGP? DES?"

PGP and DES were common encryption techniques. "No, it's called, CryptJack."

"A knock off SkipJack?"

"I don't know, Dan. I was hoping you'd heard of it."

"It's new to me."

"It's just a program, but it asks if I'm using software or hardware encryption. Can you take a look?"

"Hardware? Is it classified?"

"I don't think. I got it from a hacker's account."

"Probably public then."

"Can you do it tonight?"

"What's the rush?"

"It's part of a murder investigation. A kid."

There was a pause. A short cough. "You got it."

"How can I get it to you?"

"Transfer it over the net." He gave Tim his Internet address. "I'll call Mary, tell her not to wait up."

"Thanks, man. I owe you."

"Yeah? When you going to help us? We're always looking for good field operatives."

"I may just jump ship, Dan. You never know."

"You tell me when, Tim. I'll pass your file around."

"Thanks." Tim hung up. He probably had a few minutes before Hansen would call him in. Just enough time to log in to Hando's account, transfer CryptJack to Dan, and get out. Givens' computer sat on the desk, waiting for him.

* * *

Tim sat next to Givens, across from SAC Hansen in the large office. He felt Hansen's eyes bore into him.

"We're worried, Delbravo." Hansen held his coffee up. His voice rang out like a principal talking down at his student. "We're worried about this murderer. But we're also worried about you. The AD, hell maybe even the Director himself, is getting high-up pressure on this one."

Tim wondered if Senator Euler had bellied up to his threat against him. He felt the impulse to defend himself, vehemently even. There was no reason to just take the blame. He knew, however, that he wouldn't speak until allowed response. His two years in the army solidified that notion.

"We won't suspend you," Hansen said. "Not yet. But we can't allow you to lead the case either."

"Wait, Phil." Givens glanced from Tim to Hansen. "If he's not on the case, the murderer goes free."

"No. Delbravo will assist. I'm putting the new fellow in as case agent. The young one in Ann Arbor, at Delbravo's RA. He had some wonderful ideas about working the militia."

"Mott?!" Tim stood. Givens pushed him back down.

The corners of Hansen's mouth bent up with a sardonic twist. "Yes. That's him. Louis Mott. I like his style. You brief him, Delbravo."

"But…" Tim felt Givens' hand on his arm. Still it wasn't right. "Mott. That's ridiculous. He hindered my investigation. In fact he's one of—"

"Enough!" Hansen slapped the desk. "Your friend, Bob here, was kind enough to defend you. He sacrificed a lot to keep you on the case at all."

Tim looked at Givens, who shrugged a frown that bespoke the fight he'd given just to ensure Tim wasn't suspended. Tim knew it had been a lot by the way Givens' eyes twitched, pleading for him to just sit. He did.

"No more complaining, Delbravo. Just thank us and shut up."

* * *

Residency

When Tim traveled back to the residency, he had conflicting hopes. Kaplan usually left by five, and he would lock Tim's 9mm in his office for the night, unless Tim got there first. But getting there before Kaplan left meant arriving before Mott left. He would prefer to just miss the FOA, not have a chance to brief him.

But, for what it was worth, both Mott and Kaplan were there. So was Sherrie, copying all of their case notes. Tim immediately snatched his credentials and weapon from the RAC's office, then dragged himself toward Mott's cubicle.

"Hey, Delbravo." Mott eyed him and grinned when he sat in the chair next to him.

"Do you know what's going on, Mott?"

"Yeah. SAC Hansen's mad as fiery hell. I know that. And I know I'm case agent on your murder now."

Tim decided he would approach this from the minimalist point of view. Wait until Mott asked him, rather than volunteer anything.

"I knew you couldn't be trusted." Mott shook his head, looking disgusted. "When I heard you were coming to the Franchise, I knew you would blow it for me."

"What the hell was going on there, Mott?"

"Told you."

"You told me nothing. You were way out of line yesterday."

"Me out of line?" Mott released a loud, nasal breath. "Me? You come into my operation, almost ruin it like you did your own. You think I'm gonna play footsy with you in front of Grady?"

"No, but kicking me didn't score points with him, I'll bet."

"You don't know anything about it." Mott looked at his watch. "Look, can we get this going? I gotta keep up my work, too."

"Why don't I just save you the effort?"

Mott glared at him. "They're asking me to do it. I gotta do it. Now let's hurry it up. What's happening tonight?"

"We hope nothing."

"With you, nothing ever happens."

"Right." Tim leaned back. "We'll keep watching the Internet newsgroup for a post from the suspect."

"Yeah, yeah. Your little princess told me that much." Mott jerked a glance back at Sherrie. "Anything else?"

"You're the boss."

"Then stay out of my way, Delbravo." Mott stood and grabbed his coat.

"Where will you be?"

Mott twisted the right half of his mouth. "None of your business."

"You going to check the newsgroup, or should I?"

"Don't worry. If I need you, I'll call." He turned and left.

Tim turned and saw Sherrie, in the far end of the residency, watching him.

"A real ass," she said.

Tim nodded. They walked back to his cubicle.

"I got your notes all done." She dropped a thick folder on his desk, keeping one for herself.

"I guess I'm staying here tonight. Watch the newsgroup."

"No you're not." The voice startled Tim. He turned and saw Kaplan.

"What?"

Kaplan stood behind him and adjusted his glasses. "Mott is handling the case. You go home."

"I can stay."

"No, you can't. I want you out before I leave."

"Tim, the lawyer wants you over for dinner," Sherrie reminded him.

Tim shrugged. He still had his after-hours key. "Fine."

Ms. Downey entered. "Agent Delbravo, there's a call on the STU for you."

"You leave after that." Kaplan shook a finger at him as he went to the common area. Tim picked up the Secured Telephone receiver, flipped the key and answered.

"It's Dan Hill." His NSA friend's voice rasped more than usual. "Go secure."

Tim punched on the secure mode. It read, *MaxSL*. "What's up?"

"Where the hell did you get the encryption?"

"I told you, a hacker."

"And who knows about it?"

"What? Just me and my partner. Why?"

"You file this through official channels, Delbravo. Got that?"

"I don't understand."

"Don't tell anyone you sent it to me."

"Dan?"

"Like it never got decrypted."

"Did you?"

"Delbravo, CryptJack is another name for highly classified government code. I don't know how the hell you got it already. But you have to file officially, got that?"

"I just want the messages."

"Look, if I get you the decrypted messages, will you keep my name off the report?"

"Can you decrypt them?"

"I told you, it's in-house code."

Tim nodded; they must have a backdoor in their own algorithm. "Whatever it takes. Just send me the files."

"Not to your FBI account. It'll be my butt…"

"Dan, tell me what's so bad?"

"You shouldn't have sent it over uncleared networks. You keep me clear and I'll put the decoded messages on an anonymous server. For one hour. Then they're gone."

The phone clicked and went dead.

Kaplan stood behind him. "I hope you're keeping Mott briefed."

Tim didn't reply.

"Now out." Kaplan pointed at the door.

Tim grabbed his coat and a bag. "Come on, Sherrie. Let's get some coffee before dinner."

* * *

Café

"Man, you're a regular," the cashier told Tim at Café Connexion. He didn't reply; didn't feel like talking much. He had a lot to think about. Somehow, Hando was now hacking and stealing government encryption. A kind so new, its very leak frosted his friend, Dan, at the NSA.

They ordered black coffee and sat near a terminal. Sherrie watched him as he logged in.

"You can't stay on this computer all night," she told him.

"Why not?"

"For one thing, it closes at seven. And you're going to dinner. With me."

"To the lawyer's?"

"We could go alone." Her voice almost implied a question.

He worried she took the incident in his office the wrong way. He never meant to give her the impression that he was attracted—even if he was. But he felt unsure how to bring it up just then. What if he blurted out that he was married? What if she was just being friendly?

He continued looking at the screen. "No, I better meet with Grand, over dinner."

"Fine. As long as you take a break."

"I don't know." He looked at her. "I probably shouldn't leave the newsgroup. What if Hando posts?"

"Well, isn't someone watching it twenty-four hours?"

269

CART was, but they probably had Mott listed as the case agent. Mark Striker, the FO tech, would watch, if Tim asked. He just needed to tell Striker where to reach him. "Look, can I have my man call your cell phone? Mine got busted."

"Absolutely." She smiled. "Partners, remember?"

Tim studied the screen of the café terminal. Apparently, Hando had still not posted on the newsgroup. Nothing like waiting till the last moment, though he hoped it never happened.

"You want to call him?" She held out her cellular.

"Sure." He took the phone and dialed Striker's number. He would probably have better luck getting him on the computer. Striker answered after four rings.

"It's Tim Delbravo."

"Oh, hey." Striker sounded occupied, music hissed in the back.

"I need a favor. If you can stay late."

"You know me."

It was true. Striker never seemed to leave his computer, even staying logged in from his home system all night. Tim said, "I'll be out for an hour or so this evening. Will you check the newsgroup?"

"You think he's still gonna post?"

"Let's be prepared."

"Yeah. I can keep an eye."

"And another thing. We may be able to get the leg up, if we watch his account."

"The one at *nether.net*?"

"Yes. When he logs in, it'll be to post his story. Maybe we can get the file from the account before he sends it all over the net."

"I'll need to be inside your super account there."

Striker was asking for the account password. "I'm on a cell phone. Not sure I should give it."

"How many letters?"

"The password?"

"Yeah. I'm resourceful."

"Six. Call me if you don't get it."

"Easy."

"Thanks, Mark. And keep this between us."

"No problemo." He made a smacking noise. "You know, I heard about what happened, Delbravo. But don't worry. I'm on your side, buddy."

"Keep me posted. Don't get caught."

"I never do."

The phone clicked dead. Tim closed the lid and handed it back to Sherrie.

"So who's your man?" she asked, putting the phone in her coat.

"Mark Striker. A government hacker."

"You mean, like break into Russian computers?"

"Not exactly, but he would, given the go-ahead."

She grabbed her coffee. Tim went back to the computer. He logged into Dan's anonymous server where the decrypted messages were waiting. Tim transferred them, and read them on the café terminal. These were the three remaining messages sent by Jack Lacey Keller to Hando, which had been encrypted previously. Although he did not have Hando's replies to Keller, Tim could, from the context, guess what was going down.

Hando seemed to have a plan for abducting some children—kids he'd been surveying for a week. Something mentioned as "*overtime*." Tim remembered the document in Hando's account with the same name, and the two words inside: *Unpaid Overtime*. Keller said he would follow Hando's lead, and was waiting for him to decide if they'd meet.

In the last e-mail, dated from this morning, Keller wrote:

"All right, I know you said no about meeting. But I swear I'll be cool. Pretty please? Just take a chance with me. I want this so bad, and I got some targets here in Toledo. I know you said you would be busy for the weekend, but let's meet some evening. Just name a day and a place. I'll clear my schedule for you."

Tim noted that the message was still unread. Hando hadn't logged in for over a day. From JLK's pleading, it seemed obvious that Hando was still not ready to meet his fan. Too bad. Tim would love to have them converge so he could scoop them up together.

But if he couldn't have both, he would take what he could. In Hando's file directories, he found the mail and deleted Keller's original, unread request. From his own account, he created a mock-up of a message, a reply to Keller, as if it were from Hando.

"Okay. You've convinced me. Let's meet in two days at the Franklin Park Mall fountain just off I-23. I'll e-mail you a description of what I'll be wearing and the exact time later. Also, be careful about e-mailing me too

much here. I may need to change accounts for safety. Just wait for my signal. Don't get over excited, or I'll change my mind."

Then he sent the message and flushed any signs of his being in Hando's account. Hopefully he could set up a sting for JLK. Now he was going after two hackers.

* * *

Dining Room

"So who is Hando?" Veronica Grand asked Tim. She was Sam's wife, and she wore short hair, slacks and wide glasses, looking just like the Women's Studies Professor she was.

Tim sat with Sherrie at the Grand's dinner table, eating a pork roast with trimmings. The Grand's two children were out at friends, Sam had said.

"We're not sure who he is," Tim said. "'Hando' is an alias."

"An alias?" Veronica asked. "You mean like 'also known as Dick'?"

Sherrie passed a bowl of peas down to Tim. The food was good. Sam and his wife were very cordial. But he couldn't seem to keep an appetite while his stomach was in knots over whether Hando would post again. He also needed to call Janice, let her know he wouldn't be coming home that night. He sensed an all-nighter.

"You know." Sam put his fork down. "There ought to be laws. Penalties for using aliases on computers."

"There you go again. *Law* is always the answer," Veronica said. "Penalties for aliases—that would be like Hitler's Germany, or Stalin's Russia. 'Papers, please.'"

"As long as there are people like Hando," Sherrie said, "I'm not letting my children on the Internet—when I have some."

"Tell the Rameys," Tim said.

Sherrie nodded. "If only they had watched Bill instead of leaving it all with his tutor."

Tim did a double take. "Tutor?"

"The Rameys hired a tutor to help Bill with his computer."

"How come I didn't hear that?"

"You were...upstairs, I think."

Sam asked, "Didn't Victor teach computers?"

"He did," Tim replied. "But the Rameys weren't on the list." He just never asked them. If there was a connection, Victor had given Hando the kid's name.

* * *

Living Room

Sherrie liked spending social time with Tim. After dinner the Grands invited them to sit in the living room. Sherrie sat on the couch, making room for Tim, who was making a call at the moment. The living room was a sunken pit with a leather couch and tall floor lamps. A conversation about politics started up again, and then the doorbell rang.

"Excuse me," Sam said and rose. He went to the entry, and Sherrie could hear him greet someone. Just then, Tim returned.

"Well, my man says the post isn't up yet," Tim said, sitting by Sherrie.

"So are you two partners?" Veronica asked.

Sherrie nodded.

Sam returned with two children. Veronica introduced them all. Katie, the oldest, was ten, and Sammy Jr. was six. Sherrie thought they looked adorable, like miniatures of the parents. Both had freckles, and Katie had her dad's eyes, a long ponytail and dimples when she smiled.

"Katie," Sam said. "Tim here knows a lot about computers. Maybe he can help you fix the CD-ROM."

Katie stole a look at Tim, but said nothing. She looked shy. Like Sherrie once was as a girl. She remembered that age, spending a lot of time in her room, or in the tree-house her father built, reading books and thinking about the way things were. Now she rarely had time to think with all the *doing* she had to do.

"You have a computer?" Tim asked.

Katie nodded with her eyes darting between the floor and Tim. She kept her lower lip wrinkled up.

"Is it fun?" Tim asked.

"Yessir," Sammy Jr. said. "We look stuff up on it, and sometimes play games."

Tim's face became thoughtful. "I just got a new one last week at work," he said, "and it came with this game called Ecoscope II. Have you heard of it?"

Katie glanced up, her lips separating and grinning at him.

"She has the original Ecoscope," Veronica said. "She's been begging for us to buy the sequel. But the CD drive is not working."

"I can get to the sky-home level," Sammy Jr. bragged.

"Oh yeah?" Tim asked.

"Uh, hmm." The boy smiled. "Want to see?"

"Sure, for a minute." Tim got up. "And I'll tell you what. If you let me use the computer to make a check on my case, I'll let you two borrow my copy of Ecoscope II for a while. Deal?"

"Really?" Katie crooked her neck to watch Tim towering high above her.

"Sure. Let's go see that sky-home."

The children led him back into the hallway. Sherrie grinned. He seemed a natural with them. Her own father had been wonderful. He always had time for her, despite a full legal practice. And even though she passed on law school, he was quite proud of her advancement in the sheriff's office. They still talked almost once a week.

Down the hall she could see Katie grab Tim's hand and pull him into a room, smiling up at him. Tim had seemed quite a mystery. At first he appeared indifferent, even a little callous on the surface, but she had seen a different man in him. It was as if she knew two Tim Delbravo's, and yet hardly knew either of them. Like an M&M on a warm day, once you got past his hard shell, he was a sweet and soft gentleman. He had vulnerabilities, and Sherrie liked that. But there was even more. A troubling factor. Deeply imbedded in the soft interior, there was still something stony. Something ossifying his wounded heart.

"So how well do you two know each other?" Veronica asked her, grinning coyly.

* * *

Driveway

Tim and Sherrie stood on the front path of the Grand home, waving back at the family. Katie was especially devoted in her farewell and it made Tim smile. They turned and walked toward the driveway, where his truck and her Bronco were parked.

"What's the plan now?" she asked him.

"You should go home."

"Are you?"

He wasn't, but he didn't want to tell her. "Eventually."

She studied him. He felt exposed. She had seen his weak side when they hugged in his office. Now he knew he couldn't lie to her easily. Like he couldn't with Janice.

"Where are you going now?"

He pulled out his keys, and held up one for her to see. "Back to the RA."

"I'm coming too."

He shook his head. "I don't think you want to get tied to a screw-up like me."

"You're not a screw-up," she said. "You're just dedicated."

He didn't reply. Why would anyone not be dedicated? A murderer was putting in overtime. And Mott, Agent Johnny-Rebel, wasn't doing a damn thing, he knew.

She produced her own keys. "I'll follow you."

* * *

Residency

The RA lights blinked on slowly. Tim threw his coat and holster on his desk, and then sat in front of the computer. Sherrie sat behind him. He finished a quick check on the newsgroup—still no post. He had already called Striker and told him to go home. Striker admitted he was a little tired and would catch up with them tomorrow.

"Nice piece," Sherrie said, looking at his gun. "Does it mark well?"

"Good enough." Tim released a tired breath.

She set it down and sighed. "It's been a long day."

"Yeah."

"And you look tense." Sherrie pulled her chair behind his. Tim felt the uncomfortable quietness around them.

He felt hands grab his shoulders. At this, he cranked his head back. "Sherrie...?"

"Shhh. Just relax."

She kneaded around the base of his neck. It felt relaxing, but he tensed again as she rubbed. Hadn't he told her he was married?

His ring. The doctors had taken it off his swollen finger. He still hadn't replaced it—couldn't even remember where it was. Somewhere at home, he knew. And his family photo. He looked at his desk where it usually sat.

The second computer took up its spot. He remembered kissing the family portrait and throwing it into a drawer to make room last week. Sherrie had no idea he was married. And he had done nothing to imply the situation. In fact, he may have even encouraged her in his own way.

"Thanks, but you don't have to..."

"Shhh. Enjoy it."

He felt her hands, massaging, soothing. She was now on the outer edges of his shoulders and moving down his arms. Maybe she was just being nice, not seducing him. Her hands dissolved the tension in his muscles, making his eyes droopy and his mind shut down.

"Tim." Her voice floated in the hushed cubicle. "Where do you live?"

"Live?" He woke from the spell she cast over him. The question gave him a chance to hint. "On the west side of town. In a two-bedroom apartment."

"You like space, huh?" Her hands moved toward his chest.

"Oh, there's no room. I've got two..."

He felt lips touch his cheek, moving toward his mouth. Strands of her hair fell across his neck.

"Sherrie."

She kissed his mouth.

"I...shouldn't, Sherrie," he said through her lips.

"No one's here." Her warm breath invited his mouth to melt with hers. She really didn't know he was married. Her hand reached to his shirt.

His mind jerked awake. A hungry part of him wanted to plunge into Sherrie's invitation. Another voice shouted at him to stop it right there. If he told Sherrie that he's married, she would be embarrassed. Alone, neither she nor he had retreat, no alternative conversation to engage them. They would have to face each other and this situation. It would strain their work relationship.

He grabbed her by the shoulders, stood and then gazed into her eyes. "Sherrie."

She looked at him softly, her hands across his back.

"I want you to understand, this is all my fault. I hope you won't think badly of me, since I really respect you."

"Respect me?"

He felt her arms loosen behind him. He held her shoulders and swallowed. "It's just I don't wear the ring because I injured my left hand."

"Are you saying...?"

"Almost thirteen years. Two kids." Her hands slid off his waist. "You couldn't have known, Sherrie. Please understand. You've been so kind. I needed you today. And I want to continue being your friend and partner."

She looked at the partition and closed her mouth. Her feet stumbled back. "I...uh..."

"Don't blame yourself. I should have said something."

"No, no. It's all right." She spoke softly, waving a hand and turning her side to him.

"Let's forget this. We're a good team. We're going to get Hando together."

She turned back and forced a smile. But her eyes wouldn't lock with his.

"If you want to go home, I understand."

She hauled in a breath. "No. Let's get him."

Tim gritted his teeth into a grin.

She leaned against the desk and stared down. He knew she felt humiliated. What could he do? Talking about the humiliation would only make it worse, underscore it. Focusing on the investigation, including her in the details, keeping her involved. That would ease the tension.

He sat at the computer and grabbed the mouse. "I'll search the Usenet archives. Feed stories through the bureau's analyzer. You should read through case notes. Help make theories."

She took a seat at the table next to Tim's desk and opened the file she had copied that afternoon. She stooped over the papers, strands of her hair tucked around an ear, and didn't look back.

On the computer, he launched a web browser and went into the Usenet archives, searching the last two years of *alt.sex.stories*. Even though they were locked in a strained situation, he just wouldn't be able to leave knowing that Hando was about to strike any moment.

CASE 3

"I want to be your net apprentice.
People will revere me as the right hand of Hando."
—Jack Lacey Keller

Wednesday, February 19

Residency

Tim jerked awake. It was one in the morning. After such a long day, he had fallen asleep at his desk while waiting for a protracted analysis on every post in the Usenet archive of Hando's group. Tim must have been dreaming. It had been a strange nightmare. His mother had been younger, preparing a dinner. She called for him outside, where he had been playing with some of the kids. In the glass of the front door, he saw his image: older with a bald head, a long beard, hard wrinkles, stained white eyes and chipped teeth.

His mother became Sherrie. She smiled at him in a green and violet flowered-apron, wrapping a large napkin around his chest and back. She held up a ladle with tomato soup and dipped some into his bowl. There was tapping at the kitchen window from someone on the porch. He turned to look and saw Janice in a cap with a catcher's mitt, chewing gum.

"Come out and pitch to me," she said.

Behind her another boy, a guy—maybe a man—in shorts, smiled with dark eyes. His face seemed so familiar but not quite placeable; a face known in photos but not in person.

"Hurry up," the man said. "I've only got three hours."

Sherrie shook her head. "Not until you've finished your dinner."

The kitchen turned into a basement cell. The soup had become John Robinson's blood.

Then he woke suddenly, his heart racing, his body cold. Yet he found his new coat draped over his shoulders. He felt odd; something eerie in the dream, still vivid and fresh in his mind. The strange man's face still haunted him; it was so familiar but his conscious mind would not drag out the name. Tim shrugged off his coat, letting it slide to the floor. He breathed hard and looked around. Everything was normal, a strange late night calm. The office slumbered.

Sherrie slumped her head over folded arms on a table, sound asleep. The computer glowed at him hypnotically, still connected to the web server. The search had ended without result. Tim had fed everything from the group into the bureau's central system. But the original post just wasn't there, and there'd been no phone calls from Mott.

Mott.

He wondered about the FOA. While Mott was never quite ordinary, Grady Lonque had wanted to tell Tim something about him. With the new revelation that Hando used government code, he would've suspected Mott, had he believed the FOA was smart enough to pull off such a charade. But there were other persons with clearance that just might have the brains.

He grabbed the mouse and brought up the newsgroup reader. He scanned the subject lines and user names. The screen reflected over fifty new posts since he checked at just before eleven. *Alt.sex.stories* was busiest late at night.

About twenty posts from the end he found it. Hando's "repost" entitled, *"Romancing: rEviSiT OF a ClaSSiC."*

Tim's heart leaped as he remembered where he'd seen the title of the post. Hando reposted *Victor's* story!

"Lord, no!"

He had assumed it would be Hando's own, but his last post hadn't promised that. It only pledged a repost with which everyone would be familiar. It seemed so obvious now.

In the beginning of the message, Hando explained:

In light of the FBI roughing up my friend, Kurt Victor, I've decided to revisit his classic tale. The one that got me and everyone going.

Here's to you, Kurt!

The story would be familiar. He had read and searched it over and over for clues to help convict Victor—little good it did.

I'm just sorry you won't be there to enjoy her with me, Kurt.

Yoshiko! The Japanese girl.

Tim gunned his mind into high speed, checking the post for a time-stamp. It was posted ten minutes earlier. Still enough time. Hopefully.

He searched his head for memory of the story, knowing he had analyzed every letter and byte, even parsing the story for hidden messages in the patterns and style. He had hunted for evidence and discovered what he thought might be places Victor had originally described. At the moment, the only location that seemed to match the description was an ancient, one-room schoolhouse on Old Earhart Road.

Adrenaline pulsed through him as he sent the story to the printer. He called Mott's cellular. There was no answer. He grabbed his trench coat and 9mm, cursing and waking Sherrie.

"What's up?" she asked, glancing at her watch and rubbing her eyes.

"Hando posted."

Without another word, she grabbed her coat and gun, then left the RA with him. They got in Tim's truck, and once inside, he pointed at his car radio. "Call for backup."

"City or County?"

"Sheriff. And have them bring EMTs."

* * *

Popkins Schoolhouse

No more than forty yards down the old dirt trail, off Plymouth Road, sits a red brick school, a former part of District 7. It had been erected in 1870 according to a concrete capstone Tim had seen two weeks earlier on the north side. The dedication was inscribed just below the crumbling chimney and a sunken bell tower.

The county's planning department had told him that they wanted it to remain like the original. So they boarded the windows and bricked over the entrance. Then they forgot it.

Now in the dark, he could only see its vague outline, sitting on a slight hill. The roof sagged, looking as if it might cave in. Snow draped over the bell tower and the trees encircled behind it.

A vague feeling of déjà vu wrapped around him, and, as he turned off his headlamps, he saw the man's face from his dream; the name he knew was familiar, but his mind still refused to call it up. Imaginary facsimiles danced in the darkness around the closed up school. He started nervously, breathing rough and fast. Splashes of memories swarmed in his periphery and readied for attack. Sherrie unbuckled herself, and as if scared by her action, the images cowered into darker recesses of his mind leaving desperation behind. Unable to explain the images or what he was feeling, Tim's shoulders and hands shook.

The schoolhouse windows were boarded so he couldn't tell if there was anyone inside. He and Sherrie slipped out of his pickup quietly, closed the doors, and tried avoiding crunchy snow or other dry debris. He grabbed his weapon from inside his coat, and icy wind shot through the opening he made, causing him to shiver more.

It was cold. Even Hando wouldn't last long in an unheated room or outside. And Yoshiko...His eyes dropped to the ground. All that he had done, and she still gets abducted.

He couldn't let himself get distracted with emotional flurries. They had to make sure they went quick, but not blind. Not get sucked into a reckless hostage situation like...Like Danville.

The unknown face and Danville—it came back now. Lester Fanway was the face in his dream. Half a year earlier, Tim and his partner John Robinson had been tracking Fanway. For days he had given them nothing. Then he led them to that estate in Danville. And Robinson raced in without a plan. Tim was unable to control the situation. Hostage situations rarely went well; that one would have made the books as the worst. If they could surprise Hando this time, Tim would try disarming him before it went too far. That was, if Hando was there at all.

"What's the plan?" Sherrie whispered as they reached the front of the schoolhouse.

"Let's survey it. Each take a side and meet in back."

She looked at him. "You sure? Why the wait?"

"We don't know if anyone is even here. And we need to find the best entrance plan." That was protocol before backup arrived.

Sherrie scanned the building as they walked, tiptoeing toward the bell tower. They quietly circled around in separate directions. Tim took the southern side. He remembered from before that a cellar entrance had been there. It had been filled with dirt and trash, but maybe Hando found it and moved the debris. Or maybe he loosened a window board. Tim probed the front window-boards, pressing gently in order to remain quiet. They felt secure.

He peered through a nail hole in one board, trying to get a look inside. The small hole in the damp, swelling wood made it difficult. All he saw were figures in his mind. Flashes and children's faces.

Fanway holding Michael Miller.

Tim hadn't let himself remember for a long time. Fanway had taken Michael under his gun. But somehow it had been Tim, his own gun, that killed the boy.

He shook away his memory and kept moving. His mind battled and yelled within as he walked around to the back. *Just kick the wood in!*

No, he had to be absolutely sure this time.

He reached the cellar entrance, which was surrounded by trash. In the dark, unsure if the dirt had been removed, Tim probed the hole where doors or stairs leading down would be. However, he only felt frozen refuse and hard ground.

Nothing. He wasn't even sure if Hando was in there. Every moment was dangerously wasted. Life-saving minutes and seconds squandered on his ineptness.

Come on!

He went to another window, carefully feeling the wood over the frame. It could have been loose. Which could mean it was old, or recently moved. His mind swirled, trying to stay afloat amidst his sea of doubts. If he went in, he would have to confront another hostage situation. He remembered the gunfire, blinding flashes. The unnerving sense he might take one in the head or chest at any moment. The fear of leaving behind his family. The thunder of each shot still rang in his ears. The basement walls in Danville had echoed every sound. Tim couldn't hear correctly for days afterward.

But at least his ears survived. Michael Miller never did. The boy's eyes buried into him. He heard the screams, saw the red pooling on the cement, spilling down to a drain. Sweat ran down his brow and nose. He watched a ghostly shadow of Fanway's friend as he held another, a second boy hostage.

"Tim," a whisper jolted him into reality. Sherrie grabbed the sleeve of his trench coat. "There's a hole in the brick in back."

She turned and led the way. He wiped his forehead and panted at the memory that wouldn't quite dissolve. He couldn't let Sherrie see him like this.

"Is it big enough to get in?"

"It's pretty small."

She stopped on the west side at about the middle of a thirty-foot-long windowless perimeter. Only brick and graffiti faced them. The hole pierced the brick just above the ground. He bent down to look in.

"I did that, and couldn't see much," she whispered.

The hole was maybe thirty or forty inches in diameter. Tim would never fit his shoulders through it, but maybe Sherrie could. Then he caught a faint glow. Maybe natural gas blue.

His body froze. All kinds of images danced through his mind. Yoshiko torched with ignited fumes. Victor had written about Sterno Gel, a pink gel camping fuel that came in cans.

Yoshiko was in danger. A danger that he never thought would come after the arrest. A hostage situation couldn't be any worse than the certain death already awaiting her. The hole was small but he lunged in, striking his head on a brick with a hollow rap.

Robinson streamed across his starry vision. Blood flowed from his partner's rib cage. Fanway and his friend squeezing off rounds at them and then Tim's gun. Just his hand grasping it, blanketed by inky blackness. The barrel gleamed, sneering at Michael on the other end. Tim lunged for it, but was too late again. Yellow fire blasted from the nickel plated nose.

"STOP!"

His own scream jerked him abruptly with harsh reality just teasing at the edge of his consciousness. He was there at the schoolhouse, sitting on the ground a few feet from the hole. Sherrie stared wide-eyed at him, mouth moving open. He looked at the hole, and before he could act, Sherrie darted to it, lowering herself onto the ground. She stuck her head through.

Then he saw the flare coming from the inside. Not just a faint blue but also bright yellow and orange.

Sherrie pulled herself out. "There's a fire in there!"

His adrenaline flared up; he didn't even tell her what to do. He leaped to the north side and began pounding in a boarded window. Wet and soft, it broke easily. He climbed inside, just near the chimney where pieces of an old potbelly stove tripped him up.

He could see flames in the opposite corner of the large room. An empty room except for fire burning in a can…and someone in a chair, a tripod with equipment. Movement and noises, like crying. Tim jumped up and sprinted, the old floor creaking and dipping under his weight.

A figure behind the flames darted. Hard to see. Moving and jumping from a seated person, causing the chair to crash with its inhabitant. The shadowy ravager tumbled through a boarded window, sending back wood splinters, some of which fell across the fiery canister and caused it to spill over.

Tim looked back. Sherrie was right on his heels as he flung off his trench coat and tossed it over the flames spreading to the victim. Sherrie reached his side. He glanced, for only a split second, from the burning floor to the window opening.

"Put out the fire!" he shouted. Then he was through the opening and pursuing the assailant. Fiery images still blinded him and he wasn't sure where the man had gone. He stopped and listened for a quick moment. Sticks snapped and leaves rustled off to his right side.

Before he knew it, he was running through a snowy maze of small oaks and maples, branches whipping at him and the cold biting him.

* * *

Schoolhouse

With reflex action, Sherrie grabbed his trench coat and started striking at the flames. The flames were almost all blue, about an inch thick floating or coating the floor and pouring on the victim. They spread over the floor in many directions, reaching a tripod, trash in the corner and, just then, the victim on the floor. She squeezed the trench coat around the person, a girl, she could tell now. She tried desperately to pull or push her away from the fire. Flames first reached the girl's hair, which burned long strands, starting in bright yellow and white flames.

She overthrew wild thoughts racing through her, trying to free the victim from the flames licking all around. But the girl was tied to the chair, a heavy awkward seat. Sherrie rubbed and struck at the flames with the coat as she pushed the girl away. The girl herself didn't move or respond, and a small trickle of blood issued from her head. The fire had also reached the ropes holding the girl to the chair. With the flames rising, surrounding quickly, Sherrie felt her arms shake.

* * *

Hillside

The school sat on a hill that flowed down to the west and toward Interstate 23. At the base of the hill, a clearing descended into a small gully. There, Tim found the figure—running toward the Interstate, but still a couple of hundred yards from it.

He sprinted after him and saw the man veer northward, going parallel with the exit ramp. Following along the hilly tree line, Tim gave all he had to the chase.

He began gaining ground. The man aimed at Plymouth Road. Brown scrub tore at Tim's shins. The cold seeped into his clothing without the coat. Another twenty or thirty yards and he would have him. Through the motion of running and the wind blurring his vision, he couldn't discern anything about the man. Except that he ran fast.

Tim reached the middle of the shallow gully. The ground was hard and in the center part, ice coated the dirt. Abruptly it gave way and he slipped, falling face first into the snow and dried grass. Hard dirt pelted his chin and hands. In an instant he was up and running again. But in the same moment, he fell down once more. His left thigh sparked with pain. Hurting at the very spot where he had been shot. Paining him just like it did when he pulled himself from Priestly's wrecked rental in Milan.

He rose and hobbled as Hando, or whoever he was, sprinted away, curving closer to Plymouth Road. Tim struggled and fought against the pain in his thigh. Knowing it was useless, he turned back after watching the assailant cross the road.

Damn!

On the ramp, he glimpsed a county cruiser with flashers pushing the other cars off the roadway. Just ahead of it, Hando had apparently entered a parked vehicle. But Tim couldn't be sure in the dark. The patrol cars passed him and turned onto Old Earhart.

He jogged toward the school, praying for Yoshiko. If it was her. Limping he cursed himself for not staying to help. Chasing Hando was a waste. He didn't even get a look at him.

* * *

Schoolhouse

Before the deputies arrived Sherrie had untied the victim and managed to get the flames out. She continued monitoring the girl's air passage to keep it clear. The victim's hair had been burning for maybe only ten seconds, but she remained unconscious. Her head had a gash where it must have struck the floor. Fortunately, the bleeding had stopped.

"Where's emergency?" Sherrie shouted at a deputy.

"I called dispatch," the male deputy said. "An ambulance should be here in five minutes."

"Five minutes! It's a burn!"

"I told them—almost five minutes ago."

"They should be air-lifting her!"

"Dispatch said they'd try for med-flight. Told me to count on five minutes."

Sherrie shook her head, realizing suddenly how cold and damp it was. "Get me a blanket."

The female deputy ran out.

"Go call dispatch again," she commanded the other deputy.

He left. Alone she looked over the girl, checking her vitals again. The female officer returned with a dark blue wool cover. Sherrie removed her own coat from the girl and spread the blanket over her.

"What else can I do?"

Sherrie looked up. "Go out and see if you can find the FBI agent. He was chasing the suspect. He might need assistance."

The deputy nodded and left through the gap made by the escaping rapist. Again, Sherrie checked the girl, whose breathing rose shallow. She kept the head elevated and body covered. The bottom of Tim's trench coat was not as burnt as the top and Sherrie continued using it to apply pressure on the head wound.

The girl's face was darkened, probably by soot and ash since the skin still felt tender. Most of her burns were light. The hair had taken the brunt of the flames, protecting her face. Her scalp was a mesh of burns and gummy residue, mixing with the blood from her injury.

Scattered on the ground she saw emptied fuel cans, some rope, a broken broomstick and other items. Flames still smoldered from the equipment that sat affixed to the tripod, now toppled onto the ground. It looked like a tiny camcorder and laptop or palmtop computer. She wanted to put out the last flames, but didn't dare leave the girl. And she shouldn't touch any of it. That was for the federal forensic and investigation staff. She kept applying pressure to the girl's head, singing silently to the victim. Then she heard someone breathing. At the opening, Tim entered with the female deputy in tow. And another sound resonated above.

Whoop! Whoop!

Air lift! Lights broke through the opening and through holes in the roof. Many holes. Cold wind whipped around them as Tim knelt by the girl, his eyes searching in rhythm with his gasps. Desperation streaked his face, souring his lips.

"Yoshiko," he mumbled. "I'm so sorry."

He slid his hands under her back, gently rising with her.

What was he doing? "Tim she might be—"

"I have to!" He looked frantic as he carried her, limping through the gap. Lights enveloped him, and Sherrie could hear the helicopter touch the ground.

* * *

Tim fought the frenzy overpowering his mind. His breath rasped, uneven and heavy in his lungs. He felt like he was drowning in a sea of horror and couldn't tell what was past or what was present.

Two medics raced to meet him fifteen feet from the helicopter. They took Yoshiko from his clutches and rushed her back to their bird. He followed, a hurried limp. After they had strapped her in the anchored table, he stepped up and began finding a seat next to her.

"I'm sorry, sir," the medic told him. "No ride-ons."

"I have to."

"No, sir!"

Tim wouldn't stand and argue while Yoshiko's life hung in the balance. He stepped down. Almost immediately the helicopter lifted up and streaked into the cold like a snow owl after scooping its quarry. Tim could only pray as he watched it disappear over the trees. Somehow, Yoshiko had to be all right.

* * *

Hospital

By the time Tim got to Saint Joseph Mercy Hospital, Yoshiko had been processed through ER and seen three physicians. For a long while, he waited for someone to give him another update. Before they did, Sherrie arrived.

"Tim. Why didn't you wait?" she asked. "I would have come with you right away. I had to wait for a cruiser to free up."

"I'm sorry." He moved some magazines so she could sit next to him in the waiting area.

"I had the crime unit hold off on cleaning the scene," she said as she sat. "We'll back your unit up."

Tim nodded, scarcely hearing her words. He should probably go back, but he wanted to wait for Yoshiko to wake. She might have recognized who did this. Besides, with his mind plagued by apparitions of his past, he wanted to just stay put and wait for clear thinking.

Sherrie studied his face. An outline of worry grew over her brow. "Are you all right? When you screamed back there…"

Tim nodded.

"I guess you saw the assailant when you yelled."

He didn't say anything. His mind kept showing him Fanway's face, smiling in the basement. Robinson running up the green expanse of the estate. And Yoshiko hanging lifelessly over a burning stake. Damn, he was losing his mind.

Sherrie touched his arm lightly. "I saw you limping when you carried her. You all right?"

That was the least of his worries.

"Did you hurt yourself running?"

He didn't respond immediately. He saw one of Yoshiko's doctors—the one he questioned before. She was a thin female physician with tired eyes and gray tufts of hair. Without a word he rose and marched over to her.

"Doctor," he called before reaching her. "Doctor, is she all right?"

"Oh, there you are." The doctor pulled a pen from her pocket and exhaled roughly. "Ms. Kamahara is in stable condition. She should be just fine. Her scalp burns were minor and shouldn't leave permanent scars. However, she has a minor concussion and will need at least twenty-four hour observation."

Tim nearly fell over as the relief and, finally, exhaustion began overwhelming him. Yoshiko was not seriously injured. By chance, he really did at least stop a murder this time. But he still wanted to know the entire story.

"Doctor, what other injuries did she sustain?" He shuffled his feet. "For my report."

The physician stopped. "Well, we can send you a copy of her record once we've made a thorough evaluation. Can it wait?"

"We'll need that too. But particularly..." He didn't want to ask, but for the reports and his sanity he had to know. "Particularly, whether she was sexually assaulted."

She gazed at him with a tense mouth, then inspected the people around them. "We had been told this was an abduction. I made a cursory examination," she said quietly. "From what I've seen, and it's not a thorough evaluation, mind you, I believe the girl was not sexually assaulted. Except for the few burns and the lump on her head, she appears safe."

"Thanks." Shivers of relief ran across his skin. "Thanks a lot, Doc."

"I expect that your office will handle the press and inform the family?"

"I, uh...Sure," Tim said. "When can I talk with her?"

"Give us another twenty minutes for the tests."

The doctor walked to the double doors leading back into Emergency. Tim turned and found Sherrie still with him.

"Thank god," Sherrie exhaled. They went back to the waiting area. Tim limped up to his seat.

"You should really have someone look at your leg while you're here."

He looked at his new pants. There were no bloodstains.

"How did it happen?"

"An old injury."

"Is that where you were shot?"

Tim didn't understand how everyone seemed to know. He nodded.

"How?"

Tim looked at her. He didn't know if he wanted to answer. It was digging up what he had wanted to leave buried for so long. But after the relief just dispelled, even a feeling that he was doing right again, recounting the past was part of his absolution. Part of his final cleansing. And Sherrie wasn't part of the bureau. She wasn't a federal shrink.

"Which time?" he asked.

"What do you mean?"

"I was shot in the leg twice. Months apart."

"Months?" She studied him, her jaw open. "I mean, it's rare when an FBI agent gets shot at all. But twice? Were they connected?"

"In a way."

"Part of a case?"

"One was a case. Operation: *Innocent Images*."

"You mentioned that. What happened?"

Tim paused, feeling the old pain now. But not the same pain of digging at his open wound. It felt more like a dried-up scab, toughened and hurting because it was about to fall off.

"I was at the Oakland RA," he finally said. "California."

"How long ago?"

"Six months. I was the second most senior agent—well, so was Bob Givens. You met him in the hospital the day we came in with Olson."

Sherrie nodded. "So what was *Innocent Images*?"

"A nationwide op. Several residencies were tracking links in an international child pornography ring. Kids got abducted, and at the same time their faces appeared on milk-cartons nationwide, their whole bodies were showing up on computer screens worldwide. My partner was John Robinson. Headquarters sent us the ID of someone connected with illegal images on computer boards and the Internet."

"Another Internet porn author?"

"Not a writer. Lester Fanway, the suspect, uploaded child porn. He lived in Berkeley, just north of Oakland. We followed him and watched his apartment for two weeks with 24-hour surveillance."

"You and your partner did the stakeouts?"

Tim shook his head. "Only a little. We had local assistance for that. Some other county dips—no offense."

"None taken." She smiled.

"We would follow Fanway during the day usually. But he spent most of it at work. At a computer porn graphics studio in the east bay. They had a so-called legitimate web site of hard core material. They'd shoot photos or video of local models then doll them up with hi-res graphics, a flat blonde into a busty redhead or whatever clients wanted. Our subject was a programmer/artist."

"So he could get good porn images on the computer."

"Practically make it up himself. He did adult stuff for work, and child porn on the side, or so we suspected. But we couldn't figure out where Fanway was getting the source for children's images."

"Wait, didn't he just make them up?"

"Not completely." Tim shifted in his seat. "I mean, until just recently computers couldn't make decent human models, not ones that looked photo-real. He needed models. Images of kids were turning up on covert sites, looking like real milk-carton material, only the hair color or eye color was a bit off. A large nose turned flatter, a small mouth made wider, whatever else these perverts get off on. It was sick."

"So why didn't you just nab him?"

"Proof. We suspected his images were real, but if not, we couldn't arrest him for quote-un-quote artistic works. Even if they looked like photo-real kids."

"Why not?"

"The law hasn't caught up to hi-tech. Child porn created solely by computers, no matter how much it looks like your sister's little joey, isn't against the law. It ought to be, but we had to get proof that he was getting his stuff from real models. More importantly, we wanted to know who had the kids, as we figured he was trading photos with real child molesters, since he had a full Internet connection at home. When Fanway wasn't at work, he stayed at home. Alone."

"Then DC sent us a report about the recent image of a boy that had been kidnapped only days before. A boy named Michael Miller from Dallas."

"Dallas? As in Texas?"

He nodded. "Kidnapped while on a trip to the Bay. DC had assigned another team to haul in the guy that put it up on the Internet. But he got it from a user on his own board. A computer board back east. And apparently the user that originally put it on the eastern system was our man there in California."

"So your man was the source of original and enhanced images?"

"We weren't sure. He at least got real photos, we knew. We were told to move in but to keep our distance for the night. Hopefully, we thought, Fanway would lead us to the main source. On a Sunday in September, Robinson and I followed him to the Berkeley BART."

"BART?"

"The Bay Area's subway. It goes from the city under the bay to Oakland. Another line goes north and south on the East Bay side. He picked it up at the Liberty Square just below the Berkeley campus. Took it south to the McArthur station. We followed of course. He hopped on a second Bart—a route that went east through the hills to a large bedroom community. We couldn't understand why he was taking the BART when he had a good car. It left us without our own car and a lot of questions. We knew something was up. I had a cell phone, and called the residency to let them know where we were. But we didn't know where we were going."

"Didn't you think about backup?"

"In most residencies you have limited manpower. Having a partner is hard enough. We usually got backup from the locals. But we didn't want to blow our shadow with some spur-of-the-moment dink-ups."

"No offense taken," Sherrie interjected.

Tim smiled. "Fanway got off at Walnut Creek and took a bus south. Got off that fifteen minutes later in Danville and walked four blocks to a street with a lot of estates. We stayed back. Almost lost him. Then we found him walking up a hilly driveway. We stood back and watched the place. A really ritzy mansion."

"Why didn't you call?"

"We didn't think it was necessary just to observe."

"So you just watched?"

"For a while." Tim remembered the green grass surrounding the estate. They didn't have a plan for going in. A mistake he made again tonight. He should have just marched in to that schoolhouse. Kicked Hando in the teeth. But despite his hesitation, they still stopped Hando from killing.

"Then what happened?"

"About ten minutes after he went in, the front door burst open and we saw a boy come running out. With nothing on. Immediately behind Fanway another man ran out—someone I recognized from the place where he worked. They were chasing the boy. My partner went ape, crossed the street to the estate-gate. Before I could get to the other side, he was over the fence and on the grass. The two men hauled the boy back inside."

"How horrible!"

"It was." Even as tired as Tim felt, the memory came so easily, and the night's images of Fanway and Robinson swarmed back into his mind. What had not come since that day, he relived entirely now, remembering all so clearly in his foggy state-of-mind.

* * *

"Robinson!" Tim had yelled. But his partner was already racing up the estate green and it was all he could do to get over the gate. He groaned as he toppled over it. "Robinson!"

The estate door shut. The men and the boy were inside. Robinson had reached it. Just as Tim stepped off the grass, Robinson pumped a round into the bolt lock and kicked the front door open.

"Stop, Robinson!" Tim reached him inside the entry.

"Where are they?" His partner searched around.

"Hold on!" Tim pulled out his cellular and dialed 911.

Then they both heard the muffled scream. It came from underneath them. A basement. Robinson darted for a door off the entry.

"Robinson!"

Tim ran after him, gun in hand and phone at his mouth. "FBI. We need assistance. Have two-o-seven in progress. Repeat hostage situation in progress."

Robinson, at the bottom of the steps, cursed loudly. Halfway down the stairs, Tim caught a vague whiff of something so slight and yet vaguely familiar.

"*207?*" the phone squawked. "*Who is this? Where are you?*"

Rushing down fast, Tim jumped the remaining two steps and landed hard on the bare concrete floor. Three pairs of eyes locked on him. Around them, screens glowed with images, lewd and sickening. Video cameras and umbrella-lights piled amidst boxes and a large black bag sprawled low on the cement.

Robinson aimed his gun at one man. Two others each had boys in their grip and guns pointed at them. Tim trained his on all three in turn, still holding the cellular.

"Drop the phone and gun!" Fanway dug his gun into a boy hostage, who shrilled on cue.

Tim nodded, set the phone on a box, staying connected and keeping his gun aimed on Fanway. The subject had his own revolver on a half-naked boy.

"FBI. Police are on their way." He waited for Robinson to back him up. But his partner was muttering under his breath.

"Shut up!" The first man, who Tim recognized as Fanway's boss and owner of the mansion, held his gun on another boy. He wore Safilo wire-frame glasses and had a military haircut. "Drop your guns."

The third man, a complete unknown, stood shieldless—had no hostage, but kept his gun pointed at Robinson, who was aiming back. The man walked over to the box where Tim had lain the phone and grabbed it. He closed the mouthpiece, then threw the phone against the wall. It shattered into pieces.

"Drop it!" The unknown kept his gun on Robinson. He had perspiration on his nose, long bangs dripping over his brow.

Tim watched the owner. "Let's talk this out."

"Shut up!"

Fanway started dragging his hostage, Michael Miller, from the corner where they stood. "We're going out."

"No!" It was the first word Robinson had said.

Fanway stopped, still holding his gun on the boy. The owner watched behind his hostage. They stayed by the back wall, a dozen feet from the agents, near most of the equipment. The third, without a boy, neared Robinson, and kept his revolver aimed at the agent's throat.

"Drop it!"

"Listen to him. We will do what is necessary." With his unarmed hand, the owner reached into a pocket and extracted a knife. "We were about to dispose of this one, but it will serve as a motivator, I believe."

He flipped-out the blade, then bent down and cut open the thick black bag that lay on the concrete. From the hole, a small gray-white face peered out like a wraith from its cave.

When Tim saw the young corpse, he nearly passed out. What had been a slight odor now poured out and suffocated them. Although the body couldn't have been dead for too long—no visible signs of worm-eaten flesh—the stench still overwhelmed him.

"Drop them!" The owner held the knife up to his hostage. He dragged the blade across the boy's cheek. The hostage screamed as blood followed steel.

Tim flinched. He felt horrified as the owner wiped his blade on the boy's chest. The smell of death rising in his nostrils weakened his resolve. He could see the same confusion in his partner's eyes. But Robinson held tight to his weapon, trained on the un-shielded man.

"Put it down!"

The boys wailed. Tim slowly set down his 9mm. A flash of nerves whispered how wrong it was unarming himself, but robotic reflex had taken over his movements. Fear for the boys ruled him. He could not risk their lives; delaying until backup arrived held his hope. They needed time and peace to negotiate, not an abrupt gun battle.

The shieldless perp held his revolver up as he kicked Tim's dropped gun toward the far wall, away from everyone. He and Robinson remained locked in a show down. The man slowly edged toward the agent until he stood four feet away, their guns nearly touching. He reached out to take Robinson's gun.

It went off. Robinson fired a second round as the first propelled the man back, fluids spraying and his own gun blasting shots into the ceiling. Shots rang out from the other men. Tim dropped, trying to take cover and searching for his gun. It lay by the body of the man his partner had just killed.

"Hold your fire!" he shouted at Robinson and fixed his eyes on the boys. Their captors ducked with them under tables, still holding the hostages tightly.

Robinson swung his gun around and began firing shots at the tables, hitting computers and video equipment along the walls. Tim could see blood issuing from his right side. He'd been shot and was ranting under his breath.

"Stop it!" shouted Fanway.

Bam! Bam!

"Robinson!"

The others had quit shooting. He crawled out toward Robinson. Then he heard, barely with the ringing in his ears, the empty click of his partner's gun.

The men must have, too. Their guns lifted up. Robinson leaped to the floor, rolling toward the far wall. Two shots rang out as he scooped up Tim's gun, blood still pouring from his side.

"No!" Tim grabbed his partner's leg, and pulled himself around to grab the gun.

Robinson raised the 9mm.

The men, dragging the boys, ran toward the stairs. Robinson aimed at Fanway, who stood above Michael.

Tim reached for Robinson's hand, grabbing around the nose of his gun. "Don't! Boys not clear!"

Fanway turned, throwing Michael in front of him and directing his .357 at the agents. Tim pulled down on the gun's nose, feeling it recoil. At the same moment, Fanway fired two shots. The owner hammered out three, one of which carved deeply, throwing Tim back, his left leg going numb. Robinson's head bled.

Everything went silent. Tim looked up and saw Michael Miller's mouth hanging open. Blood poured from Michael's open chest as he slid down the wall. His eyes, Tim saw ever so slowly, the boy's eyes glaring at him. Dark pupils boring into Tim as the owner and Fanway scurried up the stairs.

* * *

Sherrie touched his shoulder as a lone tear screamed down his cheek. Without having to suppress it, he divulged the last bit.

"I was on the ground, confused as the two men escaped upstairs. I don't really remember, but somehow I managed to get on their phone. Robinson was still alive. And so was Michael Miller."

He paused, remembering the details. How after calling, he sat under a table, not wanting to see Michael. "I was sure I had killed him. He died with Robinson in the hospital an hour later."

"But, Tim. You didn't kill him." Sherrie wiped her own eyes.

It was no profound mystery. Just one he wouldn't let himself remember. And it'd happened almost as Givens first suspected. Except, it was still Tim's fault. Had he not grabbed the gun, then perhaps the men, and not Michael, would've been shot. Robinson was aiming for Fanway. And Tim pulled the gun, the aim, down.

"But I did." He could have tackled Robinson. Even stood in front of the bullet.

"No, Tim. You didn't." She studied his face. "You think you should've never dropped your gun. Or maybe you should've died instead of your partner or the boy. But you couldn't have controlled your partner."

"If I would've left him alone…He had a clear shot."

"If—a hundred things." She reached an arm around him.

"The boy is still dead."

"He would've been anyway. At least they didn't have the chance to do it their way."

That was true. Everyone had focused on the mishap, that it was Tim's or Robinson's fault Michael was dead. But he was already, in a sense.

"And the other one?"

"The other boy?"

She nodded.

"The men left him wandering outside, I was told." Not much else was ever said about the other boy.

"Then he's alive. Instead of both getting bagged in a basement, one has you to thank."

Tim wanted both alive, but he could never change that now. She was right, though, because both would have been killed. He felt his memory open further. The details and events were the same, now that he remembered them all. But, in his mind, he was no longer cowering under the table with the kidnappers. He had done everything humanly possible. And it had turned out better than it might have. He looked at Sherrie.

She smiled back and swallowed, eyes glistening at him. He felt released from a self-imposed prison. Everything inside him woke. He was so aware and alert and...

Not quite free, however. He still bowed under censure at the bureau. And Hando was still out there.

Someone stood near them. Tim looked up and saw the doctor. She hinted a smile and knelt in front of them.

"The tests are done and the patient is awake," she said. "I think you should be able to talk for a few minutes. We've given her an oral tranquilizer, so she won't be awake long."

The doctor rose and started to lead them through double doors. Tim and Sherrie followed her back and down a long corridor until they reached the short-term patient-care rooms inside Emergency. The doctor motioned at one room and they entered. In a bed, looking sleepy, Yoshiko lay sedate.

At first, Tim felt ashamed seeing her there. If he had done his job better, she wouldn't even be at the hospital. But he knew that he at least got to her before too much happened. Again, had he not done his job, she would be dead.

"Yoshiko, I'm so sorry." He crouched at her bedside.

She opened her eyes and gasped. "Agent Delbravo. I don't understand."

"What don't you understand?"

"She may have a touch of amnesia or disorientation," the doctor said from behind. "It was a good knock on the head."

Yoshiko's eyes drooped and reopened into small slits. "What happened?"

He swallowed as he examined the bandages and bruises on her head and face. Much of her hair was gone, burned or shaven. "You were abducted. Did you see who?"

"I came out of the bathroom. Then something...my head." Her mouth barely moved as she spoke. She looked so tired.

"Did you see who it was?"

She shook her head and her eyes bobbed open and shut.

"You rest, Yoshiko. I'll call your parents."

She relaxed her head and closed her eyes. Normally the bureau assigned a social worker at the field office to contact the victim's family. However, Tim felt responsible. He had promised to protect her when this started.

Hando, the cocky sonuvabitch, would pay. And this Keller fellow and Fanway. And Victor too. If Victor had been convicted for making the threat, then very possibly, Hando wouldn't have been so courageous in expanding on the original.

* * *

In the waiting area, Tim found a payphone and dialed international information with his personal phone card. It was 2:45 a.m. Eastern Standard Time, so in Japan it would be roughly early evening on the next day.

Remembering the name of Yoshiko's hometown, he acquired the phone number in Hikone, Japan. He dialed it, and as soon as it rang, realized that he had no idea if the Kamaharas spoke English.

"*Moshi moshi.*"

"I'm looking for Mr. Kamahara. I don't speak Japanese."

"Yes, this is Takashi Kamahara," the man said in good but forceful English.

"Mr. Kamahara, are you the father of Yoshiko Kamahara, studying in Michigan?"

"Who is this?"

"I'm Special Agent Timothy Delbravo with the United States Federal Bureau of Investigation."

Silence.

"Mr. Kamahara?"

More silence.

"Hello?"

"Is my daughter all right?" Takashi's voice seemed calm, but its forced manner also revealed his shock and worry.

"There has been an incident. Yoshiko is in the hospital. She's in stable condition and has a minor concussion."

After a long pause, the man replied with labored discipline. "How did it happen? When?"

Tim explained, as briefly as possible, how Yoshiko had been abducted. Her injuries. The doctor's decision to keep her for a few days. Through it all, the father kept his cool. Then at the end, he became emotional.

"I plead of you, Agent Delbravo." His voice lost its nearly perfect intonation. "Please make sure she is not alone until we get there. It will take us about twenty hours in airplane."

301

"Well, the doctors—"

"A friend. Maybe you. She talked of you to me. I know she trusts you."

"I...I can check on her every couple of hours. Make sure she is not frightened."

"I am in your debt."

They exchanged a few more pleasantries, then hung up.

Tim held the phone for just a moment, remembering what the father had said. Yoshiko had told him that she trusts Tim. He had to keep her trust. He had to find Hando.

* * *

Schoolhouse

Sherrie cringed upon returning to the bustling, overrun shanty-school. It was like finding a corpse infested with body worms. The ghostly school had filled with black uniforms and directional lights. Federal agents kept the mass coordinated and a couple of dogs trotted all around the taped-off region, sniffing everything along the hours-old threads of criminal scent. Several navy blue jackets emblazoned with gold FBI lettering acknowledged Tim as he and Sherrie moved into the grotto-like mouth of the schoolhouse. A few men studied articles inside. One looked up at them.

"Where in the hell have you been!?"

It was Tim's boss. He stood just outside the larger of several marked off areas, where ravishment had nearly occurred an hour and a half earlier.

"Doing my job, Kaplan." Tim held his ground.

"At the bureau, job number-one is investigating the crime, not pampering the victim."

"The witness is the keystone."

"Keystone? What's that, something you learned from visiting all those shrinks?"

Tim glanced around. "What do we have?"

"We? You left the scene!"

"I told you. What the victim knows can give more a lot sooner."

"Horseshit!"

Tim pressed his lips together, then spoke calmly. "Anything gleaned from digging here will have to pass days of scrutiny in the lab."

"You just up and left." Kaplan approached him with red temples. "We got here an hour after. County folks were nice enough to finally call us. The county! That was your friggin' job."

"Yeah? Where the hell is *Commander* Mott?" Tim forced a long breath through his nose. "His butt should be in the vice, not mine!"

"Well, after yesterday's little police brutality, now this, you'll be lucky if your chum Givens can save a single curly hair off your beach-black butt!"

Sherrie watched Tim stare down at the older agent. His eyes flared like snake teeth, venom dripping off. She almost decided it would be better to leave, and then Kaplan backed off. He just turned and stepped out of the school without whispering as much as a curse.

Tim rotated around and shook his head. He knelt at the border of the largest circle. Sherrie scanned the debris with him. There lay familiar objects: a folding chair on its side, several empty cooking cans, a broken broom stick, a long-handled butane lighter, rope. Circled on the ground near the south wall was a towel, smeared with the pink cooking gel. Along the west perimeter, five feet south of the hole, sat a Polaroid One-Step, all of its unexposed prints loaded and intact. An empty film carton lay crumpled nearby.

And on the ground, smoldered the charred remains of a small, digital video cam and a closed laptop computer connected to a black box a few feet away. A cable strung out of the small box and across the floorboards, leading to the wall where it disappeared under a boarded window. Tim pushed the window board and looked through the gap. Sherrie stooped down and saw that the cable terminated into something on the window ledge. The brick propped a shiny square of metal angled at a forty-five-degree tilt, like a desk picture frame, only larger. Tim let go of the board and returned to the center of evidence.

Sherrie knelt with him as a bureau photographer snapped shots of everything for what probably was the tenth time. Another had a large video camera with a focused beam affixed on top. He recorded the walls and floor and everything about the place. Sherrie wondered if the floor could possibly hold all of the weight much longer. It seemed to sag at every step the cameramen made.

From the front opening, a cold wind howled inward, sustaining the schoolhouse in a deep freeze. She heard laughter beyond the back wall. A flashlight, then a head peeked through the hole in the brick. She heard a dog bay and bark somewhere off in the distance.

Tim moved around the circle. With a tissue from his pocket, he reached out and grabbed the broomstick. After examining it, he traded it for the torch lighter. He sucked on his cheeks, holding the incendiary device by the long metal tip and studying it under the dancing light the video camera provided.

"Hey. Bring that light over here." Tim waved down the videoman, who continued recording as he drew the beam over and directed it onto the white handle lighter in Tim's pinch. Sherrie strained to see what he had found. He was measuring something with his free hand and held his bent thumb and forefinger about three inches apart. Then he unfolded them and inspected his own hand, turning it over and back again several times until he finally nodded to himself.

"What is it, Tim?" Sherrie couldn't stand the suspense. With the tissue still around the tip, he handed the lighter to her so that she could take it without leaving prints. But instead of telling her, Tim took out a pad and pen and began making notes. Sherrie had to curb an instinct to grab her micro recorder, realizing that she still didn't know what had caught his attention.

She examined the lighter carefully. On the white handle were faint traces of shiny pink marks. Not fingerprints but something probably made by a gloved hand with gel residue still on them.

Sherrie looked at Tim. "There aren't likely to be any prints on it. I'd say he was using a glove."

"Exactly." He continued in his notepad.

"What is so interesting?"

"Notice the imprints. They give a clear indication that he is right-handed."

Sherrie inspected it again, noting that the pink glove marks distinctly denoted the palm, finger and thumb orientations. Definitely the stamp of a right-handed person.

"Okay, that narrows it to 90 million men."

"Yeah, but look at the lengths of the digits."

She did and noted that they seemed a little on the short side. Not tiny, but about her small size. "So we have a shorter, right-handed male subject. Still not much."

Tim looked up at her. "Remember we have foot-track casts. Their size, the depth of the track, and the length of the palm and fingers will give us a pretty detailed reading of the subject's size and weight, along with a very probable idea of his type of bone structure. From the skin samples we have an idea of blood type and a color-match indicating the subject is probably Caucasian. All we need now is a face and exact hair color."

"Sure, but your labs never could get enough DNA from the dandruff."

"I'm talking about this sample. You didn't look closely enough."

She glanced back at the lighter, turning it over and around in a more observant audit. On the underside, in between the metal tip and handle, a thick hair laid trapped in some gel, curling sharply around the interface. Because of the gel, the color was not so easily discerned, but it looked dark.

"It could be the victim's, you know."

"I doubt it," Tim said. "It's probably an eyebrow hair with the follicle still attached. A curly one. Yoshiko has the straightest and thinnest eyebrows I've seen."

"You think it's testable?" she asked. "I mean, wouldn't that flammable gel eat away anything identifiable?"

"Something in it will be." He turned to the photographer. "Call in the rest of the clean-up crew. Vacuum it all and I want everything bagged, in and out of the circles."

He stood and motioned at the open window frame. "Come on, Sherrie. Let's go look at some tire prints."

* * *

Residency

Tim felt fatigue settle in as he and Sherrie returned to the RA with the schoolhouse evidence in bags and containers. Sometime just after eight that morning, a courier would come and take them for delivery to the lab. Tim grabbed the two largest containers and carried them to his desk. Sherrie followed and sat in the spare seat next to him, while he pulled out photographs taken earlier.

Photos of casts taken from the swamp and in Milan, where Olson was hurled, showed two different sets of tires. Tim studied them, comparing each set with his notes and memory of the tracks they had found near the schoolhouse before leaving the scene. It had not even been an hour, but already his bone-weary memory was fading. Once the Laboratory Division had the new casts, all three sets would undergo a thorough comparison.

"Look here," he told Sherrie.

She bent down to look at the pictures.

"See the new treads on the last two. And wheel separations are close."

"Same car?"

"Could be."

At least two things were clear. The treads from Milan and the schoolhouse formed a more likely match, if memory served. The set from the swamps, bald and worn tires, had completely different prints. Still, tire separation measurements at each location indicated that all three sets had nearly identical frame sizes. Possibly even the same car, but with new tires since the Ramey murder.

He set the photos down and pulled open a drawer. From it, he lifted the command module for his tracing equipment. It had an LCD screen and five buttons in addition to the phone keypad. He attached its cord to the phone jack and, looking in his case book, punched in the number to *nether.net*. Once connected, the command module downloaded a complete dump of information from the trace equipment on the other end. The dump included every calling number, the time and duration of the connection.

It finished. Tim scrolled through the list on the LCD, looking for the correct time stamp. It was twenty-eighth down the list. The number was local.

Sherrie watched the screen also. "Hando's phone number?"

Tim nodded, then grabbed the keyboard on his National Crime Information Center terminal. He logged into the reverse index database server.

"That camping fuel he used," Sherrie said, "is it pretty common?"

"Fairly. We might even get a make in local stores."

The reverse index found a match. The number belonged to U-M's Phone Branch Exchange, a phone network.

"Where is that?" she asked.

"One of the university lines that their internal phones connect to for outside calls."

"So it's someone that works at U-M?"

Tim logged out. "Perhaps, or maybe just visits and uses a public phone. Could be anywhere on campus: Med-school, library, even family housing. He has a laptop."

"But it was with him at the schoolhouse."

"He uploaded the post just before going there, I guess."

"From campus? But then why take the laptop?"

"Good point. Maybe he has a computer on campus. Maybe he set it up to automatically send the post at a pre-specified time. I'm betting he only uses the laptop and camera to capture digital video of his slaying."

Sherrie scrunched her face into a disgusted snarl. "At least we can get the university's phone records, right?"

"Yeah, but campus doesn't wake up for a couple hours."

"Get a warrant."

"Maybe, but by the time we wake and convince the judge, they'll be at work. Then I can get the phone logs without a warrant."

"What till then?"

He stretched back on his seat. "Why don't you get some sleep?"

"And you?"

"I can't. There's a lot to do."

She sighed, then grabbed her coat and rose. "Actually, I am tired. And I need to feed my cat. Catch you in a few hours?"

"See ya, partner."

She smiled and snatched her stack of notes. "I'll put myself out, rereading the background."

He watched her leave, then turned to the large evidence containers by his desk. They opened easily. Inside, he pulled out clear, zipped pouches containing items collected from the schoolhouse. In one was the digital video cam, melted and blackened. Even through the plastic bag, he could smell the acrid tang of burnt plastic. Another bag contained a large lead-cell battery with six terminals for powering three devices during extended outdoor use. A third bag held a small and mysterious black box. Its simple design, just painted aluminum casing outside and unlabelled electronics inside, did not look commercial. A fourth bag contained the metal square that had sat on the brick ledge outside the schoolhouse.

The last bag held the laptop, which he carefully unzipped. Before pulling out the computer, he rose and walked to the common area. He grabbed a box of surgical gloves and put on a pair, then returned to his cubicle.

The laptop smelled like the video camera and black box. He extracted it and turned it over in his gloved hands. Taking the four main components, he connected them in series, as he had first seen them at the scene. The digital camera plugged into the back of the laptop, which in turn connected to the homemade black box. Lastly, the box attached by a long fat cable to the metal square that had sat on the outside ledge.

Tim did not doubt that this setup transmitted Hando's video. It was much more complicated that the typical laptop wireless card, or cell-modem setup. No, Hando would easily understand that modems—even many wireless cards—cannot transmit full motion video. And there was no wireless service at the remote schoolhouse. The key here was in the last item, the flat metal square. It was something Tim had seen once during his stint in the Army almost fifteen years earlier. A high speed transmitter. A two-dimensional phased-array antenna, used to send digital signals. Very high tech.

The army had used a larger one-dimensional version for classified operations. On a war game field, telemetry and positioning signals were sent from tanks and ground vehicles via phased-array antennas to hilltop receivers. Only recently, Tim read that cellular phone companies were testing it and improving the design for commercial communications. Like digital cell phones.

How had Hando gotten a hold of such technology? And to what receiver was he relaying his video? It had to be big for his video to reach all the way around the world. Perhaps data on the laptop's hard drive held the answers. Tim would send the evidence to DC, where the lab, with its racks of electronics, would dump everything they could from its hard drive, assuming the fire had not destroyed it. He would attempt some diagnosis himself, but he didn't want to disrupt any forensic evidence on the cover, in the likelihood the files were not retrievable.

On the back cover, he found the laptop model number and less than half of the serial number. In a couple of hours, the manufacturer would open, and then he would use the partial serial number to get a list of owners. Maybe even Hando's real name, if he was a registered owner.

He picked up the phone and dialed Mott's cell phone. It rang four times, then someone answered.

"Mott?"

"Hmm?" His voice was muffled and labored.

"Where were you tonight, Mott?"

"Who is this?"

"Tim Delbravo."

"Go to hell."

Click.

Tim put the phone down. He really couldn't believe Hando was Mott. But Hando, a local hacker, had access to government computer code. He used drugs. DC's profile said he was a *complex psychopath.* That much fit could Mott, but Hando was smart and short with dark hair, which ruled out Mott with his blonde head of low intelligence.

There were a range of people in the region working for the government in a variety of auspices. Defense contractors, university scientists, and a host of other federal enforcement agencies in Detroit.

But few, if any, would fit the whole profile. No one except...Mark Striker.

The FO technician was clever. He was local. He might be crazy, use drugs. He had dark hair. And Tim gave him Hando's account.

But he remembered from his visits to the FO that Striker kept his mouse pad on the left side. Hando was likely right-handed. Then again, a right hand on the lighter didn't exclude left-handed or ambidextrous persons. Striker, it seemed, suddenly topped the list of suspects. He called Striker's number at the Field Office, but no one answered at the early hour. There wasn't enough evidence to arrest Striker. Not yet. He needed to place Striker at the scene, if it was the technician. He just didn't see how.

Tim sighed and put the evidence back in its containers. His mind couldn't function well with so little sleep.

* * *

Residency

The phone rang, waking Tim on the second bell. He glanced at his watch before picking it up. It was eight-thirty in the morning.

"Hello?"

"Tim, it's Bob Givens."

"You hear about last night?"

"I did." He cleared his throat.

"And did you know Mott never showed last night?"

"I squeezed it out of Kaplan this morning. Called him at home, which didn't make him happy. As far as I'm concerned, you're lead again."

"Good news. Thanks."

"Also, I called the Associate Director about the campus incident."

Campus. Tim had almost forgotten about a suspension. So much had happened in one night.

"I got the senator's name out of the AD. Ever heard of Jack Euler?"

"Unfortunately, yes."

"Well, he seemed nice on the phone. We agreed that he wouldn't push for removing you off the case."

"In exchange for what?"

"Well, nothing really." Givens paused. "Just if I agreed to testify on behalf of some bill he's pushing on the Hill."

"Hey, thanks, but I can't ask you to do that just to save my butt."

"Don't worry, Tim. Euler actually complimented you. Said you were a damn fine agent, really. Was sure you would catch the subject."

"Well, somehow his confidence doesn't enthuse me."

"In any event, Tim, we looked at the news photos and sent your side of the story to Quantico. I got the AD thinking about going to bat for you."

"Great."

"There is one thing."

"What?"

"The student's lawyer called Hansen's office first thing; before I got through to DC. He wants to meet with us after conferring with his client this morning. He's going to discuss the possibility of settling out of court. Just in case, I'll have legal counsel on conference call from Washington. Doubt he's got anything. My contact thinks we can freeze the whole suit."

"Good."

"We just need you near a phone."

"A phone?"

"During the meeting here."

"What time? I'm real busy with this. So close, you know."

"I know. We need you at one to two in the afternoon."

"I'll try."

"Tim, be there. Okay?"

"All right, Givens."

He hung up and rubbed his eyes. Still tired, he called the university's communications services. No one answered and a recording told him their hours went from nine to five. He dialed the computer manufacturer in New Jersey that produced the laptop they bagged at the school. After the fifth transfer, he spoke with someone in the legal department. He grew frustrated when the man wouldn't give him any information.

"I just need the names of owners with serial numbers matching the partial I've got."

"Sir, we can't divulge that. Not without a court order." The representative had a nasal arrogance riding over his voice. "Why, I don't even know if you're really with the FBI."

"Call Washington. Check me out."

"Why don't you send a representative with the court order."

"Look, can you at least tell which batch this computer came from? A date?"

"Support does that usually. But…I guess I can do that much. What's the model and serial number?"

Tim told him.

"That model is fairly new, six months at the most. There's…" He paused. Tim heard keys clicking over the line. "There were two production batches. But the serial number you gave me is incomplete. Without the last half, I can't tell you anymore."

"Thanks."

Tim hung up, rose and carried his evidence containers to the entrance. Ms. Downey looked up at him from a novel.

"These are ready for courier," he told her. "Tell Kaplan not to soak his trousers. The FO account numbers are on the boxes."

She nodded.

He passed the other cubicles, noting that no one seemed to be in yet. It was late, but then everyone had been up late. Everyone except Mott. Tim remembered that Lonque had wanted to talk. He reached his desk and grabbed the phone book, then dialed the *Franchise*.

"*Founder's Franchise,*" a familiar voice answered.

"Mr. Lonque. Special Agent Delbravo. I got your message. Sorry I didn't get back, but things have been busy."

"I can imagine. See, the reason I wanted to talk is because of that Jim Staples fellow. He's been involved in some really crazy stuff."

"Yeah?"

"I don't normally tattle on my fellow Americans, but I have a reputation to keep as you know. I sort of sense I can trust you."

Tim got the feeling that he was being conned, manipulated. Like Lonque was telling him just what he wanted to hear. Behind, he heard someone entering the offices. He stretched around the cubicle wall and saw Mott taking off his coat at his desk.

The timing was incredible.

Grady was saying, "And the militia has been getting a lot of flack for this kind of stuff."

"Stuff?"

"Well, I don't like doing this but…" Grady stammered.

"What?"

"I think Staples is involved with the Klan. We try to encourage our members to stay away, but sometimes they don't. The day you were here, Staples even invited me to a weekend retreat at Waters, Michigan. I asked him what he was doing there and he said that it's a secret. Said I could find out by going."

As Tim listened, he detected a change in the man's accent. Just a perceptible shift from woodsy and rough to refined and stuffy.

"Now I know these Klan types are very furtive and do some pretty cruel things. I once knew of a couple types that were involved in a shooting. A black man in Ohio. They got arrested and all and I was harassed by the police because I knew them."

"Who were those men?"

"I only remember one's name: George Williams. I'm telling you this because I want to be up-front with you so I don't get in any hot water again."

"All right," Tim said, looking over the cubicle wall at Mott. "Anything else you can tell me about, uh, this person…the weekend?"

"Not really, but I'm willing to keep you posted if I hear anymore."

"Fair enough. Thanks."

Tim hung up and tapped on the NCIC terminal at his desk. He had already looked over the notes on Lonque and never saw any mention of a scandal with George Williams before. Searching under the name of George Williams, Tim pulled up a long file on his indictment on murder charges. A white supremacist with a long history of dealings in the Klan, and most recently with a known militia activist named Albert Sorenson. But nothing indicated that Grady Lonque was ever a part of the investigation. Not a mention of him or the Michigan Militia in connection with Williams.

Why would Lonque lie? He turned from the screen, wondering what to believe. He rose, walked out and saw Mott sitting quietly at his desk.

"Mott."

The agent regarded him. "Do you prank call regularly?"

"What the hell happened to you last night?"

"I did my work. I checked the newsgroups all evening. There was nothing so I went to a party. Can't hang a man for having a little fun, can you?" Mott imitated an innocent grin.

"You are really weird, Mott."

"And you're like a breakfast cereal: fruity and nutty." Mott roared at his own joke.

"I just got a phone call from Lonque. He claims you went to Waters, Michigan, for a weekend retreat."

Mott's face went bland. "What the hell does he know? He's no one."

"Joining the Klan, Mott?"

The agent sat silently, looking down at his desk.

"Trying to build a new career in case you blow it here?"

"Like *you* know how to make it big in the bureau." Mott glared back at him. "You blew it already. Next thing you know, you'll strike it rich on the daytime talk-show circuit."

"Don't change the subject. You're going to have to account for your whereabouts last night until two in the morning."

"Why? What do you care?" Mott seemed to get more agitated.

"Because I'm watching you, Mott."

"Go to hell. You're not my boss-man and it's none of your damned business where I was. I am lead on this case now."

"Not anymore. Call Givens."

Mott paused, shaking his head. "Even so, that doesn't give you the right to tell me what—"

Tim grabbed his shoulder and gripped the muscles stretching from his neck. "Yes it does. A girl was nearly murdered."

"Stop touching me!" Mott shook off Tim's hand. "I told you, I was at a party."

"You got alibis?"

"What!" Mott scowled. "You accusing me of murder?"

"It was attempted murder. Be glad she'll live." He knew he could get in trouble for saying this to a fellow agent. And he didn't quite believe it, but Mott *was* up to no good.

"You bastard ape-man! Do us all a favor; go back to the beach and just sit on your big black ass."

Tim glowered at him, thinking how to act. He waited for his anger to rise, but remained calm. Then he heard buzzing from the entrance. Mott continued sneering at him.

"Tim." Sherrie came around the cubicle.

"Don't leave town," he mumbled at Mott and turned to Sherrie. "Hi. What's up?"

"I couldn't sleep and went over the case notes, all the way back. Now I have some questions. Also, Olson left the hospital. He's at the sheriff's office getting a sketch from our artist. You want to go and see?"

"Of course." He began to walk with Sherrie toward the exit.

Mott blurted, "Look! Before you go off and round up a posse, I think you should know I'm starting a special operation. Talk with SAC Hansen or Kaplan later today, after my meeting with them."

Tim turned back. "I will."

* * *

Bronco

Tim entered Sherrie's Bronco, shivering at the cold gripping the air. They'd had record lows this year, and Tim had been fond of California's warmer temperatures. He moved a stack of papers from his seat and latched the belt across his chest.

"I hope it starts," she said, turning the ignition. "I've had to jump-start it twice this winter."

It started fine, but the engine idled rough. Tim shuffled the papers, her copy of the case notes, that were on his seat. She put the vehicle in reverse and pulled out of the underground parking stall.

"So what's your questions?"

"First, tell me what the university found with the phone number."

Tim looked at his watch. "They'll be opening in five minutes. I'll call from the sheriff's office. I'll probably have to go on campus."

"Well, I can take you there first."

"That might be best. Olson's sketch can wait over getting the phone number." He reached for his cellular phone, realizing he still hadn't picked up a new one. "You got a phone?"

She pointed at the floorboard, where a car phone sat in its charging stall.

He picked it up and dialed. University Communication Services were still not open. He replaced the phone.

"Another question," she said. "You know me, not much for computer details."

The Bronco lurched over some ice on the street as she pulled out into the busy downtown traffic. She spoke again. "I was looking over all the e-mail, and noticed it had a lot of information at the top."

"Headers."

"Right. And I noticed how similar all the headers are."

Tim looked down at the stack in his hands. He thumbed through them and picked out some of the e-mail. "Headers are created by the e-mail servers, machines on the Internet Service Provider. Many fill in similar information."

"Right. The names and dates looked different. Can you use that information to find Hando?"

"That's what I've been doing. And how I found his e-mail account."

"Hmm. But not his real name," she said softly. "Somehow he is getting access to the Internet. Wouldn't the provider—what's it?"

"Internet Service Provider."

"Right. Wouldn't they have his name?"

"Not sure which ISP Hando uses. He forged the headers."

"Everything?"

"All but the date and time. At least since the Ramey murder when he posted to the newsgroup."

Traffic got wild as they turned onto State Street and headed south. Over the road, the city had put up banners about activities for Black History month. Most of them already come and gone.

Sherrie asked, "What about Kurt Victor?"

"Headers were real. Victor used the university's system."

"Computers on campus?"

"From his dorm."

"Oh, so he called on a modem from his own computer—the dorm isn't high-speed yet."

Tim nodded. He glanced at the papers, noticing the phone transcripts for the first time since the day he was at Victor's dorm. The university ISP phone number had been highlighted by the campus police. There were many calls made during December and January—three or four times as many calls as the number of messages Victor sent. Which, suddenly, seemed a little strange to him.

He looked over the header dates on Victor's e-mails to Hando back in December. He found a corresponding phone call for each. And in between, he found one or two phone calls where Victor had not sent messages.

In the case notes, he found the replies Hando had sent to Victor and checked the dates. When he saw the correlation, he felt stupid.

"Holy Toledo!"

"What?" Sherrie looked at him.

"These phone transcripts. They correlate."

"What, Tim?"

"Every time Hando e-mailed to Victor, the dorm computer had called the ISP phone. It was connected at the same time."

"How? Hando used the dorm computer?"

Tim nodded. "And remember Victor's roommate?"

"Ned Lovanah?"

"Spell both names."

Sherrie whispered the letters, counting on her fingers. "...D-D, V-V...Alven Hando—Ned Lovanah. I can't believe it."

* * *

Lawrence Hall

Tim couldn't believe it was so simple. The names: Alven Hando—Ned Lovanah. Anagrams. Almost too convenient.

"All this time, Victor's roommate," Sherrie mumbled. "And you noted that there were a bunch of computer books in the dorm. You assumed they were Victor's."

"Yeah, but that's what Lovanah told us." Tim shook his head. "Victor wasn't even there when we did the search."

"You were more worried about Victor, I suppose. Left tracking Hando to the Canadians."

She was right; he could do only so much with his limited time.

They moved down the hallway, where all was quiet just after nine in the morning. Two deputies Sherrie had called followed behind them. Tim guided them to Victor's dorm room, remembering the last time he had been there with the campus police.

"Hang back," he told the two deputies. Sherrie strode along his side as they quickly closed the distance.

Tim rapped hard on the door and loosened his gun-snaps. Sherrie stood at his side, hand over the butt of her Glock. Both deputies spotted places behind.

After a moment the door cracked open and a loose-shirted kid peered at him. He was a blonde, lanky, surfer type and his blue eyes perked-up when he saw the uniformed deputies behind. But Tim didn't recognize him as Lovanah. Or Victor.

"Yeah," the student said timidly.

"FBI. We're looking for Ned Lovanah."

The student crinkled his brow. "Never heard of him."

"Who are you?"

"Bill Stuzon."

"We're looking for a kid that lives here. An Asian-Polynesian student."

"Oh. You mean Victor's old roommate, right?"

"Old roommate?"

"Back before his suspension. You here for Victor? He's not here."

"We're looking for Lovanah."

"I think Lovanah is just down the hall. My old room. When Victor came back, they switched us."

"Show us."

The kid came out in his underwear with hardly any apprehension. He took them to the end and stopped at the last room. "Here."

Tim pounded on the door. It opened wide, a Chinese student looked up at them and nodded at Bill behind them.

"Is Ned Lovanah here?"

The Chinese student nodded and pointed at one of the beds. "He is sick."

Tim entered, followed by Sherrie and the deputies. Lovanah lay in the bed, sweat drenching his brow. His eyes were closed.

"I take him to the doctor in the middle of night," the Chinese roommate said.

Tim turned to him. "Middle of the night?"

"To emergency. We were there until two in the morning. He has food poisoning. He sleeps now."

Another thought struck Tim at the same time. How did Lovanah, a foreign student, get access to government encryption? Something felt wrong.

"Did Ned go anywhere else last night?" Sherrie asked the roommate.

He shook his head.

"What doctor did he see?"

"Dr. Phelps. Bad dorm food. They pumped his stomach." The Chinese student held up a yellow paper. "Cost him two hundred dollars."

"Let me see that." Tim took the sheet. The doctor's orders and a date with time-stamp labeled the sheet. Lovanah had been at the hospital before and at the same time Yoshiko was there. The same time Hando abducted her.

Tim scratched his chin. Sherrie looked around. "Do you have a computer?" she asked.

The Chinese student shook his head.

From the doorway, Victor's new roommate, Bill, asked, "So what's going on? Did Kurt do something to that guy?"

Tim put the sheet in his pocket. He couldn't actually arrest Lovanah without good probable cause. Was the name correlation just a coincidence? The time of the phone records and computer usage just couldn't be coincidental. The key was the computer. Tim remembered finding Victor's stories on it. As he left the dorm room, he also recalled the oddity of the satellite tracking software. The strange video transmitter found at the scene could use a satellite for relaying the signal all over the world, if he knew how to tap into it. Just maybe the old roommate was still using Victor's computer...

"Hey, wait!" Bill followed him into the hall. "You know, I heard about Victor's arrest. But I find it hard to believe that he'd actually want to do some girl."

Tim didn't like the sound of "*do some girl.*" He walked back down the hall, remembering the specks of solder he had found on Victor's desk and floor. Or did Lovanah, who could still have a key to his old dorm room, leave the solder? Solder that came, no doubt, from making the black box in the video setup.

"What do you mean?" Sherrie asked the kid.

"I didn't think he liked girls."

Tim jerked his eyes to the student. "What?"

"I don't think Kurt Victor likes the ladies."

"Why do you say that?"

Stuzon smirked at them. "You didn't know?"

"No. Please educate us."

"Yeah. He was out-and-out queer. At least with me."

"What makes you so sure?"

"He's come on to me several times. A real lovebird."

"What do you mean, *come on* to you?"

"Last few nights I come home late from studying, you know, and he's all decked out in some crazy sado-maso fit. He calls to me in this fantasy voice like some Freddy Kruger and tries dirty lines on me. I'd just leave again."

"You're talking about Kurt Victor, right?"

"Yeah. No wonder Lovanah wanted out. The kid's a real psycho. He even uses another name at those times. Something like Linus. Linus Boltz."

A gate opened in Tim's head. "Is your last name spelled S-T-U-Z-O-N?"

"Yeah. Why?"

Bill Stuzon—Linus Boltz. Another anagram of another roommate.

"Tim…" Sherrie had written out the two names on a sheet.

"Yeah. I know." He turned to the roommate. "And where is Kurt Victor?"

"Hell, if I know. Or care. I haven't seen him since yesterday. Never came home last night."

"You two stay here. Arrest Victor if he comes back." Tim motioned at the deputies, then hurried down the corridor. Sherrie followed behind.

"Hey! What's going on?" Bill asked as they left.

* * *

Attorney's Office

Tim remembered Victor was supposed to meet with his lawyer some time in the morning before the attorney would call the bureau. Sherrie called for two more deputies, giving them the address and a time. It was mid-morning when they all arrived at the bright doorway of Daniel Clevor, Attorney at Law. Tim remembered the arrest, and the red Celica, Victor's car, that had been parked outside only a few weeks ago. The same red car used in each crime, and that Tim never got a warrant to search when he first arrested Victor.

"Oh it's you," Clevor said when he saw Tim at the entrance. It'd been almost three weeks since they last saw each other; outside the court the day Judge Truante gave Sam Grand a slim chance at staying Victor's release.

"Is Kurt Victor still here?" Tim asked through the small door-crack Clevor offered them.

"No, should he be?"

"Didn't he meet with you to discuss the settlement?"

"What settlement?" The door opened a little wider.

"The settlement you're working out in the Detroit Field office this afternoon."

Clevor shook his head. "You're confused. Kurt and I only spoke briefly yesterday about a possible suit. But I told him I would need at least a week, and a good-sized retainer this time. He seemed impatient with that, and said he'd already spent the money given him on a laptop. After all I've done for him, he threatened to find a new lawyer."

"Do you know who?"

Clevor shook his head and began closing the door. Tim put his shoe in its path.

"Do you know where Victor is right now?"

"Nope." The door pressed hard.

"If you see him call the bureau immediately. He'll be needing your services again." Tim moved his foot and the door slammed.

* * *

Residency

A manila envelope waited for Tim at the RA late in the afternoon. He had just returned from searching Victor's dorm, and from a trip to Communications Services on campus. Both had yielded positive-proof results of his theory, that Victor was Hando. The solder, he was sure, came from building the black box used in transmitting Victor's snuff video. And Tim had a good guess where he obtained the phase array antenna.

He ripped open the envelope. From it he extracted a collection of pictures and notes: the images he had printed of the girl in the faked video at the bakery, and a letter from the Ypsilanti police. They had sent the girl's picture out, like he requested the week before. A teacher in Ann Arbor recognized the girl. Her name was Laurie Dunlap. Currently, she was in Moscow with her folks. But the year before, she had attended a private junior high school in the area.

Tim recognized the name at once. Dunlap had been the man who alerted the university and FBI about Victor's story. How Victor got her picture, he couldn't understand. Unless, of course, Victor knew her before she moved to Moscow. Or, perhaps, he met her on the Internet.

He sat at his computer and searched the web for the girl's name associated with Ann Arbor or Moscow. It located two relevant hits. Both were personal web pages. One had a collection of pictures. Different shots of two girls, Laurie with a friend named Paula. Several of Laurie's photos looked identical to the ones he had printed from the faked video that Hando posted the week before.

In Victor's file, Tim found the name of the company that employed his father. Victor's dad worked as a field engineer at Digisat, a communications firm that consulted many satellite companies. He brought up Digisat's web page and read about their work with Microsoft's Teledesic, which was building the "Internet in the Sky"—a wireless network that would connect everyone worldwide by digital satellite communications. A free roaming, global Internet. The new system would come on line soon, and Digisat was providing proof-of-means studies and tests by borrowing satellites already in low earth orbits.

Tim called the office where Victor's dad worked, and introduced himself as a federal agent. The first technician assured him they were up to snuff on FCC regulation. Tim received royal treatment thereafter, and they transferred him to the lead engineer. He asked general questions about their projects, and learned that they indeed tested systems to "broadcast" high rate video data worldwide.

"It's pretty simple," the engineer told him in a whiny voice that grew more and more excited. "A lot like Digital TV—you know, DirecTV? In fact, we're borrowing one of their open channels, though on another LEO sat, for the first phase of tests."

"Can anyone transmit through the test satellites?" Tim asked.

"Well, sure if they know our protocol, but we keep that quiet. Otherwise, the system just down-links whatever appears at the uplink frequency. You have to physically sit in line of sight with the satellite. That requires some sat-tracking, you know, and a couple watts of signal—like, car battery power. But basically, if you can get a signal up there, it'll just bounce it across the other four test sats."

"And what about receiving? Who can receive the broadcast?"

"Well, you have to be under the sats, but like I said, you can use a standard digital TV receiver on the borrowed down-link frequency. We've been sending Microsoft software ads on our channel. With only five sats, we have big gaps in coverage, but we've picked up transmissions everywhere from Russia to South America."

Tim wondered if they saw the ten-minute videos Hando sent on their satellites. "One last question," he said. "Does Jacob Victor work on these systems?"

"Yeah, Jake leads our sensors group, and helped design the antennas we use remotely."

Tim bit his lip. Jacob Victor, Kurt's father, had either given his son the information or left it out someplace where Kurt got access. Kurt only needed to build the box, borrow an antenna designed by his dad, and track the test satellites in order to broadcast nearly worldwide.

* * *

Detroit

Tim drove into Detroit that evening, joy still bouncing through him since he discovered the truth. Everything with this case was falling into place. Hando was neither a phantom in Canada nor Victor's old roommate, but actually Victor himself!

There was no meeting between the bureau's attorneys and Victor's lawyer or anyone else. He guessed the afternoon appointment was probably a ruse to throw them off the trail. Probably called in by the subject himself. Tim wondered where Victor got all of his free time. But then, some college students seemed to have a lot of time with the little studying they apparently accomplished.

Nearly every other implication fit as well. The police sketch based on Olson's description of the third person from Zig's band was a portrait of Victor—Victor who sometimes called himself Hando. Tim couldn't believe it when he saw it. Only an hour before, the lab confirmed the size and weight of his body from the evidence they had collected from the glove prints and shoe tracks. All of it basically matched Victor's physical features. The eyebrow they had extracted would get tested in a few days. The blood type from the skin flakes at the swamp matched. He knew blood typing was rarely enough to convict but it was all a good start.

Also, Victor's current roommate, Stuzon, confirmed that the redhead Fairborne had visited Victor in the past week. It was another small piece that led to guilt by association. With a warrant obtained late afternoon, Tim had searched the dorm room and found several consistent markings of his theory that Victor was Hando. Besides the same computer books as before, Tim found electronic parts left over from the black box and more confirmation that Victor was indeed using Digisat's test satellites. It amazed Tim that he could do it, but that was exactly what the companies aimed for—a wireless digital connection for everyone in the world. Victor just got a jump start on the rest of the world through his dad. Tim wondered if Senator Euler would have heart failure when he realized that the whole world was about to become a billion global broadcast stations, each with the potential of sending porn and whatever else the user wanted. As for the faked rape, the synthetic video at the bakery, Tim made a few calls and learned that two years ago when

Victor first came to U-M he had worked part time for a month at the bakery in Depot Town. He'd even said as much to Hando in their last e-mail exchanges.

Also in the dorm, Tim found more depraved files on Victor's computer: stories about rape, mutilation and so forth. And a receipt under the bed from a camping surplus store on Liberty Street. Although it didn't have an itemized list, the amount of one entry was the exact price for a four-pack of canned cooking fuel. Another receipt in the desk indicated that Victor had recently bought new tires for his red Toyota. And lastly, the university matched the phone call from his trace at *nether.net*—Jager's system—to Victor's dorm telephone.

Tim kicked himself because the clues had already been staring him in the face: the computer logs, the books, the satellite tracking software, and the tutoring rich elementary kids. One of which turned out to be a victim. And he bet the fibers they had found at that scene came from a dye unique to Africa. Probably from a sweater Victor's mother had acquired during her anthropologic research.

Victor's whole manner from the beginning; all indicative of the profile Tim had received from DC last Monday. A past-grown schizophrenic with leanings toward a *"complex psychopath."* Someone with irrationality problems and deep-rooted deviancy. Having what essentially equated to an electronically-linked multiple personality disorder.

But now Victor or Hando, or whatever he was calling himself today, had disappeared. The bureau immediately sent a team to his parents' home in Illinois. His dad had not seen him, of course. The assailant could be with Zig hiding out somewhere. Tim didn't know, but they seemed to have disappeared days apart. He believed Victor was alone—well, as alone as a multiple personality could be.

The only thing that still didn't make sense was the government encryption. But now Tim was betting that Jack Lacey Keller had given it to Victor/Hando. JLK was someone with secret access. Who?—Tim had his suspicions: Striker, Mott...

In any event, there was an All Points Bulletin out for Victor. Every police department in the Midwest would fax and transmit the APB across their own version of a network. It wouldn't be long before they had Victor in custody. He had little cash and he didn't fit the profile of someone that robbed for money. Either they'd find him using credit cards or he'd surface at a friendly place like home. And a surveillance team would jump him instantly.

It was all going well. As if a 2000-piece puzzle Tim couldn't even start a couple of weeks ago was now really looking like the box cover; the end was in sight. He should have felt proud and appeased and victorious.

Yet by nightfall, his body had tensed and his mind twisted in anxiety. Something had begun gnawing at him and distressing him. Not the case. Not his job. Not even his family.

It was the timing.

He just couldn't seem to get out of the cycle of time. Like the case was turning back on itself or doing a replay. Events in time, playing a trick on him.

Early in the evening, he parked his truck just off a driveway in the neighborhood. The first place of *time* or memory for him. Where his mother still lived. Not sure why, he'd come back. Maybe to find comfort or just to see it one more time before...

"I'm just getting pre-arrest jitters," he told himself as he stepped onto her porch.

He had felt it all before—just before closing down a New York wire fraud ploy, prior to hitting a software hacking ring, and when he set up child pornographers. In each case everything had turned out right. All except for Danville. Even that had ended now. Only a little more to go and he would be finished with this era. His life would make that turn. A transition he had sensed coming for weeks now. He only needed to snap those last couple of pieces into the gaps and it would be picture-perfect.

It was harder than it sounded. In the past, he'd found that the last few details could cause as much or more grief than everything preceding. Sometimes he almost became overwhelmed by the details and bureaucratic crap at the end. That was when it became necessary to go back to the beginning and see why and how it all started. And for some unknown reason, Tim found himself at the entrance to his mother's home.

He rapped with the lion-face knocker and a slow moment later, the door opened cautiously. When his mother saw him, a broad smile seized her face.

"Tim!" She hugged him.

"Hi, Mom." He entered and kissed the top of her netted hair, hugging her back.

"Ohh," she fussed, letting go of him and holding her hip.

"What's the matter?"

She reached for a kitchen chair. "Oh, my hip and back have been giving me problems again."

Tim helped her with the chair. "Have you seen the doctor?"

"Yes. He said I may have a rheumatoid problem or something."

His mother was aging. Tim hated to see it happen. The one person that was always a pillar of strength for him, now crumbling with old age. "Is there anything I can do for you, Mom?"

"Just hug me again, softly."

He bent down and kissed her cheek.

"I just cleaned up from dinner, but I could get you a dish of ice cream, if you want." She started to lift herself from the seat.

"No, stay. I'm fine. Ate a big dinner before coming." He hadn't actually had dinner. He had wanted to take her out. But he arrived later than he intended and it didn't look promising.

"Well I was about to watch a show. You want to join me, or should we just talk?"

"Either."

"Let's talk for a while."

Tim nodded a smile. "You want to sit on a softer seat in the living room?"

"Sure."

He helped her up and they slowly went to the couch. Sheets were folded on top of it and a comforter laid on the floor. His mother sat on the sofa and Tim took the recliner.

"You expecting company for the night?" Tim asked, looking at the bed linen and blankets around the room.

"No," she sighed and grabbed a pillow to put behind her back.

Tim also noticed drawers. His mother's dresser drawers were filled with clothes and stacked all around the living room. A large pile of dirty clothes sat in one corner, barely hidden by an old chair.

"Are you doing okay, Mom?" She'd never been one for having a cluttered home.

"I guess," she said quietly, her face reflective. "A little lonely."

"Anything need work? Like your bed or dresser?"

She looked around at her clothes. "It's just a lot easier than going up and down those stairs so many times a day."

He wondered. "Let me take a look, okay?"

"Suit yourself. But you have to tell me what's happening with you. And with my grandkids."

"Sure, when I get back down." Tim rose and headed for the stairs.

"Back down? Where're you going?"

"Just a check."

As he climbed the stairs, he noticed several items were stacked on the first three steps. All objects that normally belonged upstairs, like the second phone, her bedroom lamp and several books and the Bible she usually kept on her nightstand. He reached the top stair and flipped on the hall light. The bulb flashed and then died. It hadn't been used for a while.

He reached the bedroom and turned on the light. Her room was in disarray. The dresser was just a frame, the bedding was messed up and the floor was spotty with all kinds of particles and dirt. The furniture looked dusty. He wondered how long it had been since she stayed in her room. It had been only a few weeks since he visited last. He went into hall and entered the bathroom. It appeared somewhat bare. No soap or toothpaste. Shampoo and towels missing. Just a half-roll of toilet paper and other odds and ends mixed in with the accumulating dust. The second bedroom had the same telltale signs of desertion—long before the first.

He descended the stairs with an uneasy feeling. Before going back into the living room, he entered the kitchen and opened the cupboards and refrigerator. He found more signals of a problem. The shelves were starved of food items. Mostly just some basics like bread and cereal and a few apples in the cupboards. The fridge had some old condiment bottles and pickles and a spoiled container or two. There was a small, half carton of Vanilla ice cream in the freezer. Not much to live on.

"Tim? Are you in the kitchen?"

"Yeah, Mom. I'm getting a glass of water." He turned on the faucet briefly, feigning his explanation.

It was so hard to see it all like this. His own problems he could live with, but to find his mother in such circumstance was almost unbearable. He returned to the living room with a forced smile. His need for comfort had turned into a need to comfort his mom.

"Sit down," she said. "You're making me tired."

He sat, not knowing what to say. Wanting to take the pain from her.

"You look pretty good," she said. "A little thin. You need someone to cook for you. All of that fast-food is doing you no good."

"Probably." Tim wondered how she was managing to keep weight. She still looked the same size. But her eyes were baggy and her face was drawn down, more worn than he remembered from just a month earlier.

"I was just remembering how good-a-eater that boy of yours is. Reggy can eat me out of house-and-home."

Tim nodded, recollecting the growth spurt the boy had that two summers ago when they visited her for a week. Reggy was constantly hungry. Somehow he had convinced his grandmother that he wanted a coconut in the store. Tim objected over the price. But his mother had insisted that coconuts were "the best thing for growin' boys."

"And you don't bring them by enough. Janice gets too busy too." She patted her lap and gazed at him through her glasses. "I called there yesterday. You were out working late, as usual, getting yourself hurt, I hear."

"Mom."

"I know. You love it. Now Janice's going to work, she says."

Tim had nearly forgotten about that. His children were missing both of them.

"And those kids are growing so fast. You don't bring them here enough."

"You said that already."

"So I did." She sighed. "I remember when you were Reggy's age. You were a good boy, Tim. So was Cedric."

Cedric was Tim's younger brother. A real good kid. Never got into trouble. He was the last one Tim had thought deserved to die like he did. On leave from the army, he came back to Detroit to visit Mom. A mile from her house, he saw some guy assaulting an old woman. He stopped the taxi, got out and struggled with the mugger. The man pulled a gun and shot Cedric in the chest.

"You were a good baby, too." She grabbed a framed photo of Tim and Cedric as boys.

He watched her eyes sparkle with water. "You were—are—a good mother."

"Well, sometimes."

"No, always."

Tears welled in her eyes, filling them completely. She began reminiscing. "I can't forget the time when you were walking and climbing a lot. We had a crib that finally broke after Cedric used it for a couple of years. One night you figured out how to climb out, and could also open the door. You were about two. I was trying to sleep because I had an early shift at the factory. But you kept getting up and I would put you back. It went on five or six times through the night and by four in the morning, I couldn't stand it."

"I'm sorry, Mom." Tim remembered long nights with his own two.

"I was so tired and got upset at you." She stopped and released a single sob. "I spanked you real hard. About an hour later I found you sleeping out of bed on the floor with your pajamas off and a big purple spot on your back-end."

"It's okay." He reached for her hand.

"I felt so bad," she cried. "I hardly could do my work that day, thinking about you and wanting so bad to go back and hug you and ask you for forgiveness. Then that afternoon I picked you up from my mother's, and you greeted me with a hug and a smile. It hurt so much and I told you I was sorry, but you didn't understand. You had forgotten all about it."

"It's all right, Mom."

She wept some more. "I just want to see my grandchildren, Tim." She looked at him with a sorrowful, pitiful simper. "Family is all I have now."

Tim gulped at the thick wad developing in his throat. Somehow he had to do something. His mother needed him now. She needed love and care and him. So did his family. He knew his priorities had been skewed. And now, for some odd reason, he felt it might be too late to fix them.

Thursday, February 20

Residency

Ms. Downey badgered Tim about paperwork and messages when he entered; it was late already. He had over-slept after staying up at his mother's home, cleaning, grocery shopping and sitting at a Laundromat with her clothes.

Mott barely looked up as Tim passed his cubicle, only glaring from the corner of his eye. But Tim didn't want to confront him at that moment. Sooner or later he'll have to apologize to Mott about the insinuation. Kaplan had told him that Mott was now working on a special op. Something apparently administered out of Hansen's office. Some kind of special assignment that had Mott working the Klan because he was such a shoo-in there. Between that and Lonque, Tim still had his doubts, wondering whose idea it really was and why. But that was another problem he just didn't need right now. He had all he could handle.

During a brief moment the day before, he set up an appointment with Jack Lacey Keller, Hando's friend, using Hando's double email account. JLK would meet with their undercover Hando that afternoon. Tim just needed someone for the part.

He reached his desk and wrapped his black parka around the chair. His trench coat had been burned beyond use. Before he sat, he grabbed the phone and began dialing. About halfway through the sequence for Bellow's office, someone tapped him on the shoulder. He turned to find Sam Grand.

"Hi, I barely missed you in the hall," the lawyer said. He reached in his dark suit pocket.

"I was just on my way over after one phone call."

"No problem. I've got everything here." Grand pulled out a thick envelope.

"Warrants?" Tim rolled out his seat.

"For Keller, when you catch him. Conspiracy to commit murder."

Tim took the envelope. He wanted Keller, but the charges paled compared with what they had against Victor and his two friends. "Thanks, Sam."

Grand smiled. "My daughter has been asking about you. She wants to know if you can show her how to load the CD-ROM drivers on our computer in case they go south again."

"Sure. I'll come over some time." Tim reached for his desk drawer. "And give her this." He handed Grand a CD game.

"Now she'll be asking me to invite you more often. She'll love it, thanks."

"No problem."

Grand waved the disc and said good-bye. Tim went back to the phone. On the third ring Givens answered.

"Givens. It's Tim Delbravo. What's the latest?"

"Neither us or the Toledo police have any files or ID on a Jack Lacey Keller. The name is nowhere. But we haven't actually sent any requests to DC yet since you gave us such short notice about your plans."

"Well I didn't say anything because I thought I was getting suspended."

"We'll have to wing it, I guess, and use only local know-hows. What's your plan?"

"We'll send someone to meet Keller. I'll listen to the wire from here, see what evidence we get."

"You don't want the part?"

"I've been in the news too much to impersonate Hando. I would suggest Olson, but he's still recovering."

Givens said, "I don't think we can spare anyone here. The only one I can think of is Louis Mott because he knows the computer jargon and the subject might want to talk it up. Any ideas at your end?"

"Not him," Tim said. "What about Spike Cobbs?"

"Who? You mean Taylor Cobbs there in Ann Arbor?"

"Yeah, we call him Spike. He could do it, but may not be well versed on computers."

"Good idea. Can you spend an hour and brief him on the technical nature?"

"It may take more like two, but I'll get him started. You authorizing it?"

"Yes, and did you get the paperwork?"

"Just saw the U.S. Attorney."

"Good."

"Since I'll be busy prepping Cobbs, I'm leaving the procedure up to you guys. When can I expect it?"

"I'll schedule cooperation from the Toledo RA, then fax the plan to you on the secured line."

"Okay. I'll look for it then."

"Go over it with Cobbs. I want you to review every detail."

"Got it."

Tim hung up. The plan was moving. Today they'd get Keller, if all went well. And next he'd find Victor.

* * *

Residency

By lunchtime, Tim was drained. Spike breathed and moaned under the weight of the task. He was smart, but no one could be expected to learn so quickly what it took even a computer hacker weeks to pick-up.

"About the best thing you can do," Tim told him in conclusion, "is to put him off. Say that it's a secret. And you'll reveal it after he's proven his commitment."

Spike nodded. "So if he starts asking about how I, I mean Hando, keeps so concealed on the Internet, I just make like it's some kind of rites-of-passage?"

"Yep. You'll do fine." Tim slapped Spike on the back. He had three hours before meeting agents in Toledo. "Go get some lunch. We'll meet for one more hour after a short break."

Spike sighed and rose, holding a thick stack of papers in his left hand. Tim shook his head as Spike left. There was no way anyone could expect Spike to learn all of this. The computer lingo, Hando's past posts and his stories and e-mail with Keller. All together with the Field Office's plan for the sting, it was a lot to demand. But Cobbs kept moving fast.

He rose to leave with pangs of hunger driving him out. Just before he escaped the RA, Sherrie Marshall showed up at the entrance. Her face was minus its usual smile.

"Hi. What's up?" he asked.

"Guess who us county-dips just rounded up?"

"Victor?"

Sherrie shook her head. "Sorry. Just Fairborne and Ponke. They were hiding out in Pittsfield Township at a nightclub."

"And Victor wasn't with them?"

"No. I questioned them myself. They know him, but don't know where he is."

"Where are they?"

"Don't know. I tried to call you, but your boss got on. Said someone else would pick them up. They could be in Detroit."

"I'll find out. At least we got them."

Tim reached in his parka—not as many pockets as his trench coat. He pulled out the envelope and removed some papers. "I have warrants for everyone now."

Sherrie looked them over. "What about drug possession?"

Tim sucked his lower lip. "When we first applied, Grand told me we didn't actually have evidence of drugs. Nothing was found in the dorms. But now the DEA can sweep up that part."

Sherrie rubbed the top of his desk. "Tim, now that the case is breaking, and there's more help coming, I may need to spend full time on my own cases."

"I appreciate what you've given." He hoped she wasn't leaving because of what happened between them the night before.

Her lips remained straight. "I'll catch up with you later tomorrow or the next day."

* * *

Toledo, Ohio

Spike Cobbs entered the Franklin Park Mall in North Toledo, carrying the designated rainbow-colored umbrella in his hand, and an undesignated wire under his shirt. It would transmit a mile away in open areas, shorter in the mall. At the proper moment he sat on a bench in front of the Star-Pro shoe store and began watching for Jack Lacey Keller. He hadn't been given a photo or sketch or any indication of what the subject looked like. The ASAC had said he would have to wing it on their devised dialogue.

The mall was typically laid out. A large main hall with store-fronts lining the walls, and little carts, benches, displays and a fountain shielding the middle. At two in the afternoon, the crowd was still slight, but growing larger for the evening rush. Somewhere around him, there were three other undercovers, borrowed from the Toledo residency for a couple of hours. They would watch and follow, each with their receiver connected by airwaves to his small wire transmitter. They suspected that the subject would want to travel, and they had three separate cars for the tail. He wouldn't code-call them until they had absolute ID or proof of wrong doing by Keller.

Cobbs watched several people stroll by him. Most of them were ladies, many with kids. Few if any were young men. At five after two, a young woman with short dark hair and brown, bell-bottom jeans walked up to him and sat down at his bench.

"That's a bright umbrella for such a dark day," she said. It was the code Keller had designated in e-mail for first contact.

Spike was so stunned when the girl said Keller's line that he completely forgot his own.

"I said that's a bright…"

"Yeah. I…" Spike faltered. Was she Jack Lacey Keller? "I need it to, uh…make some rain." It was, inexactly, supposed to be his formulated reply.

"Are you Hando?" she asked.

Spike wondered what was going on. Maybe he should bail, stop the operation. A girl meant either another accomplice, or that Keller was the pseudonym she used. Or, could it be she was setting up Hando? Someone acting independently of the FBI?

She shook her head confusedly and began to get up.

"Yeah. It's me, Alven Hando." Spike rose and dodged in front of her. "You just caught me off guard. I was expecting…"

"A guy?"

"Yeah."

"Come on." She began walking to the exit, carrying a dark jacket in her hand. Spike noticed her white T-shirt fitted tightly and revealed full breasts despite the horribly loose bell-bottoms below. Definitely a woman.

"I've got a car outside," she said.

"So do I."

"We'll take mine. I know the way."

"Way to where?"

She didn't reply. He followed this young, unabashed female as she slipped on her coat and pushed through the exit. In the parking lot she made a line to a fifteen-year-old Firebird with gray and red primer for paint. After she unlocked the side door Spike got in and sat on torn upholstery. The Firebird, a Bondo-plated memorial with shoe-sized holes in the floorboard, started on the girl's third attempt. Then Keller, or whatever her name was, pulled away and drove out of the mall parking lot. She turned the crumbling vehicle down Regis Street and silently maneuvered it like a station wagon, making slow turns and letting everyone else pass her. She lit a cigarette and smoked it casually.

"Are you Keller?"

She didn't respond.

"Where the hell are you taking me?"

"Just be patient," she said. She wore green and brown camouflage bands around her wrists. Her coat remained open. He could see something tucked in a pocket of the lining—a small handgun, a .22 cal probably. By the looks of her, Spike didn't question whether she could use it. He wondered if she was on to him.

"That's it. I want an explanation, or I want out."

Abruptly, she opened all four barrels in her Autolife carburetor. They sailed down one-way streets at twice their speed limit. The Firebird moved into the heart of Toledo like a torpedo. After going through three red lights, into a parking stall, out an alley, and down three side streets, she resumed her grandmotherly motor skills and offered a short explanation.

"Just to be sure you weren't followed."

Spike felt his stomach gurgle. He suppressed an urge to look back for his tail. If she lost them, he might have to fight, even kill her. She didn't look too tough, but without a gun, he was at a disadvantage. He had been expecting a man, a guy with intentions and an obvious plan, a crazy fellow that practically idealized Hando.

"Are you a cop?" he asked, although he just couldn't believe it. Nothing she was doing met with any sort of protocol he had ever heard.

"Don't worry. See, this is your lucky day," she said.

Don't worry?

He glanced at her. She drove slowly, like they were going to church. Maybe she was a religious-freak, a cult member. Or part of some kind of weird, underground cyber-punk gang. A gang meant violence. And, according to instructions, Spike hadn't brought his credentials, let alone a gun. At the start, he had every reason to believe he wouldn't need them with all the back up. Now he had no way to prove he wasn't Hando without the supporting undercovers.

"Look, you," he said. "Where's Keller? I didn't come to meet with some bitch. I'm the one in charge here."

"You are, huh?" She kicked the accelerator. They shot down a narrow street and abruptly turned, tires squealing, into a lot—a motel lot. The Firebird came to a screeching halt and she cut the ignition.

"What's going on?" he asked.

Without a word she got out and motioned for him to follow. He slowly opened his door and watched as she pulled a key from her coat and began unlocking a motel room whose door met the sidewalk on the outside.

"What the hell are we doing? Where's Keller?" Spike closed the car door, causing large chunks of Bondo and rust to fall off. He reached out and grabbed her arm at the doorway. She didn't even look at him. Just pulled her arm and swung him inside, away from the door. She slammed the door and jerked his hand off her elbow.

"Sit down," she dictated—not in a cruel or harsh tone. Almost pleasantly she added, "I've got something to give you. Don't worry."

The cheap motel room was ordinary to the extreme. A bolted down 13-inch TV sitting on a small dresser-table, a single bed with a single painting above it, lamp on a table by the far window and a bathroom. It looked just maid-prepared and was empty except for one very small duffel bag on the bed.

"Open it," she told Spike. "It's a gesture of good will, I'm told."

Cautiously, he went to the bag and began unzipping it.

"There should also be a note at the bottom," the girl said.

"A note? What about?"

"Haven't read it, can't say. I'm not supposed to touch anything. But they said the note should explain everything to you."

"They?"

"Just read the note."

The bag contained three stacks of bills. Twenty-dollar bills stacked in sets of probably fifty, equaling something around three thousand dollars. And under those was the note she had mentioned.

"Use it wisely." She went to the door and then turned back. After wiping some keys with a cloth, she tossed them on the bed. "You should stay here tonight. It's already paid for." She winked and dragged on her smoke. "Wish I could stay the night, honey, but orders is orders."

She opened the door, wiped the knob, and began to leave.

"Wait!" Spike started after her. "What's this about? Where's Keller?"

She shrugged, then walked out, leaving the door open. Spike's mind exploded with impressions and ideas, causing him to dash to the bag and rifle through it for the note. Then he ripped the wire from his chest and slammed it to the bottom of the bag. After throwing a single stack of bills on the bed with the note and the keys, he hauled the bag and its remnants out and sprinted to the Firebird that was nearing the lot exit. He smacked the window and motioned for her to roll it down. She complied. He tossed the bag on her lap.

"I don't want this. Take it back to whoever put you up to it."

She looked at him blankly and waved her head. "Your choice."

The car, pitching gravel and ice with 18-inch wide treads, screeched out of the lot. He ran back to the motel room and called the Toledo Residency, giving them his location and some scant details that would hopefully allow the tails to keep following her.

* * *

Residency

In Ann Arbor, Bob Givens sat with Tim in his cubicle where they were monitoring a conference call from Toledo. With three tails, the girl had not lost all of them, and one had kept right up with her from the time she left the motel. Spike's quick thinking left them listening to everything going on in her car, which for the moment wasn't more than some muffled music—muffled because the wire was in the zipped bag under two stacks of bills. They couldn't even determine the exact likeness of the music for now.

"I guess we should up-rank this op," Givens said quietly. "I'll send a short task summary to DC since we never fully briefed it."

Tim didn't have to worry about administrative protocol at this level. He just sat and took it all in. Toledo had the pick-up from the wire being repeated across the phone on the conference call, and he listened casually as he re-read the faxed copy of the note that Spike had pulled from the duffel bag. It was a few, simple lines, typed and left unsigned.

Here's a little something to help you keep posting. Try to go south, if you can. You're doing good work, we really appreciate it. In your next couple of adventures, add Jack Lacey Keller as a guest star. Once we see you can continue, we'll contact you with more assistance. Make us proud!

Several things could be harvested from the note. One, they had a little cash, maybe more, but weren't willing to spend all that much on someone like Hando just yet. Spike had told Toledo that all the twenties looked crisp and new. Now the Toledo residency was trying to decipher their origin by serial and time on the street. At least it would be known which bank had originally received it, and when.

Next, they liked the work, appreciated the effort Hando was making. Oddly, they wanted the likely mythical JLK to be a part of the snuff stories. Strange motives meant peculiar people. And part of their plan included Hando going south. Why, was anyone's guess.

Also, they had a way to contact Hando, presumably by e-mail. Keller's account had assuredly been forged like Hando's, making it obvious that whoever they were, they were techno-savvy.

Last, "We" meant more than the girl. They, probably many more than one, were likely more advanced in technique than the girl. The girl, Tim bet, was a gopher. Other than the note and her features caught on video at the mall, not much else was known about her. The Toledo RA ran a check on the license of the Firebird and came up with a stolen plate.

Currently, the girl headed out of Toledo, going just past Rossford by way of back roads. And even with the stolen plates and innuendo of conspiracy with a known fugitive, the FBI wouldn't haul her in until they knew what was really happening. Until the surprise was understood.

When the garbled music on the speaker finally died, Tim was contemplating what kind of motive this group must have to encourage someone like Hando. An organized effort, no less.

"Okay, she's pulling back onto a main road," said the undercover agent over the speaker. He was still tailing her. *"We're now on Rawlson Ave, just past Ford Road. Going east."*

When they realized what Spike had done, Givens contacted Detroit and enlisted an audio engineering expert there to gather all the sounds and analyze them on the fly. Now they had Toledo, Ann Arbor and Detroit on the conference call. Fortunately most everyone was busy listening and not talking at the same time.

Tim kept his NCIC and Internet terminals ready, so when information was needed immediately, he could grab it fast.

"We're pulling into a...motel. The Cavelier, off Rawlson."

Then the speaker phone relayed several curious sounds, probably the engine dying, the car door creaking open, and the unmistakable sound of the door slamming shut. There were other noises, stuff he couldn't make out.

For a long moment, everything was silent.

"She's gone inside," the tail said. *"It looks like she didn't even stop at the front desk. I'm heading in."*

"How's your juice?" someone from Toledo asked.

"The wire should be good for another hour. It's the cell I'm transmitting from that'll be dead soon. One of the others should have an extra—"

Fweeeep! They all went quiet when they heard the sharp reverberation. It was a zipper being opened, and stuff being shuffled, maybe from the bag or a coat.

"She's probably in a room," the agent whispered. *"Not sure which."*

No one spoke further. And for another eternal moment, they listened to clearer indications of movement and breathing and just silence. Then just as Tim thought she had gone to sleep or maybe had left, they heard some more movements followed by the far off, yet distinct, two-tone harmonics of a push-button phone. Numbers were being pressed. A call was being made.

"Givens," Tim whispered. "Get the engineer."

"Yeah. I'm ahead of you." Givens, in the adjacent station, had picked up another phone.

"It's Rainbow Girl." The voice of the subject was fairly clear, despite being soft. Tim turned up the volume a little. Too much and it would reverberate through every phone on the conference. So he muted the mic on his end.

"Yeah. I found him."

A pause.

"Sort of good-looking. Short hair, maybe kind of punk....No, a perfect gentleman of all things."

Another moment of silence.

"Far from smooth...Up till we got to the motel, then he went over the edge."

From behind, Givens, who had been whispering in the other cubicle, returned.

"Didn't go for it. Gave the bag back...What?"

Givens handed Tim a note.

"*Well,*" the girl said, and noises engulfed the transmission, hissing or scraping sounds. "*The note's gone…No, just two stacks. Why?*"

The note had a phone number. The audio expert in Detroit had deciphered the dual-tone signal from the transmission revealing the area code "708." Tim lifted an eyebrow at Givens.

"*No, there're only two.*"

"South Chicago suburbs, I guess?" Givens whispered.

"*You never told me.*"

Tim quickly logged on to his terminal and fired up a connection to the reverse-index database.

"*What now?*"

Within a moment, Tim was looking at an address to a restaurant called the Wrangler Inn near Calumet City, south of Chicago. The phone number belonged to a public pay phone there. Whoever she was talking with, he would be gone after finishing the conversation. He pointed at the restaurant's address and Givens wrote it on a slip before running back to the other phone.

"*See, I didn't know the plan,*" the girl was explaining.

Something triggered Tim's memory. After turning up the volume all the way and listening further, he grabbed his desk phone and programmed it with the number. Set to speed-dial.

"*Just tell me what I should do with the bag.*"

Faintly, Tim thought he might have heard the other voice. Something familiar in it.

"*Okay, I'll call you when I get there.*"

As soon as he heard what sounded like a phone going down against a receiver, Tim pressed the speed-dial. It rang only once and then someone answered.

"What now?" the person, a man asked with an unforgettable voice.

"Who is this?" Tim asked anyway.

The phone clicked dead, but Tim had pretty much confirmed his suspicion.

Givens returned. Tim rotated in his chair. "How fast?"

"Twenty minutes for an agent. Five for local Calumet City police. But we don't even have a description. At most, we'll maybe get prints off the phone or possibly an eyewitness." He looked at Tim's desk. "Were you just on the phone?"

"I called the number right after the girl got off."

"Delbravo! You might have spooked the guy."

"Yeah, but I had a deep suspicion. It's all connected, Givens."

"Of course, but how?"

"*Ann Arbor, should we grab her?*"

Tim held up a finger at Givens, then he reached out and tapped the conference mute back off. "Tim Delbravo in Ann Arbor here. I think I know what might be going on. Yes, haul the girl in now. Set up for questioning. I'll fax you everything within five minutes."

"You coming down?" asked the Toledo RAC.

"It'll take me over an hour to get there. I have to make a quick stop first." He hit mute and grabbed some paper to write his theory.

"What's going on, Tim?" Givens studied his note. "Who was on the phone in Chicago?"

"Dan Buck."

"And that's…?"

"One of Senator Euler's aides."

* * *

Hospital

Visiting hours would be over long before Tim could return to Ann Arbor, so he visited Yoshiko quickly before going to Toledo.

"We can not thank you so much. Please, accept our gratitudes." Takashi, Yoshiko's Father, bowed for what was the tenth time.

His wife still held her head down, uttering, "*Domo arigato gozaimasu.*"

Both were dressed formally in business-like apparel. Behind them, the doctor moved to Yoshiko, checking on her temperature.

Tim bowed back, embarrassed and unsure. "I'm so sorry about your daughter."

Takashi smiled, then turned and dashed back to a corner, where he pulled out a bag. From it, he extracted a box and returned it to Tim.

"Please, accept this gift," he offered, holding out the box.

Tim took it. The packaging had Kanji lettering, but the picture on it indicated that it was some kind of electronic device. Something made by Sony.

"We heard you work with computers. That is a pocket computer. The best in Japan." Takashi puckered and stood straight, like nobility.

"I don't know what to say." Tim looked back at the couple. Holding out a hand, he said, "Thank you, but I don't deserve this."

"Agent Delbravo," Yoshiko called from the bed, where the doctor had finished. "I'm so glad you have come to visit me again."

Tim smiled. How should he comfort or reassure her? He didn't know what to say. It was his fault she got hurt at all. If he had not wasted time with fears, if he had rushed into that school the moment he got there, then he could have saved her the burns.

Yoshiko swallowed painfully and flashed modest eyes at him. "I hear what you did. And what the other police did. Thank you all so much."

Tim could hardly look her in the eye. "We feel so badly that this happened. I'm so sorry we didn't get there sooner."

She nodded gingerly. A small smile formed on her bruised lips. He turned his glance away again. Looking in her eyes reminded him again of Robinson's daughter, right after her dad died.

* * *

Toledo

The residency in Toledo, like Ann Arbor's, did not have a formal interrogation room. The Firebird girl, Francine Draveson, sat in the office of their Resident Agent in Charge. Another agent, SA Thompson, sat with Tim and the girl.

Draveson still wore her T-shirt and brown jeans. She looked drained, as she would after a two-hour grilling. They hadn't charged her yet, and so, didn't ask her if she wanted a lawyer. She didn't seem to know the rules and never asked for one. She was just beginning to cooperate.

"So what happened next?" Tim had been asking most of the questions.

"Well, like I told you already..." Draveson's words came out weak. She was tired, he could tell. "I told the guy on the phone that some of the cash was missing. He said to hang tight at my place, only not in so few words, you know. Like some kind of hot shot Harvard grad. Big words and all."

"You don't know him well, then?"

"What am I getting? I'll tell you, but how do I know you can make me a deal?"

"If you want a deal, we have to charge you with a crime. You'll ask for a lawyer, then spend a couple of nights in jail before we even get to negotiations."

"So why the hell am I being held?"

"All you got to do is answer our questions, and you go home tonight without a charge. Not even for stolen plates."

"I told you, I found them at the dump." She looked at the door. "I want a smoke."

"No," the RAC said.

Tim leaned forward. "You tell us a little more, then we'll buy you a whole carton."

"I like unfiltered."

"Right. So what did he want you to do?"

"I was told that orders were coming. The next morning. Then I hung up and minutes later, you goons stormed my room."

"And you don't know anything about computer accounts?"

"I told you, nothing. I never heard nothin' about a computer. I hardly know what they look like."

Tim suspected she wouldn't have any information about the encryption or forged accounts. She was just a chauffeur, it seemed.

"How did you get the bag with the cash?"

This was only a little further than she had gone before. She sighed and looked at the RAC, who hadn't said much yet. SA Thompson took notes.

"Can I get a drink at least?"

The RAC nodded at his agent, who rose and grabbed a coffee pot. "Black or cream?"

"Black," she said.

"And about the cash?"

She didn't speak.

"Have you met your contact, face to face?"

She took the mug from Thompson and drank quietly. Tim had been through the questions so many times, he felt like a auctioneer.

"You live in Chicago?"

"No."

"Toledo?"

"Are you kidding? I spent a year here one weekend. Real boring place."

"How did you meet the contact?"

"I like unfiltered."

Tim looked at the RAC. He shook his head.

"Did he hand you the cash?" Tim asked.

"No."

"How did he give it to you?"

"It was just there—at the motel. He told me there would be cash in the bag. Told me it was less than what I would make that month helping him. But I didn't know the exact amount or anything else about it. It was already there when we got to the motel. I was to make sure that I got the guy from the mall to the motel, leave no prints, and make sure no one followed. Nothing illegal." She turned to the RAC. "Can I have a smoke now?"

"Not in here," The RAC said.

"Then you get shit."

Tim leaned over to the RAC. "Just get some," he whispered.

The senior agent sighed, then nodded at his man again, who rose and left the office.

Tim looked back at Draveson and asked, "Did you ever meet your contact another time?"

She took a sip from the mug, then set it down. "I need a smoke."

"It's coming."

"I'll wait."

"Did your contact give you the name Keller?"

"He mentioned it."

"And Alven Hando?"

"Yeah, but I wasn't supposed to give out names."

"On the phone?"

"Yeah."

Thompson entered, carrying a new pack of menthols, filtered. He handed them to her. The RAC pulled a lighter from his desk and tossed it across the table at her. She exhausted half of her first cigarette in the first drag.

"Ready?"

She looked at Tim, holding up the pack. "I wanted unfiltered."

"You'll get cancer."

She finished the cigarette, throwing ashes on the floor.

"Had you met him?"

She took out another cigarette. "What the hell. All right. I doubt this guy is dangerous. Just weird."

"Name?"

"I don't know. Never said it."

Tim slid a photo set of men to Draveson. He had shown them to her three times already. "Is he one of these?"

"What did I do that was so illegal, besides grabbing plates out of the trash?"

"Ms. Draveson, you tell us about your contact, and we'll give you a new set of plates free."

"And the carton? Unfiltered?"

"And two cartons."

She smiled, then looked over the photo set. She shook her head. "Not one of these."

"What about this set?" Tim slid a second photo set to her.

"There's the little shit." She pointed at the last. A photo of Dan Buck.

"And he never mentioned a name?"

"No names. But I heard him say something about a guy in Nebraska. Someone that was setting up the account, whatever that means."

"Money or computer account?"

"I don't know."

"Where in Nebraska?"

She sucked down on the cigarette, then exhaled a long hazy breath. "Don't know, but you could probably line up the whole state in this squad room. Just a bunch of farmers."

"So you've been there?"

"Not even a weekend. Look, I've told you everything I know."

"Then we'll go through it some more."

"Again?" She coughed.

"One last time with a court reporter." Tim sat back. "And a video camera. We want to get this on record."

Friday,
February 21

Residency

Tim woke late again, after arriving home well into the early morning. His family had been asleep, and he sat on the couch for another half-hour, anagramming "Alven Hando" on a notepad. His favorites included: "an old haven," "held on a van," "a novel hand," "have nodal," "vend anal ho," and "halved anon." Many of them could relate to Hando/Victor both on and off the online world.

He left the house with only a short apology for the late hours. Janice seemed to handle it well, saying she would be working that day as a substitute for a kindergarten class.

When he entered the RA Ms. Downey handed him a message. The note came from the DC lab. They had made a match on the first fibers, the ones found at the swamp. Tim had guessed correctly. The dyes came from a North African plant-dye and some kind of unique wool used typically around the Mediterranean.

He put the note in his case file, then sat behind his computer and logged into the bureau's server to check his e-mail. Mark Striker, who almost only communicated by computer, should have some messages for him. The technician was up all night breaking JLK's password, to retrieve his e-mail.

He opened the large wad of messages Striker had sent him. All of them were from Hando, since JLK never e-mailed anyone else. Dan Buck was under surveillance for the day. By tomorrow, DC agents would arrest him with a long list of charges. Tim hoped they could use it as leverage to figure out what was going on. And whether Senator Euler was involved.

One thing was sure, though still not confirmed: The encryption came from JLK to Hando. And it was the same encryption that Euler was adopting in his famed D-chip. Why they gave it to Hando, Tim couldn't understand exactly. On the computer, JLK's e-mail included the half of the conversation that Tim was missing from before. Although he couldn't really trust anything in Keller's messages, it was Hando's replies that Tim needed.

In the second e-mail from Hando to Keller, he found another mention of an abduction. The "Overtime" he'd seen mentioned before.

"It's a real pain to have to keep a low profile," Hando wrote to JLK on the 17th. *"I'd love to know what these cops think of my techniques. But the next couple times I strike they'll know exactly who I am and what I can do.*

"Sure, the Asian bitch will be great, but it's just a warm up for what I'm planning next. Back pay for Overtime. It's the overtime they'll regret. The plan is nearly perfected. Two kids in four days. I'll send you the story that goes with it. I'll even send it earlier so you can see it before the group. But I don't think I want help this time. Maybe in a few weeks."

Tim's blood went cold as he read it. *Two kids in four days.* That meant today or tomorrow, depending on how Victor counted days. Two, assuming Yoshiko was one, meant one more any time now. And Hando or Victor was building the story for the honor of punks like Keller. On the run and without a personal computer, Victor might not be able to do it. Unless it was hidden somewhere in his computer account, because like the Café Connexion, there were numerous places around town for Victor to go and get online.

Tim accelerated his log-in to *nether.net.* He moved into his twin-account that enabled him to play the part of Hando. There, he hoped to find some link of information to break Victor's game. If he could get the story before Victor began to put it into action, Tim would win.

In Hando's file directories, there were a couple new documents that Tim had not seen. File dates on these indicated that Victor had indeed been in the account since yesterday. Even with the trace and other online monitors, somehow Tim and CART missed it. Hando had found another way to enter, apparently, a way to remain unseen. Perhaps he used a secure telnet or rologin and erased his tracks afterward. In any event, Tim would camp out and wait for Victor online, assuming he could spy him any more easily.

* * *

Elementary

It was her third day substituting, and already Janice felt tired of the job. Even though she was subbing a kindergarten class this week and the days were shorter, it still zapped her strength. Children at this age required twice the energy, and a half-day felt like more than a full day of sixth grade. At least subbing for K-classes let her get home about the same time as her children.

"Mrs. Delbravo!" yelled Sally Abrahams, a little girl with thick glasses. The students were finger painting and several wanted her opinion.

She wandered over. "Yes, Sally."

The girl pointed to a figure on her sheet. "What color should I make it?"

Janice stared at the finger smears, trying to figure out what the girl's masterpiece could be. "That's a tricky one, isn't it, Sally? Maybe you can tell me about it. That way I can think about the best color for you."

"Why, it's for the prettiest dress in the whole world!" Sally declared. "Well, it's supposed to be. I'm not sure what color to pick."

"Is it your dress?"

"Oh no, it's for Patty."

"Patty?"

"My sitter after school."

Janice nodded. Another child that chooses to paint her sitter. "I'll bet she's pretty."

"Oh yes! After my dinner, she's always brushing her hair and puts on lipstick and make-up. I watch her because she gets to go out every night after my dad picks me up."

"What color dresses does she usually wear?"

"I don't remember."

"How about your mother's dresses?"

Sally thought about it. "The black one. When she comes home after I have to go to bed."

Janice wondered how much longer it would be before she had to get a sitter for her own children.

* * *

Residency

In an hour, Tim had searched and *grepped* every byte of Hando's account for an indication of what he was planning. He found some UNIX shell scripts that contained some of the messages Hando had posted before. One of these, the first post that had threatened to mire the University of Michigan, had a sleep delay. Apparently, Victor had written the poem earlier, then programmed it to get posted much later when he could get an alibi. Little did he know he would be in jail when the post was uploaded automatically. That was why it had not mentioned the arrest, even though it came afterward.

Besides the older messages, only one very small file gave Tim a clue about Hando's next move. He had seen the document name before—overtime.doc. It had some new material, two short lines:

UNPAID OVERTIME

I like children, especially these two. We'll have a tea party.

He was planning to take *two* more children. But no mention of who, where or when. Tim studied the phrase, trying to find some hidden meaning. He issued the command to close out the file. Before it closed out, however, a prompt asked him if he wanted to overwrite a copy of the file. It confused him. What copy?

He gasped. Another copy of the file had been opened and some changes had been made to it. Now the computer wanted to know if it should save his version in place of the more recently opened version.

It meant Hando was logged in and had opened his own copy of overtime.doc. If Tim overwrote it, it would erase whatever Hando was writing and alert him to Tim's presence. Without hesitation, he declined to save his session and tried to move out unseen. He knew he should just hang quietly in the shadows or even logout before Victor noticed that someone else was logged into the account. If Victor knew he was being watched, it would spook him. But Tim needed to see what the perp was writing. He would trace his whereabouts, and get a copy of that story as Victor wrote it and then act quickly to dispel the plan.

Before logging out, Tim picked up the phone and called Mark Striker in Detroit.

"Striker. Tim Delbravo. I've got Hando logged in at the same time I'm in."

"Hando logged in?" Striker repeated, keys clicking audibly over the phone. "Are you sure? There's nothing on my monitor."

"I think so."

"Don't see how."

"Someone is in," Tim assured him.

"You still on?"

"Yes."

"Tell me what users are on."

Tim typed the command and the screen on his desk displayed two names. One of which was "Hando" logged in from *root*. The other root-user came from *gypsum.fbi.gov*—Tim's host machine.

"Damn, Striker. My FBI machine is being listed. I can't get off. I've got to watch him."

Logging out would make them blind. Tim could get back on in ten-minute intervals and check Hando's creations afterward, but they might risk losing all information if the suspect took the files away.

"And is the real Hando online?"

"He's logged in through *root*." Breathing fast, Tim tapped out, list overtime.doc.

"He's found a way to get back on to their main drive. He got real root again. Get out of there!"

"One more second."

The file displayed a new line:

A tea party with children of the…

Abruptly his connection died. Somehow forced off. Tim sat motionless and stunned until Striker spoke on the phone.

"Are you out?"

Tim closed his eyes. "I'm off, but I didn't log out. It dumped me."

"He found you, Delbravo."

* * *

Residency

Tim ate a late lunch from the vending machine, then returned with iron clad butterflies running from his belly through his throat. It felt as though they were pounding at the base of his skull. The online collision with Hando had him distressed.

He logged in to check the status and see if Victor had come back. When Tim was logged out, Hando logged off too. Striker thought maybe it was a system-wide failure. Tim checked his mail. The first mail-message shocked him. The return address, a new one, was *hando@DeathsDoor.com*. Sent at 2:54 p.m., directly to Tim.

Subject: Not so fast!

Dear FBI snoops:

I know all about your little craft.
Tricking that JLK made me laugh.
No more snooping in my stuff.
Now I'll start to play it rough.
Even in hard times just like this,
I'll get the G-man's kids that I wish.
Retaliation for your lies.
By day's end, hear their cries.

—Alven "fiercest freedom fighting" Hando

Tim's mind jumbled the words until they made no sense. He had to read them a second time and nearly fell off his chair when the stanza did come clear.

Hando was going after "the G-man's kids." Tim's own!

For a long moment he stalled. Standing and bolting in place. Then sitting and reading and searching the header of the e-mail, trying to make it all go away, or tell him what to do. How to feel.

His mind exploded with a half-dozen scenarios of Hando abducting, raping and torturing the two children he had not hardly paid attention to for months. It just wasn't right. It just didn't seem possible.

With the computer message glaring back at him, he grabbed the phone and began dialing. Twice he had to redial and on the slower third attempt, he finally got it right.

His home phone rang and rang. Then the machine turned on. Damn! Janice, he remembered, had taken substitute teaching jobs. But where? In the county there had to be over thirty elementary schools. He'd been so involved with breaking his case, he didn't know where she was today.

Beep.

"Janice. It's Tim. Call me at work. It's urgent."

He pushed the plunger on the phone base, still holding the handset and thinking of his next move. Tasha attended Mack Elementary. Reggy went to Forsythe Middle School. Although Janice had met their teachers, Tim hadn't visited either. He didn't even remember their names at the moment. The schools would tell him. He lifted the plunger and dialed information.

"City please?"

"Ann Arbor." Because he worried more about Tasha with a strange man, he asked for the number at Mack Elementary. He got the number and dialed the school.

Sam Grand entered his cubicle. He smiled at Tim, holding up a CD. A game or something. Tim held up a hand. He couldn't afford the distraction.

Sam reached up and put the disk in Tim's open palm. The phone rang. He bit his tongue, telling himself to remain calm, to speak professionally.

"Mack Elementary," answered a receptionist. Her smoker's voice sounded uncaring.

Sam mouthed, *Thanks.*

"I need the principal."

Grand left. Tim didn't see anyone else in the offices. He felt like he was wasting time, but knew phones were quicker than squad cars.

"Who's calling?"

"Special Agent Tim Delbravo. FBI." *Come on!*

"One moment."

Every second seemed an eternity. The elevator music on the other end was cheerful and made him feel even more antsy. He thought about his children with Hando, little mousy Victor. Reggy had become aggressive in his Aikido, and Tim worried his son's bravery would only enrage Victor. The phone rang, a seemingly infinite number of rings before the principal answered. Her greeting sounded more irritated than sunny.

"This is Special Agent Delbravo," he announced. "We have a kidnapper targeting a child in your school."

"Excuse me. Who are you?"

"FBI. SA Tim Delbravo. A kidnapper—"

"Yes, but…" She paused, coughing into the receiver. "I can't take directions over the phone."

"What?"

"Do you know how often we receive bomb threats, fire alarms, false—"

"This is not a threat!" He stomped his foot. Sweat gleamed on his brow.

"I can't just take your word. How do I know you're with the FBI?"

What? "I am!"

"But we have protocol here."

Tim knew this, but he didn't have time to go through local channels. "Look!" Tim exhaled and held his anger. "My daughter," he said with clenched teeth, "is at risk."

"I see…Your daughter." She chirped the words. "And this is about a custody battle?"

"I'm not lying!"

"Call the police, sir, if there's a real threat."

"I'm telling you…"

The phone clicked dead. Tim wanted to throw the handset. Slam it onto the desk. Damn. What the hell did she expect? Call the police? He was the police!

Even if he called the locals, they'd get there twenty minutes after Hando grabbed his children. He turned, ready to bolt out of the office. At this point, he had little choice, but first, he would make an attempt with Reggy's principal, then grab a cell phone and get backup while he moved to the elementary. Damn, he hoped the principal at the middle school had more smarts.

He called information, asked for the number at Forsythe Middle School, then let it dial. Again a receptionist answered. She transferred him to the principal's office, a man this time. He tried a different approach with him.

"My son is enrolled there. I just received a report that he is being targeted by a kidnapper."

"Who is he?"

"Reggy Delbravo."

"Just a moment."

Tim looked around the cubicles during the pause. He was still alone as far as he could tell.

"And, who are you?"

"His father, Timothy Delbravo."

"You're listed, but not registered."

"What?"

"You're not registered. We require new parents to meet with the principal. At least the teacher. Have you come in?"

"Look, we just moved here. I couldn't get off work."

"Your wife is registered. Can she call?"

"What? No!" Tim slapped the desk. "My son is going to be kidnapped, dammit!"

"Sir—"

"School is letting out. I'm asking that you have the teacher watch him until I can get there."

"I'm sorry, sir. But only a registered guardian can give us instructions for a student. He's scheduled to take the bus, unless we have written authorization from a registered guardian. You need to get the boy's mother to contact us."

Tim huffed. "And if Janice Delbravo called, how would you verify it was really her?"

"We would…" A pause. "She would have to indicate her name and the boy's name. If she came to pick up her son, then we would verify her before she would be allowed to take the boy."

And you people educate our children? "But she isn't coming."

"Have her call."

"That's just it. I can't locate my wife!"

"I'm sorry, sir."

Tim slammed the phone down and fumed. "Sons-of-bitches! Damned fools!"

Did all schools handle a security problem or parental request this way? It seemed so disorganized.

He grabbed his parka, praying that he could get there in time. As he zipped his coat, Kaplan poked his head into the cubicle.

"I heard the swearing, Delbravo. What the hell did you do now?"

"Kaplan…" Tim didn't have time to mess with his boss. "Look, Victor e-mailed me. He's after my children. I'm going."

Kaplan's mouth gaped. "Your children!"

"I need a cellular. Loan me yours or call backup to the schools."

"You didn't get assistance there?"

He didn't want to spend time explaining why he never registered at his children's schools. "I gotta go, Kaplan."

"Wait! You got e-mail? Have you told anyone else? CART should examine it, and Detroit needs to know."

Tim was afraid of this. Next they'd be asking him to verify it on tape and fill out a detailed report in triplicate, all while his children remained unguarded at school.

* * *

Apartment

Janice dropped the mail on a table and removed her coat. Thankfully, she had made it home before the kids' school let out. She would have just a little time to get some cleaning done.

She began clearing dishes left from morning, when she saw the blinking light on the answering machine. She struck the playback button.

"Janice. It's Tim. Call me at work. It's urgent."

His voice sounded frantic. Like it had the day he called her to tell her about his brother, killed in Detroit. She snatched the phone and speed-dialed the RA. His phone rang several times, then transferred to the receptionist.

"This is Janice Delbravo. I'm looking for my husband."

"Oh, he's just walking out. Hold on."

She heard the secretary calling Tim's name. Then it was quiet. She felt pains in her stomach, waiting just inside the kitchen.

"Janice!"

"Tim, I just got back. What's wrong?"

"Look, I need you to call the schools. They wouldn't take orders from me."

"What? Our kids' schools?"

"Call the schools. Tell them to keep the kids and watch them."

"Why? School just got out."

She heard him curse under his breath. "Someone threatened to kidnap them."

"Oh my heavens!"

* * *

Residency

"Just give me the cellular, Kaplan." Tim walked past the doorway again.

"You give us the password for the e-mail. Then you can go."

"I'm leaving. The technician in Detroit can watch the account."

Kaplan followed him to the elevator. "You're not going alone. Mott or I'll go with you."

"No thanks." He pressed the call button.

While he waited for the elevator, a dozen thoughts shot through his mind.

It was strange. After chasing kidnappers in California, he had worried that something like this would happen to his own, that he would never be able to protect his children. Now he felt confident. Strong and able. He worried, but only that he wouldn't be there. If he could get there, they'd be safe. That much was certain.

Or was it? Why was it suddenly so different? Was everything better just because he remembered Danville?

No matter how he sliced it—accident, misfortune or otherwise—he had still been unable to save that boy or stop those men. And he did not completely protect Yoshiko. Was he really so certain he could save his own children? But now was not the time to lose faith. He had paid the price for his mistakes. If only he could cash in on Victor.

He looked up at the indicator lights. The elevator was tied up on the level below. He turned and started for the stairs.

They crossed back in front of the residency. Ms. Downey poked her head out.

"Agent Delbravo, it's your wife."

He stopped. "On the phone?"

She nodded.

He deliberated for a split second whether to just go or catch her message. The police he had called were on their way to both schools. But Janice would know if the children were still safe and now being watched by the school. He returned to the offices, grabbed a phone on the nearest desk. "Transfer here, Tammi!"

The phone hardly rang before he had it up to his ear.

"Janice, the kids?"

"Both schools had them in the office already. School security is watching Tasha. Reggy is with the principal."

Tim relaxed and landed in his seat. "Well that's a relief. They were so uncooperative."

"What's going on, Tim?"

Tim heard Kaplan speaking loudly with someone in the hall. "I really should get down there. My perp might be at one of the schools."

"Tim, I'm so scared."

"It's all right now, babe."

"Delbravo!" someone screamed from the residency entrance. It sounded like Sam Grand. Tim turned around to find Sam running in, shouting, "He took my kids!"

Sam's eyes were red, his face flustered and clothes ruffled. "I heard you knew he would do it. You've known for a while, you bastard!"

He lowered the phone, lifting his eyebrows. Sam stood with his legs spread, and then threw his jacket down. He lifted his right arm, cocked it back and swung hard.

The impact came fast. He dodged most of Sam's fist, but it still hurled him into a cubicle partition. His cheek stung and his mind was trying to make sense of it all. Sam's kids? Not Tim's.

"Sam." He tried to get up. "Slow down. What's going on?"

"My kids were taken." Sam's voice shook. "My wife just called. The police were sent to Thurston Elementary because my kids were taken just as they were leaving. And SA Kaplan said you knew it would happen, you sonuvabitch!"

Kaplan stood right behind Sam, ready to spring at him.

"I thought he was after my kids." Tim held up a hand. "He e-mailed me directly. Besides, we don't know for sure if this is at all related."

"They never made it on the bus. A friend saw Sam going into a strange red car."

"Just a minute." He lowered his hand and picked up the phone. "Janice?"

"I'm still here. What happened?" she asked.

"I've got to go. Look, you stay with the children. But it may not be them after all. Someone else's children were abducted. They need me here right now."

"Call me soon."

"I will." Tim hung up, then turned to Sam. "I'll find them, if it's my man. I promise."

* * *

Residency

For an hour, Tim checked the newsgroup at two-minute intervals. In between, he monitored his e-mail for the post, just in case Victor decided to make it personal again. Either way, Hando/Victor, always uploaded the plan. And it still hadn't shown up.

The city police remained on standby and had sketches and photos of Victor and the children. The APB and his car license was heralded across police radio again. A team was assembling and preparing at the residency. Sherrie had just arrived, with two deputies at her disposal. Sam Grand had gone out and then returned with his wife an hour earlier. Veronica, still in tears and frantic, hadn't stopped asking about everything. Tim didn't say so, but he actually wished Sam would take her out. At least she was calming down a bit.

According to a faxed report, local police had scoured the school grounds for any piece of evidence. Tim would've gone, but he knew he did his best work on the computer. And the most likely scenario was what they were guessing. Victor had taken a "G-man's kids." A government attorney's children. Tim felt embarrassed that, in selfishness, he assumed Victor would kidnap his own children. He took it for granted that even Victor himself had called both Grand and Delbravo *G-men* during their failed plea bargain at the penitentiary two weeks earlier. Now he had to make up for it.

"So we have only one eyewitness?" Sherrie asked.

"A friend of Sam Junior's," Sam said. "He saw Sam and Katie get into a red car."

"And Victor owns a red Celica," Tim added. "I remembered that yesterday." The red car matched it all. The carpet fibers on Olson and the tire marks at the school. Victor had a charge on his credit card for new tires, which would match, Tim was sure. He had alerted the city, county and state police with Victor's plate number, vehicle description, and other pertinent information.

Sherrie asked, "Didn't he use a truck in that post about the Ramey boy?"

Tim hesitated, looking at the Grands. He didn't want to remind them of Victor's first success. "Victor probably wanted to throw us off. I'll bet the truck was a ruse."

"But why our children?" Veronica Grand asked again, nearly choking on the words. She wrapped Sam's arm around her, and he patted her shoulder.

Tim shook his head and shrugged. They'd been asking that question over and over without any real answer, except revenge. But more important was where the hell he had taken the children.

Ms. Downey entered the cubicle area. "Anyone want some coffee?"

No one responded. Veronica buried her head in Sam's chest, sobbing again. Her husband whispered into her ear. His eyes looked strained, fighting back tears of his own. Tim understood. Only moments before it was his children. Yet…when it was his own kids the adrenaline had boosted his confidence, a confidence that was waning now. When it was his kids, he was eager to leap in front of a bullet for them, be the instant superhero. Hell, taking a bullet was always honorable, twice if for your own children. It was the living for them that scared the hell out of him. His stomach ached when he went home to his "regular life," to those thankless tasks day after day. It took real guts jeopardizing a promotion to keep the promise of watching Reggy's hardball game or to play tea party with Tasha. There would be no fanfare or news articles, no commendations or medals. It was just plain self-sacrifice and heroism at its purest.

In the seat next to him, Sherrie flipped a page in the case file, studying intently on details. A deputy talked on the phone with local police, gathering more resources. Even Kaplan checked weapons and their field equipment. Everyone in the RA seemed focused on saving Grand's kids, and it was valuable and praiseworthy. But it was their job, and they got the rewards when they did it right. Sherrie glanced up at Tim then back to her notes. He remembered the other night. He had acted foolishly with Sherrie, almost destroying his wife's trust. It had been a work-related injury that made him pocket his wedding band. It had been his fervor for the case that induced him to put his family photo in a drawer. Tim wished he could undo the last few months. He was no longer the fearless FBI agent tracking down criminals in hopes of glory. Now he was also a father, too long away from his own children, driven by his job to save everyone else, losing himself and his precious family in return.

He turned back to the computer, checking again. It was already after four-thirty. There was one new post in the last five minutes, from another user. Nothing from Hando.

"Does he usually write where he'll be?" Kaplan asked from the back of the room.

Tim kept his hands on the keyboard. "With a little guesswork, we can determine it. If it's not obvious, we'll split into teams and try the most likely places. Keep in tight radio contact."

Veronica sighed, shivering a bitter frown.

"Tim," Sherrie said, looking up from her notes. "Do you remember the profile said that this kind of assailant tends to place his crimes at places correlating with the reasons he takes certain victims?"

"Yeah. So far it's the swamp and then the old school. You see a connection?"

"The swamp observatory is owned by U-M. The old school is probably along a similar vein."

"So he's into academics."

"That's our first clue."

Tim nodded. "Each has been remote. Either abandoned or secluded."

"But the profiler warned that this type of personality may go for a place that gets crowded later. All for getting more attention."

"Okay, so it's just more likely to be secluded."

Sam stood and whispered something to Veronica. She nodded and they both walked out of the residency. Tim hoped that the talk didn't offend them. When he went over the details, it was often done professionally, perhaps even too insensitive for the Grands.

"What's this? A party?" Spike had entered, wearing his militia duds.

"Grand's kids have been kidnapped by my subject."

"The U.S. attorney?"

Kaplan nodded.

"Need help?" Spike asked.

"Absolutely, all the manpower we can get. We'll be going out when the story comes down. Maybe even split up."

"When we going?"

"Any moment, I think."

Tim turned to check the newsgroup again. And it was there—Hando's post.

Subject: A tea party with children of the law.

Exactly two weeks ago, my friend Kurt would have been released from prison, but a nosy attorney delayed it for another day.

It was unpaid overtime.

This is for him.

I always thought tea is appropriate during anniversaries and children love to play tea party. The children, our attorney knows. The tea, he won't.

Now the story.

"It's here." Tim scrolled down reading further. The plot was similar to the last two. A common theme of painful death ending in fire. This time he called the accelerant "tea."

"What does it say?" Sherrie leaned behind him.

He didn't respond. He was searching for clues about where Victor had taken the children. The only lines that gave them a lead came near the beginning. Tim read the lines aloud.

"Through the jagged rim of glass spikes we hiked. Into the deepest recess of the beast's lair we went. The beast that started it all by throwing my friend out. Down the wooded slopes, to a deserted hole whither the beast seldom preys. My bag, the guests and their innocence followed me."

Sherrie squinted. "The beast that started it all?"

"Who acted first against Victor?" Tim lifted an eye, then spun around. "Call campus police. And have a burn-crew from U-M's hospital on transit immediately."

* * *

Dark Room

Katie was so frightened that she hardly wanted to open her eyes when he finished checking the rope on her hands. It was the first time he had really touched her skin since they stopped here. It sent shivers through her. She wanted to cry, but the pain in her stomach and the confusion, it all stopped the tears. In the darkness, she could see the man check Sam Junior's hands. Then he took his small packet from the bag again and dumped some of the powder

360

in his hand. He had done it in the car too—put his nose on it and sniffed hard. Drugs.

Her eyes were adjusting to the darkness. Her hands were tied firmly, but her gag was gone. She doubted anyone could hear if she screamed, and it would only anger the man. She wiggled and squirmed, only moving up her blouse and baring a little of her stomach. She stopped squirming and started working on the ropes. The man didn't even notice; he was so busy with the powder...Sniffing. The man hadn't said anything to them since they came into the house. And before that, only threats, telling them to get in his car, holding a knife at Sam, grabbing her so fast that she couldn't react. When he stopped at a computer store, he gagged and tied them, pushed her over Sam onto the car floor, tossing a blanket on them. She was in the seat and working the door handle when he had returned. He slapped her face, held his knife to her throat until it bit the skin, threatening to kill her if she tried to get away. He had spoken again when they stopped a few blocks from this place, telling them to follow him without a sound. He had kept his knife at her back and held Sam by the arm.

She had wanted to run, but he jabbed the knife at her kidney and held her brother so tight; Katie couldn't leave him behind.

She watched him again. The man lifted his head up slowly. He gazed at her, head swaying, droopy cheeks and his mouth hanging open. A tiny smile passed across his lips. She turned her head, gasping at his ugly eyes. Big dark, lifeless marbles. Monster eyes.

She felt choked. Smothered in fear, wriggling against the cords on her hands.

The man breathed loudly, watching the ceiling. Then he closed his eyes like he might be sleepy. Katie could hardly watch him, but wanted to be prepared. There had to be some way out. Again, he took the packet and put it to his nose, breathing deeply. Sniffing hard. Awkwardly, he settled on the floor and laughed quietly to himself. She rubbed her hands on the cold cement floor, feeling for something to use as a weapon.

They were in a basement room with a low ceiling, a drain in the center, stacks of wood shelves at the back. The shelves, too far to reach, held bottles. Fancy bottles. With wine, she recognized. It smelled musty and she saw a lone fogged window back by the shelves. Very little light came through it. It was late afternoon.

Sammy began sobbing. Katie writhed on the floor until she reached him. She wanted to sob too, but instead whispered the words from a song their mother sometimes sang. Before she got to the second verse and before Sam calmed, the man sat up.

"Be quiet!" he shouted. Then he laughed hideously. "It's time."

He grabbed the duffel bag that he had carried and took out mason jars. Seven bottles of what must have been clear water, laying them out in an arc by the door. Then he pulled out a long stick and a candle. With the long handled-stick-thing, he sparked a flame and lit the candle.

She could see his face more clearly now. Shadows danced wildly across his glasses and a thin mustache. Dark lines appeared on his forehead and cheeks, staining him with inhuman features. Katie shivered as a quiet tear slipped down her temples.

He moved the candle back, then grabbed a jar and opened it.

"Please…"

"Shut up, bitch!"

Sam sobbed louder.

"I said shut up." He kicked at her brother.

"Don't!"

"I warned you, little bitch." Sneering, he lifted the opened jar and poured its contents over her.

Not water, it stung!

Her eyes burned and her shoulders and hands, especially where she scraped herself on the floor. It smelled like the stuff her mom used to clean her sores. Alcohol, Katie remembered. Yet different somehow. Sweeter smelling, more like wine except clear.

The man drank from a second opened bottle. He dump the last half on Sammy, who cried louder. Then he pulled out a plastic basin and poured the remaining bottles into it. Except for a small amount, with which he filled six paper cups.

"It's tea. Drink up!" he said, lifting a cup to her lips.

Tears fell, soaking her ears.

* * *

President's Office

"Come in, Miriam." President John Kladstein was just about to wrap it up for the day.

"John, campus police just informed me that they received a report of an incident at the home."

"The home?"

"The presidential home."

"Oh, the mansion." The century-old estate that many say Kladstein had the gall not to live in. He was the first president that chose to buy his own home instead of residing in the old campus mansion. The renovations would have cost him out of his own pocket more than a new home. And he couldn't get the Regents to subsidize it with university funds.

He turned to her. "An incident?"

"A break-in. A burglary, I guess."

"Holy mother! I have my wine stored there." His Bordeaux 1982 Lafite Rothschild collection!

He rose. "My books."

His rare book collection was in the master bedroom closet. An original of *The Mansion* signed by Faulkner himself. The home was only used by infrequent, esteemed visitors, and as an occasional tour for wealthy alumni. In its disuse, he had thought it would also serve as storage.

"Let's go." He picked up his briefcase and overcoat. "Lock up, will you?"

* * *

President's Home

Tim assembled his five-member team in front of the mansion. With him were Spike and Kaplan from the bureau, Sherrie and two more deputies from the county. Campus police assisted as well, guarding the front entrance and posting someone along the rear and side fence perimeters. A nine-foot tall fence wrapped the back and most of the sides, but the front remained open. Tim hoped they had the right place; it was all he could think of from the post. Victor's red Celica was not anywhere on the street around the estate.

"How do you even know this is the right place?" Kaplan asked, rubbing his belly. Tim didn't reply; he surveyed the grounds. The senior resident muttered something and pulled a small bottle from his coat. He unscrewed the lid and took a large swig, leaving a pink Pepto-Bismol coating on his lips.

Tim walked from the south side to the front. It appeared large and unoccupied—a Victorian-styled, whitewashed mansion built before the turn-of-the-century. In the dusky light, Tim hoped they could see well enough once they went in. None of the interior lights were on. Electricity was shut off from the basement utility box, campus police had told him.

And in the basement, he suspected, was *the deepest recess of the beast's lair.* That's where he'd find Hando. If he was inside.

He looked at his team. "Everyone, ready?"

Some nodded, others grabbed their sidearms.

"Let's wait for Hostage Rescue," Kaplan said, holding his pink bottle.

"No." Tim moved toward the door.

"I said, we'll wait." Kaplan followed him.

Tim turned. "Wait for what? For a little girl and boy to get tortured?"

"Hostage Rescue handles this kind of situation all the time."

"Like with McCurty at the convenient store?"

Kaplan took a swig of his antacid bottle and muttered a curse. "You take the blame, then. I wash my hands."

Tim turned back to the entrance, starting up the steps.

"What kind of weapon does he have?" asked a deputy.

Tim approached the two campus police posted at the front door. "I don't think he'll have a gun. It's not something he's used in the past. But a knife and fire are sure bets."

He nodded to the campus police at the front entrance. One officer took a key and unlocked the door.

"How did he get in?" asked the second deputy.

"He mentions something about broken glass in his story," Sherrie replied.

Tim nodded. "I saw a smashed window on the north-side." He entered first, then turned to one of the campus cops. "The stairs down?"

"It's been a while, but I think it's around the living room, at the east end of the kitchen."

"Okay, I want the two deputies to survey the upstairs just in case." Tim pulled out his sidearm. "Marshall pairs with me and, Kaplan, you're with Spike."

They all nodded and then entered.

* * *

Campus

"Hurry!" the president said to Miriam.

From his office just off the student diag, the home was only three buildings away, a quarter-mile at most. It had been planned that way when people walked more than they did today. He skipped ahead of her, winding along the walkway that bent east toward the fence at the back of the estate.

A few students strolled along the path, sporadically falling in his path and making him dodge them. Students. With their wrought-up anti-capitalism propaganda and their joy-of-sex free-speech protests. He'd taken a beating from disciplining the worthless speech. And for making lucrative advertisement deals in behalf of U-M's athletic department.

"Do you have the key?" his secretary gasped.

"Of course. We can enter from the rear."

"What if the burglar is still there?"

Silly woman. "Why would the campus police already know about it, unless they caught the idiot?"

* * *

President's Home

Inside, they split up. The plan was to meet up in the back area if nothing was found. Tim and Sherrie paced back to the kitchen, and upon entering, heard the sobs. He turned around an isle counter and headed for a door on the back side. Tim found the door opening to the cellar stairway.

Kaplan and Spike entered the kitchen just then.

"We heard the noise," Kaplan said. "Someone's down there all right."

Tim glanced at him. "Get the deputies, Kaplan."

Kaplan scratched his head and then nodded. Once he had left, Tim performed a quick check of his weapon's safety. It was on, just in case. Spike and Sherrie did the same and then they flew down the steps as quietly as they could. At the bottom, the steps creaked.

"Help." A muffled voice. Katie's. No waiting around this time!

Tim aimed himself toward her voice, hastening to a door. No waiting, no hesitation. He cranked the old knob and rammed the door with his shoulder.

The fragile door was no match for his weight and broke from the upper hinges. He flew into the room, somehow maintaining most of his balance and a grip on his gun.

But he tripped up in some kind of basin, water or liquid flying all over him. He landed on one knee and an outstretched hand. His pants and parka soaked with a familiar smell. Booze or straight ethyl alcohol. It burned as he blinked it out of his eyes.

"Freeze!" shouted someone. Tim, through bleary vision, saw figures in the dimness of a candle. His eyes adjusted with alcohol still dripping from his nose and eyebrows. He could see Katie and little Sam lying on the floor, stomach down.

"Stop!" Victor knelt over the kids, pressing a six-inch blade at the base of Katie's skull. He positioned the weight of his upper body so that if shot, he would fall with his mass on the knife, piercing Katie's brain stem and killing her. From his other hand, a flame shot out of a long-end lighter. "Don't come any closer or they'll both go up!"

"Kurt, don't do—"

"Kurt?" he said.

Sherrie and Spike stayed in the entry. Footsteps on the stairs told him that Kaplan and the deputies were coming down.

"I'm Alven Hando." Victor sneered.

"Right." Tim was closer to him than the rest, who were still at the doorway. He knelt just outside an arm-stretch of Victor and the kids.

"Drop your guns or I'll light them!" Victor lifted the lighter over Sam. Katie shivered, still wet with accelerant and under his blade.

"Okay, Alven." Tim tried to stand.

"Don't move!"

"Okay, just calm down."

"Everybody throw down your guns and kick them to that wall." Victor pointed to the wall off to his right.

"Okay, don't do anything rash." Before he would consider dropping his gun, Tim got his bearings. The door sat opposite a row of shelves with a window above. Bare walls everywhere else. Victor crouched just in front of the wine shelves. Spike and Sherrie and the rest stood in the entry facing him. Tim still knelt on a leg just off to the side.

Then it hit him hard. He was in a basement again, trying to stop another child-killer from hurting another victim. His life rehashed.

"Now!"

Victor spun the flame onto Katie's hair, singeing a dozen strands. She shrieked. Tim raised and lifted his gun. The assailant, holding the lighter above Sam Junior now, pushed the tip of his blade into Katie's skin. The lighter's flame almost licked Sam as he did, and Tim saw a trickle of dark fluid appear on her neck.

"Okay!" Tim shouted, throwing his gun down in the middle of the room. "Stop!"

Katie's hair smoldered as Victor pressed on it with the forearm holding his lighter. Tim wanted to leap on the jackass. And he would have, but the subject kept his blade on Katie's neck.

Victor set the lighter down and smiled. Tim readied to jump again, when Victor snatched a cup on the ground.

"Guns over there." Victor lifted the cup above the children and poured alcohol over them, then replaced the lighter near Sam just as quickly.

"Now!" Victor demanded.

The rest threw their guns against the far wall. Tim's mind cycled for a plan. But all he could think of were Michael Miller's eyes and Robinson's bloody head. The whole thing happening almost like before.

* * *

Fence

Kladstein unlocked the gate and moved through it. Miriam caught up, breathing hard and leaving the gate open behind her. The president felt incensed that anyone would dare attempt to steal his valuables. He'd have them prosecuted to the full extent.

"President?" a voice said from the outer side of the fence.

He turned to find a campus police officer. These dimwitted campus rookies couldn't seem to do anything right. Where the hell were they *before* the burglary?

"I don't think you should go in there, President."

"It's all right. I'm just going to see what happened."

"You mean it's over?"

Kladstein glanced at the officer. Obviously a bright banana-green recruit that hadn't been informed of anything. "Yes, it's over! I was called a while ago."

The officer entered the yard. "But—"

Kladstein waved him off and went to the back door. Without responding, he slid his key into the lock.

"I'll escort you in," the officer said.

* * *

Cellar

Weaponless and with only a vague plan, Tim sat, sweating each moment. "Now what?"

"No one move." Victor looked around, up at the window. "I'm going out."

"How?" Sherrie asked. "You won't get far."

"Shut up, bitch!"

Tim was just a yard from him, directly to his side. The children were under Victor and the lighter moved back and forth as he talked. In the other hand, he kept his blade biting into the base of Katie's skull. He pulled at Sam's pants, then on Katie, moving them inch-by-inch back.

Tim and his team could wait. Let the alcohol evaporate. But Victor still had his knife, and he was inching further from them. At this angle, Tim might leap and propel Victor back such that the thrust pushed the knife away from Katie. It was risky. He had to time it just so the flame didn't land on Sam.

The lighter. Tim had been doused with alcohol, too. Still wet. If he got near that tip, he would surely go up. And so would the children. It would take time, too much time for it to evaporate. The longer it took, the more likely an accident...He had to act now. Somehow, he had to save Grand's children.

Victor pointed at him and then to his gun. "You reach out and without picking it up, slide it to me."

Tim stalled for a moment. If Victor got the gun, it would be even harder to end this without incident. It'd be over.

The flame crackled in Katie's hair, singeing it again. She sobbed.

Victor spat. "Now!"

Tim leaned forward, touching the gun, pausing before actually sliding it. Then he heard a creak. Footsteps on the stairs. He looked at Victor who was watching him closely, lighter dangling only inches from Sam, blood trickling under the blade still on Katie. Tim halted.

"Do it!"

He slid the gun across the concrete, away from both he and Victor. Just as it left his reach, someone from the stairwell yelled.

"To me, dammit!" Victor kicked a jar across the room, shattering it on the cement walls.

"My wine!" a man's voice called from the stairs.

Abruptly, Victor shifted his focus to the doorway, carelessly moving the lighter from the children and his weight off the knife.

The gun too far, Tim hurdled forward, leaping madly onto Victor and converging on his hands. Pulling with all his strength away from the kids. Focusing on the knife.

The moment he felt the flame hit him, he wondered if it was the right thing. He clung to Victor. There was no turning back.

* * *

Sherrie had turned at the shout. A man in a suit entered, then the whole room lit up. Her eyes jerked back, trying desperately to understand what had happened. She saw Tim writhing, flames rising and growing big. But on the other side, she could not clearly make out Victor or the children. Nothing except Tim's burning scream.

Oh my God!

She had to do something. Her mind raced through half a dozen scenarios in less than a half-second. But none seem logical or plausible.

* * *

Tim's mind was engulfed. The flames reached everywhere. Especially his black hemp parka. Like dry grass and gasoline touched by a spark, nothing he did stopped it. He could feel skin burning, peeling. Stinging like nothing he'd ever felt.

In his hand he felt Victor slipping. Escaping from his clutches. The pain and the heat overwhelmed his conscious effort to bring down Victor. Then his grip clutched air. Victor was free. The kids…!

With hands emptied, he darted and moved, trying to find hold, to roll and see them.

* * *

Sherrie's mind pushed her forward. Victor squirmed on the other side of Tim. Everyone dashing toward the scuffle. The growing flames stood between them, causing her to pause only for a moment.

On the ground sat Tim's gun, glistening in front of the scalding blaze. It all happened so fast. She scurried to the gun and aimed it, but was blinded with the brightness and the heat. Everyone rushed around her, uniting around the children and Tim, trying to get a hold of them. Shouts and clatter. Blazing shelves falling over and bottles breaking. A leg or a foot, pushing over racks. She watched something slide through the window above the shelves.

A person escaping.

It was Victor. She knew it had to be Victor. Aiming through the heat and watery eyes, Sherrie began squeezing the trigger on Tim's gun.

* * *

Tim saw Sherrie grab his gun. Aim it just over him. Fire leaping around. And flashes of Robinson with his scared eyes. A gun pointed toward the children.

"Don't shoot!" he tried. But the air was sucked from his lungs. His mind ached. Stretching, he reached a hand to the gun. If only he could make her drop it, loose it, like with Robinson…No, he had to trust his partner, that she could make the shot. He dropped his arm. Hands grabbed at him.

Crack!

The gun blasted, ringing in his ears with the rushing sound of oxygen around him.

Katie! Sam!

His eyes dodged through the flames and the boundless pain. He scarcely saw them; just enough to know that there were not injured. They were fine! Scared, but not hurt and not under Victor's control.

Their faces. Sweet and frightened. Safe. Other faces now. The pain was immense. "Janice!" Hands rolled him. "Reggy!" His body whirled uncontrollably. "Tasha!"

Then he felt nothing, relaxing in the control of others. Entirely meaningless and void of care. All except thoughts of his family. Their faces standing out there watching him. They seemed to move away. Then his eyes defocused, melting like smooth butter on a warm summer day.

* * *

Campus

An instant after missing, Sherrie was past the human blaze and out the window. The figure of a man whirred forward, running off the estate yard past an open gate. He slammed the gate door. She was only a dozen yards behind, gripping Tim's gun and hoping he'd be all right. The gate opened easily. She heard a campus officer shouting from the house. Something she couldn't understand as she flew onto campus grounds. Over a thin coat of snow.

Victor raced across a walkway, running with incredible speed. Energized, no doubt, by synthetic chemistry. She pushed herself, leaping over a barren flowerbed onto the sidewalk. Faster, she streaked past several students bundled for a cold night, her breath puffing and sweat peaking under her coat.

The assailant reached the border of the diag. Students on the path ejected out of his way and she passed by their startled squawks right behind. Victor leaped over a stone bench and past a closed shanty, running beyond and into a small, forested area at the edge of campus. Sherrie dodged fallen branches and skipped around trees.

But she could barely see him in the dark, a shadowy figure outlined just perceptibly above the ground. She slowed and lifted Tim's gun, aligning the aim on the figure.

"Halt!"

He didn't and she fired. The bullet cracked into a tree, and Victor vaulted to the side, falling over. She raced forward. He lifted up and ran. She aimed again. But he disappeared.

The grassy forest was small and dim. Behind her it led to campus. The other end dumped into a series of store-lined streets. Over the past couple of years students took over sections of the grounds, declaring it "People's Place." They planted copses of small trees and bushes wherever they felt academic construction had deforested too much. Campus administrators tolerated it with forced grins. Now it was a disjointed park of short and tall trees, bushes, benches, rocks…Victor could be behind any of them.

Sherrie halted and listened. Moving her eyes from tree to bench to the next tree, waiting for any sound. Then she heard hard breathing as two campus police officers arrived behind her.

"Be ready," she told them. "He's in the trees."

Both smiled narrow eyes at her and cocked their bold heads as they began stomping around trees one by one. Sherrie started on the other edge, cautiously scanning the gray dusky horizon.

Suddenly several lights tripped on. Night detectors sent electricity to bulbs all around campus and at the edge of the forested area.

Then a blood-chilling scream as one of the officers fell about twenty yards from Sherrie. Victor hopped from him and rushed deeper into the trees, away from the lights, and hid around some bushes. Sherrie could hardly aim her gun before he disappeared again. The other officer ran to his partner.

"He's been stabbed!"

Sherrie moved quickly toward the spot where Victor had cloaked himself, stopping just at the edge of a tangle beside a large oak. She raised the gun. The bushes grew between two medium sized pines with low bows. She could detect no movement or sound except the groaning of the officer on the other side.

About thirty feet to her left she caught sight of a line of flashing barricades. A four-foot deep trench flowed from the far streets through the grounds and ended at a wall outside the UGLI—the undergraduate library. Telling herself to push on, she inched toward the trench. A sign near the edge, by the wall of the library's computing center, said that the university was putting in fiber optic link for connection to "Internet 2" as it would be called. Light from street lamps and orange flashers lit the trench. Sherrie scanned the line from the building to as far as she could see. There was no sign of Victor hiding in it. The barricade tape was intact and unbroken.

Behind her, she heard faint rustling of leaves. She pushed back to the underbrush and trees. "Come out with your hands up!"

It felt so eerie to her. Once on the campus at Ohio State a man had chased her. She was returning from the library when he leaped at her from behind a pillar. She ran for ten minutes. Even lost the book she had checked out. He hadn't caught her, but she never felt safe on campus again. The same dread spooked her now.

"Come out!" She drew closer to a large bush. Abruptly a figure rushed at her from the oak behind. She jerked around and grabbed the attacker's hand as he tackled her. They both fell, shrieking to the cold ground. She almost lost her grip on his fist—the one with the knife—and she had to let go of the gun to use both hands. She pulled and pried at his fingers. Just before she could loosen them from the knife, he pushed it away and tumbled from her. He rolled to an upright position, then flew through the trees and sprinted away.

Sherrie searched frantically for the gun, finding it under snow and decaying leaves. Her hand gripped and raised the gun without her mind directing it. Once she had the subject spotted she squeezed off a round. But in the darkness she lost aim, and it whizzed past him. She opened both eyes and caught Victor's outline approaching the barricades. She squinted and aimed at the running figure, then held a half-breath and pulled again.

Crack! Thunk!

This time he went down, crashing through the construction tape and into the trench for the fiber link. She exhaled a stale breath and jogged toward him. Victor writhed in the hole, tangled in cable housing, moaning and cursing, arms wrapped around his leg and shouting. "It hurts! Damn it hurts!"

Behind her, two more campus police and a deputy arrived.

"Pull him out...and cuff him," she told one, between gasps, dropping her aim. "I'll go call...for an ambulance."

She began sprinting back. She had to know if Tim was okay. Students had collected at the edge of the forested area. She passed them, and they cheered for an encore of more shooting. Before she reached the other side of the plaza, she heard the shrieks of an ambulance. Lights flashing in the direction of the estate. She dashed to the fence and saw Spike coming through the gate.

"How's Tim?" She panted.

"The medics just got here. They worked over him with a ventilator. Otherwise..." He shrugged.

Sherrie dropped her hands onto her knees and panted hard.

Spike stopped in front of her. "And Victor?"

"Shot in the leg," she huffed.

"It's over, then."

Sherrie nodded slightly. "Campus...dips," she said in honor of Tim, "are cuffing him now."

Saturday, February 22

Quantico, Virginia

Special Agent Brahams watched senatorial aide Dan Buck, not the video playing in the conference room. Buck gulped, causing his larynx to bulge against a green bow tie below it. His eyes darted over the screen, which displayed Francine Draveson wearing a T-shirt and brown bell bottoms. She was finishing her recorded statement, given after agents at Ann Arbor and Toledo had picked her up from the motel in Rossford.

"What about this set?" SA Delbravo, from the day before, slid a second photo set to her. Next to her sat a lady-lawyer and a court reporter. The camera perspective zoomed in, flushing the lawyer and agents out of view. It focused on both Draveson's face and the photos, close enough to discern particular features on the three men displayed in this set. And confined enough so the frustration Draveson had been feeling was very apparent.

"This one." She pointed at the last.

Brahams looked from the video to Dan Buck in the conference room. Buck's face, exact to the one identified by Draveson in the scene, was going white at the moment. He watched her finger him. It gave cause for a long overdue smile on Brahams' face. He saw that the bureau attorney sitting across from Buck had one too.

"That's him."

"And he never mentioned a name?"

"No names. But, like I said already, I heard him say something about a guy in Nebraska."

Brahams got up from the table, straightened his red tie and walked to the television. Before it went any further, he shut it off and stared at Buck.

"Such odd behavior for a senate-aide, don't you think, Mr. Buck?" Brahams asked.

Buck sat with his lawyer at the conference room. Both had on pinstripe suits. Buck wore a green bow tie that seemed to hold up his large larynx. The larynx bobbed passionately up and down as he replied: "I indubitably don't know what you're talking about."

"Setting up rendezvous with alleged murderers by falsified computer accounts. Hiring a chop off the street to carry through with the meeting. Paying the killer to continue something which your boss, Senator Euler, has emphatically and openly combated for years."

The aide's lawyer whispered something to Buck and then answered in his place. "None of these superfluous charges have any substance. You're holding my client on a whim."

The bureau lawyer strode over to a small briefcase and pulled out four sheets. He threw two on the table. "A copy of a memo found only two hours ago in Mr. Buck's office at Lexington. Let's read it together, shall we?"

The lawyer looked at Buck, who didn't return the glance. His attorney took a sheet, holding it up so his client and he could read it. But Buck only took a quick shot at and then darted his eyes against a far wall.

"I'll do the honors." Brahams held up his copy and began reading.

"Memo. January 19. To: Members of Rhino Team. Regarding: Designation of infusement task. NOT FOR DISCLOSURE."

He looked at Buck. "Can you tell us about the Rhino team, or the infusement task, and why this isn't supposed to be disclosed? And why wasn't this signed by anyone?"

"That's a private memo. I've advised my client not to talk," the lawyer replied. "If you don't have a charge, then I suggest you stop this now, and return all documents back to him. Regardless of your internal warrants, this is a blatant attempt to slime my client and his associates."

Brahams caught a glance at the bureau attorney and then cast his eyes back on the memo. "Let's continue."

"C.J. market deals with FH and NCC mitigated with excellent response.

The attention has been growing, but DB's infusement plan will divert this as we go to a vote. Once the deals are completed we will baptise the task."

"Such a simple memo, but very unclear upon first glance," said the federal attorney. "However, I think we're starting to figure out a bit of it."

Buck didn't reply.

"For a political committee, your memos sound awfully corporate to me," Brahams added. "I'm guessing that baptise is an obvious one. Burn All Paper Trails. *BAPTise the task*. What are you hiding?"

Neither Buck nor his lawyer said anything.

"And C.J.?" the bureau counsel said. "I'll venture it stands for CryptJack, the encryption in your decency chip. NCC, maybe, National Communications Corp. FH? Well that one's a mystery still."

"But not DB." Brahams walked around the table. "You were assigned to spearhead the infusement task. And Draveson, your employee, was working on some part of that assignment yesterday. Something for which you were paying her, and trying to pay a murderer to continue."

The aide's lawyer cracked a belligerent smile. "This whole piece of fiction is a work of great novelty—no pun intended. You've got nothing here that wouldn't be laughed out of the courts faster than you could file it."

"Maybe the acts are laughable, but the charges are serious: Conspiracy to enact murder. Unlawful employment."

Buck looked at Brahams, his mouth jutting open.

"What about stolen plates?" the federal attorney continued. "Electronic wire-fraud? And endangerment to an FBI agent?"

"You're out on a limb!" the lawyer clamored. "You might be able to charge that girl...that hussy on the video, but it won't stick on my client."

"What if," Buck began. "What if I decided to cooperate?"

His lawyer glared at him, then whispered into his ear.

"We'll cut a good deal," Brahams promised. "We want Senator Euler."

"It won't hold up!" the lawyer shouted, looking at his client, not the feds. "They don't have a shred of evidence. It's all circumstantial and hearsay."

"No evidence?" Brahams asked with a snide grin. "We have Bank of America records from the senator's slush account showing a withdrawal three days ago of three thousand cash by Mr. Buck's Washington subordinate. Withdrawn bills matched by serial numbers to the cash at the scene, whose numbers were assigned for drop by the U.S. Mint to the same DC branch of Bank of America only two days before."

The bureau attorney joined in. "We have agents gathering corroborating testimony from a William Preston at Nebraska State U, who is promising to swear under oath that he was hired to create an e-mail account for the made-up name 'Jack Lacey Keller' and whose cash payment can be similarly traced to earlier transactions at the same bank in DC. Agents in Nebraska tell us he's already recognized a photo of your Nebraska office assistant as the one that gave him the first payment."

"And," Brahams added. "That very office assistant, which has no knowledge of the task, is willing to corroborate that Mr. Buck gave her instructions to keep Preston's employment off the record."

"Then there are your credit card purchases on Thursday," Brahams' partner said. "An Avis car rental in Chicago. Gas at the Texaco across the street from the Wrangler Inn where you bought a beer. Two witnesses recognized your photo, placing you at the Wrangler at two-thirty in the afternoon."

"We have letters from your office to several chip makers listed on the legislation, about adding encryption to the D-chip, which the NSA admits holds a backdoor, and—"

"All right!!" Buck stood. "Enough!"

"Oh, but there's more and we've only been at it for a day now," said the federal attorney. "We have more than enough for grand jury indictment on conspiracy charges."

"We want Euler, Mr. Buck," Brahams said. "He's already denounced you. Claimed you set the whole thing up yourself. But we know better, and we need your help to get him."

The lawyer was pawing Buck's suit, trying to get him to sit. "I want to confer with my client."

The bureau men looked at each other, masking their optimism.

"Alone," the lawyer added.

They understood and walked out of the conference room. In the hall, the federal attorney smiled at SA Brahams. "We got him."

"Yeah, for a deal maybe. We're just scratching the surface."

"Don't worry, we'll get a warrant for at least Euler's congressional office."

"The motive is still so strange. They're dealing with chip makers and have a backdoor encryption on their chip, but then this infusement task?"

"Corporation payoffs and politics," the attorney answered. "A three-ring campaign circus."

"But why the craziness. A senator conspiring with psychos?"

"To generate publicity, maybe."

"For what? The D-chip?"

The attorney nodded. "It's not so popular. Not with Internet activists."

"But promoting by hiring a killer?" Brahams shook his head.

"I don't know. Maybe it's a shield for diverting attention from the corporate telecommunications bill the D-chip legislation rides on."

"If Buck weren't sitting in the next room, I'd say we were crazy."

"Politics is crazy. And confusing." The lawyer leaned against the wall. "I'm still going through the D-chip bill—all 1000 pages of it."

Brahams shook his head. "So big. All those bills are that huge. And who has time to read them all?"

"Not the senators. Not with all the campaigning and sound-biting they do."

"Then who writes all of those bills?"

* * *

Washington, DC

"That sonuvabitch!" Senator Euler cursed. He slouched in his tall leather-back antique at his Capitol Hill office.

"And we have little time, my sources tell me," Senator Hillard said, leaning on the hundred-year-old oak desktop.

"Time for what, dammit?!"

"Warrants. Buck gave them an ear-full, a complete bargain."

Euler's limbs felt like jelly. "But warrants would require the AG's authorization. The bitch is on our side."

"And she'll have to give in once the press gets wind. No Attorney General would take the heat for this."

"We need a smear. Buck has to be completely cut off, *bastardfied*. But now, I can't afford to go through normal channels; they'll be monitoring me. Could you...?"

Hillard nodded. "I can ruin him, but we'll have to stop all transactions for a while. And you know public opinion will plummet."

"It was all for nothing." Senator Euler cupped both hands over his head. "Our corporate deals, all the work, the decency shit—a waste, then."

Hillard only nodded.

"Holy shit!" Euler held his forehead. "We have to clean up everything. Holy shit!"

"Jack, just tell me one thing," said Senator Hillard. "Who's idea was it to contact those Internet crazies?"

"For your sakes, John, you don't want to know."

* * *

Hospital

Janice kissed Tim for the tenth time. He felt happy, even though he had no eyebrows and his skin had second-degree burns in places, all which would heal in time. The worse part, he was stuck eating hospital food for another three days.

Tasha and Reggy watched him at his bedside, not saying too much. He grabbed them both in his arms.

"Are you staying home for our time?" Tasha asked.

"Our time?"

"Mom said, this was your time. Will you be home more? I want…" She gulped. "I miss you, Daddy."

"Oh, honey," Tim said as he wrapped his arms around both of them. "I promise I'll be around more."

He had focused so much on taking back his place within the bureau, chasing after madmen who hurt children—children often ignored by parents too busy in their own pursuits. Politicians believed they could fix the problem. But Tim knew what had to be done. He was just as guilty.

"Your mom called." Janice sat on the edge of the bed. "She wants to come and visit. I told her we could pick her up later today."

Tim gulped. "Janice, I know this may not be the best moment to decide, but I was thinking she could stay with us for a while."

Before Janice could respond, Bob Givens entered in his black poly-cotton suit. He smiled at Tim. "I'll bet getting stuck here is the worse part of your whole case."

"Are you kidding? I got cable TV." Tim smiled. "So what's up, Bob?"

Givens didn't reply. He greeted Janice and the children then asked them, "Could you excuse us?"

Janice gathered Reggy and Tasha, arching an eyebrow as if to tell Tim she would be back for an explanation. Givens watched them leave and then turned to him.

"What's the latest on Lonque?" Tim asked.

"We checked your tip." Givens paused. "Mott admitted it."

"So did Lonque and Mott have it planned all along?"

"I'm not sure." Givens shook his head. "I don't think that Lonque knew from the beginning who Mott and Cobbs were, but somewhere along the line Mott confessed to him that he was an FBI plant. We suspect Lonque and he worked up an elaborate plan to pass bureau information to the Militia and Klan through Mott."

Lonque had lied, big surprise. Their militia branch had direct ties with the Klan. And Mott lied. "But why would Mott risk the suspicion of proposing a detailed mission in the Klan?" Tim asked. "His best bet would have been to lay low if he only wanted to be an informant for the militia."

"Well, from the papers that Spike retrieved from Lonque's store, we suppose that Lonque actually wanted to frame the bureau with some kind of tie to the Klan. As ridiculous as it sounds, we think he urged Mott to propose the operation with SAC Hansen. He was out there the night your Japanese girl was attacked."

"You mean Lonque was using Mott as an informant and setting him up at the same time?"

Bellow nodded. "Yeah. Lonque had a real conspiracy of his own going. As good as the federal conspiracies they howl about."

"Well with Senator Euler's plot, they may not be far off."

"You're assuming we'll nail Euler with his aide's testimony. Senators are awfully slippery—getting warrants for a senator is unprecedented." Givens sniffed. "At least we have Lonque."

Lonque, the manipulator. Even Tim had seemingly fell under the man's charisma. He purchased a flammable coat from a white supremacist and, not that Lonque could have planned it, the coat almost ended up sparking another Klan burning. Although the coat lit up fast, fortunately the others were there to put it out before it finished the parka. And him.

Even Mott was being used by the jolly racist. "And I thought Mott just hated me because I'm black," Tim replied.

"That too. But in this case, he also didn't like you stepping on his toes. Probably thought you would figure him out." Givens smiled. "And sure enough, with your tips…"

"How many arrests?"

"By noon today, we'll have Lonque and three other Militia-Klan members. Charged with conspiracy and illegal weapons offenses. And Mott will be indicted with at least the collaboration and security breaches."

"Mott arrested for spying against the bureau," Tim mumbled, still shocked. "And I almost pegged him to my case."

"Well, you got your subject, Tim."

"Yeah." Tim sighed with content. The thought of Victor's capture made all of the sores and pains worthwhile. "So, where is Victor now?"

"In Wayne County jail after getting released from the hospital early this morning. The warden promised to pair him with a big, bald, shower-loving inmate."

"Not funny, Givens," Tim said. Even Victor didn't deserve that kind of treatment. "So the case moving fast? I mean, with all of the evidence..."

Givens paused, looking away briefly. "You don't have to worry, you did an excellent job collecting evidence."

"But what?"

"It's fine, Tim."

"Right. Don't fool with me."

Givens leaned forward. "Well, Grand's assistant already met with defense counsel this morning. They're going for an insanity plea."

"Whose insanity? The lawyers or Victor?"

Givens chuckled.

"Is Grand thinking about a bargain."

"No, no. He's being taken off the case. Conflict of interest. He wants to nail Victor real bad. His daughter is getting long-term psychiatric care."

"That's too bad. Victor should hang."

"Not likely. My impression is the insanity plea has a lot of credibility this time."

"That's ridiculous."

Givens shook his head. "Your profile, the split personality; they all say Victor's gone mad."

"But he passed all those psych-evals at the university and with our own psychiatrist."

"What can I say? Personality disorders aren't always caught."

Tim shook his head. "I can't believe it will stick. We have a lot of evidence saying he planned this all along. He was sane enough to calculate and manipulate many people."

"I hear you, Tim. And he'll probably manipulate again. The judge and jury this time."

Tim wanted to scream, but he knew it would hurt too much. In California, his perp got away—was probably out there hurting other kids. Now Victor, who hunted children and brutally tortured one to death, would get a slap, at most a few of years in a mental health facility. Victor was hardly getting more punishment than Tim went through for a misunderstanding in California.

"I just don't understand it all, Givens."

"Me neither. I guess only the defense lawyers do."

There was movement at the doorway. Sherrie Marshall stood there.

"Sherrie," he murmured.

"Hi, Tim." Sherrie entered. "I didn't want to disturb you."

"No, no."

"I'll leave this card on the table. It's from the guys at the residency." She placed an envelope on his empty food cart. "Come see me when you're released."

"I will, Sherrie. Thanks."

"Welcome, and get well." Sherrie waved, then disappeared.

"I better go, too." Givens grabbed his coat. "When you get out, we'll make sure to give you something with upward mobility."

"I don't know," Tim said. "I need some time. Maybe a long vacation with the family, and rethink everything."

"Don't leave us. Who's going to help retire Kaplan even earlier?"

Tim smiled. "We'll see. I just need a change of scenery."

"Good. Do something different. Take advantage of the bureau's tuition reimbursement program. Get a master's."

"As long as I don't have to live in the dorms." Janice would love to get him out of the bureau, or at least on a desk job. "How about your job?"

Givens chuckled. "See you, Tim."

END

Lightning Source UK Ltd.
Milton Keynes UK
UKOW051354300512

193637UK00001B/38/P